Harley's job as a Memphis tour guide is about to become even stranger than usual...

She had a bus full of Elvis impersonators. As soon as she dropped the guys off at the hotel for their contest, she intended to go to the nearest drug store and buy ear plugs.

When she pulled into the covered parking area to unload her passengers, she managed a smile as she told them she'd be back for them at eight, and reminded them that if their schedule changed they were to call her cell phone or the offices at Memphis Tour Tyme.

A rather portly Elvis paused in the door and said, "Thank you, thank you verra much," as he got out. If she had a nickel for every time she'd heard that or would hear that in the coming month, she could retire.

However, she just said, "You're welcome, Elvis. Good luck."

As always, she glanced back to make sure everyone was out before she left, and only one guy remained in the van. He was in the very back on the last seat.

"Hey," she called, "last stop for all *Elvi*. This is it, sir. Sir?"

He didn't respond, just remained in his seat staring out the window. Maybe he'd gotten cold feet. She didn't blame him.

Grown men dressed up like Elvis and sweating on a stage had to be daunting. She should know. After all, her dad, Yogi, went every year. It was his only brand of religion, other than his government conspiracy theories. The last she understood, but the first she found inexplicable. "Sir? Hey, Elvis?"

He still sat there staring out the window, and with a sigh, Harley got out of the van and went around. She'd get him out with a can opener if she had to, but dammit, he was getting out. She deserved someplace quiet for a while before she had to deal with the ride back to their hotels.

"Hey, buddy," she said when she reached his seat, "we're here. Time to go on stage and sing your heart out. Knock 'em dead."

When he still didn't respond, Harley put a hand on his shoulder to give him a slight shake out of his trance. He slumped forward, his head hit the back of the seat in front of him, and she jumped into the aisle. The hilt of a knife protruded from his back. She froze. This couldn't be happening. Not to him, not to *her*.

Maybe it was a mistake. A bizarre, cruel joke. She leaned closer, and the rusty smell of blood made her stomach lurch. Backing slowly away, she fumbled at her waist for the cell phone that she now kept tethered to her with a chain, and hit speed dial. The police dispatcher answered quickly.

"Nine-one-one?" Harley said in a voice that sounded a lot calmer than she felt. "We have another dead Elvis."

Other Books from Virginia Brown

Virginia Brown is the author of more than 50 novels in romance,
mystery and general fiction.
Bell Bridge Books is proud to publish these Virginia Brown titles.

The Dixie Diva Mysteries

Dixie Divas
Drop Dead Divas
Dixie Diva Blues
Divas and Dead Rebels

The Blue Suede Memphis Mysteries

Hound Dog Blues
Harley Rushes In
Suspicious Mimes

Mystery/Drama

Dark River Road

Historical Romance

Comanche Moon * Capture the Wind

Also Available

Savage Awakening * Defy The Thunder
Storm of Passion * Wild Heart
Legacy of Shadows * Moonflower
Desert Dreams * Heaven Sent
Wildfire * Renegade Embrace
Emerald Nights * Hidden Touch
Wildflower * Wildest Heart
Jade Moon * Highland Hearts

Suspicious Mimes

The Blue Suede Memphis Mysteries
Book Three

Virginia Brown

Bell Bridge Books

Bell Bridge Books
PO BOX 300921
Memphis, TN 38130
ISBN: 978-1-61194-099-2

Bell Bridge Books is an Imprint of BelleBooks, Inc.

Printed and bound in the United States of America.

Originally published in trade paperback as Evil Elvis, by ImaJinn Books, Canon City, CO
We at BelleBooks enjoy hearing from readers.
Visit our websites – www.BelleBooks.com and www.BellBridgeBooks.com.

10 9 8 7 6 5 4 3 2 1

Interior design: Hank Smith
Front cover art and design by Don T.

:Lms:01:

Dedication

To Elvis Presley, the man who changed the direction of music worldwide.

He'll not be forgotten, nor should he be. There will never be another like him.

And to Vivian McMahon, who makes Nana McMullen look slow. I miss seeing her smiling face over my fence, and I expect to be invited to her 100th birthday party!

Disclaimer

No animals or Elvises were harmed in the writing of this book.

A few were terribly annoyed, however.

"If life were fair, Elvis would be alive and all the impersonators would be dead."
—*Johnny Carson*

One

"Elvis lives." Harley Jean Davidson didn't really mean that, but what else could she say when her father was looking so expectant, waiting for her to comment nicely? "I'm sure he'd be pleased if he could see you dressed up like him," she added.

Yogi grinned and twirled so that his jeweled white cape flashed in a glitter of green, red, and blue stones her mother had carefully sewn into what looked like eight yards of satin. Sunlight coming through the front window gleamed off the stones, almost blinding her. *Good Lord.*

"This year, I've had to turn down gigs. I've been practicing." Yogi struck another pose, this time with one leg behind him, the other bent at the knee in a half-crouch, his arm flung out in front like he was trying to hail a taxi.

Harley barely kept from rolling her eyes. She dreaded Elvis Week. It came every year in August, the momentum building up to a climactic frenzy of Elvis-related activities downtown and at Graceland. Perhaps she wouldn't dread it so badly if Yogi hadn't made a habit of tugging on a white jumpsuit and impersonating The King, whom he still admired more than twenty years after Elvis's death. It'd been greatly humiliating when she was younger and more concerned with the opinion of her peers. Now it registered a lesser blip on her radar screen.

Over the years, she'd learned there were far worse humiliations her parents could generate than an unnatural attachment to a long-dead celebrity.

When she looked over at Diva, her mother said to Yogi, "This is the year you'll be famous."

Strong accolade, considering Diva's uncannily accurate predictions. She might miss some of the details, but lately she'd been right more times than not. That should please Yogi.

"Of course," her mother added, "it won't be quite as you

expect, but your name will be linked with Elvis's in a spectacular way."

That was a little unsettling. In light of the past few months of unwanted publicity, Harley would have preferred anything but spectacular. "Our family has been in the news quite enough, thank you verra much," she said, her accent on the last phrase a really bad imitation of Elvis. It made Yogi smile, as it always did.

"This is the year I'll win first prize," he said jubilantly. "Always a runner-up, but now I think I have a real shot at it. Preston Hughes dropped out."

Preston Hughes was Yogi's archrival in the Elvis impersonator contests. His rendition of *Love Me Tender* brought down the house every time. The judges loved him.

While Yogi could imitate Elvis fairly well, he didn't have the vocal range Hughes did.

"I'll do what I can to be there," Harley said, "but August is our busiest month, you know. All those tourists wanting to do Graceland means we have every van full. It's still July, and I did eight runs yesterday in twelve hours. I'd take a load out there, drop them off, go back for another one, bring another group back, take another one. I don't know how Tootsie kept it all straight, who went where, and when, but he did. He's amazing."

Diva smiled. "The candlelight vigil this year will be interesting. Perhaps you should skip it, Harley."

Harley looked at her. "I'd love to, but that's our busiest night. All drivers are needed. Mr. Penney would fire me if I missed it. And I'm on shaky ground as it is after all that's happened."

"I know. But I have a feeling that you should miss it anyway."

"I wish you hadn't said that. I'm already committed. Tootsie would get into a snit if I tried to change on him now. I'd really like to keep my job."

"You seem very content these days. I'm glad."

"I am content. While I admit driving a tour bus isn't the best-paying job around, it does pay my bills. I like doing it. The hours are flexible, the people are usually nice, and when they aren't, I soon get rid of them and never have to see them again. Look in your crystal ball again. Are you sure that warning isn't meant for someone else? I'd hate to bail on Tootsie now."

"Whatever you think best, Harley."

Harley hated it when her mother said things like that. It always felt like she'd made a bad decision when Diva tranquilly agreed with her.

"Okay. I have to ask. *Why* do you think I shouldn't go?" By now Diva was headed to the kitchen and Harley followed along behind her, something she could have done even in the dark since her mother liked wearing tiny bells sewn into her loose, flowing skirts. Diva still dressed much as she had in the late sixties and early seventies, with her pale blonde hair long and down her back, tunic tops and skirts to her ankles, sandals and bracelets and necklaces that she made herself out of crystals and beads and leather. Diva and Yogi lived in their own era, and it didn't much matter to them that time had moved on.

Diva's reply drifted back over her shoulder. "It's your choice, Harley."

"Yes, I know it's my choice. That doesn't mean I'll make the right choice. Come on. Give me a clue here. You know something I don't, apparently."

"Rama and Ovid are concerned."

Harley couldn't help it. She rolled her eyes. "What do Rama and Ovid have to do with me? They're your spirit guides, not mine."

"What you do affects me. You're my daughter. But perhaps it's best that you do go. It will help your father feel so much better."

"Oh, good lord. That sounds ominous. I'm not going to have to get up on stage at one of his shows and throw my panties or anything like that, am I?"

Diva laughed. "I'm sure not. Oh, will you let King in? The pet door is broken."

Recognizing she wasn't going to learn anything else until her mother chose to tell her, Harley went to the back door and opened it. King, her father's black and white Border Collie named for Elvis, trotted inside. His paws were muddy, and seeing as how there'd been no rain lately, that no doubt meant he'd been up to mischief again.

"I thought the higher fence Yogi put up kept King from getting out," she said as she gave the dog a pat on the head that promptly elicited an ecstatic wiggle of his entire body.

"It does. Why?"

"His feet are wet. I'll bet he's been fishing in Mrs. Erland's pond again."

"Perhaps he's just been in the garden. Yogi hooked up a watering system. King likes to go back there and sample tomatoes on occasion."

That explained the glazed look in King's eyes. Yogi's illegal tobacco grew right next to the tomato plants, and the crop of both had a relaxing effect on those who indulged. Since King couldn't roll his own and smoke, he'd obviously found eating the tomatoes a nice substitution. Well, whatever kept him from being the neighborhood scourge had to be an improvement.

"He seems much better behaved now," she remarked. "Maybe he's settling down."

"The obedience classes helped, I think. How kind of the Border Collie Rescue to help out."

"They just didn't want to get stuck with him. But I'm grateful for anything that keeps me from having to go looking for him at three in the morning."

"You have an affinity for animals, Harley. I don't know why you resist it. That's a lovely talent to have."

"Right. If you don't mind pet hair over all your clothes, on the floor, on the furniture, in your food—"

"So how is Sam?"

Harley sighed. "He's fine. I can't believe I let Cami talk me into keeping that cat. I had to pay Mr. Lancaster a pet deposit. A hundred dollars just so I can clean out a litter box and pay good money for a scratching post and toys that I use more than he does. He looks at me like I'm crazy when I try to get him to play with them. I think I've been had."

"We don't often choose animals. They choose us. They're on a higher spiritual plane than we are and can sense people with good hearts."

"Which explains why Sam is so picky about who pets him, I suppose. It's rather nice having a cat that's smarter than people."

"He's not necessarily smarter, just isn't burdened with preconceived ideas about how things are supposed to be. He sees with all his senses. Just like King."

While Diva smiled at the dog, who seemed to know good things were being said about him and wagged his tail so hard it should have flown across the room, Harley reflected on the simple truth that animals had some kind of pipeline to objectivity. They never let anything like concern about their next meal interfere with behavior patterns that bordered on criminal. If it wasn't for the cuteness factor, dogs would never have been allowed into that first cave. And she wasn't at all sure they were domesticated. Cats were definitely still undomesticated, despite the popular belief that they were house pets. They weren't. They just had good PR agents.

"Listen to this," Yogi said from the kitchen doorway, and Harley turned, wincing a little at the sight of him still in his Elvis getup. At least his pot belly had shrunk, and with his long sideburns, once he got his annual haircut he'd resemble Elvis pretty closely—if *closely* included cherubic cheeks and a nose that was a bit short, lips that were a little too thin, and height a couple of inches below six feet. The Elvis contest was the only time he ever cut his hair; the rest of the time he kept it in a ponytail.

"We're listening," Harley said as her father hit a few chords on his guitar.

Yogi launched into a pretty good imitation of Elvis singing. *Suspicious Minds.* He really wasn't bad. Even his guitar playing had improved.

"I've been taking guitar lessons from Eric," he said when she complimented him on how good he sounded. "This is the year I'll win. I just know it."

Harley couldn't help a big smile. Yogi was always so certain he'd win, and when he lost, always so determined to win the next time. "I'll just bet you do win this year."

He did another Elvis stance. "Thank you. Thank you verra much."

Time to go. Harley left after the usual farewell rituals and stood on the front porch a minute before heading to her car parked at the curb. Huge oaks hung over the street on both sides, shading it save for a few patches of sunlight.

Her parents' house was only a few blocks from the University of Memphis—formerly known as Memphis State, and before that, Normal State, the latter no doubt changed when it became obvious it was a more hopeful than realistic name. The Normal neighborhood had gone through many transitions over the years. In the thirties up to the fifties it'd been full of young families, then older families. In the sixties, college kids and hippies painted flowers everywhere, grew pot in closets with sophisticated lighting, then melded like chameleons into yuppies and left it all in a shabby air of neglect.

In the past decade or so, the transition had started all over again. Some of the older families like hers had stuck it out, but some of the houses were divided into rented rooms for university students. Now younger families had started buying and renovating the older homes in the area. Most of the families at this end of Douglass Street were older. On the other end, swing sets and kids' toys littered yards like some kind of plastic nuclear blast.

A wide front porch ran the length of her parents' bungalow-style house. In summer it held chairs, in winter it held hardy plants. Now it held Harley's younger brother. Eric was just coming up the steps onto the porch. Tall, thin, and nearly always dressed in black, he smiled when he saw her. "Hey, cool chick."

"Hey, dude." Standard greetings over, she asked him about his art classes the coming year at the University of Memphis, the heavy metal rock band he was in, and if he'd be going to the big Elvis finals competition with their parents. Provided Yogi made it that far.

He shook his head, and afternoon light glittered off the earring in one ear. "Not this time. We've got a gig that night. Thank god."

Harley completely understood. "Yeah, I have to work. I hope. What color do you call that on your head? It looks pink."

He brushed a hand over the gelled hair standing four inches high on his scalp. "Fuchsia. It didn't turn out quite like I wanted."

"That's a relief. I'd hate to think you were going for that look."

"I'm thinking of shaving my head and tattooing the hair on."

"Now *there's* a look guaranteed to break a mother's heart. I'll be glad when you grow out of this difficult stage. Think it'll be any time soon?"

Eric just grinned. "Maybe. Maybe not."

That was the thing about her family. They just drifted along at their own speed, heedless of convention or opinions, happy to just exist. Why couldn't she be like that? No, she had to be in this phase where she questioned everything about her life: her job, her direction, why she was still unmarried at nearly thirty, and even if she ever wanted to get married.

Not that she did without male companionship. While she refused to think of it as a bona fide relationship, she certainly enjoyed all the perks of keeping company with Mike Morgan, the hottest undercover cop in Memphis. Three months, and things just got hotter. She liked to tell acquaintances that they'd met over murder. It was certainly a conversational icebreaker. And very nearly true.

So what if the beginning of their relationship had been a little rocky? It'd smoothed out. Perseverance and tolerance helped. Given his line of work, the sharp edges were understandable, if not always desirable. While most of the time, she saw only a killer bod, electric blue eyes, dark hair that was usually a little shaggy around the edges, and a grin that made her stomach do funny flips, he had another side that she wouldn't want to confront in a dark alley. Or even at high noon. She'd only caught a glimpse of it a few times, and wasn't especially eager to see it again. She liked him much better when he was agreeable, even if a little intolerant about her stumbling over corpses.

Later that evening, Morgan reminded her about his intolerance of her new direction in life. "Over two months without you finding a body or two lying around." He blew into her ear and she shivered. "I'm glad to see you've reformed."

"I like to think of it as keeping better company, thank you."

"No jewelry thieves, no smugglers—what do you do with all your spare time?"

She slanted her eyes at him. "When I'm not being asked annoying questions by a naked man in my bed, I knit scarves for the homeless and hang out on street corners. It's not like I *tried* to find bodies, you know."

"So you say. Baroni must be delirious with relief."

"Bobby," she said, "is a jerk."

"That's not a nice thing to say about an old friend. How would he feel if he heard you?"

"He's already heard it and didn't seem too bothered. We're not speaking at the moment. Sometimes we do that."

Mike laughed softly. "Do I want to know what happened?"

"Probably, but I'm not going to tell you."

He rolled over on top of her and pinned her arms back to the pillows. "I have ways of making you talk, y'know."

She looked up with a smile and whispered, "Do your worst, copper."

"How about," he whispered back as he moved over her in a most intriguing way, "I do my best instead?"

"I'm up for it."

He smiled. "So am I."

Oh yeah.

Tootsie looked a bit frayed when Harley showed up for work a little earlier than usual the next morning. The phone was ringing, and paperwork had piled up on his desk.

"You look like you had a bad night," she said, plopping the leather backpack she used as a purse down atop his desk. "Want me to help out?"

"Grab the phone. Take a name and number and tell them we'll call back." He looked up at her, frustration in his eyes. "This time of year is always a bitch."

"Isn't it?" She answered the phone for a few minutes, and when it finally stopped ringing, blew out a breath of relief. "I don't know how you do it. Some of these people are downright rude if they don't hear what they want to hear."

Tootsie batted his eyelashes. "I use my Southern charm. Works every time."

She grinned. "Must be why I'm not very good at it. I failed that class."

"You just spent too much time in California. It was all that commune living as a child. Southern charm is usually a requirement here."

"Not for everyone. You do recall my Aunt Darcy and cousins?"

"Ah yes. There are those who don't show up for class. What's up?"

She got up from the chair and perched on the edge of his desk while he got back to the computer. "I don't suppose you'd schedule me for airport runs during the candlelight vigil? Or taking tourists to Beale Street? Or Victorian Village? Or AutoZone, or—"

"I'd be happy to, but Charlsie already put in for the airport, and Jake got Beale Street, and Sharon took Victorian Village. Since your time off, they have seniority. I did have a Dixon Art Gallery run, but you're still banned from there so I sent Lydia. Sorry, baby."

Harley sighed. "I understand. I don't like it, but I understand. Of course, if any of them get sick, I get first chance at their run. Deal?"

"Deal." Tootsie laughed. "Just don't get any ideas."

"You know me so well." She smiled. Thomas "Tootsie" Rowell was really one of her best friends. He'd hired her immediately when she'd answered the ad in the paper, and they'd gotten along famously ever since. She even attended his shows at times, where he dressed up like Cher or Madonna or Liza Minnelli, or whoever caught his fancy.

Hard to admit, but Tootsie was more gorgeous as a woman than most women. He wasn't much taller than she, only about five seven to her five six, and borrowed her dresses from her corporate days of wining and dining. She hated to admit he looked better in them than she ever had. But then, she was much more comfortable in jeans and a tee shirt anyway.

Evening dresses had never been her style, and it probably showed every time she wore one. Most of the time liked her job as a tour driver and occasional taxi service. That depended on where she was needed most, since the company had recently branched out into offering short runs as well as the regular tours. It'd taken a while to get the licensing and regulations straight, and required more training for the drivers so everyone could get their piece of the financial pie. But more vehicles were added to the fleet and all the drivers qualified.

It wasn't like her former job in corporate banking. If she disliked the clients, she got rid of them at the end of the day, where before she'd had to deal with them on a regular basis. Not to mention several tiers of former bosses, some of whom were nice but most of whom were stereotypical jerks.

Maybe she should have finished college, but at the time it hadn't seemed nearly as important as it did now. Ah, her shallow youth was behind her. She was now entering the halls of maturity. Things could be worse.

Tootsie snapped his fingers in front of her face. "Hello? You in there?"

"Sorry. Just thinking how lucky I am to still have a job."

"Baby, you just don't know."

"Sure I do. You went to bat for me. I'm convinced you've got something on the ogre. If you didn't, I'd have been out the door back in May."

"Don't get too comfortable. And for pity's sake, don't go around finding any more dead bodies."

"Which makes me wonder—is there such a thing as finding live bodies?"

Tootsie rolled his eyes. "Sometimes you act so blonde."

"I *am* a blonde."

"I know. But you're usually a smart blonde. There's a run you can take this afternoon. I know it's one you'll like. Elvis impersonators."

"A taxi run? I thought I was scheduled for Tupelo."

"They cancelled at the last minute. Fortunately for you, we have this one."

She sighed. "I'm in hell."

"Not until two o'clock, baby."

By two-thirty, Harley was rethinking the entire tour guide thing. Just getting around town was a feat of luck and persistence. But now her ears hurt as well. All the Elvises sang at the same time—*is the plural of Elvis called Elvi?* she wondered, then winced at a particularly loud mix of *Blue Christmas, Don't Be Cruel,* and *Kentucky Rain.*

Normally—and separately—she liked those songs. All at the same time, however, they made her want to ram the van into the nearest telephone pole. As soon as she dropped these guys off at the hotel for their contest, she intended to go to the nearest drug store and buy ear plugs.

When she pulled into the covered parking area to unload her passengers, she managed a smile as she told them she'd be back for them at eight, and reminded them that if their schedule changed they were to call her cell phone or the offices at Memphis Tour Tyme.

A rather portly Elvis paused in the door and said, "Thank you, thank you verra much" as he got out. If she had a nickel for every time she'd heard that or would hear that in the coming month, she could retire.

However, she just said, "You're welcome, Elvis. Good luck."

As always, she glanced back to make sure everyone was out

before she left, and only one guy remained in the van. He was in the very back on the last seat.

"Hey," she called, "last stop for all Elvi. This is it, sir. Sir?"

He didn't respond, just remained in his seat staring out the window. Maybe he'd gotten cold feet. She didn't blame him.

Grown men dressed up like Elvis and sweating on a stage had to be daunting. She should know. After all, Yogi went every year. It was his only brand of religion, other than his government conspiracy theories. The last she understood, but the first she found inexplicable. "Sir? Hey, Elvis?"

He still sat there staring out the window, and with a sigh, Harley got out of the van and went around. She'd get him out with a can opener if she had to, but dammit, he was getting out. She deserved someplace quiet for a while before she had to deal with the ride back to their hotels.

"Hey, buddy," she said when she reached his seat, "we're here. Time to go on stage and sing your heart out. Knock 'em dead."

When he still didn't respond, Harley put a hand on his shoulder to give him a slight shake out of his trance. He slumped forward, his head hit the back of the seat in front of him, and she jumped into the aisle. The hilt of a knife protruded from his back. She froze. This couldn't be happening. Not to him, not to *her.*

Maybe it was a mistake. A bizarre, cruel joke. She leaned closer, and the rusty smell of blood made her stomach lurch. Backing slowly away, she fumbled at her waist for the cell phone that she now kept tethered to her with a chain, and hit speed dial. They answered quickly.

"Nine-one-one?" she said in a voice that sounded a lot calmer than she felt. "We have another dead Elvis."

Two

"Give me a description of all the other passengers."

Harley stared at the uniformed officer. "Black hair, long side burns, white jumpsuits—you're kidding, right? They all looked like Elvis."

This was crazy. She had twelve passengers listed on her schedule of pickups, but there had been thirteen on board. None of the twelve remaining passengers on her list of pickups knew the extra, or so they said. Somehow, he'd slipped in on her. She should have counted heads as they boarded. Then maybe she'd have noticed an extra passenger.

Shivering despite the afternoon's heat, Harley once more gave the officer a run-down of her schedule. The crime scene unit white van and a van from the morgue had arrived, and the area swarmed with police cars. Yellow tape screened off her MTT van, flashing blue lights cordoned off the parking lot, and there she stood in the middle of it all. It was just too familiar.

"Dammit, Harley."

She sighed. That was familiar, too. Unfortunately. She turned, managing a smile as Bobby Baroni approached. As a homicide detective, he always found things out too quickly. As a childhood friend who'd been party to—and often instigator of—one too many pranks in their old neighborhood, he knew her too well. Not only that, Bobby had that Italian macho thing going on, where he always had to be right. Or maybe that was just a male thing.

Even in the heat, he had on a suit and tie, a world's difference from the clothes he'd worn as a teenager. Somehow, the suit made him seem more remote, almost like a stranger instead of a guy she'd hung around with all through junior high and high school. College really did change some people. Or maybe life did the changing.

When he reached her, she tried to sound casual and asked, "Hi, Bobby. How's it going?"

He shook a cigarette out of a pack he took from his pocket, lit it, and squinted at her through the smoke. "Funny you should ask. I was sitting at my desk, happy I'd gone nearly two months without you being involved in a murder, and then came the phone call. I should have known better."

"Really, Bobby. I'm not involved. I'm just the unlucky—and I'd like to point out *unwilling*—witness."

"Yet you are here. With a dead man in the back of your van. How do you explain that?"

"You have such a suspicious nature. Does your mother know you're smoking again?"

"I get paid to be suspicious. And there are things my mother is better off not knowing. Can you tell me how the vic got stabbed in a van full of people without anyone noticing?"

"A bomb could have gone off and no one would have noticed. They were singing. All at the same time, and all different songs. It was horrible." She shuddered again. This time it wasn't because of the singing, but the memory of the dead Elvis slumped in the back seat of the van.

Bobby looked at her a little more closely. His family was Sicilian, a long line of shopkeepers and merchants who'd immigrated to America for a better life sometime in the middle of the nineteenth century. It was entirely possible her Irish ancestors had done business with them way back then, since many of the early Italian and Irish immigrants to Memphis had first settled along the river front. Her Irish ancestors had branched out to become farmers, and his family had done well with grocery markets and liquor stores. Both had no doubt dabbled in bootlegging. It'd been quite profitable during Prohibition.

"You okay?" Bobby asked, and she shrugged.

"I should be getting used to dead bodies by now, but somehow, I'm not."

Bobby nodded, took a last puff off his cigarette, then dropped it and ground it into the hot pavement. "Don't leave town," he said as he walked off to interview the other passengers.

Maybe she should leave town. Bad things seemed to happen to people in her vicinity. It was as if she was a murder magnet lately. She'd gone nearly thirty years with no trouble at all, and suddenly *poof!* Bodies began popping up everywhere around her. It was crazy.

Sitting glumly on the edge of a concrete planter overflowing with petunias, she had to bite her nails instead of smoke a cigarette, which she really would have preferred. But she'd quit before she'd started her new career as a cadaver dog.

When her cell phone rang, she hesitated. It wasn't going to be a good conversation, and it didn't matter who was on the other end. Maybe she shouldn't answer it. No point in getting even more depressed. But *Dixie* played louder and louder, so she finally gave in and answered the persistent caller. It was Tootsie.

"Harley, what the *hell?*"

"I take it you've been notified."

"You could have called to warn me, you know."

"I could have . . . should have . . . *would* have, but it was kind of a shock finding him like that with a knife in his back."

"Hon, it seems to me you should be used to that sort of thing by now."

"Well, perhaps, but does anyone ever really get used to finding bodies? Except maybe the coroner? Or the police? Or soldiers, they must be used to it. Oh, and doctors—"

"Focus, baby, you're sounding a little hysterical."

Harley took a deep breath. "I've bitten my nails down to the first knuckles. I have nubs for fingers. If I don't stop it soon, I'll consider bumming a cigarette."

"Don't. Too hard to hold with nubs. Listen, I'll send someone to pick you up as soon as you're released by the police."

"What should I do about the other Elvises . . . Elvi? What's the plural? I was wondering about that just before . . . before I found a dead one in the back seat."

"Jesus. You really are a basket case. Don't worry about the other Elvises. I'll get someone else to take your return trip. I don't think you need to be driving right now."

"I'm just fine."

"Darling, not even close. Stay there. I'm sending someone to get you."

Maybe Tootsie was right. Her hands were shaking, and she curled her fingers into her palms. Violent death had no resemblance to peacefully laid out bodies in funeral homes, with the soft music and sweet-smelling flowers, the hushed voices and cushioned furniture. This was ugly, abrupt, and seemed a lot more final than lying in a plush walnut coffin wearing make-up and best clothes. She tried not to think about the Elvis's face, that vacant, sightless stare into eternity.

Another shiver trickled down her spine. She clasped her hands together, crossed her legs at the ankles and waited for someone to arrive to take her away from death.

Just her luck, Mike Morgan showed up as her ride. What was Tootsie thinking? He should know that Morgan had much the same view on her being in the same vicinity of a body as Bobby had. It was terribly inconvenient and very annoying that they now viewed her as some kind of lure for murder.

Mike was in his own car, a vintage red Corvette that he left parked by one of the squad cars. She watched him saunter over to Bobby Baroni and talk to him for a few minutes, and both of them looked toward her. They were talking about her, of course. She had no desire to know what they were saying. It was never complimentary when this sort of thing happened.

It'd be so much easier if Morgan didn't make her stomach feel all squishy inside when he looked at her. He had that lean-hipped, dangerous look going on, dressed in a black tee shirt, faded black Levis, and what she called his SWAT boots. Somewhere on his body—close to all the masculine equipment he'd been born with—he had probably stashed a few weapons of the lethal variety. Tools of his trade, he called them. She liked his natural tool best.

When he finally started toward her, she got up from the concrete planter. She put her hands on her hips and watched him walk across the driveway. As did a few other women. She didn't mind. They couldn't help it. Morgan seemed to have that effect on women.

The best defense is a good offense, she thought, and said aloud, "Damn, what took you so long? My butt's asleep from sitting on this concrete for the past three hours, and the only thing I've had to eat is my fingernails."

He didn't smile. "Are you going to make a habit of this?"

"Biting my nails?"

"No, Harley, finding bodies. Baroni thinks you may be a serial killer."

"Bobby's still mad because I told him to stay away from Cami unless he was serious. She takes things to heart and he's a serial boyfriend."

"Stay out of Baroni's love life. Dammit, what the hell is going on with you?"

She stared at him incredulously. "You're mad at *me* because some Elvis got stabbed in my van?"

He looked frustrated and angry. "Has it occurred to you that one of these days I'll show up at a crime scene and find *you* laid out? Do you ever think about that?"

"No," she said sarcastically, "I'm just always happy to see you, too."

Blowing out a harsh breath, he looked away from her, raked a hand through his dark hair and obviously struggled for control. When he looked back at her, his voice was reasonable but his eyes were still dark blue with frustration.

"How do you think this looks to the department? Next thing I know, internal affairs is going to be breathing down my neck, wanting to know why I'm seeing someone who leaves behind a trail of bodies wherever she goes."

"Isn't that *your* line of work?"

Morgan said grimly, "Most of my arrests are of live bodies, not dead ones. You've found more corpses in four months than I've found in four years."

"Well, pardon me if I've inconvenienced you. It's not like I go around looking for them, you know." She glared at him. Her throat hurt. This was their first real fight since becoming a "couple," and with her nerves already shredded, tears would be just too humiliating.

"Don't bother giving me a ride. I'll call a taxi," she said stiffly, and turned to walk away.

Mike grabbed her arm right above the elbow and turned her around. "Christ, let's not argue about it. I'm giving you a ride."

She pushed his hand off her arm and squared off from him, bristling. "Touch me again and I'll punch you."

His brow shot up, but he didn't reach for her again. "Okay. So it's going to be like that. If I say I'd like to take you home, please, does that sound better?"

"That depends. Is this an 'I want to take you home because you're upset' thing, or an 'I have to take you home to make sure you don't find another body' thing?"

"Mostly the first one. Some of the second one."

She thought about that for a moment, and then nodded.

"Okay. That sounds fair."

The ride home was quiet, except for the radio. Uncle Kracker sang *Follow Me*, and Harley drummed her fingers to the beat and stared out the window. Fortunately, it wasn't too far to her apartment. Pea gravel crunched under the Corvette's tires when he came to a stop in back of the red brick house divided into four apartments.

"You don't have to come up," she said, opening her door and putting her feet out before he even had the brake set. "I'm fine."

"I'm sure you are. I'm coming up anyway. Unless you tell me I can't."

"No, I'm not saying that. I have a feeling it wouldn't do me any good if I did." She looked at him over her shoulder.

He turned off the ignition. "You know better than that."

"Yeah. I guess I do. Okay. Come up if you want."

It felt so awkward and stiff, when she really wanted it to be like it'd always been before. She wasn't good at this kind of thing. She did just fine as long as things went along smoothly, but the first bump in the relationship road, and she came unraveled. There was a string of past boyfriends to prove that. Only one long-term love in her life before Morgan, if she didn't count George, the fish she had released in the Audubon Park koi pond. And, of course, Sam the cat, who'd wheedled his way into her life with a pair of big blue eyes and a few moves that had twice saved her from disaster.

But she'd begun to think Morgan might just be The One. She should have known better. Her track record of failed relationships was nearly as bad as Bobby's.

Sam greeted her at the door with a disapproving *miaoow* that escalated into a chorus of complaints until she poured more dry food into his bowl and added a little canned food to the top of it. Siamese cats could be very vocal, not that she minded too much. She and Sam made a nice duet.

"I have leftover takeout," she said to Morgan, "if you want anything to eat."

"If it's Taco Bell, no thanks. That's better fresh."

"Chinese."

"Sounds good." He seemed to feel as awkward as she did, and

she didn't know quite how to take that. Was he working up to a break up or just still upset about the dead Elvis in her van?

Only one way to find out.

"So," she said when she put the heated plate of fried rice and egg rolls in front of him, "is this a break up?"

He gave her a startled look. "What are you talking about?"

"Me finding bodies. You not liking that. Us. Maybe we need to talk about it."

"Yeah. Well. I'm not really good at that kind of conversation."

"Me either." She sat down in the chair opposite him, and Sam immediately jumped up on the cushioned arm to sniff her plate. He purred. Little beggar. She gave him a piece of rice and he gave her a horrified look. Then he leaped down to cross to Morgan, who had chicken fried rice.

Morgan obliged the cat with a piece of chicken, and then looked over at Harley. "Maybe we just need a break from each other. Just for a couple weeks or a month. Something like that. Give us time to think about . . . things."

Her throat got tight, but she nodded casually. "I think you're right. I don't want you to feel like I'm jeopardizing your job, and lately I can't seem to stop tripping over bodies. I don't know what it is. Some kind of murder magnet, I guess."

One corner of his mouth tucked into a wry smile. "Any chance you can get rid of it?"

"Always a chance, but since I don't know how I got it, I don't know how to get rid of it."

After a moment of heavy silence he said, "It's just that we've got this big case going on, it takes a lot of time and all my concentration. Sometimes it's a good thing that you're a distraction. This isn't one of those times. I think about you when I should be thinking about the case. Now you're mixed up in another screwy murder case, and I'll be worrying about you. If I knew—"

"No, it's okay. Really. I understand. And I don't blame you. I worry about you, too, and when you're on an undercover assignment, you don't need to be thinking about anything else. I couldn't stand it if I caused you to be hurt or killed."

It was even more awkward after that, and when he left, she gave him a kiss on the cheek and closed the door behind him. Sam, perched atop the back of the off-white cushioned chair in the living room, paused in washing his face with his paw to look up at her quizzically.

"Looks like I blew another one," she said, but it didn't seem to make any difference to the cat. He went back to washing his face. She threw out the rest of the Chinese, washed up the dirty dishes, cleaned cat hair off the chair and poured herself a glass of sweet tea from the pitcher she kept in the refrigerator. Then she went out to sit on the small balcony that overlooked Overton Park and the zoo. White concrete banisters curved into graceful knots next to red brick walls. She sat in her chair, propped her feet up on the railing, and sucked down nearly half of the tea in one or two gulps. Early evening silence began to settle on the neighborhood. Rush hour traffic had eased, joggers and mosquitoes came out, and people walked their dogs in the park.

It was a great place to live. A stately, dark-red brick structure that looked more like an old house than an apartment building because it had once housed a single family, it now held four separate apartments. Concrete balconies and curvy masonry trim were kept a bright white, and the magnolia tree in the front yard looked to be at least thirty feet high. It had survived all storms so far, and creamy blossoms that smelled lemony sweet grew big as dinner plates every year. Oak trees shaded the back, and hedges along each side of the green front yard muffled noise from the street and provided shelter to so many birds it sounded like an aviary most of the time.

The neighborhood was a mix of one-family homes and apartment buildings like this one, a quiet area of Memphis, or as quiet as it could be with the busy thoroughfare of Poplar Avenue only a stone's throw away. At night, she heard the shriek of peacocks and the roar of lions and tigers in the zoo. During the day, the grumble of city bus engines drowned out other sounds. In the summertime, the nights held the busy whine of mosquitoes looking for their next meal. She slapped at one on her arm and thought about going inside.

Her house phone rang. Suddenly, going inside wasn't that appealing. Phone calls these days rarely held good news. There was the chance it could be a harmless call, but why be foolish? While she debated, it rang again and her answering machine clicked on. Diva's husky alto drifted out the open doors. "Harley, nothing is forever, not even the bad times."

That was so Diva. She always seemed to know things.

Very disconcerting. Of course, Diva could mean anything from *Sorry you found a dead body* to *Sorry you can't find that ten dollars to balance your checkbook*. But knowing Diva, it was about the other calamity in her daughter's life. Morgan.

Sighing, Harley got up and went inside to pick up the phone. "I know," she said into the phone.

"This will pass, Harley. Then all will be well again."

Sam jumped onto her lap when she sat down in the chair, and she started stroking his soft fur with her free hand. He began to purr loudly and, oddly enough, it made her feel better.

"Any chance I can hold you to that?" she asked her mother.

Diva laughed softly. "See? You'll be fine. The circle must be completed."

A soft throb started behind her eyes, and Harley put her fingers to her temples. "What circle? Or do I want to know?"

When Diva went off into her talk of mantras and chakras and chi and spirit guides and all that other stuff she believed in, Harley thought about the baker's dozen of Elvises that had been on the van. One of them had to be the killer. The guy didn't stab himself in the back. If she went over the list of passengers to be picked up at the hotels, maybe she could remember who got on where. The odd man out would be the killer. This time, though, she intended to give the info to Bobby and not go off on her own. It only caused more trouble.

And right now, that was the last thing she needed.

Maybe she should go on vacation. Get some fresh air, see new sights, leave town for a while until this all blew over.

"Harley?" Diva said, sounding like she'd said her name a few times before.

"Sorry. Just focusing on what I should do instead of what I did do."

"You didn't cause anything. It's just that your life force is so strong it generates energy that attracts negative as well as positive. There's a reason for that."

"What is it? I'd give a week's pay to know."

Diva's laugh was soft. "It will come to you."

"Right. Let's hope it comes in time."

"It will. Your spirit guides are keeping you safe."

"I think my spirit guides took a flight to Vegas. How come they never show up when I need them?"

"But they do, Harley. They're always with you."

"Today they're on a winning streak at the blackjack tables. Looks to me like it's time to get them back on the job."

"No need. It was the Elvis who died today, not you." Diva had a point.

Harley thought about that while she was brushing her teeth before bed. There had been some narrow escapes lately. Bobby had said it was sheer dumb luck that kept her alive, but what did he know? He never gave her enough credit. And Morgan—well, obviously he didn't give her much either.

Not that she could blame him. A brief inspection in the bathroom mirror was reason enough for any man with half-decent eyesight to run the opposite way. The gelled blonde spikes of her favorite hairstyle had gone limp. She looked like a drowned hedgehog. Her hair was a little too long to stick up like it should, anyway. Maybe it needed to be cut again. Or grown out. Such a major decision required another opinion. She turned to look at the cat sitting atop the closed toilet lid.

"What do you think, Sam? Should I let my hair grow out or get it cut?"

Sam offered no opinion either way. He continued to clean his face with a paw and ignore her plight. Just like a male.

Never there when you really needed them.

That made her think of her latest purchase. A sexy pair of red silk panties she'd bought at Victoria's Secret and tucked into her underwear drawer for a special occasion. She'd planned on wearing them for Morgan. A surprise for him since her usual choice was plain white cotton bikinis and a sports bra. Not exactly sexy, but she'd never heard any complaints.

Now, of course, he'd miss the red silk panties. Damn him.

Three

"Leave it alone, baby." Tootsie frowned and leaned closer to her. "It never works out good when you start meddling."

"I'm not meddling. I'm investigating. And I intend to turn over anything I find out to the police, so you don't need to worry about me going off on my own anymore."

"Uh hunh. I seem to remember you saying that a time or two before. And look how that turned out."

Sitting in a chair behind the reception desk with the print-out he'd gotten for her, she dismissed the reminder with a wave of her hand. "This time is different. I'm only going over this list of passengers to see if I can match the name to the face. The one I don't recall will be the killer. It's very simple. Some guy snuck on the van in the middle of the other Elvises, and for some reason, killed one of them."

"Right. And this became your problem how?"

"When I found a dead Elvis with a knife in his back, for starters."

"You know what I mean, honey. Let the police handle it. They'll match names to faces and figure out who was supposed to be where. Somehow, they usually manage to find the perp."

"The perp? I love it when you talk cop to me. So how is Steve?"

Steve was Tootsie's significant other, though Harley had never met him and had serious doubts as to his existence. Still, it was polite to ask about him, and a good way to change the subject.

Tootsie grinned. "Gorgeous as always. How's your cop?"

"Gone." She tried not to flinch when she said that. For some reason, Morgan had gotten to her more than any guy ever had. That should have been her first clue that he'd take off.

Tootsie sat back in his office chair and stared at her. "What do you mean, *gone?*"

"Like the wind, you know—*pffit!* Off to play with the bad guys and leave us bad girls behind, I guess."

"I don't believe it. He's crazy about you."

"Apparently not. I think it's my habit of hanging around with dead guys. Seems to make some cops nervous."

"Understandable. Harley—what's going on?"

"I don't know. Maybe it's just time for us to be over. We had a pretty good run, I guess. May until July isn't too bad."

Tootsie rolled his eyes. "And they say men aren't monogamous. What are you going to do now?"

"Figure out which of these guys wasn't supposed to be on that van, and then call Bobby. After that, I've got a run to Graceland, right?"

"Right. But if you aren't up to it—"

"I'm fine. It's not the end of the world, just a guy." She left it like that, and after a minute Tootsie went back to work at the computer and answering the phone. Good thing. She wasn't at all sure she felt that way this time. Dammit.

The best antidote for uncertainty was work. Or so she'd heard.

It was harder than she'd thought matching the names to faces, especially when she hadn't really looked at them. They all looked the same, some taller, shorter, thinner, fatter, but basically all alike. And photos on driver's licenses were notoriously bad anyway. Her photo looked like a demented David Bowie, for instance, her lip curled in a sneer that she'd meant as a smile, and hair standing up atop her head like she'd stuck her finger into an electrical socket. It was the only picture of her where the resemblance to her brother could be seen.

Except Eric's eyes were blue, hers were green, and he had chameleon-color hair while hers usually stayed light blonde with a few darker streaks.

By the time she had to leave to pick up the van for her run to Graceland, she still hadn't figured out who was who. She'd only matched four names with Elvis faces, and that was because she figured out the tallest, shortest, fattest, thinnest. Maybe she couldn't help out after all. Not a bad thing. Her efforts at help in the past had only led to disaster anyway. This had to be a karmic sign. She needed to think about something else for a change, so she picked up her van and headed out.

One good thing about driving in Memphis—it required the concentration of a NASCAR driver to get to a destination without playing bumper cars. An excellent distraction.

Poplar Avenue traffic was always heavy. Today, as always, there were Memphis drivers who celebrated sunshine with their usual disregard for courtesy or traffic lights. A driver with Tennessee plates on his rusty El Camino leaned on his horn and yelled "Mississippi driver!" at a transgressor, and the driver in the shiny new SUV from DeSoto County, just across the Mississippi state line south of Memphis, returned the welcome greeting with a snappy one-finger salute. Tourism at its best. West Tennessee, North Mississippi, and a wide strip of eastern Arkansas formed the Mid-South, or Tri- State area. Memphis was the crossroads for trucks, trains, and planes delivering merchandise in the Southeast and up the Eastern Seaboard. Home of Federal Express, Nike, a Northwest Airlines hub, Elvis Presley, BB King, and the Grizzlies basketball team—all lucrative enterprises—Memphis was the last stop before I-55 dipped into the Deep South. It also made quite a handy route for drug traffickers transporting their products out of Mexico to customers up north.

Changes in the past three decades included a lot more than integrated schools and a black mayor. Martin Luther King had died in a shabby motel downtown, bringing Memphis infamy back in the sixties, but Elvis had already integrated music with his love of Negro gospel and the blues. Once known as just a "big country town," Memphis had imported more than its share of residents from as far away as China, and quite a few from places like New Jersey and Michigan. Chinese restaurants and Sharp manufacturing employees were welcomed, and longtime residents greeted them with friendly curiosity.

For all its veneer of recent sophistication, many old-time Memphians had never forgotten Union occupation during the Civil War and considered Southern general Nathan Bedford Forrest a war hero. A statue of Forrest stood tall and proud in a small park on Union Avenue in the heart of the medical district, marking his and his wife's graves. On the river bluffs downtown, despite some efforts to rename it, Confederate Park overlooked the Mississippi, its cannons aimed at invisible enemies. Tom Lee Park celebrated the heroics of a black citizen who'd pulled people to safety after a horrific boiler explosion on a riverboat, and the site hosted the annual worldwide barbecue every May. Riverboats docked at the river daily, and it was a big deal when a passenger paddle-wheeler stopped on its way downriver to New Orleans. Nineteenth-century bricks made walking to the boats rough, barges slogged down the middle of the river dragging wide wakes, and smaller paddle-wheelers made daily trips along the riverbanks for tourists. The city skyline had the glass Pyramid at one end, and President's Island with a toxic waste dump and dusty concrete plant at the other. Sandbars and wide expanses of muddy water lay on the southern horizon. Despite—or maybe because of—all its diversity, Memphis had a reputation for Southern hospitality.

Born in California and transplanted in Memphis fifteen years before, Harley was glad to do her part at welcoming paying tourists. It beat dealing with former bosses at a banking corporation.

The group she picked up at their hotel was pretty sedate. They were English, and not only excited to be here, but polite. The excitement in the van increased as the tourists saw the billboard and Graceland exit signs when she got off the Interstate at Brooks and Elvis Presley.

"Has it always been named Elvis Presley Boulevard," one of the ladies asked, "or was it named that after he died?"

"After he died. Before then, it was called Highway 51 on this end, and Bellevue inside the city limits," Harley replied. "My mother met Elvis back in the sixties. Ann-Margret and some other celebrities were there, riding motorcycles in the horse pasture. She hung over the stone fence to get his autograph."

It was just a little tidbit of personal information that Elvis fans usually liked to hear, as well as the regular spiel.

"Did he act like just a regular bloke," one of the men asked, "or was he shirty?"

Harley grinned. She loved the way the English talked. "Elvis was always courteous. He really appreciated his fans, even though it meant he was almost a prisoner in his own house."

"Sad, the way Elvis died. Too bad he couldn't have the street named after him before he went. Guess that's the way it is, right? Most people aren't truly appreciated until they're gone," the lady commented rather sadly.

Harley thought about that after she let them out behind the

tourist shops to get on the EPE—Elvis Presley Enterprises— van that'd take them across the busy street to the Graceland mansion. The tourist was right. People took others for granted far too often, and she'd been just as guilty of that as anyone else.

Mike came to mind. It wasn't that she hadn't appreciated him, because she had, but she hadn't thought about how her actions affected him or his job. She felt a little guilty. It was a lot different than with Bobby because, after all, he was just her friend, not her boyfriend. Besides the ribbing he took from cohorts, Mike had to be put in an awkward position every time she stumbled across another body.

But damn, it wasn't like she was trying to infiltrate undercover operations or anything. He had to know that. Didn't he? Maybe he'd just been looking for an excuse to cut out. Her finding bodies may have been the excuse he'd needed to move on. It was possible. She'd done the same thing herself a few times—grab at the first thing she could to make a graceful exit from a relationship that wasn't working. Sometimes her tongue outpaced her brain, but being unkind wasn't her style. Not like that. Hurting others was unnecessary. Most of the time.

Harley had a brief guilty pang about her caustic relationship with her cousins, but that was the way they'd always communicated. Though after risking her own life helping them out of a tight spot with a smuggler, murderer, and possible prison terms, their relationships had greatly improved in the last couple of months. It'd certainly make future family reunions more pleasant.

Anyway, now that she was on the receiving end of the "take a break" letdown, it still stung, no matter how nicely it was meant. A lesson for the future. An honest "this isn't working" was better than waiting for a phone call that would never come.

Diva was right. As usual. Karma had a way of biting you in the butt just when things seemed to be best.

As she was contemplating past sins and thinking about a cold Coke, a scream came from one of the other tour vans parked nearby. The hair on the back of her neck stood up, and she stuck her head out her still open van window to see what was going on. It was another Memphis Tour Tyme van, one of the larger ones that held two dozen people. Once it had been a Head Start school bus, but that was before the renovation of white paint and fancy blue lettering.

She didn't get out of the van because, after all, it was probably just a scream of frustration after listening to two dozen Elvises all singing at the same time. But then it came again in a shriller tone. Damn. She recognized that high pitch—Lydia Free.

Sighing, she got out of her van and crossed the parking lot. Waves of heat came up from the asphalt, shimmering. A canvas canopy covering steps leading to the shops and ticket booths flapped in an erratic breeze. The MTT bus door was open, and she saw Lydia standing on the second step, craning her neck to peer inside. Lydia had brown frizzy hair that Memphis humidity didn't improve, pale skin dotted with freckles, and a nervous tic under one eye most of the time. Her skinny frame looked frozen in place, one foot on the top step, and one foot on the second, white-knuckled fingers clutching the sides of the open door. Wheezing sounds came from her open mouth.

"Hey Lydia," Harley began, but Lydia turned and launched her body outward like an Air Force rocket. She landed on Harley. Immediately engulfed in a babbling, hysterical grip, Harley made some wheezing noises of her own before she got out, "Let go!"

When Lydia didn't release her strangling hold, Harley used a move she'd learned in a recent course on driver safety and self-protection, and twisted free. Mr. Penney's money had not been spent in vain. There was no need to use a stun gun at all.

"Jeez, you've got a grip like a python," she said when she could breathe. She firmly held Lydia at arm's length in case she coiled around her again. "What happened?"

"B-b-b-obby," Lydia got out, and Harley frowned. "Bobby? Bobby who?"

"No!" Lydia took a deep breath and said clearly, "*Body!*"

"As in—dead?"

Lydia's head bobbed energetically up and down.

Oh no. "Are you sure the person isn't just napping?"

Now Lydia's teeth were chattering. "Pretty s-s-sure. But maybe . . . he is?"

Probably not. Lydia would have scared him awake by now.

Harley felt queasy. She didn't want to deal with this. Maybe it was a mistake. Maybe the man was deaf. A lot of old geezers got all dressed up every year and wiggled their drooping butts, remembering a better time. That had to be it. She looked at Lydia. "I'll check." She stepped up into the bus. Lydia was known to overreact. Why Mr. Penney allowed her to take a vehicle onto the Memphis streets was beyond comprehension, but apparently Lydia was his niece or cousin, or something like that.

Sitting in the fifth row by the window, an Elvis impersonator sprawled halfway off the seat. Harley's heart thudded into overdrive. Her stomach twisted when she got close. He certainly looked dead. His mouth hung open and his eyes were half-closed. She leaned closer.

"Sir? Elvis?" Nothing.

She didn't want to touch him. You'd think she could tell a dead person from a live one by now, but apparently it didn't work that way. He could just be asleep. Her cousin Maddie slept with one or both eyes open, a really freakish thing to see in the middle of the night.

Finally, she squelched her squeamishness and put out a hand to give him a slight shake. It didn't help that Lydia screeched from the bus door, "Don't touch him!"

"If that voice doesn't wake the dead, he's past help," Harley muttered, but determinedly gave Elvis a gentle shake.

His head lolled forward on his chest at a crooked angle, and that was when she saw the tiny object sticking out from his neck. It looked like a penknife that kids used to carry, but obviously it could be pretty lethal. A thin stream of blood trickled down his neck and under the collar of his white jumpsuit. *Oh boy.*

She turned to look at Lydia still hanging back in the doorway.

Eyes as big as duck eggs looked back at her. Lydia's lips worked, and then she whispered, "Is . . . is he . . . ?"

"Dead as last Sunday's dinner."

"Why are you here? This isn't even your jurisdiction." Harley couldn't believe Bobby had shown up. As if she wasn't already feeling queasy and lightheaded. She'd never get used to death up close and fresh. Now he'd make it worse. "Isn't Graceland in the South precinct?" she asked crankily.

"Yes. I'd ask why you're here, but that'd be redundant. There's a body here, so of course you're here, too."

"That's not fair."

"The list of unfair things is too long to contemplate right now. Who found the DB?"

"Lydia Free."

"And again, why are you here?"

"I had a van full of tourists. They're up at the mansion right now."

"Where is this Lydia Free?"

"Follow the shrieks. The EMT's had to give her oxygen. They shouldn't have. It's only made her louder."

For a moment, Bobby stood looking at her where she sat in the driver's seat of her own van. He didn't look angry, but sort of perplexed, like he was trying to figure out the square root of an isosceles triangle or some other complicated math problem.

Harley stared back at him warily since he got so testy whenever she was in the vicinity of a dead body. "Harley," he finally said in a tone she recognized as bordering on the edge of angry, "are you trying to piss off everybody you know, or just me?"

"Just you, of course," she snapped back, "no one else is as much fun."

"One more reason you go through boyfriends so fast," he observed. "You've never forgotten how to make men go crazy. Still trying to get over me?"

She glared at him. Apparently, he'd already talked to Morgan. How else would he know they'd split up? Not that she cared. It wasn't like Bobby could brag about longevity in relationships. If it wasn't for the fact they'd long ago decided platonic worked better than any of that physical stuff, he'd probably be just a faint memory anyway. At the tender age of sixteen, she'd spent a most interesting night on the backseat of Bobby's car with Meatloaf playing *Paradise By the Dashboard Lights* on the radio. Not long after that they'd both come to the mutual conclusion they did a lot better as just friends. Bobby had that sexy Italian charm going on, but he tended to get a little too possessive, a trait that made her a little too homicidal.

"Don't flatter yourself, Bobby," she replied in reference to his conceited inference that she'd never gotten over him. When he kept looking at her, she said, "What? Do I have dirt on my nose?"

"I'm trying to decide if that's hair gel or horns on top of your head."

"Very funny."

"I'm glad one of us is amused. How do you do it? How do you go nearly thirty years without getting anything worse than traffic tickets, and then in the space of three months run across five corpses?"

"Just lucky I guess. And this makes six. Don't forget the guy in the warehouse." This conversation was eerily similar to the one she'd had with Morgan, and she'd had enough. "Since I'm not really involved, I'm going to pick up my passengers and take them back to their hotel. Am I released?"

He snapped his notebook shut and jammed his pen in the breast pocket of his suit coat. He looked rumpled and tired. And pissed off. "I'll need your official statement."

"I can find my way to the precinct with my eyes closed by now."

"Which explains the unusually high rate of traffic accidents lately."

She didn't dignify that with a reply. Haughty aloofness was a much better response.

Bobby stepped back as Harley got out of the van and headed for the shops to find her tour group. They were in one of the gift shops across from Graceland, mulling over ceramic replicas of the mansion mounted on top of music boxes, and discussing the exchange rate between pounds and dollars. She pulled out a calculator and helped them figure it out, then accompanied them to a store that specialized in Elvis CDs and tapes. Elvis videos played on one of the TV sets, a continuous stream of different songs. As much as she came here, Harley was always reminded anew of Elvis's sheer talent. Dark walls in the small museum built behind Elvis's house had rows upon rows of gold and platinum records to attest to that. There had never been anyone like him before he burst onto the music scene, and there would never be anyone else like him, a man recognized the world over the moment his distinctive voice was heard.

Finally they left the shops and headed for the van. Police tape stretched around the bus, and cruisers with lights still flashing barricaded it. Bobby was still there, talking with other officers. She'd been hoping they'd all be gone by now.

"Bloody hell," one of the men in her group exclaimed, "what happened here?"

Not wanting to alarm the tourists, Harley just said that a passenger had died. Let the cops get them alarmed. They were better equipped to handle hysteria than she was. Of course, the police took down names, addresses, and any pertinent information from each one, and a statement as to what they saw or didn't see. That took a while, so Harley got into her van and turned on the AC. Might as well be comfortable while waiting.

A familiar tingle in her right jeans pocket signaled an incoming call on her cell phone. She ignored it. Bobby had unnerved her. Dammit. Why did this keep happening to her?

Okay, it was bad enough it seemed to be happening to Elvises, but it was beginning to look really bad that she always seemed to be around when it did. She rested her head against the steering wheel and closed her eyes, waiting for the police to finish taking statements and move some cruisers out of the way so she could leave. In a few minutes the cell phone vibrated again, humming against her hip.

Finally, giving in to the inevitable, she played back the messages. Tootsie. Three times. All sounding a little frantic. "Harley," he said on the last call, "Lydia's tourists need a ride and all the other vans are too far out to get there quickly enough. Call me, girlfriend. I'm getting desperate here."

She called him back to tell him she'd have to drop her group off first, and then she would have room to take some of Lydia's tourists to their hotel.

"Thank God." He sounded relieved. "Charlsie can pick up a few, but she's in the small van. By the way, darling, I'm glad this body wasn't found in *your* van. I don't think the police would appreciate it right now."

"Yeah, so I heard. Lydia didn't like it too much either."

"Let the group know that we're sending vans for them, and that there'll be no charge. We sure don't need to scare away paying customers. Two dead guys in two days isn't at all good for business."

"Can't say it's done me any good either."

Harley hung up and made sure the van's air conditioner was full blast to cool off the group, then went to assure Lydia's group, huddled close to the yellow crime scene tape, that they'd soon be returned to their hotel.

"Your day is comped for your inconvenience," she added, "courtesy of Memphis Tour Tyme. Please wait for your ride to the hotel in the coffee shop, and we'll get you safely back."

By the time she got back to Graceland for them, Charlsie had picked up those she could. The ones left behind had indulged in a few beers and were feeling fine. One of them, a rather chunky guy who was obviously feeling no pain, sat up front with her since there was no more room in the back. She didn't normally allow that, but this guy seemed genial enough, good-natured and not belligerent, and since there wasn't room for him in the back, she was out of options anyway.

"I should'a known something was wrong with that guy," he said once the van was on the Interstate headed for their hotel. "He acted kinda weird."

"What guy? Oh, you mean the dead man? Most Elvis impersonators act a little weird." *My father not excluded,* she thought wryly.

"Naw, it wasn't that. Didn't want to share his seat. Acted like he'd get robbed or hit in the head. Put up a little fuss until the other guy said something to him, and then he settled down all right."

"Did you tell this to the police?"

"No, didn't think about it. Maybe I should have, huh? Was the dead guy sick?"

Harley thought for a moment. Apparently he didn't know that the dead Elvis had been stuck in the neck with a penknife.

How had he been killed so quietly and without anyone noticing?

It took a lot of nerve to do something like that in a bus full of tourists—nerve, or insanity. Or maybe a little bit of both.

"So he knew the other guy?" she asked, and the tourist shrugged. "Couldn't tell. No one else knew him, but we didn't know either of them anyway."

"Wait—weren't they part of your group?"

"Never saw 'em before. Figured they were just along for the ride."

Just like the extra guy had been along for the ride in her van. That was very interesting.

"Can you give me a description?" she asked.

"Black hair, long sideburns, white jumpsuit—"

"No, not the dead man, a description of the other guy."

"I just told you. Black hair, long sideburns, white jumpsuit, and gold chains."

"Both of them were Elvis impersonators?"

"Yeah. Maybe that's how they knew each other."

Sounded logical.

"But what's weirder," he said in a bit of a slur, "is that only one of them was s'posed to be on the bus. If that twitchy gal's right, that is."

"Twitchy?"

"Yeah, the skinny little driver. She's kinda excitable." Good description for Lydia.

"Did she say one of the Elvises wasn't supposed to be on there?"

"Not exactly, but she kept reading over that list on her clipboard and doing a head count when we got to Graceland. Like it wasn't coming out right."

"Where was the other Elvis?"

"Don't know. He got off the bus with the rest of us—except for the guy that died—but there were a lot of other Elvises around there, so I guess he just joined up with them. Some kind of concert under a tent."

After a moment, Harley said, "You really need to tell all this to the police."

"Sure. If you think it's important. Can't see why though."

"It's important." Let someone else tell him the guy had been murdered. It sure wasn't her job.

Tootsie met her at the garage when she returned the van. He looked frazzled. His hair was all loose around his face and straggling out of the ponytail he kept it in for work, and his silk shirt was half out of his pleated-front pants. Not at all normal. He was always immaculate.

"What's up?" she asked in concern, and he gave her an open-mouthed stare.

"Two . . . dead . . . bodies. On *our* vans! When this gets out we'll have cancellations all over the place." He cupped a hand over his mouth, words coming out all muffled. "This is worse than being embezzled."

"I'd think so. Although Sandler does look the type. It's always the quiet, snarky ones."

"Not always. Believe me, it can be someone you least expect. Anyway, I'd settle for that right now instead of this. At least it wouldn't run off a lot of our clients."

"Speaking of running off clients, you look pretty frightening at the moment."

Tootsie went back to pacing, his Birkenstock sandals slapping against the concrete floor of the parking lot. "This is unbelievable. Unbelievable!"

Harley looked at him. He seemed awfully upset for a mere employee. Could it be that he had a personal stake in the company? Like financial? She'd often wondered just how the ultraconservative Lester Penney had been induced to hire a man who painted his fingernails in the office and wore women's clothes after hours. For that matter, how had they even *met?* That could be a very interesting story. Now wasn't the time to ask, but one day . . .

"What can I do to help out?" she asked when he stopped pacing and leaned his forehead against the concrete wall with a big blue number two painted in the middle.

With his head still resting against the wall, Tootsie cut his eyes at her. Silence stretched, and then he said, "I can't believe I'm even asking you, but could you help find out who's behind this? Quietly, and without publicity?"

Harley blinked. "Wait—you're *asking* me to help?"

"I know. I can't believe it either. But you do seem to have a knack for it."

"I have a knack for getting hit in the head, crapped on by a goose, and whacked with a wooden penis. Although technically, I did most of the whacking with the last one."

"As if I need a reminder of your newest hobby. Not wooden Johnsons. Dead bodies." He turned to lean back against the wall and briefly closed his eyes. "Jewel thieves, smugglers, now dead Elvises. Your career has taken quite a different turn."

"Who'd have thought it."

"But somehow, and I have no idea how you manage it, it all ends up good."

"For the police and aspirin corporations."

He opened his eyes. "You didn't do too badly last time, if I remember correctly. Ten thousand dollars is a nice reward."

"You're offering me money?"

"No. But I'll keep you on the payroll even when you aren't doing tours."

"Can you do that? What'll Mr. Penney say?"

"Just let me worry about that. Think you can do it?"

"Why not? It'll be a great distraction for me right now. I can't promise there won't be publicity, though," she warned. "There usually is."

"Just please, *please*, try to keep it to a minimum."

"No promises," she repeated, and Tootsie sighed.

"As long as it's a Tour Tyme employee who solves the murders, that can only be good. Just be sure you help solve the murders and save the publicity until after it's over, okay?"

"I'll do my best."

Four

It was much too quiet in Harley's apartment. The Spragues next door didn't have their music up loud for a change. Maybe the honeymoon had worn off. Not that she was complaining. Right now, listening to rather vocal lovebirds would be like throwing a bucket of water to a drowning man, completely unwanted.

Thoughts of Morgan had changed from regret to resignation. In some weird way, she understood his reasoning behind putting distance between them. For a guy in his position, this new habit she'd somehow acquired had to create career conflict. It'd be like her Aunt Darcy going to work for the Republican party, when everyone knew she'd rather give up all her Manolo Blahniks than vote anything but a Democratic ticket.

Understanding and liking it were two entirely different things, though. Usually, she could see the end of a relationship well before it finally hit the skids. This one had blind-sided her.

"Maybe you're so upset because he did it first," Cami said when Harley called her later to complain about Morgan. "You know how you've always been the one to walk out first." Camilla Watson had been her best friend since junior high and knew far too much about her past loves and crimes, just like Bobby. That could be inconvenient, but also helpful at times.

This wasn't one of those times. She didn't want truth. She wanted sympathy and righteous indignation.

"That's not true," Harley said. "Remember Alex?"

"How could I forget? And you still walked out on him first. Yes, you did, because you called me from Oxford to say you were moving out and needed a place to stay for a night."

"Oh. Yeah. That was my third year of college. Stupid of me to quit college. Alex should have been the one to leave. One more day of living with him, and I'd have kicked his ass down the stairs. I guess I should have waited him out."

"He called me for a year after that, you know, asking about you."

Harley was surprised. "He did? I never knew that."

"Yep. Couldn't get over the fact that you'd dumped him. It surprised me, too. I'd always thought Alex was the great love of your life."

"So did I. Wonder why I left him? I can't even remember now."

"Neither can I. Anyway, it proves my point that you're mostly upset because Morgan left first."

She thought about that a moment. Then she said, "No, I think I really miss him. The jerk."

"At the risk of sounding like Diva, if it's meant to be, he'll be back."

"I'm glad you didn't quote that 'Let it go free and if it's meant to come back, it will' crap that annoys the hell out of me. I prefer the other version."

"Which one is that?"

"Let him go free and if he doesn't come back, hunt him down and shoot him."

Cami laughed. "I've heard people say that when you live long enough, you know you're better off with a cat anyway."

Harley glanced over at Sam. He sat on the arm of a chair washing his family jewels. Or what he had left of them. "That's entirely possible. He's the only male in my life or bed right now."

"So, other than your tawdry love life, how are things?"

"I take it you haven't been watching the local news."

"Oh God."

"Why is that the reaction I usually get from you?"

"Who died?" Cami asked with a sigh.

"Elvis."

"This may shock you, but rumor has it that he died in 1977."

"I've heard that. This Elvis, however, was stabbed in the back of my van yesterday. It was not a pretty sight."

"Oh, I did hear that. It was *your* van? I should have known. Have you ever considered that you may be some kind of magnet for murder?"

"Now see, that's just what I said to Morgan. I can't figure it out either. So today, when I was minding my own business, going right along with my usual tour guide stuff, another dead Elvis pops up."

"*Another* one? Harley, they're going to put you under the jail."

"It didn't happen in my van. It was in Lydia's tour bus. But here's the really strange thing—two Elvises were on that bus. Sitting together. One of them ends up dead, and one of them ends up gone. Ring any bells for you?"

"Yes, warning bells. Stay away from this, Harley. Remember the other times you got mixed up in this kind of thing."

"Here's the kicker—Tootsie asked me to investigate." When Cami didn't say anything, Harley waited a moment to allow the shock to sink in. Sam had curled up in her lap for a nap, and she stroked his soft fur with one hand. His body vibrated in a loud purr. Just as the silence on the other end of the line stretched a little bit too long, Cami asked, "Are you sure?"

"Yep. Shocked me, too. I didn't know he had so much faith in me."

Cami wasn't as pleased as she'd expected. Instead, she sounded horrified. "You do realize he was probably just being sarcastic?"

"No, not at all. He was dead serious. Ha! I made a pun. Anyway, he said he'd cover any time I missed and still pay me, as long as I keep things as quiet as possible and find out who's killing people on our tour buses."

"Harley, Bobby is going to freak out when he finds out you're getting involved. You know that."

"You're not going to tell him, are you?"

"Of course not."

"Then he's not likely to find out. I'm going to be very low-key. And since Morgan isn't around to rat me out, it ought to be a lot easier."

"It won't work. You know it won't work. Something's going to happen, you'll end up in big trouble and Bobby will have to arrest you. So don't do it."

"Take a deep breath and have some faith, Cami. Everything'll be just fine. Tootsie says I have a knack for this."

"A knack for murder? There are nicer things to have, Harley. Like typhoid."

"Unbeliever."

After they hung up, Harley reflected on the two murders.

They had to be related, but it had occurred to her that they had two slight differences. One Elvis had been killed by an unknown Elvis in a bus full of Elvises, while the other Elvis had been killed by an Elvis he knew. If it was the same killer, he—or maybe even she—adapted to the situation. But why pick on Elvis impersonators? There had to be a common thread. Had the two dead Elvises known each other? Were they all in the same competition? Business together? Neighbors? There could be any number of motives, but none of them jumped out at her.

Since she had to start somewhere, it made sense to find the connection between murderer and victims and go from there. To do that, she had to start with the victims' connection to each other and work backward.

Fortunately, she had experience in working backward. Tootsie was quite willing to do his computer magic and use his police connections to find out what he could about the victims. The first Elvis's real name was Derek Wade and he worked at the local Kellogg's plant in his other life. The second dead Elvis was a thirty-six year old man named Leroy Jenkins.

One lived in Midtown, the other lived in North Memphis, and neither of them had any known connection to the other except that they were both contestants in the Elvis competitions.

"Maybe if I talk to their families, I could find out if they knew one another," Harley said the next morning, and Tootsie nodded. He looked a little haggard, with bluish bruises under his eyes and a frown line between his brows. "Sounds good to me."

"I'll need some kind of official sounding reason, though. You know, without being too obvious."

"You're a Memphis Tour Tyme employee. You're there to offer condolences and ask if there's anything we can do. Of course, our insurance adjusters will handle any claims that may arise, so don't get sucked into discussing that. Especially admitting fault in any way. We have to be very careful about that, and let the lawyers and adjusters handle that kind of thing." Tootsie paused, and then said, "I'll print you out a few business cards with our logo and phone numbers so they'll feel more comfortable about allowing you to ask questions."

"Good. I ran out of mine. Put my cell number on them, too,

okay?"

"Don't you think that's a waste of ink? It'll be broken by the end of the week anyway."

"I haven't broken a one since I started clipping them to my belt loop. My record is now at nearly six weeks."

Rolling his eyes, Tootsie said something about *too little too late*, but printed out the cards on the laser jet printer, and handed her the perforated sheet of thick paper. "Be careful, girlfriend," he said, and she nodded.

"I always am." She flashed him a bright smile meant to reassure him that the problem was in good hands, and then blew him a kiss on her way out the office door. She thought she heard him shout after her *Don't do anything stupid!* but could have been mistaken. She always tried to be careful.

Armed with business cards, her cell phone, and a full tank of gas in her '91 silver Toyota, Harley set out for Midtown and the family of Derek Wade. He'd been forty-two, lived at home with his parents—which explained a lot—and worked as a raisin counter at the local Kellogg's. Apparently it paid well to count raisins. She wondered how they did it, one by one, or with a scoop like in the commercials, "two scoops" in every box. That *was* Kellogg's, wasn't it? It was hard to keep up with the battling cereal corporations' ads.

And it was much harder than she'd imagined interviewing the grieving parents. She had to remind herself it was for a good cause, finding his killer, but she still found it difficult to deal with their pain. It put real faces to the victim's family, something she'd never had to deal with before. Statistics were cold. Grief was not. How did the police do it day after day? How did they deliver such terrible news after seeing broken and bloody bodies? No wonder so many officers retreated to emotional apathy while performing their jobs. It'd be suicide to empathize with all the victims and families they must encounter on a routine basis, and lessen their competency and effectiveness.

The interview with the Wades yielded little information she didn't already know, and she considered avoiding her visit with the Jenkins family. But that wouldn't get the job done. So she steeled herself for another emotional hour and drove to the North Memphis address. It was in a shabby area of the city, the houses smaller and rundown, litter in many yards, not to mention the broken trees from a storm several years before. The media had dubbed it Hurricane Elvis, the straight-line winds fierce enough to knock down old oaks and keep electricity off for weeks in many neighborhoods. Just a few streets over in the same part of Memphis, houses were compact but neat, with fenced yards and obvious pride in ownership. Houses here still had tree rubbish, but at least it was piled up.

She parked at the curb in front of the house and checked the house number twice on her list. Could it be wrong? This couldn't be the house of the recently bereaved. The front door stood wide open, and laughter and music drifted out. Maybe they hadn't been notified yet. That thought made her queasy.

While she sat there indecisively as the sun beat down ferociously on the windshield, one of the kids running in and out of the house hollered that another cop was sitting out front. Okay, she could at least figure out if they'd been told, and if they hadn't, make up some excuse and come back later.

A woman came to the front door and leaned against the frame. Skinny, with dirty blonde hair piled on top of her head like some kind of bizarre bird's nest, she squinted across the yard littered with broken toys and trash, a lit cigarette hanging from one corner of her mouth.

"You the cops?"

Harley got out of the car and approached the house. "No. Are you Mrs. Jenkins?"

"When it suits." She laughed at her own joke. "Who are you?"

"Ms. Davidson. With Memphis Tour Tyme. I wonder if I could ask you a few questions."

"This about Leroy? He's dead."

So she knew. And apparently hid her grief well.

"Yes," Harley said, "I know. Please let me offer my condolences and assure you that the company is cooperating fully with the police to find his murderer."

"Yeah, yeah. So how much money are you offering?"

Harley blinked. "Excuse me?"

"Money. A settlement. You're with the insurance company, right?"

"No, with the tour bus company. Your husband was on our bus."

"In that stupid Elvis getup, I guess." She blew a stream of cigarette smoke in Harley's face and snorted. "Dumb bastard. Leroy never had a lick of sense anyway. Always off spending good money on shit like that instead of groceries. That's why I threw his ass out last year. Not good for nothin' around here." Her eyes narrowed slightly. "But he left me with his kids, so maybe I need to sue the tour bus company for letting that good-for-nothing idiot get killed."

A little boy peeked at Harley from behind Mrs. Jenkins, big brown eyes wide and his hair hanging over his eyebrows. All he wore was a pair of ragged blue shorts. Behind him, bare floors were littered with empty cereal boxes and discarded clothes. Flies buzzed and a window air conditioner competed with the heat. Home sweet home. It made Harley greatly appreciate her parents, for all their flaws.

"Mr. Jenkins didn't live here? I was given this address—"

"Just told you. Threw his ass out last year. Why are you here if not to offer money?"

"I'm gathering any information that might assist the police in apprehending his killer. As I said—"

"I don't care nothin' about that. He probably got what he deserved. All I'm interested in is how much money I'm gonna get to support his kids. It'll be the first time he's ever helped out, that's for damn sure."

The little boy clinging to his mother made a sniffling sound, and Harley saw his lips quiver and his eyes fill with tears. That made her mad.

"You know, Mrs. Jenkins, whatever your problems with your late husband, I'm sure his children loved him, so maybe we can discuss this in private."

"Hell, his kids know what a rotten bastard he was, so no point in—"

"Step outside and close the damn door," Harley snapped, "or I'll report to the insurance adjusters that you're uncooperative." She had no idea if she could do anything of the kind or if it'd matter anyway, but this troll of a woman obviously needed to be dealt with in language she'd understand.

It must have worked, because she shoved the little boy back into the house and closed the door. Then she turned to look at

Harley, arms crossed over her chest and her eyes narrowed. She had an expression like a thwarted weasel. Well, that didn't matter, because Harley had experience with weasels, too, and she intended to get the information she needed.

By the time she left, she'd learned that Leroy Jenkins had moved in with a roommate in Frayser, that he worked erratically as a mechanic at a repair shop on Watkins, and that he'd been attending Elvis competitions for five years. He'd been a favorite last year, making the finals.

It wasn't much, but it was a start. As far as she'd learned, neither man knew each other, at least not well, but must have been acquainted with one another at the competitions. Maybe she needed to investigate the competitions next, how they were conducted, prizes offered, etcetera.

Yogi should be able to help with that.

"There's a Super Bowl competition for Elvis impersonators?" Harley had to keep from rolling her eyes, speaking loudly to be heard over the whine of Yogi's electric treadmill.

"Yep," her father replied, puffing a little as he tried to keep up with the treadmill, "it's called an ETA Super Bowl and it's held in Memphis at the *Images of the King* competition. This year it's August eleventh through the sixteenth, right up until the candlelight vigil."

"Why is it called ETA? Shouldn't that be EP something?"

"Elvis Tribute Artists." Yogi missed a step and slid backward on the treadmill, barely catching himself before he fell. King watched intently from under the dining room table, muscles quivering as if he intended to jump on it, too. Maybe that was a good idea, in light of the fact the dog was so high-energy.

Harley turned her attention back to her father. "So what does the winner get? A lifetime supply of fried peanut butter and banana sandwiches?"

Yogi gave her a reproachful look. "There's a cash prize as well as the prestige of being the grand champion."

Aha. Motive. "A big cash prize?"

"It's not the cash prize that's the most important. If he wants, the grand champion gets a lot of gigs during the next year, and appears at the annual ceremonies the next year to present the trophy. It's a big honor. And I intend to win."

"Just because you feel the money isn't important doesn't mean everyone does. Y'all hide your money in pickle jars instead of keeping it safely in a bank. You're just asking for trouble." Yogi stopped to look at her but the treadmill kept going.

He fell forward, caught himself, then went backward, staggering as his arms pin-wheeled. Harley tried to catch him but missed. He landed on his butt with a heavy "whoof!" The empty treadmill kept going, and King took advantage to jump on the moving black band. While the dog kept pace with the treadmill, Harley helped Yogi to his feet.

"Are you all right?" she asked when she got him upright again. He looked dazed. His eyes were the bright green of a traffic light, and he kept blinking them.

"I think so . . . " he finally got out, sounding breathless.

"You need to work on your dismount technique. You're supposed to turn the machine off first, and then stop walking. It's much easier that way."

"Maybe so."

"Well, at least you now know how to exercise King on rainy days. He thinks he's a race horse."

Yogi sat down on a dining room chair and wiped his brow with a paper towel he pulled from his pocket. "King gets on it more than I do. He loves it. I hate it. But I don't want to insult Elvis's memory by being too fat or busting out of my jumpsuit. If I could lose enough weight, I'd wear the same black leather he wore at his comeback in sixty-eight."

Harley sighed. It was beyond her comprehension. Not even in her days of intense worship of Steve Perry from Journey had she idolized a singer as much as her father worshiped Elvis. Of course, she recalled dressing up like Stevie Nicks once, layered dress and boots, long hair loose around her face, singing *Stand Back* while Cami used her parents' Super 8 camera to film it. All traces of that humiliation had since been destroyed, she hoped. So maybe Yogi wasn't so alone in his rock star adulation after all. He'd just kept at it too long after adolescence.

"I understand," Harley said to her father when they both knew she really didn't.

He smiled. "Thanks."

She smiled back at him. He really was a great father, even with this insanity he indulged in every year. And really, everybody had their quirks, didn't they? It just seemed that her family was a bit more blessed with them than most, or maybe it was just that they didn't mind keeping them unapologetically out in the open.

"So tell me what goes on at these competitions," she said. "Like how many contestants there are and who the judges are, that sort of thing."

"It varies from year to year by how many contestants show up, but only twenty-four are in the finals." Yogi got up and turned off the treadmill. Sweet silence filled the dining room.

King hopped off the treadmill when it stopped and went into the kitchen, presumably to get a drink of water. Yogi wasn't far behind him. "Sometimes the judges are other contestants from previous years, but occasionally we get a celebrity or two as judges."

She followed him into the kitchen. As she'd suspected, King lay on the kitchen floor with his head in his water bowl.

Just his ears and eyes showed above the deep bowl, reminding her of a flop-eared crocodile, and slurping sounds came from his vicinity.

"Like who as celebrities?"

"TV people, news columnists, those kind. Did you drink my root beer?" he asked with his head stuck inside the refrigerator.

"You know I don't like that organic stuff Diva buys. Where is she, by the way? Burying the pickle jars?"

Yogi shut the refrigerator and twisted open a bottle of peach flavored water. "I think she went to pick up some more supplies. We've got a big flea market coming up soon."

Their main source of revenue. After inheriting his parents' house when Harley was only fourteen, they'd moved back to Memphis from a California commune. Diva read tarot cards and sold crystal jewelry and dream catchers, and Yogi made metal garden trolls and windmills to sell at local flea markets. They made enough money to buy food and pay utilities and taxes, though Yogi always had to make his annual protest over the latter. Government conspiracy was a familiar theme. He'd never quite recovered from the mindset of the sixties. Not that Harley didn't sometimes agree with him, but she stopped short of picketing the Federal Building or protesting for animal rights outside the meat packing plants. More than once she'd had to provide her parents bail money and a ride home from the police station.

Since Yogi chose to ignore her references to their banking system of pickle jars buried in the back yard, she gave up for now. It would come up again. She'd make sure of that.

"So is that it? That's all the Elvis tributes are, just contests and a little prize money?"

Yogi sighed. "After all these years, you'd think you'd have paid more attention."

"You would, wouldn't you? It's not that I'm not interested in you. It's just that I've never been that interested in all the fuss made about Elvis every year. Sorry."

Yogi looked sad. "There's never been another one like him, never will be. He created an era all on his own, a poor boy from Mississippi with only his talent and determination. Now he's known worldwide, and most of the rock music today is here only because of him. I don't mean that stuff your brother plays, that's just noise. A waste of talent."

"We certainly agree on that. And it's not that I don't admire Elvis, because how could I not? Every week I tell tourists about how he started out in a two room house in Tupelo before his talent got him to Graceland. And sometimes I tell them that because of my father, I've listened to Elvis's music all my life."

That pleased Yogi. "You do?"

"Sure. And sometimes I tell tourists about one of the times Diva met Elvis, and knew how he often got so lonely he'd walk down the highway from Graceland to visit with the night attendant at the Shell gas station. Almost everybody knows about how he had to rent amusement parks and movie theaters to be able to go out and not be mobbed by fans, but not many realize just how lonely he got at times."

Yogi nodded. "There's a muffler shop at that Shell station now. My dad worked there a long time ago, when it was still a Shell station. He was a mechanic. The night attendant, Clyde, would tell him how he and Elvis talked sometimes, maybe shared a nip or two, and told dirty jokes. People forget that at heart Elvis was still a small-town boy from Tupelo stuck in a big-time world with too many boundaries. Talent made him, but it ruined him, too. Nobody ever thinks about how much he gave up sharing that talent."

Now her father looked so sad Harley had to change the

subject to cheer him up. "Hey, want to go to McDonald's while Diva isn't here?"

That did the trick. As a closet carnivore living in a vegetarian household, the occasional cheeseburger or Big Mac was a guilty pleasure for Yogi. No doubt Diva knew about his lapses, but chose not to make an issue of it.

So Yogi, Harley, and despite her halfhearted protests, King, got into her car and drove to the McDonald's on Highland, only a few blocks away. She bought her father a Big Mac and King a cheeseburger, and herself a fried pie. All three of them were blissful with grease.

"You know you're going to have to do extra jogging to work that off," she said to Yogi as they left the parking lot, and he nodded.

"It's worth it. Got any breath mints? I don't want your mother to smell McDonald's on my breath."

"For you, but King will have to wing it. You can always claim he got in the neighbor's garbage again. That's usually true anyway."

"He's been doing much better. Except for yesterday, when he got in Sadie's flowerbeds. I have to replace two azalea bushes and some kind of orangey flowers. He was digging for moles. I told Sadie those humps in her lawn were mole trails, but she didn't listen."

"How did he dig up two bushes? Those were pretty big."

"Oh, he didn't dig those up, he ate them. Or chewed on them, anyway."

Harley glanced in her rearview mirror. The culprit didn't look at all ashamed. He had his nose pressed against the back window as he surveyed the passing panorama of neat houses, the neighborhood head shop that sold bongs and other drug paraphernalia, a tattoo parlor, the St. Ann's Catholic school Harley had attended, and a music store. Businesses and residents changed through the years, but some things always remained the same.

"Well," Harley said, "Mrs. Shipley doesn't get mad about that sort of thing as long as you replace them. For a busybody and neighborhood gossip, she's really pretty nice."

"She's been a good neighbor," Yogi agreed, and wiped his mouth with a napkin to scrub away any remaining traces of McDonald's as they got close to home. Eating meat was his biggest crime to date lately, and he and Diva hadn't been arrested for protests in a while. Maybe they were growing out of that stage at last.

Really, as frustrating as they could be at times, Harley decided, she needed to stop complaining about her parents. She could have been stuck with a horror of a mother like that Patty Jenkins. No wonder Leroy left her. Too bad he didn't take the kids with him.

"Hey," she said as an idea occurred to her, "when is your next Elvis-fest?"

"A concert Friday night at Dad's Place on Brooks. Why?"

"I thought I'd tag along if you don't mind."

"Mind?" Yogi grinned so big his eyes looked like slits. "I'd love it. You can give me a few pointers, maybe. The big competition is way too soon and I want to be at my best."

"I'll be there." It would give her an excellent chance to scope out the contestants and see which one of them might be a killer.

Five

"Why are we here again?" Cami looked around the huge room filled with Elvises and noise.

"To find a killer."

Cami winced. "Arrest that guy over there. He's killing *Don't Be Cruel.*"

"I can't make an arrest, Cami. Even for murdering a song. The judges will have to do that. I just want to scope out these guys and see if any of them look familiar. The killer was on my van, so I should be able to spot him."

"Wasn't he dressed as Elvis?"

She sighed. "Yeah. That might make it a little more difficult."

"I'll say. And anyway, even if you see the guy who killed the Elvis on your van, there's no guarantee he's the same guy who killed the Elvis on the other bus."

"That may be true, but there's got to be a connection. Two dead Elvises in two days? Say, do you know if the plural of Elvis is Elvises, or Elvi?"

Cami gave her a skeptical look. "You've really lost your mind, haven't you. I think it started back in May, but now you're past help."

"We've already discussed this. My insanity began at puberty. I've just refined it."

"Bobby's right. You're dangerous. I can't believe I let you talk me into coming here with you. Where's Yogi? And how soon do we get to leave?"

"Don't listen to anything Bobby says about me. Yogi and Diva are here somewhere. I said we'd meet them at the bar when it's over. Have I told you how good you look tonight? Your diet has really paid off."

"Atkins was right. Low-carb works. I'm a size four, but I'd kill for a loaf of French bread or a box of Krispy Kremes. Maybe that's what set off the guy who's killing Elvises. A case of Diet Derangement."

"No excuse. There aren't any carbs in gin or vodka."

"Good point. I'm headed for the bar. You'll find me with a Diet 7-Up and Absolut."

"Good thing I'm driving," Harley called as Cami walked away. She really did look great, but almost too skinny. That's what fooling around with a man did for women. Turned them into sticks or cat ladies. Harley wasn't sure which one she qualified for, probably both. Her jeans had gotten loose and now she slept with a cat every night. Things were not looking up.

Not that she didn't look nice tonight. She'd worn a thin-strapped top with a low neckline edged with a broad band of glittery embroidery, a new short, flared purple skirt, and sandals with heels. She almost never wore skirts, much less heels, but she had tonight. And she'd blown her hair dry instead of gelling it into spikes, so it feathered around her face in wispy strands. It was a disguise. Her own parents wouldn't recognize her. Cami's mouth had dropped open when she'd seen her.

"I forgot you could look like that," she'd exclaimed, and Harley had told her to shut up and never mention it again. Cami had just laughed.

Harley got a Coke and wandered around the crowded room, peering at Elvises over the top of her glass, looking as nonchalant as possible. On the bandstand, different impersonators sang their hearts out, songs ranging from early Elvis to gospel. Some were really good, and some were ludicrous.

Now she understood Yogi's determination not to mar the memory of his favorite performer. A really fat Elvis with a bad wig attempted to reenact one of the Las Vegas shows, but split his pants when he went down to one knee. Or maybe that was part of the impersonation.

She knew it wasn't going to be as easy to recognize the guy from her van as she'd hoped. While dressed in different Elvis eras ranging from fifties to seventies, they all blended together, it seemed. Except for physical size, the faces were nearly indistinguishable, save for the Asian, black, and Hispanic impersonators. This definitely wasn't going to be easy. Maybe not even possible.

Leaning up against the wall, Harley watched the crowd. She didn't see Cami. Maybe she had run off with an Elvis or taken Harley's advice to find a one-night stand. The latter was not at all probable, and the first was impossible. Cami's musical preferences drifted more toward the David Lee Roth, Jon Bon Jovi type. But she hadn't been exposed as much to the eclectic music of Harley's childhood.

The announcer at the mike said a familiar name that grabbed her attention, and Harley looked at the slightly raised stage against the far wall as he introduced her father. Yogi came onstage with a flourish, swirling his white jeweled cape in over-the-top Elvis imitation. He belted out a favorite hit, *His Latest Flame*, that brought a round of applause and seemed to impress the crowd. It was the best she'd ever heard him sing. The applause verified it.

Just as Yogi left the stage, someone grabbed her arm and said, "Don't blow my cover."

She'd been taking a drink of her Coke, and barely kept from spilling it. She looked up angrily. Then she choked, spraying the Elvis with Coke. Coughing and spluttering, she suffered a few blows on the back before recovering enough to say, "*Morgan?* What the hell are you doing?"

Dressed in black leather pants, his dark hair styled in Elvis of sixty-eight, he narrowed his eyes while he brushed recycled Coke from his black leather jacket. "What does it look like?"

"You're an Elvis impersonator? Dear God—why didn't I know about this dark side of your personality?"

"Let's go over here where we won't be overheard."

Harley allowed him to guide her into the carpeted corridor outside the room, where she stood looking at him in the dim overhead lights. He even had a gold TCB necklace around his neck. Damn, for an Elvis impersonator, he really looked good. "I'm working a case," he said softly, "so don't blow my cover, okay?"

"You mean gang-bangers and drug lords dress up like Elvis, too? Or are gunrunners smuggling weapons inside their jeweled capes and pink Cadillacs?"

Mike's mouth thinned. "Very funny."

"No, what's funny is seeing you like this. Are you wearing *make-up?*" She couldn't help it. She had to laugh. And the more she laughed, the more he scowled, but she couldn't seem to control it.

Mike leaned back against the wall and crossed his arms over his chest. "Believe me, it wasn't my idea. I didn't volunteer, that's for sure."

Finally able to talk without giggling, Harley wiped her eyes. "I believe you. I can't imagine what kind of case you'd be working that would require dressing as Elvis, but—"

She stopped. He looked at her and she looked at him. Even though she knew he'd never admit it, she said, "You're working the dead Elvises case, aren't you. The police know the killer is another Elvis or someone connected to these competitions, don't they? I knew I was on the right track."

"And just what the hell do you mean by that? Harley, if you're messing around in that case—"

"I never said I was." Instant irritation set in. "Yogi is performing tonight, remember? I've got as much right to be here as anyone else. I just figured it had to involve an Elvis impersonator after the last murder, that's all."

Morgan didn't look trustful, but after a moment he nodded. "All right. Just don't *you* get involved. Whoever the murderer is, he's bold enough to kill in plain sight of two dozen tourists. I don't think he'd hesitate to kill anyone else who got in his way."

"Well, I don't have to worry about that since I don't intend to get in his way." That much was certainly true. She intended to pass along any information she learned to Tootsie and let him pass it on to his roommate, Steve the cop. Any credit for identifying the killer would only be made public after the police had made an arrest. While the most important thing was catching the killer, Tootsie hoped good publicity lessened any negative press generated by the murders on Memphis Tour Tyme buses. And it wouldn't hurt Harley, either. She'd love to prove Bobby wrong, as well as Morgan. She wasn't always a screw-up.

"I hope not," Mike was saying, "'cause your luck may not hold out."

"And here I thought it was more than luck that kept me alive."

"Right, but there won't always be someone around to rescue you."

"Rescue me?" She put her hands on her hips and glared at him. "I don't recall anyone around in that warehouse, or showing up before I got away from that last maniac who intended to kill me."

"We seem to remember things differently. I showed up at the warehouse, and again last time right in the middle of the shooting."

"Yeah, but I'd already escaped. Mostly." He just looked at her and she felt a little guilty. "Okay, I concede that part. But I probably would have gotten away both times."

"Guess we'll never know."

"Guess not." An awkward silence fell between them. Then he looked toward the door as the announcer's voice came over the speakers. "They're calling my name. Got to go do my stuff."

"You're actually going to sing? Good God. Can you sing?"

"I do all right."

"I've got to hang around to see this."

"Don't stay on my account. Feel free to leave."

"No way in hell. I'd give a week's pay for this entertainment."

Morgan groaned. "I'd give a month's pay to get out of it."

"And yet here you are."

"Here I am. Do me a favor. Go away."

"Sing to me, Elvis baby. I'll be the blonde at the bar."

"In the short purple skirt." He looked her up and down, and something in his gaze made her stomach flip. He still had a powerful effect on her libido. Damn him.

It seemed forever but could only have been a few seconds before the announcer's voice came over the speakers again, his words incomprehensible over the roar in her ears as her blood surged like ocean surf. She could almost smell the seaweed, see the moonlight, feel Morgan's hands . . .

"Later," Morgan said, snapping her out of her brief trance, and she blinked as he turned and walked away.

Why did she have to run into him again? She'd been doing all right. Now she had to wait a minute for the blood that had rushed from her head to work its way back up before she tried to walk. By the time she got back inside Morgan was performing his rendition of *Suspicious Minds*. He would. It was her favorite Elvis song. The rat.

He gathered more than a few interested looks from the women in the crowd, swiveling his hips in a pretty good Elvis imitation, the tight black leather pants leaving little to the imagination and sparking more than a few memories. Why did they have the heat on in this place? She fanned her face with a bar napkin and tried to think of something else.

Cami found her leaning against the bar. "That guy onstage right now looks pretty familiar to me, Harley. How do I know him?"

Without taking her eyes from the stage, Harley said, "He's Morgan's twin brother."

Cami squinted at the stage. "Really? I didn't know he had a twin."

"He doesn't."

Cami set her drink down on the bar, but missed. Ice and vodka spilled across the counter and onto Harley's arm. "Damn. Sorry about that. I missed the bar. Why doesn't he have a twin?"

"You'd have to ask his parents. I'm not going to have to carry you out to the car, am I?"

Considering that, Cami said as the last lyrics faded into a riff of guitar chords, "I don't think so. I've only had three drinks. I'm still functioning."

Harley turned to look at her while Morgan left the stage. "Just not so well, it seems."

Cami smiled sloppily. "I'm fine."

"Uh huh. Here come Yogi and Diva. Straighten up, and we'll leave soon."

Yogi was smiling broadly. "Did you hear the applause? They loved me!"

"I'd have been shocked if they hadn't. You were great."

"Got any pointers for me?"

"Yes, a little less melodrama with the cape. Other than that, don't change a thing."

Yogi nodded happily. Diva smiled serenely. Harley sighed enviously. It'd be nice to live in their world.

Her world currently required that she get her drunken friend to the car, however. Of course, they'd had to park in the very back of the crowded lot. I-55, an abandoned hotel, and a chain link fence edged the parking area, and she tried to remember just where she'd left her Toyota. Headlights of passing cars on the interstate and overhead vapor lights provided enough illumination for her to walk Cami across the asphalt without falling into a pothole, though she wasn't navigating much better than her friend. Stupid of her to wear sandals with heels. Not used to them, she wobbled like a drunken sailor.

It took luck and skill, but she managed to get the passenger side door open and Cami safely wedged inside without too much damage to either of them. Humidity and effort took its toll, however. This year summer had swung between steaming heat and monsoons. She wasn't sure which was worse. At least it wasn't as hot as previous years, though tourists unfamiliar with southern summers found that hard to believe.

Leaning back against the side of the car to catch her breath, Harley happened to look over when a vehicle stopped in the aisle between cars. An Elvis impersonator opened the back door to the taxi, and when he straightened up and looked in her direction, something about him struck her as very familiar. She'd seen this guy recently. It wasn't until the taxi had pulled away to go out the exit that it hit her—the missing Elvis!

"Hey, wait a minute," she shouted, and started running after the taxi, but it'd gone around the far end of parked cars by then. She kicked off her heels to run faster and try to catch the taxi driver's attention, but that didn't help. As it passed under a vapor light, she saw the Elvis looking back at her.

Harley spent the better part of the next morning at the Memphis Tour Tyme office tracking down the taxi and driver that had made a pickup at Dad's Place around ten. How did the police do it? No wonder it took them so long to solve cases, when they had to follow so many leads that ended in dead-ends before they got lucky.

"Where are you going?" Tootsie asked as she stuck the paper with the name and address into her backpack. "And leave your cell phone on. Just in case."

"Just in case what? Never mind. Stupid question. I'm following up a lead, talking to the taxi driver who picked up the missing Elvis last night to see if I can get an address where he took him. With any luck, he took him home and we can get a name as well."

"That wouldn't be luck, baby, that'd be a miracle. If the guy recognized you running after him, he's probably smart enough not to go straight home. Not with that taxi driver, anyway."

Harley sighed. "I know. I wasn't thinking. I was just so

surprised to see him after I'd looked all night, watching all those Elvis guys onstage—and some of them are really bad—that when I recognized him as the extra Elvis on my van, I just took off. And let me tell you, it's not a good thing to run in parking lots in your bare feet. I'll have bruises for a week." She'd already told Tootsie about Morgan, and knowing he'd never endanger an undercover cop, it was important for him to know that the police were obviously following in the same direction in their investigation. They'd gotten on it pretty fast, sending in an undercover guy. Of course, there'd be a lot of pressure from the Convention and Visitors Bureau, as well as the city officials, who'd want any hint of danger for tourists to be quickly squelched. That'd be a lot of dollars to lose in a month-long Elvis celebration.

Tootsie leaned back in his chair. He was once more his impeccable self, well-groomed and his shoulder-length auburn hair tied in a ponytail at his nape. The lines around his mouth had eased, but he still had bags under his eyes that told her he hadn't stopped worrying. He smiled slightly.

"I don't even want to know why you weren't wearing shoes. And remember, don't try to talk to this guy on your own. All you have to do is—"

"I know. Get you the information. You'll take it from there."

"Right. Whatever the reason this guy is taking out Elvis impersonators, I don't want him doing it on our buses. It's not good for business."

"Not good for the Elvises either."

"No," he agreed. "It's not. The thing is, we aren't really sure it's about Elvis impersonators anyway. It could just be a guy with a grudge against the victims for some other reason. Maybe they had a disagreement, lover's spat, a difference of opinion over politics, religion, women, whatever. The police are checking out all those leads, but you're the one who can possibly identify the killer."

"So can Lydia, if we can get her to be coherent. I don't think the police were able to get much from her that made sense. Anyway, I could be remembering the wrong guy, you know. Maybe it's just one of the other passengers that had absolutely nothing to do with it."

Tootsie nodded. "The process of elimination will determine that. Meanwhile, see if you think this guy's a likely suspect, and if you find out his name, I'll turn it over to Steve. I guess you've already given a description of him to the police?"

"As much as I could. I mean, he looked like Elvis. I gave his height, approximate weight, and all that, but I couldn't remember any distinguishing features for the police artist. All I can say is that he had a different walk. Yeah, I know, that sounds stupid, but it was something about the way he moves. Really, it's the perfect disguise, hiding as Elvis in a bunch of Elvis impersonators. I mean, they may dress a little differently, in white jumpsuits, or in baggy suits of the fifties, or in black leather, but they're all so similar it's hard to pinpoint any big differences between them."

Except for really sexy undercover cops in tight black leather, she thought before she could stop herself. She had to quit doing that. It got very distracting.

"Gotta go," she said then, and heaved her backpack over one shoulder. "Wish me luck."

"*Good* luck, I presume."

"What else?"

She found the taxi driver in line at The Peabody Hotel. Taxis waited in an area by the parking lot off Second Street, while valets scuttled out to open car doors and usher in guests. On Union Avenue, horse-drawn carriages waited for tourists.

There'd been a lot of discussion about the horses being allowed to wait or even pass by restaurants. Something about manure and diners. Harley had her own opinion about that—City Hall spread around enough manure that a few more piles here and there in the streets shouldn't matter in the least. After all, the horses wore diapers, but politicians weren't required to wear muzzles. The horses won out, but the politicians were still there. Unfortunately.

So far, no law had been passed about the politicians.

After finding an empty parking spot just outside the employee door opening onto Third Street, she stuck a few coins in the meter and cut through the alley. The taxi was still in the same spot, his ID number on the light atop the roof. The driver sat inside, a craggy-faced man wearing a Memphis Redbirds baseball cap.

"Hey," she said, stepping up to his open window. He looked up from his newspaper to squint at her. "Mind if I ask you a few questions?"

"You want a ride somewhere?"

"No, I'd just like to ask you about a fare you picked up at Dad's Place—"

Rattling his paper, he looked back down at it. "I ain't no information booth. Be glad to take you anywhere you want to go, that's it."

"This won't take but a minute, I just want to know—"

"Lady, I done told you. Want information, ask at the front desk of any hotel. Want a trip to the airport or wherever, hop in back."

"Fine. Give me a ride to the Orpheum."

"That's only two blocks away. Walk or take the trolley."

Harley got irritated. "Your customer service attitude sucks. Do your supervisors know what a jackass you are to paying fares?"

Now he looked up at her with a scowl, chewing on the unlit cigar in his mouth. "Ain't got no supervisors, just dispatch. I own this cab. I take the fares I want, and I don't like short hauls."

"Okay, round-trip to West Memphis then. Or isn't that far enough away?"

"Depends. Where in West Memphis?"

"Oh, for the love of—" She paused to remind herself that she needed the information, so counted mentally to ten, then said in the sweetest voice she could muster, "Southland Greyhound Park, please."

He folded his paper and slung it to the frayed leather seat beside him. "Get in. I got the meter running."

Before she had the door closed, he'd started off, the taxi jerking forward. Second Street was a one-way street so he headed south, then turned toward Riverside Drive. Probably going to take I-240 west across the new bridge to Arkansas.

West Memphis was a collection of truck stops, restaurants, and motels that catered to truckers, the greyhound race track, and all the businesses and homes that formed an easy, laid-back small town. Just across the bridge, residents enjoyed the slower pace, with the conveniences—or annoyances—of Memphis a short ride east over the Mississippi River.

"So," Harley said, sliding open the little Plexiglas window that made a barrier between the front and back seat, "where did you take the fare you picked up last night on Brooks Road? A hotel? A residence?"

"I pick up lots of fares during the day. How should I know where I took one?"

"Because you keep a log, as required by law. It was around ten. The guy was dressed like Elvis. You can't get too many of those."

"You'd be surprised this time of year."

"Probably not, but that isn't important. I just want to know where you took him, what he might have said, and a description."

The driver glanced in his rearview mirror. "You a cop?"

"No. Just an interested party."

"Look, Blondie, I ain't getting mixed up in some messy divorce."

"No, *you* look, Mr.—" A quick glance at his registration card reminded her of his name, "Todd, it doesn't matter to me in the least what you're interested in. These are not hard questions. It won't take much effort or time to answer me, so give it a try."

From her position on the back seat she had an excellent view, and she saw his cigar stub go up and down vigorously for a moment. "Is there a tip in it for me?"

"*Extortionist,*" she muttered under her breath, but he must have heard her.

He shrugged. "Ain't extortion if you want answers, little lady."

"You're right. Pretty please?"

"Ask me the questions again, and if I know the answers I might tell you."

"Where'd you take the Elvis you picked up last night on Brooks Road, and did he say anything unusual?"

"Took him to the corner of Poplar and Highland, dropped him off in front of the pancake place."

"You mean Perkins Restaurant?"

"That's the one."

That was only a block from Memphis Tour Tyme's main office. Coincidence? Maybe. And maybe not. "What'd he look like?"

"Elvis."

"Right, but I'm sure you can do better."

"I just give 'em a ride, I don't look at 'em."

Harley thought about Tootsie's use of Southern charm to deal with clients, and decided to try it. Couldn't hurt, and it might even help. She put on a big smile.

"Now I don't believe that. You seem like an observant kind of man, someone who knows what's going on even when others don't. I bet you know a lot more than you let on."

He glanced at her again in the rearview mirror. "Maybe. Maybe not."

"Sure you do. You could probably give me his shoe size."

"Well . . . guess I did notice a few things. About six feet, I'd say, maybe a hundred seventy-five pounds. Kinda long face, short straight nose. Full lips, white teeth, but the kinda white that's bright like paint, y'know? I'd say he might be thirty or so."

"Did he say anything in particular? Anything that might have been odd, or unusual?"

"Kept kinda quiet, just said to take him to Poplar and Highland."

That was disappointing. She sat back in the seat and tried to think if there was anything else she should ask, something that would set this guy apart from everyone else. But she drew a blank. Damn.

Instead of going straight and taking the exit to Arkansas, Mr. Todd took a right on Poplar to pass by the jail and courthouses, then took another right on Jefferson, going toward the river again.

"I know how to get to West Memphis," she said, "so let's not take the long route."

"Do you really want to go to the dog track?"

"No."

"Then how about I take you back where you found me and you just give me a really nice tip, Blondie."

"Works for me."

The taxi bumped over the trolley tracks and turned left on Riverside Drive. Barges passed by on the river, skirting Mud Island, an inelegant name for a spit of mud and sand that now had half-million dollar homes built on it. The hot summer sun shimmered on the Mississippi that looked deceptively calm. Undercurrents could take a foolish swimmer down in seconds. Sometimes she felt like she was swimming against river currents.

When they got back to Second and Union, Harley gave him a twenty dollar bill and opened the back door to get out. He stopped her.

"Hey, Blondie, that guy did say something a little weird."

"He did? What?"

"Asked me if I'd ever wanted something so bad I'd do anything to get it."

"What'd you say?"

The cigar switched to the other side of his mouth as he shrugged. "Just said I already had everything I wanted."

"Then you, Mr. Todd, are a lucky man."

He grinned. "That's just what he said."

Great. Now she was thinking like a killer. Or possible killer. She had no real evidence he was the same man who'd killed the first Elvis, and wasn't at all sure he was involved in the death of the second Elvis. It just seemed likely.

When she got back to her car, a parking ticket was stuck under the windshield wipers. It fluttered in the hot breeze as if mocking her. Dammit, she'd stuck money in the meter. How could it be out already? City Hall was going to hear about this, by God, because this was one ticket she didn't deserve, especially after paying those tickets she'd gotten back in May. Oh no, they weren't going to get away with this. She looked up to see a man standing at the meter by her car, shoving coins into the slot.

"Hey, that's nice of you to pay for my parking, but I've already gotten a ticket."

He looked over at her. "I'm not paying for your parking. This is my meter."

"Your meter?"

"Yeah, looks like you parked in the loading zone."

"Oh." Grabbing her ticket from under the wiper blades, she unlocked her car and stuffed the ticket into the glove compartment next to one she'd gotten the week before. Half her salary these days seemed to go to unnecessary parking fines, and the other half to buy new cell phones. Keen observation didn't appear to be one of her strong points.

She sat for a moment with her hands on the wheel, letting the air conditioning cool off the interior. Maybe she was wrong. Maybe the guy she'd seen last night wasn't the same guy who'd been on her van. Obviously, she wasn't that great an eyewitness. Bobby had told her about some studies they'd done to test eyewitnesses, and how almost every one of them had missed vital evidence in a mock crime. Conflicting stories had veered from totally fictional to pretty close. No one had given a perfect version of what had really happened. There was every possibility she was on the totally wrong track. It could have been any of the passengers who'd killed the Elvises, with the guilty party glibly laying the blame elsewhere.

Still, what had been said to the taxi driver was pretty odd, any way she looked at it.

Just as she put the Toyota into first gear and pulled out into traffic, her cell phone rang. Law of probabilities at work again. Go to the restroom in a restaurant, and your food would come while you were gone. Finally find an interesting article in a five year old magazine, and you'd be called back into the doctor's office. Go to shift gears in a five-speed, and your cell phone would ring. Never failed.

A car horn blared behind her, and when she looked back the driver was gesturing wildly for her to get out of the way. She had to go forward, so she drove down the street until she reached a church, then pulled into the parking lot. If she tried to juggle phone and gears with the traffic, she was bound to screw up one of them.

Tootsie said, "Have I got you or the answering service?"

"Which one sounds sexier?"

"The computer voice, darling. Where are you?"

Harley squinted out the windshield. "The church on Third by the interstate."

"It must be fate. Go in and have some prayers said for your soul."

"What? Why?"

"Bobby Baroni just called here looking for you. He doesn't sound like his usual jovial self. Or maybe he does and that's the problem."

"What could he be mad about?"

"Didn't you say you ran into our favorite undercover cop last night?"

"No. He wouldn't tell on me. That rat!"

"I'm not saying he did or didn't. You better talk to Baroni before you go jumping to any conclusions. Just wanted to give you a heads up. He'll probably be calling you soon."

"Right now the only thing I feel like jumping is Mike Morgan's ass. With a two by four!"

"It must be love," Tootsie said sweetly, then laughed and hung up when she gave her opinion of his comment in two short, pithy words.

Fuming, Harley sat there for a moment, cell phone in hand and the air conditioning doing nothing to cool her off. How dare Morgan tell Bobby she was investigating the Elvis murders!

And how had he known? She hadn't given him any reason to think that. Her appearance at the Elvis contest was perfectly reasonable since Yogi was a performer. Not only that, but Mike had asked her not to rat him out. Then he went and ratted her out! Oh, there would be vengeance involved. And it was best served cold.

Bobby called as she was turning into the lot behind the two-story buff brick building that housed the offices of Memphis Tour Tyme. She looked at her cell phone. Might as well get it over with.

"What's new, Detective?" she asked as cheerfully as she could manage.

"I was going to ask you that." Bobby did not sound cheerful. He sounded mad. "What's this I hear about you visiting the families of the victims? Mrs. Jenkins was really upset."

Oh. Maybe Morgan hadn't been the one to rat on her.

She'd reserve judgment on the vengeance thing. And fortunately, she'd had enough time to think of a reasonable response to likely questions.

"As a Memphis Tour Tyme representative, we wanted to extend our deepest sympathies to the families in their time of bereavement," she said primly.

A moment of silence was followed with, "When did you start talking like a Hallmark card?"

"Right after I found a dead Elvis in the back of my tour van."

"Well stop it. You didn't go out there to console anyone. Admit it. You're messing around in our investigation again."

"Bobby, you wound me."

"Don't give me any ideas. Look, we've been friends a long time, but you know I can't let you go around getting in the way and possibly contaminating evidence or interfering with a witness, not to mention an ongoing investigation. To you, this is just one big game, but to the police, it's serious business. You're going to end up in trouble. Big trouble. You've been damn lucky so far, but that's bound to run out. Then you'll put officers in the position of endangering themselves and others to protect you. It's not right, Harley, and besides that, it's illegal."

Guilt replaced indignation. He had a point. She stared out the windshield of her car at the hedgerow that provided a barrier between the parking lot and the next yard, and thought that maybe the days of her amateur sleuthing should end.

"Okay," she said, "even if someone is murdered in front of me, I'll stay out of it. I'll just be Harley Jean Davidson, tour guide extraordinaire. That make you happy?"

"Delirious with joy. Do I have your word on that?"

She hesitated. Anything could happen. Breaking her word to a friend was serious stuff. If something beyond her control happened, it'd hurt their friendship. She'd rather make him mad now than risk irreparable damage later.

"No. Look, Bobby, I don't intend to get in trouble. I promised Tootsie I'd help out all I could, but I'll tell you everything I've found out and you do with it what's necessary. Of course, the way things have been happening around and to me lately, I can't promise I won't get involved at all. The best I can do is say I'll do my best to stay out of police business."

After a short silence, Bobby said, "If you weren't my friend, you'd probably have already faced charges. Next time you obstruct or interfere in a police investigation, you'll be treated like any other Memphis citizen. You'll be arrested."

Gulp.

Six

"So what did you say when he said that?" Tootsie's expression was part fascination, part concern. Harley sat in the office chair across from him, bare legs crossed, swinging one foot and debating her future.

"I just said 'Fine' and then told him what I'd found out. We hung up, but it wasn't on the best of terms."

"I'm sorry, baby. This is my fault."

"How is it your fault? You're not the one committing murders. The only thing you've killed lately is a little time listening to me whine. I'm done now. You can go back to work." She stared glumly at the chewed tips of her fingers. Not a nail left. They'd been growing out pretty well before all this happened. Now it looked like rats had been gnawing at her hands.

Tootsie sighed. "I shouldn't have asked you to investigate for me. If I hadn't been so desperate, I'd have known better."

"Desperation seems to be contagious lately."

"Look, let the police handle it. Don't risk more trouble. It's not worth it."

Harley looked at him. "Then I guess those bags under your eyes are the newest fashion? It's worth it, girlfriend. If for no other reason, so you won't keep looking like a reject from a Salvation Army sale."

Tootsie's gasp of horror as he put a hand to his mouth made her immediately feel guilty. His eyes got big, and his lips quivered. "Salvation Army?" he echoed in a high voice.

"No, no, not really," she said hastily, "I used the wrong words. You just don't look like your usual snazzy self, that's all. It's nothing a good night's sleep and peace of mind wouldn't fix quick enough. I swear it." She got up to put an arm around him, patting his shoulder to soothe his ruffled nerves.

He put his face in his palms. His voice was muffled. "I can't sleep. All I can think about are those dead men and some vicious beast running amok on our vans. It's not just business I'm worried about, it's the danger to our clients. Is it just *our* company that's the target? Why is it happening only to us?"

The last came out in a kind of wail, and Harley didn't know quite how to react. This was a Tootsie she wasn't used to seeing. She kept patting his shoulder, covered by a wrinkled blue silk shirt. This was so unlike him and indicative of his distress.

"I don't know," she said finally, "but I intend to find out. Maybe it's just coincidence it's always Tour Tyme vans, or maybe there's a reason for it. Look, I know the police are a lot better than I am at doing this kind of thing, but I can talk to people who might not talk so freely to the cops. If it's okay with you, I'll keep on asking questions and digging around. All right?"

"You'd do that?" Tootsie looked up at her, spreading his fingers across his face to stretch away the weariness and doubts. "And you'll be careful?"

"You bet. So don't keep stressing about it. The MPD is one of the best in the country at tracking down criminals, and hey—they've got me to help."

"Oh God." Tootsie laughed a little shakily. "Don't tell them that. I have a feeling it wouldn't be in your best interests."

"And I have a feeling you're right. Now here." Harley dug in her backpack and pulled out a new tube of lipstick.

"Estée Lauder. I was saving it for a special occasion, and I think this qualifies."

Tootsie opened the box and pulled out the tube. "Ooh, scarlet red! You sure you don't want this?"

"It's not my color. Actually, I got it for you anyway. Free with my purchase of mascara. It's you. Really."

The phone console lit up with a call, and saved her from any further lying. Happier now, Tootsie answered the phone with his Memphis Tour Tyme spiel and took down a message on pink paper.

As another call came in, he handed it to Harley. "Put this on Rhett's desk for me, will you? He should be back soon."

"Ah, the charming Retch Sandler. Has he found his missing personality yet?"

"Still missing. But he's a good accountant and hasn't stolen anything yet, so don't make him mad, okay?"

"I'll do my best. As long as he still hands out the paychecks, anyway."

Harley went down the hall and put the pink message slip in the middle of Rhett's desk, on top of a neatly stacked set of ledgers that sat atop a spotless desk, in a small office that was more like a hospital room than most hospital rooms. Sanitary, hygienic, and sparse. Just like Rhett. No personal photos, no sports souvenirs, no plants. Just stacks of ledgers and a computer. It looked a lot newer than the one Tootsie had at his desk. Sandler had a new computer to use in his work, while Tootsie still used an older computer. It was most likely a thorn in Tootsie's side that he didn't have a new one at the office, but he did have a state-of-the-art computer at home.

Sandler's computer hummed, the monitor still on. *Curiosity killed the cat, but satisfaction brought it back*, Harley said to herself, and hit a key to take a peek at the screen. Accounting had never been her forté. Even though she'd worked for the bank, it had been in the marketing department, where creativity counted a lot more than spread sheets. They'd been about to outsource all the marketing when she'd decided she couldn't stand another minute of her bosses, and a transfer to one of the branches was her idea of hell. Thus began her sojourn into the world of tourism.

And murder. Who would have thought it?

Now she reflected that she should have paid more attention to the accounting class she'd taken at Ole Miss, because all this looked like hieroglyphics to her. A few things stood out, not the numbers but the initials. LOP. TAR. What on earth were those for? Tar she could figure out, probably something to do with repaving the parking lot, but LOP? What was a *lop* and why did it cost so much?

Footsteps slogged down the hallway, and she headed for his office door. Sandler met her in the hall, his eyes narrowing a little when he saw her come out of his office. He was the kind of man you'd never really notice, ordinary, with sandy hair he kept short, slight build, and regular features. He always wore a suit, black in the winter, tan in the summer, and bowties that still didn't hide his prominent Adam's apple. Black glasses with thick lenses balanced on the bridge of his quite ordinary nose. His only distinguishing feature was a mustache that he clipped short and curved, so that when he talked it looked like a brown caterpillar riding his upper lip.

"May I help you?" He spoke in a nasal monotone, like the guy on TV who did the commercials for eye drops.

"Just leaving a message on your desk. That's all." She gave him a bright smile and a little wave of her fingers as she passed by, certain he suspected of her snooping. She didn't mind. She had been snooping, so it seemed fair.

Tootsie was on another call, speaking persuasively into the headset he wore over his right ear. It was a skinny piece of plastic that curved around to his mouth, and every so often he'd reach up to adjust it, like the person on the other end just wasn't understanding him.

"Yes, I know," he said calmly, "but the police are working on it. There's no indication this is anything other than sheer coincidence, perhaps a personal grudge between two of the— I see. Of course, I understand that this is just business, but with it so close to the anniversary date, I think you'll find it quite difficult to book—you have? I agree your first responsibility is to your clients, but Memphis Tour Tyme has an impeccable record of service and reliability. This is just an aberration—I understand. Certainly. Perhaps next year."

He pushed a button and sat for a moment with his shoulders hunched, then looked up at her. "Fifth cancellation in two days. Not just the hotel groups we get, but agencies that book well in advance." Slowly, he bent forward until his forehead rested against the desk surface. "We're ruined," he said in a moan. "Ruined."

"No, not yet. People are just nervous. They get that way around dead bodies and murder. Just as soon as the guy who's doing this is caught, business will pick up again. Hey, there's no shortage of tourists who want to see Graceland and Jerry Lee's house, not to mention Victorian Village and Beale Street. It'll work out. Besides, the taxi and limo service are still going strong."

Tootsie perked up. "We have had increased business with Elvis week so close. Too bad we didn't get our licenses in time for prom season. We could have made a killing. Oh. Bad term to use, I guess."

Harley gave him a pat on the arm. "See? It's going to be just fine. I'll do what I can, and you know the MPD is doing what they can. Two murders so close together have put them into high gear."

"I know. Steve's working long hours."

"Ah, the mythical Steve. Over a year and I've seen no sign of him. Are you sure he's not a ghost or figment of your imagination?"

Pursing his lips, Tootsie gave her a sly glance. "Anything but, darling, anything but."

With Tootsie in a much better mood, Harley took off for the main library down Poplar Avenue. The bank of computers there came with help, and she didn't have to waste Tootsie's time or listen to his exasperated comments about her being technologically deficient. Here, they expected it and had a couple of geeks to help out.

The main library had recently moved to Poplar from its long time location at Peabody and McLean, the old brick building demolished to make way for high-priced condos. This library was modern and sleek, with lots of glass, concrete, and a wide-open spaciousness to it. Somehow Harley missed the former one even though it'd seemed dark and dusty and had that scent peculiar to old wood and years of use. It'd had character. As beautiful and efficient as this one was, it felt cold and impersonal.

At first she tried finding out information that would connect Leroy Jenkins and Derek Wade. Hours of Internet research didn't indicate any connection between the two victims. She'd hoped to find something on the Internet site for the Elvis competitions, but all she found were photos and mentions of winners and runners up for the past few years. There was a photo of Yogi, too, a serious look on his face as he struck a pose for the camera. She smiled. As crazy as her parents made her at times, she wouldn't trade them. Curbing some of their tendencies toward protests in public places and flaunting of the laws would be nice, though.

So much for the easy way out. She'd just have to put some mileage on her car and shoe leather, it seemed.

Harley attended another Elvis concert and interviewed Yogi and other Elvis contestants, careful not to imply police involvement or cross any lines that might get her arrested.

Bobby had been serious. She'd heard that tone in his voice before. Spending time in a cell at 201 Poplar didn't appeal to her, and spending time with jail inmates dressed in orange jumpsuits had never seemed that attractive anyway.

None of the contestants were helpful. Most of them were a little puzzled at best, suspicious at worst. So far, all she'd learned that she didn't already know was that there were fierce rivalries among a few, but for the most part all the contestants viewed one another as extended family with the same shared interest in Elvis. Annual contests were often more of a reunion than any kind of rivalry. She'd narrowed the list down to a handful of those who didn't view the contests as a good-natured competition. Getting their names had been a real struggle. Most of the contestants were reluctant to speak badly about others.

Their wives and girlfriends, however, had been a lot more talkative. She had a nice list of names, both professional and personal. Those were the ones she'd check out first.

Plopping her leather backpack down on Tootsie's desk Monday afternoon, right before the office closed for the evening, she gave him a bright smile. He looked back at her a little warily.

"Should I ask what's up?"

"I have a list of names. The only way to check them out is a little one-on-one, so that's my next step." She held up her hand, palm out, when he started to speak. "As I've been advised not to take any risks or I'll face severe penalties, I've chosen a bodyguard to go with me."

"Excellent idea. I approve. Who?"

She tilted her head. "You."

"*Me?*" Aghast, he stared at her. "Do you have a death wish? I weigh less than you do. Together, we might hit two hundred pounds. Hardly an intimidating team."

"You weigh more than I do, and anyway, it's not brute force that matters, it's brains. Or so I was recently informed by someone who likes to dress as Madonna and sing *Material Girl.*"

"I didn't mean it." Tootsie sat back in his chair and shook his head. "Everything I said was a lie. You just needed cheering up."

"Uh hunh. Get up, boss man, and put on your mojo. We're going to tag team a killer."

When Tootsie left his house that evening—one of those older, remodeled Midtown houses worth a fortune now, when once they'd been considered slums—Harley gave him a pained look. "What, you couldn't find anything more noticeable?"

"Well excuse me, Vera Wang. I think this is fashionable investigative wear. You don't like it?"

"It's not that I don't like it, it's just a bit flashy when we need to blend in without drawing attention. And who's Vera Wang?"

"No wonder your wardrobe consists of jeans and tee shirts." He opened her car door and slid into the passenger seat, crossing his silk-clad legs with an elegant grace she'd never be able to manage. Black silk pleated pants coupled with a black silk shirt were all right, but the vest he wore sparkled with gemstones and some kind of glittery stuff that caught the light with his every movement.

"You look like a night light," she muttered, but let it go. At least he wasn't wearing a bra and mini skirt.

When they reached the hotel and nightclub, it was already crowded. Tootsie stared at the rows of cars thoughtfully. "Who'd have thought there were this many Elvis devotees? I think it's rather nice they're so loyal after all these years."

"Are you an Elvis fan?"

"I appreciate his music and talent, but my first love is the blues."

"Blues? I thought you were a big Madonna and Cher fan."

"Oh, I am to a certain extent. I like impersonating them. I don't think an impersonation of Muddy Waters or Little Laura would be quite the same thing on stage, however."

"Probably not." Another facet of Tootsie's personality that was new to her. He really was an intriguing person, and despite his often over-the-top penchant for cross-dressing, one of the most stable people she knew.

That was a depressing thought.

It was as crowded inside as it was in the parking lot. Harley winced. The noise level hit the decibel range of a jet taking off. She should have brought ear plugs.

Tootsie leaned close to her ear. "Who should we talk to first?"

"What?"

"I said, who should we talk to first?"

"I heard what you said, I just thought you'd have some idea about that."

His brow lifted. "Remember, honey, you're the brains, I'm the brawn."

"Then we're in deep doo-doo on both counts. Here's the list. I have it narrowed down to nine. I chose them on grounds of competitiveness and personality, not to mention the nasty things said about them by the wives and girlfriends of the other impersonators."

"You're so thorough." He took the list and scanned it. "So where do we start?"

"With the ones who are about six feet tall and a hundred and seventy-five pounds. Rule out any who don't fit that description, then we'll go from there."

"And we find these guys how? They're not wearing name-tags."

"You'll think of something. Improvise. Say you're looking for Sam Doyle, or whoever is on the list. Here. You take the top four, I'll take the bottom five. I already have your own list for you."

"Surprise, surprise. Aren't you the efficient little thing," Tootsie muttered, but he didn't look too unhappy.

"I have my moments. You take that side of the room, I'll start over here."

An hour later, Harley had eliminated three names from her list, one too short, one too fat, one too female. When had they let women in these things? It seemed self-defeating, seeing as how the point of the competitions was to look and sound as much like Elvis as possible in order to win. But who was she to judge?

Finding Tootsie was not a challenge. Even in a room full of Elvises dressed in capes and draped in gold, his twinkling vest stood out. He was deep in conversation with an Elvis impersonator that wasn't even close to six feet tall. Maybe it was a lead. Or a fellow cross-dresser. That thought led to the speculation that no one had ever dressed up as Priscilla Presley to her knowledge, and she wondered why. Did they ever have Lisa Marie impersonators? And if so, did they hang out with the Michael Jackson impersonators?

"Oh, you found me," Tootsie said when she nudged him.

"It'd be impossible not to, with that GPS system you're wearing."

Tootsie ignored her. "We were just discussing the blues and how they affected the early years when Elvis was growing up. Gospel, rhythm and blues, all those old spirituals played a vital part in forming his musical talents."

"Muddy Waters on the slide guitar, Pinetree Perkins on the piano, had to be his musical base," the Elvis agreed. "Elvis was happiest when he sang gospel, would stay up all night with the Memphis Mafia, singing his heart out."

As much as she appreciated Elvis's talent, Harley had a mission. "Yes, he was remarkable. There'll never be another like him." She leaned close to Tootsie. "Are you ready to go now?"

"No, but I assume you're ready. It was very nice talking with you, and I hope we meet again," Tootsie said to the Elvis, and to Harley as they walked away, "That was rather rude."

"You're right. Sorry. I've been told I'm compulsive. What'd you find out?"

Sighing, Tootsie shook his head. "Two don't fit at all, one of them is a maybe, and one is worth looking at further. And that's obsessive, not compulsive."

"Right. I've got two names on my list. That means we have three definites to consider, and one maybe, none of which are here at the moment."

"So what about the guy you thought was on your van? Have you seen him tonight?"

"Not a trace of him. If he's targeting just Elvis impersonators, maybe he's decided to skip the concerts and wait until the main competition starts."

"Which leads to the question, why come to some concerts and not to others?"

"I know." Harley sighed. "Maybe it really is just about some personal grudges, and no one wants to admit to it. But doesn't it seem odd that neither family knew about any grudges?"

"Maybe not. Some people don't take work problems home with them."

"Again, neither of the victims worked together, and as far as I can find out, they had no other contact. I even checked to see if Derek Wade had his car worked on at the auto shop where Leroy Jenkins is a mechanic, but nothing panned out." They stood outside on the covered sidewalk. Dull light gleamed in the stones on Tootsie's vest. Music from the concert blared out the open doors. It was a muggy night, damp heat pressing down like a wet electric blanket.

"If that's true, then you're right about the conflict or motive stemming from the contests," Tootsie reflected, frowning down at a piece of lint on the silk sleeve of his shirt. He flicked it off. "It's really the only logical conclusion."

"I know. But it seems too obvious, if you know what I mean. Why would anyone kill over a trophy at an Elvis competition?"

"Why would anyone kill over a five dollar loan, but it happens every day." Tootsie put his hand under her elbow and turned her toward the parking lot. "This has been most illuminating, and I'm glad I was able to assist. And the best part is, we've not been assaulted, insulted, or shot at the entire evening. See what you can do when you put your mind to it, girlfriend?"

"How kind of you to notice."

"Don't feel bad." He put his arm around her shoulders. "It's a good thing, just like Martha Stewart says. No shooting, no mugging, no fuss."

"I guess that's supposed to mean I'm responsible for all those things," she said crossly, but didn't really take offense. It seemed to be true. How annoying.

"Tomorrow I'll run those names through the computer and see what we can find, and then we'll figure out what to do next. I have extra access, you know, that lets me hit quite a few other databases."

"Would Steve investigate for us?"

Tootsie shook his head. "No. He's a lot like Bobby. He tends to want to abide by the rules. Inconvenient at times, but I've learned a lot just listening to him talk about past cases. It's amazing how easy it is if you just pay attention."

"I've figured out that observation isn't my strong point," Harley said as they reached the row where she'd parked her car. "Maybe that's why I end up in trouble at times."

Tootsie halted, grabbing her arm to stop her. "It's dark back there. The vapor light is out."

"Oh. Was it on when we got here?"

"I think so. Wait a minute."

He talked softly, and the hair on the back of Harley's neck tightened. It *was* dark. Lights on the interstate could be seen passing by, but the area where she'd left her car was pitch black. The building next door was unlit, and the hotel lights in front didn't reach this far back.

"Do you think something's wrong?" she whispered after a moment.

"I don't know. It just feels wrong."

That was it. It didn't have to be lights flashing and bells ringing—it was the feeling that something wasn't right that provided a warning. It'd saved her butt a few times.

"So what do we do now?"

"I'm not sure." Tootsie looked around. Tension vibrated from him. "It seems okay. It's just . . . "

"Dark," she finished, and he nodded, his body silhouetted by the light behind him.

"Yeah. Too dark back there."

"And I left my Mace in the car, dammit. Maybe it's just a coincidence that the light's out. Do you think?"

"Could be. Well, we can either go back inside for a security cop, or keep going. What do you want to do?"

"The security guard is drunk and dancing alone. I'm not sure he'd be much help." She thought a moment. "You may be right. After all, who'd be dumb enough to jump us?"

"The same guy who was dumb enough to sit on a van full of people and knife a guy in the back, I presume."

"Oh. That guy." She shivered despite the muggy heat. "Twice, if my suspicions are right."

"Okay, we're going to the car." Tootsie sounded determined. "This is ridiculous. Here we are cowering in the parking lot because a vapor light is out. I refuse to let my imagination rule my intellect. The probability of someone waiting in the dark to jump us is much less than the probability of faulty lighting. Come on."

"Right behind you, my fearless leader. This is really dumb, but you sound so brave I'm not scared anymore."

That wasn't quite true. She grabbed his arm and kept in step with him, not behind and not ahead, so that they had the ungainly gait of contestants in a three-legged sack race. "You're hurting my arm," Tootsie said after a yard or two.

"Sorry. Is that my car just ahead? It's so dark back here. The only light is from that damn vest you're wearing."

"Then it's come in handy, hasn't it. I think that's your car. Home free, baby."

Harley breathed a sigh of relief. "Well, a little terror is good to get the blood running, but I feel kinda stupid now."

"Me, too. These murders hitting so close to home make me realize how you must have felt a few months ago. I take back what I was thinking about you. Or some of it, anyway."

"I can't believe you were disloyal."

"Not disloyal." He stopped behind her car as Harley fished in her jeans pocket for her car keys. "Just uninformed."

"And now you're well-informed?"

"Better informed, anyway. What are you doing?"

"Looking for my keys. I thought I put them in my right pocket."

"Maybe they're in your purse?"

"You know I don't carry a purse. My backpack is much more efficient. Ah. Here they are. I put them in the other pocket. Hold my pen and notepad, will you?"

As she transferred the legal pad and her pen to Tootsie, she dropped her keys. Bending to pick them up, she heard Tootsie shout and jerked to the side just as something hard struck her in the left shoulder. Reaction set in and she dropped to the asphalt and rolled to the right. Footsteps sounded loud on the rough pavement, and she couldn't see anything but a vague blur over her, so she lashed out as hard as she could with both feet. She connected with something. A grunt and curse was followed by a high-pitched yell that sounded like Tootsie, but the language was unknown.

More grunts and thuds mixed with scraping footsteps, but by the time she got to her feet, the assailant was running away.

A little dazed, she looked toward Tootsie.

"Are you okay?" they both asked at the same time, and then both answered, "Yeah."

Harley inhaled a deep breath and tried to get her hands to stop shaking. "I don't suppose you got a good look at him?"

"No. Tonight Elvis wore black, including a mask. You sure you're all right?"

"Just all shook up." She laughed without real humor at her own joke. "Except my left shoulder hurts. What'd he hit me with, anyway?"

"He had a knife. *Omigod*, you're bleeding. We need to get you to the emergency room. Do you have anything to put over the wound?

"A *knife?*"Lightheaded, Harley pointed to the trunk of her car, and Tootsie pulled out a couple of rags she kept in there for emergencies. He tucked one inside her shirt against the cut, and gave her the other to apply pressure.

Despite the pain in her shoulder, a cold chill went down Harley's spine. The sparkling stones and glitter on Tootsie's vest blended together in a colorful blur, a dull light in the darkness around them. She put out a hand to grab Tootsie's arm. "But if it's the same Elvis who's been killing the others, why did he attack *me?*"

"Can we worry about that later? Get in the car. I'll drive, as soon as I find your keys."

It took him only a moment to find the keys where she'd dropped them and he unlocked the passenger side door for her. "Why me?" she asked again, dropping awkwardly to the seat.

As Tootsie lifted her suddenly heavy legs into the car, he said, "Sugar, he has to know you and Lydia can identify him. I'd say he's eliminating witnesses."

Oh God. She leaned back against the headrest and closed her eyes. Her arm and shoulder began to throb painfully. As Tootsie started the car and shifted gears, she opened her eyes and said, "Someone needs to warn Lydia."

Seven

Fortunately, Harley only had a flesh wound. If she hadn't bent for her keys, it might be a very different matter. Tootsie took her home from the emergency room, doped up and bandaged, and helped her into her apartment.

"You should have let me take you to your parents," he grumbled. But even as drugged as she was Harley knew better.

"No way. Diva would cleanse my aura and do all this mantric stuff, and Yogi would get a tire iron and go looking for the guy. I don't need a review of the seven chakras or a hernia getting the tire iron away from Yogi."

"You're probably right. Want me to put you to bed?"

Harley shook her head. "Please. I know you're just one of the girls, but I'm not an invalid. Not yet, anyway."

Sam had perched atop the back of her cushioned chair. As Tootsie lowered Harley gently into it, careful not to touch her shoulder, the cat let out a shriek and leaped down.

"*Jesus*," Tootsie gasped with a hand pressed to his chest, "that scared me almost as much as the Elvis."

"*Now* you're scared? Why didn't you ever tell me about this Rambo part of your personality? Not that I'm complaining. It definitely came in handy. What was that foreign language you were speaking?"

"A little self-defense class I took a while back. You're supposed to do these yells with it. You know, to unnerve your opponent."

"It unnerved *me*. So . . . it's karate or something?" Her tongue felt thick and her voice came out all strange, slow and slurred.

Tootsie's hazy face hovered above her, but she thought he was smiling. "Or something. Stay here. I'm going back to the car to get your takeout, and Steve is coming by to pick me up in a little while."

Maybe she nodded her head. She wasn't sure. Her eyelids felt so heavy that she had a hard time holding them up. Waving the hand on her good arm, Harley got out, "Taco Bell. Food of . . . the . . . gods."

As if through a fog, she heard Tootsie say, "This is your brain on drugs. Close your eyes and give your brain cells a chance. I'll be back in a minute."

Lovely, lovely clouds wrapped around her, taking away the pain in her shoulder. Nice. If she stayed real still and didn't breathe too hard, maybe she'd float away on them. Why not? She was already light as a feather, drifting along, drugs relaxing her muscles, taking away pain . . . *wait.* She couldn't open her eyes, couldn't lift her arms, could barely wiggle her fingers. Oh yeah. Now she remembered. She didn't like drugs. Anything that took away self-control and left her helpless as a slug was a bad thing. No . . . she had to get up, not let freewill be sucked away. That's what she had to do. Was going to do. In just a minute . . .

She must have dozed off, because when she woke up, she was alone and Sam was curled in her lap. Groggy, mouth dry as the desert and probably smelling like a litter box, she sat up gingerly. It was dark outside, and cool and quiet inside, with a single lamp lit. Tiffany-style, it glowed on an end table in warm colors of ruby, emerald, brilliant blue, and amber. It was on low and didn't put out much light. Squinting, it took her a minute to find the note propped up on the table beside her. She had to blink a few times, careful not to do it too fast or her head might fall off, and peered at it.

Didn't want to wake you, you looked so peaceful. Your grease is in the fridge, the phone is next to you, and your cell phone is charging. Keep your door locked and don't take candy from strangers. By the way, your hair could use a trim. Call me if you need me. Tootsie.

Harley lay back on the cushions and smiled. Good girlfriends were nice to have.

After a few minutes of testing her extremities one by one to see what worked and what didn't, she abandoned the chair and cat and made her way to the kitchen. She'd just opened the refrigerator door when a sudden loud whirring close by made her jump, banging her bandaged arm and shoulder against the open door.

"Damn!" she yelped, clutching at her arm while her heart pounded and Sam's four paws thudded across the wood floors as he dashed for safety under her bed. For a moment she stood there.

Then she recognized the whirr of the self-cleaning litter box in the little alcove off the kitchen. She put her good hand against her forehead and stood there letting the cool air of the refrigerator chill her feet. "I've got to get hold of myself, "she muttered. "Next thing, I'll be hiding under the bed with the cat."

She grabbed a two-liter bottle of Coke and swigged from it, relishing the sharp bite of the carbonation that went a long way toward waking her up. Then she burped, a long, satisfying sound, ignoring Grandmother Eaton's frequent admonitions that *ladies* did not make unpleasant bodily noises. She'd often wondered just what ladies did. Keep it all inside until they swelled up like hot air balloons? But of course, she'd never said that to Grandmother Eaton. She recognized that her grandmother's efforts were to make up for fourteen years of lost time learning table manners, social graces, and all the things that Diva, her eldest daughter, had left behind. Maybe her grandmother thought she could correct with Harley everything she'd not managed to perfect with Diva. But then, Diva was doing quite well without social graces and knowing which fork was the shrimp fork and which knife was the fish knife. And she was very happy, something Grandmother Eaton had finally begun to recognize.

Who'd have thought it would turn out that way? Certainly not the Eatons. They'd been horrified and disapproving when Diva—still called Deirdre by her mother—ran off with a totally unsuitable young man by the name of John Davidson. It'd been a family scandal at the time, but since Diva and Yogi were in California by the time it got around to all the relatives, they'd never been concerned with disapproval. They just went on being happy and living in vans, moving from one place to the other, mostly staying in California. That had been during the heyday of the early seventies, when women burned bras, free love was everywhere, and staying in one place was "a drag, man."

If Yogi's parents hadn't died and left him the house he'd grown up in, Harley would still be in California, though probably not living in a van. Somehow, she was more like Grandmother Eaton in many ways—not exactly insistent upon appearances, but not really crazy about living like a nomad, either. It'd been a relief to move to Memphis and go to a real school, one that taught English, math, and spelling, not herbal remedies and the importance of the fourth chakra. Not that love, compassion, and acceptance weren't important, of course.

Harley took the Taco Bell sack out of the refrigerator, hoping she'd ordered her usual. It heated better later. Ah. Bean burritos and nachos. Tootsie may try to convert her, but at least he knew her favorites.

By the time she'd reheated her bean burrito, Sam had emerged from hiding. He expressed his disgust with her choice of meal by throwing up a hairball on the kitchen floor. She cleaned up after him and took her food back to the chair. Her head was clearer now, and she set her plate on the glass-top coffee table. The thick bandage and sling on her left arm made it a little awkward. At least it wasn't hurting badly, just a dull throb. Bearable, if not desirable.

Eating a bean burrito with one hand wasn't all that easy, she discovered when the hot filling oozed out the end of the flour tortilla and onto her lap, so she loosened the straps holding the sling. Much better. Maybe she should learn some of that stuff Tootsie had done, the "Hi-ya!" yell and upward kicks. It'd been almost too fast to catch, especially in the dark, but his vest had been a rapid blink of color as he turned and whirled like a ballet dancer. Graceful, if lethal.

She shuddered at the thought of what could have happened if he hadn't been there. Maybe Morgan was right. There was always someone close by to rescue her. One of these days, her luck was bound to run out, despite the spirit guides Diva said were with her—unless Tootsie qualified.

Thinking of Tootsie reminded her again how close she'd come to disaster. Maybe their attacker was just a mugger. Or maybe he'd just been ticked off because they'd gotten his parking space. But if it *had* been the killer, why would he think only she and Lydia could identify him when there had been two busloads of tourists along for the rides? That didn't make sense. There were dozens of other witnesses, but the killer focused on her, and perhaps Lydia. Because they knew him? Was he a former employee? Parking lot attendant? Delivery guy? Damn, there was any number of choices to track down. She really wished she could find out what the police knew.

First, Lydia should be warned to be careful. Since it had to be done delicately instead of bluntly—not Harley's specialty— she hoped Tootsie had already taken care of that. Dealing with a hysterical Lydia would make her forget the fourth chakra.

With that unappealing thought in mind, she took the remnants of her Taco Bell meal to the kitchen. Instead of putting it in the fridge she threw it away. Morgan was right. Warmed- over burritos weren't very tasty. The microwave did something nasty to the sour cream.

Sam curled around her ankles, looking up at her with slitted blue eyes and purring, his tail straight up like a flagpole. He wanted something, of course.

"Just like a man," she said to him, and he purred even louder, "always wanting something else and never happy with what you've got. All right, you little fur ball, how about a kitty treat? The pet store clerk said cats love them, so I'm sure you won't."

Harley was right. Sam sniffed it a few times, and then walked away with the equivalent of a cat shrug. Really, that was one of her favorite things about him, his individuality and sense of independence. Not at all like King, slavering drool all over her shoes and wiggling ecstatically just for a word or two. They didn't even have to be kind words.

Cami said there were cat people and dog people. She must be a cat person. She'd never say it to Cami, but she'd gotten really attached to Sam. If she let Cami know that, she'd end up with a dozen cats running around her apartment, so it would be a well-kept secret.

After pulling the curtains over the French doors to her small balcony, she checked the lock on the front door and turned out the lights. A couple of nightlights shed a small glow so she could find her way in the dark for midnight raids on the fridge, and so Sam could find his litter box for a night deposit. She'd bought one of those expensive electric ones that automatically scooped after him and saved her the necessity of continuous scooping. Other than a little bit of scattered litter and the whir it made while cleaning, it worked out fine for all concerned.

As she turned toward her bedroom, she heard her front door knob rattle, and froze. Didn't most visitors have the decency to knock? Heart hammering, she fumbled one-handed on the counter that divided her kitchen from her living area, searching for anything she could use as a weapon. At least the front door was locked, so the intruder would have to break in and that would be noisy enough to alert her neighbors—just as her fingers found a small, hard object, the front door swung slowly open.

A dark shape silhouetted against the hallway light stood there a moment, and Harley flung the object in her hand at the head. Not waiting to see if it hit the target she grabbed for something else to use, hampered by throbbing pain in her left shoulder.

"Oww, dammit, Harley!"

She paused with her hand on a heavy candle and solid brass holder. "Morgan?"

He said something under his breath, and then said aloud, "I see that you're not at death's door like I was told."

Harley flipped on the lights. Mike stood rubbing his cheek.

"What are you doing here?" she demanded, not sure if she was glad to see him or not. He had a big red spot on his left cheek and didn't look at all happy as he rubbed at it. He worked his jaw from side to side, apparently testing it for fractures, then blew out a heavy breath.

"Tootsie called. He said you'd been stabbed, so I came to check on you. What'd you hit me with this time?"

"I don't know—oh *dammit!* My cell phone." It lay in several pieces on the gleaming oak floor, and looked beyond repair. Again. "You could have called first, y'know," she said crossly.

"He said he'd left you sleeping. I didn't want to disturb you. I should have remembered to wear a helmet and faceguard."

"So what were you going to do, sneak in and watch me sleep?"

He shrugged. "Something like that, I guess. Just wanted to see for myself that you're all right."

"Obviously, the wound isn't fatal."

"Obviously."

He stood there with the door still open, looking so good in his usual black jeans, tee shirt, and SWAT boots that she had a hard time not saying something stupid. Like *Come lie down for a while*, or *Stay with me*. That would never do. He'd wanted a break, so she'd give him one.

After a moment, he said, "Got everything you need? If not, I can run to the store for you."

"I'm fine. We stopped at Taco Bell and I have cat food. I'll make it until tomorrow."

"You know the assault's been reported."

Damn. She hadn't thought about that. Of course, the emergency room attendants would have to report it even if Tootsie hadn't. Gunshot wounds, stabbings, things like that were always reported to the police.

"I don't remember talking to the police. Who did?"

"Tootsie. You were out of it, and Baroni told them you could be released to go home. A couple of uniforms took the initial report from Tootsie. Expect a call from Baroni."

She sighed. "I'm *so* not looking forward to that."

"I don't blame you. If you're okay, I'll go back to my stakeout."

"Stakeout? You have a suspect for the Elvis case? And don't bother denying that's what you're working on, because I won't believe it. There's no other reason you'd have been in black leather pants and a TCB chain." She sat down on the arm of her cushioned chair. Morgan looked at her left arm and shoulder in a sling, and then shook his head.

"Have you ever thought of applying for the police academy? Use your talents for good instead of evil?"

"Stick to the issue. I've tried to stay out of sight and out of trouble, but tonight this guy attacked me. Tootsie thinks he might be trying to get rid of witnesses. What about the tourists on the buses? Aren't they witnesses, too?"

"Yes, but most of them were from out of town. They've given statements and gone home, except for a few."

"Oh." She thought for a moment, and then something occurred to her. "If you're on a stakeout and it's for this case, am I the one you're staking out? Or Lydia?"

He just cocked an eyebrow.

Harley didn't know whether to feel better or worse. If they were staking out her apartment to see if the guy came after her, then she was protected, but that also meant they thought she was in danger. There wasn't really a good side to this that she could see.

"Go away," she said. "My drugs are wearing off and I might get cranky."

"Wouldn't want that. You're always so sweet."

"Sarcasm to a poor invalid. Really, Morgan, that's police brutality."

"So report me."

Catching her by surprise, he closed the distance between them in two long strides, put his hand under her chin and kissed her. It was short, sweet, then over. Except for that tingle in the pit of her stomach. Damn. How did he do that to her? She stared at the closed door for a moment before getting up to lock it. Even with pain killers, it was going to be a long night.

"What are you doing here?" Tootsie shook his head and scowled up at her. "You should be resting at home."

Harley plopped her backpack down on his desk, a familiar ritual. "I've got some errands to run. Besides, I'd get more rest lying in the middle of Poplar Avenue. Did you send out a chain letter announcing my injury? Even my great-grandmother called this morning to tell me I need defense lessons. Which reminds me—why didn't I know that you could do karate?"

"You never asked." Tootsie took another call, and then looked up with a wink. "Someone like me has to know a few defensive moves. There are always guys who want to prove their manhood by beating up someone smaller, especially when he's wearing a blonde wig and boobs."

"I guess that could be a problem."

"Only if you can't defend yourself."

Harley sat down in the chair close to Tootsie's desk. "You always seem so well-adjusted it's hard for me to think anybody wouldn't like you."

"Strangers don't bother me. I just consider them ignorant. It's the family members who say and do things that get to me. You'd think after all these years I wouldn't care, but sometimes I do." He shrugged. "Everybody has a right to their own opinions and lives as long as they don't infringe on others, so I try to overlook it."

"I'm sorry."

Leaning back in his chair, Tootsie retied his ponytail with the elastic band, adjusted the phone headset and said lightly, "Don't be, darling. We can't choose our family, just our friends."

"Good thing. Think of all the therapists that'd be out of business if we could."

"You always have the right answers. Ah, the delightful buzz of more cancellations. Do excuse me, bankruptcy is calling."

Three lines had lit up at once on the console next to the

computer. The console was new, the computer not. Tootsie had seemed disappointed about the latter, but managed to make do. He'd loaded a bunch of new programs in it that made his life a lot easier, he said, especially when she observed that he was on the Internet a lot for someone supposed to be booking clients. Since computers were among the things she found convenient but uninteresting, she took his word for it so he wouldn't go into detail about gigs, megahertz, and other incomprehensible terms.

Musing about differences between friends and family members, Harley thought about her own family. Which led to thoughts about Patty Jenkins, which progressed to speculation about Leroy Jenkins. He'd moved in with a roommate in Frayser. She really needed to talk to him even though the police most certainly had already done so. Maybe there was something she, as a non-police officer, could find out. People were usually more comfortable talking to civilians in a casual situation than they were the police, especially if they'd ever transgressed in some way. All she had to do was make a quick visit. She still had that address written on the back of one of the Memphis Tour Tyme business cards Patty Jenkins had refused to take.

"How do you drive one-handed?" Tootsie asked during a lull in cancellations.

"Slowly. I just have to hold the wheel with my knees and shift gears with my right hand. The bad thing is, I can't drink Cokes while I drive right now. By the way, I've got a bone to pick with you."

"Pick away. But if you're going to bitch at me about calling Morgan, it won't do you any good. You know you're glad." He leaned back in his chair and pursed his lips in that bitchy little way he had. It turned into a smile when she flipped him a one-fingered salute.

"But why *him?* You could have called Cami."

"Please. You two together are just double trouble. I wanted someone to watch out for you who actually can watch out for you."

"I don't need a keeper."

"Baby, as many bodies as you run across, you need a scorekeeper. Here." He grabbed his car keys off the desk and held them out. "Take my car. It's an automatic. You're less dangerous on the streets that way. Just don't spill any Coke on my leather seats."

"Did I ever tell you that you're my favorite person?" She took his keys. "I'll leave you my keys in case you need to go somewhere."

"That's all right. You'll be back before I leave. Won't you?"

"Of course. But you know, I'm sure, that my best intentions somehow get screwed up on occasion, right?"

He held out his hand. "Right. Give me your keys. Just in case."

Tootsie had a four year old Acura with leather seats and all the bells and whistles any hedonist would need. Harley sighed with pleasure as she snuggled into the buttery-soft seat. She had thought about buying a new car since she had that extra money in her savings account, but couldn't justify it. She had her Toyota, after all. It ran just fine and never gave her any problems. Now that her Harley-Davidson Softail Deuce with over-under dual exhaust and a Twin 88 cam belonged to her and not the finance company, her only bills were her Visa card and the basics like rent, phone, utilities, and food. And of course, her monthly cell phone replacement. That ran pretty high lately. It'd be nice if they made a rubber one.

There were three errands on her list—cell phone replacement, a chat with Leroy Jenkins's roommate, and a visit with Lydia Free, who also had a paid leave of absence. Being related to the ogre apparently had perks.

It took only a few minutes to replace her cell phone. The clerk recognized her in the parking lot, got out a new cell phone and had it ready by the time she reached the counter.

"See you next month, Ms. Davidson," he called as Harley left, and she just barely kept from saying something really rude. If there hadn't been children in there . . .

Leroy had lived off Frayser Boulevard, in a duplex that had seen much better days. Harley set the alarm on Tootsie's car and managed to get up the sidewalk without tripping over chunks of broken concrete uprooted by a huge dead tree. It looked bleak, not like the other houses.

After knocking a few times, the door opened. A guy who looked to be in his late twenties to early thirties stood there. He had brown hair that looked like he cut it with an electric fan, hard eyes, and grease streaks on his face. Must be the roommate. He wore a greasy shirt with his name on the pocket.

Darren. He leaned against the doorframe and gave her a gap-toothed grin.

"Well, hello, green eyes. Did it hurt?"

"What?"

He pointed at her arm. "When you fell from heaven."

She barely kept from rolling her eyes. "As a matter of fact, yes. Do you mind if I ask you a few questions about Leroy?"

Darren's grin disappeared. He narrowed his eyes at her. "You a cop?"

"No. I'm with Memphis Tour Tyme. Leroy was killed on our van. Here's my card." She held it out and after a moment, he took it. He had grease blackening his hands and nails, but an auto mechanic usually did.

"So, what cha wanna ask me? I don't know nuthin' much about Leroy. He just crashed here when his old lady threw him out. Paid his rent on time, and that's all I cared about."

"Did you ever go with him to the Elvis events?"

"Hell, I didn't even know he was a freak until a few weeks ago. Comes in with all that Elvis crap, looking like a dumbass and sounding like shit."

"Uh huh. I'll take that as a no. Did he ever say anything to you about a fight with other contestants, maybe a dislike of any of them?"

Darren shrugged. "We didn't talk that much. Worked together, might watch a few ball games together, but not much else."

"Did Leroy ever talk about his wife?"

"Talk? Hell, all he ever did was moan about how she kept him from his kids. Wouldn't let him see 'em. Said he had to pay to play." He frowned. "How does any of this have anything to do with a tour company? Sure you ain't the cops?"

"Mrs. Jenkins has requested monetary damages, and there has to be an assessment of the amount lost by her husband's . . . demise." A half-truth. She smiled. "I'm sure you understand."

"That greedy bitch. Wouldn't surprise me none if she had him killed. Did you talk to her yet?"

"Once, but I'm sure I'll talk to her again."

"Then give her this, will ya? I forgot to put it with the rest of Leroy's stuff." He left the duplex door open when he stepped inside to pick up a stack of envelopes from a table littered with empty beer cans, overflowing ashtrays, and half-eaten pizza.

Along with unwashed body and probably decaying food, the sharp smell of marijuana drifted out the door. He held out the envelopes. "It's Leroy's mail. I don' know what else to do with it, so she might as well have it."

"I'll see that she gets it."

Darren smiled at her again, showing empty spaces where a couple of teeth had been. "I bet a hot number like you has lots of guys after her, huh."

She took a step back. There was no good answer to that. "Thanks for your help," she said, and walked away with him still in the doorway looking at her.

"Anytime you feel like goin' for a beer, stop by," Darren called after her, and she pretended she didn't hear him.

Harley looked over the mail when she got in the car, wishing she was brave—or stupid—enough to open the envelopes. Most of it looked like bills or junk mail, but a postcard with Elvis on the front lay wedged under a Publisher's Clearing House envelope. Shamelessly, she turned it over to read it.

Words that looked like they'd been printed by a computer Inkjet nearly jumped out at her:

"There's to be a special interview with Channel 3 before the concert August 2. Dress as you would for the competition, and take the Memphis Tour Tyme van that will be at the Omni Hotel at 2:00. Do not tell the other contestants about the interview, please. There's only room for a few of the best. Claude Williams will meet you in front of Graceland."

The postmark was dated July 30th. So who was this Claude Williams? Maybe she should find out how Leroy had been chosen. And why he'd been told to board her van when he wasn't on her passenger list. There had to be an explanation.

Harley decided to take Leroy's mail to Patty Jenkins before she visited Lydia, with only one side trip. She didn't need a Federal charge hanging over her head for tampering with the US mail, but she rationalized making copies wasn't really tampering.

When Patty came to the door with a cigarette hanging from one corner of her mouth, she narrowed her eyes at Harley.

"Thought I told them cops to do something about you."

"So you did. I just thought you might want your dead

husband's mail."

Patty hesitated and then took it from Harley's outstretched hand. "I don't, but I'll take it. Get out of here."

"I'm on my way." She stepped back, and then turned just before Patty shut the door. "By the way, did Leroy know about you and Darren?"

It was one of those shot in the dark things, just something to see what she'd say or do, but Harley didn't expect her reaction. Patty went white, then red.

"Damn him! What'd that sonuvabitch say to you?"

"Enough. Do the police know?"

Patty stepped out of the house and shut the door. "Listen, it wasn't like that. Only once or twice. No big thing. But if Leroy found out, he'd have used it against me. Taken the kids."

Harley thought maybe they'd have been better off with him, but didn't say it. She just shrugged, and then winced at the pain in her shoulder.

"So why'd Darren break up with you?"

"It wasn't like that, no matter what that asshole says. He had to go and tell Leroy he could move in with him, and I wasn't going to take any chances. I told him to leave me be after that."

"Maybe Darren didn't take it so well."

"That ain't my problem," Patty said. "Dumbass. Guess he thought it'd be funny to sneak around on Leroy while he's got him living with him."

If that was true, Harley thought after she'd left, then it gave two more people motives for getting rid of Leroy. Which, of course, didn't explain Derek Wade's death. She mulled that over for a few minutes, and then decided to visit the Wades again. Maybe Derek had received a card.

Though a little perplexed, the Wades were gracious enough to look in their mail basket.

"I may have thrown away his mail that didn't seem important," Mrs. Wade said as she shuffled through papers in a wicker basket. "He didn't get much anyway, just a few things—ah. Here it is. Yes, Derek did receive a card from the Elvis competition people. He was very good, you know."

Scanning it, Harley looked up at her. "May I borrow this, Mrs. Wade? I'll return it to you as soon as possible."

"Yes, of course you may. You don't have to return it." Tears welled in the older woman's eyes. "He doesn't need it now."

Harley didn't know what to say so she just put her hand on Mrs. Wade's arm and nodded. It felt awkward, yet at the same time as if a connection had been made. An image of Derek as he must have looked to his mother flashed through her mind. How sad.

Once in Tootsie's car, she held the card next to the photocopy she'd made before taking Leroy's card to Patty. Almost identical except for the dates. Derek was to meet Claude Williams the day after Leroy was killed. So who had sent them?

And why? A lure? But to be so bold as to kill intended victims right in the middle of a crowd? It just didn't seem logical. If it wasn't logical, could it be true? Damn.

This was evidence the police needed. She'd turn it over to them. After she made a copy of Derek Wade's postcard, of course. There was a limit to her cooperation, though the main thing was to catch the killer. It didn't really matter now who managed it first. She just didn't want Bobby to accuse her of obstruction when she was only trying to help.

Lydia Free rented a room near the Dixon Art Gallery off Park Avenue. Harley found the house easily enough since it was down the street from the very first house Elvis had bought for his mother on Audubon, and frequently on her tour route. She parked in a separate parking area in the back, next to Lydia's car. It looked like the back door was the main entrance, so she rang the bell and waited.

No one came. She rang the bell again. It was a pretty big house, so maybe it just took some time to get to the door. When no one answered after a few minutes, she opened the storm door to knock, figuring there might be trouble with the electricity since several MLG&W trucks were on the street. If someone had hit a light pole on Park, it'd put out lights for the entire neighborhood.

Her first rap on the wooden door swung it open. It'd been left ajar. Harley got an uneasy feeling. Other than hers, Lydia's was the only car in the driveway, but that didn't mean Lydia was here. She could have gone walking, or ridden with someone else. Still . . .

Maybe she should call the police and have them check out Lydia's apartment. But what if she was just taking a nap, or jogging around the block? Or lying out in the sun? Harley walked over to the tall wooden fence, took a plastic bucket left in front of the garage, upended it and used it as a ladder to peek over the top. A tree had fallen over and just lay there with the leaves still green. Bushes were high and the grass needed cutting, but no Lydia.

She retrieved her new cell phone from her car, locked it, and went back to the house. This time she stuck her head in the open door and called, "Lydia? You home? It's Harley."

Nothing but silence.

She got that tingling again, like the time she'd gone into Mrs. Trumble's house and found her dead on the floor. This couldn't be the same thing. Could it?

Sucking in a deep breath, she stepped into the hallway.

Straight ahead was a laundry room and to the right was a closed door. A spiral staircase climbed to a room overhead, and to the left she saw a living room with doors leading into other hallways and rooms. She had no idea which one was Lydia's. Might as well start with the closest.

She rapped lightly on the door, and when there was no answer, opened it. A huge room cluttered with musical instruments and tall speakers opened onto the back yard. French doors were wide open, letting in hot air and flies. Odd, but hardly ominous.

Closing that door, she went on to the next. A check of three more downstairs bedrooms, the kitchen, dining room, and living room, didn't produce Lydia or anyone else. Harley began to feel like a burglar. If someone came in, how would she explain her presence?

Okay, just a quick look upstairs and she was done. A flight of stairs off the living room seemed the most likely for an apartment, and she went up as quietly as possible. When she got to the top, she called for Lydia again. "Lydia? You here?"

No answer.

She put a hand on the knob and turned it slowly. The door swung open and she peered in. A big dormer window let in light that fell across what was obviously a small sitting room that led to the bedroom. A kitchenette lay off the sitting room, small but efficient. Thick carpet cushioned her feet as she crossed to look in the bedroom. Clothes lay discarded on the floor. Beyond the bedroom, the sound of rushing water seeped out from another closed door.

Relieved, Harley felt like a fool. Of course. Lydia was taking a shower. That's why she didn't hear the doorbell or knocking. What an idiot she was, looking for trouble behind every door. She really had to get over this. Recent experience made her much too jumpy. She'd wait in the sitting area for

Lydia to get out of the shower, and hope an unexpected visitor didn't scare her too badly.

Nice little place, really, small but fairly tidy except for the clothes on the floor. Even the kitchenette off the sitting room had sparkled with cleanliness. She'd always figured Lydia for the sloppy type. Which only proved Diva was wrong about her daughter having keen perceptions.

Halfway back to the sitting room, Harley paused. Something about those clothes on the floor . . .

She went back and looked at them more closely. Dark red splatters stained the tee shirt and shorts. A strong smell hit her when she knelt down to look at them, and her heart began to thud rapidly. Blood?

Looking up at the closed bathroom door, Harley rose and moved cautiously toward it. She dreaded what she'd find in the shower, images from the movie *Psycho* flashing through her mind. The bathroom door was unlocked, and she pushed it slowly open. Steam billowed out and fogged the mirror over the vanity sink. A black shower curtain had been pulled across the tub, hiding it. Heart still thudding hard enough to break a rib, she held her cell phone ready in her left hand and put her right hand out to pull back the shower curtain. She jerked quickly, and then stared. Blood ran down Lydia's face onto her shoulders and made red puddles in the tub.

Harley screamed.

Then Lydia screamed.

Eight

"Tell me again why you're here?" Lydia, wrapped in a huge towel and shivering, glared at Harley.

"I wanted to talk to you about the murder on your bus."

"You couldn't have called?"

"In retrospect, that would have been a much better idea. You shouldn't leave your doors unlocked. Why are you dying your hair red?"

"Not that it's any of your business, but my therapist said a change might be good for me." Lydia pulled a smaller towel from her head. "I thought dying my hair red might be a good start, but then I spilled it everywhere, on my clothes, and now it's on my face—I must look horrible."

"You do resemble an accident victim, but a little baby oil ought to take care of that. I can help, if you'd like. I've helped my brother dye his hair a few times, so I have experience."

Lydia looked uncertain, but Harley convinced her that she could be useful. It didn't take long to scrub the dye stains from Lydia's forehead, cheeks, and neck. When Harley realized one of the smaller stains she was trying to scrub away was a freckle, she stopped.

"There. All done."

"How do I look?"

Lydia peered up at her, and Harley didn't have the heart to tell her the truth. Diplomacy would work much better. "As good as new."

"Red's not my color, is it."

Now there was no escape. Harley shook her head. "Not really. I think you'd look good as a blonde, though."

"Do you?" That seemed to please Lydia, because she smiled. "Maybe I'll try that."

"Go to a professional next time. Just in case."

Lydia nodded. "So what'd you want to know about the dead guy on my tour?"

"Not really so much about him as about the guy who sat down next to him. Was there any distinguishing feature you can remember that might identify him?"

"I already went through all this with the police. They were just two Elvis impersonators. I get a lot of them this time of year, reduced rates since they're part of the entertainment, just like you do."

"I know. But my van was all Elvis impersonators, while you had only two. I thought you might be able to recall something different about either of them."

Lydia frowned. "Does Uncle Les know you're doing this, asking all these questions?"

"You mean Mr. Penney?"

"Well, yes. He's my uncle, you know."

"I've been asked by the company to do what I can to help the police find the perpetrator." That sounded middle of the road, true without straying too far into details.

"Oh. I didn't know. Okay, I'll tell you what I told the police. The other Elvis was tall, I guess somewhere around six feet, not fat but not skinny. He had on a black wig but the sideburns looked real. I didn't pay too much attention to him. It was so noisy in there, everyone talking at once, and I was just trying to get through the day."

To Harley's surprise, Lydia blinked away some tears. "I told Uncle Les that I'm not good at this sort of thing, that I wanted to work in one of the other offices as a receptionist or in the accounting department, but he said I had to start out at the ground floor first."

"Maybe now he'll transfer you," Harley said sympathetically.

"I'm not going back if he doesn't." She shuddered. "Finding that man dead . . . And the man who killed him was right there, and he could have killed all of us."

"I think he picked his victim before he got on that bus."

When Lydia looked hopefully at her, she added, "And I think they knew each other. One of your passengers told me that there was a disagreement over seating."

"Now we know why."

Harley nodded. "Were there any words between them, maybe, anything you might have overheard?"

Lydia shook her head. "They were sitting too far back. Even if I'd wanted to hear them, I wouldn't have. Everyone was making too much noise."

"Talking?"

"Singing. Someone started that Jerry Lee song, *Great Balls of Fire*, and then everyone started singing it. It was like one of the detective shows on TV, when he figures out the guy used music to disguise the murder."

"Uh huh." Lydia was known to consider all TV shows reality, but this time she might be right. Singing would mask any noise the victim might make when stabbed.

Still, it didn't make a lot of sense. It was too risky. No one in their right mind would plan a murder in a bus full of people.

Would they?

"The mistake you're making," Tootsie said, "is assuming that a murderer *has* a right mind. Except for a crime of passion or self-defense, any murderer is basically unbalanced."

"Is that you or Freud talking?"

"Please. Don't insult Freud." Tootsie got up from behind his desk. He switched off the desk lamp and picked his keys up off the counter. "These murders were bold, yes, definitely risky in a crowd, but no one can identify a killer who looks like a hundred other people who all look like Elvis. In its way, it's a perfect disguise."

"That's what I said." Harley leaned glumly against the desk. "I'm sure the police have recovered evidence, though—fibers, fingerprints, shoeprints—something that'll identify him."

"This isn't TV. It's not going to get solved in an hour—forty minutes without all those commercials. It takes a while to gather and process evidence. It may take weeks or months."

"Oh great. Well, I'll do what I can, but I'm about at a dead-end here."

"That's all right." Tootsie smiled wryly. "It was a crazy idea of mine anyway. The ogre wasn't at all happy to hear I'd asked you to investigate."

"I can imagine."

They'd started for the door when the office phone rang.

Tootsie paused. "Damn, I forgot to switch it over to the answering service."

Harley waited while he answered it, leaning over the counter to punch the buttons and give his usual spiel. She looked at her fingers and the nails chewed to the quick. There must be a better habit to have. This one was unattractive. She dug in her backpack for some gum and found the postcards. She'd forgotten to mention them to Tootsie. Maybe he'd know what to make of it.

Then she lifted her head to look at Tootsie when he said, "What? When? Okay. We're on our way. Just don't touch anything."

He hung up, pressed a few buttons and looked at Harley.

"There's been another murder in one of our vans. This time at the hotel where they were taken after a concert."

The police got there before they did. Cruisers flashing blue, Charlsie Spencer stood by the door and stared blankly ahead, her face reflecting nothing but flashing blue lights. Harley knew just how she felt.

"Want to go inside and sit down?" she asked her, but Charlsie shook her head.

"No. I just want to wake up."

"I know. A nightmare, isn't it?"

Charlsie turned to look at her. "How do you do it? Deal with it, I mean. Death is so . . . ugly."

"Murder is ugly."

Charlsie was married with two little kids, a pretty woman with soft brown hair and blue eyes, a little on the healthy side but not fat. Just rounded, a Marilyn Monroe kind of round. She shivered despite the heat.

"Yes," she said, "very ugly."

Harley hesitated. Maybe she shouldn't ask her any questions. She looked pretty rattled. It could wait.

But then Charlsie turned to look at her, eyes a little glazed as if she was seeing something horrible, and said in a whisper, "I thought he was asleep. I went to wake him . . . I touched him on the shoulder and he . . . he just fell forward. Then I looked at my hand. There was all this blood on it, so bright red and sticky . . . like my little girl's finger paint. I didn't know what it was at first, and then I realized . . ."

She began shaking again and Harley put an arm around her shoulders. "It's okay. You'll be fine. Has anyone notified your husband?"

Charlsie nodded. "David's on his way."

Harley waited with Charlsie until her husband arrived, and the look on his face when he saw his wife was a mix of panic and relief. They held on to each other for a few moments before he let her go, and even then, he kept an arm around her shoulders.

Looking at Harley, he asked, "Can she leave now?"

"You'll have to clear that with the police. If she's given her statement, I imagine they'll let her leave."

When they left, Harley found Tootsie. He stood talking to the police, not far from one of the smaller vans. If this kept up, they wouldn't have any vehicles left. Two vans and a bus were out of commission until the police ended their evidence gathering. It put a cramp in scheduling tours during their busiest month. Though cancellations were cutting into that.

One bright spot was Bobby's absence. He must be on another case. Thank God. She didn't think she could deal with him right now. He'd ask questions she didn't want to answer, and he knew her well enough to know when she was lying or evading. That was never good.

Finally, Tootsie came to stand beside her. He looked stressed. "You okay?" she asked.

"No. Three vehicles from our fleet are temporarily sidelined. Even if I get back the van you were driving, I'll be two short next week, during the busiest season. Not to mention the bad publicity, with all these guys getting killed on our buses. Fifty thousand people will be here soon, all probably using other tour companies."

"Let Mr. Penney worry about that. Besides, this is only temporary. You've got friends at the TV stations and the paper. Get them to put a different spin on it, how Tour Tyme has taken extra security measures to ensure the safety of their clients during the festivities or something. I've got a friend in the security business. I'll ask Butch to give us cheap rates."

For a moment Tootsie just stared at her. Then he nodded, though he didn't look less stressed. "That'd be great. Security. It might help. Then again, it might backfire. What if tourists think it's too dangerous to come to Memphis?"

"It's too dangerous to cross the street anywhere these days. That doesn't stop anyone."

"True." Tootsie looked a little relieved. "It might even work."

"See? You feel better already."

"I'll feel better when I see a healthy bottom line after all this is over."

"Sometimes I just can't figure you out. I know job security is important, but why should you get so upset about profit and loss?"

"Think of it this way, baby. A healthy profit means a healthy payroll. Besides, you don't have to work close to Lester Penney every day, and I do."

"Ah. There is that to consider. It pays to keep the ogre happy."

"A logical conclusion."

"Speaking of logical conclusions, I know I've said this before," she said as they headed toward Tootsie's car, "but it's just not logical for someone to take such a big risk killing these guys on tour vans. Why not kill them at the concerts? In the bathrooms, or outside diners, or in alleyways, at home? Somewhere it's not so crowded. Why stab Elvises right in the middle of a group of tourists sitting on a tour bus?"

"Why stab them at all? Why kill just Elvis impersonators?"

"I take it this last death is—"

"An Elvis impersonator. Last seat in the back row, stabbed right in the heart."

"While the other people were singing *Great Balls of Fire*." When Tootsie gave her a strange look she said, "I talked to Charlsie. She told me they were singing. I'm sure it helps hide any, uh, noise."

Once in the car, Tootsie said, "I'm beginning to think these victims aren't random, but specifically chosen. Maybe there's a connection between them that we're missing."

"I used library records to check everything I know to check—work, family, friends, even looked up their old schools all the way back to kindergarten to see if they might have known each other. Nothing." In the pause, she pulled out the two Elvis postcards from her backpack. "Except these. Both victims were sent these postcards directing them to take a Memphis Tour Tyme bus and ask for Claude Williams when they reached the concert."

"Who's Claude Williams?"

"I thought you might know, but it's definitely something we

need to find out."

"Have you informed the police about this yet?"

She shook her head. "Not yet. I don't want to talk to Bobby. He can be such a jerk."

"Maybe you should talk to Morgan, give him the evidence."

"Even worse. Besides, if I call him, he's liable to think I just want to see him, and I don't want him to think I'm chasing him."

"How sixth grade of you."

"Oh, shut up."

Tootsie laughed and said, "I'll call Bobby if you want."

"Would you? I'd just as soon not get arrested if I can avoid it."

"Then I'll be discreet."

Harley sighed. "He'll see right through that. He's almost as good at it as Diva."

"I think cops develop a sixth sense. At least, the good ones do."

"Then Bobby must be one of the best. So, what do you think? There has to be some kind of connection between the two cards and the dead Elvises. I'm willing to bet this third victim got a postcard, too."

"If he did," Tootsie said grimly, "then we've got a serial killer targeting only Elvis impersonators."

"Yeah, but not randomly. He's got some kind of devious plan. It must be one of the Elvis contestants trying to knock off the competitors."

"That makes more sense than anything else."

"So maybe we need to find out if these victims were any competition, and who's listed as the favorite this year."

Glancing at her, Tootsie nodded. "That's where we'll start."

"I'll ask Yogi who the favorites are. He always knows that kind of stuff."

"Preston Hughes was favored to win this year, but he dropped out of the competition." Yogi lowered his voice as if they were in public instead of his own living room. "I heard he got disqualified because of an incident last year between him and a few other competitors."

Harley stared at him. "And you didn't think it might be important to mention that to me?"

"Why? He's not in the competitions this year."

She bit her lip. "Okay. So, who were the guys he got into it with last year?"

Shrugging, Yogi put aside the crystal necklace he'd brought in from his shop. "I don't know. One of them was Derek something, I think."

"Derek Wade?"

"Could be. Preston claimed Derek stole part of his act."

"How can you steal part of an Elvis act? There are only so many songs and so many suits you can wear."

"Harley." Yogi looked horrified. "Each act is individual, with certain songs and costumes, the way you move and sing and connect with the audience and judges—it's what counts the most in a performance. It's not like just anyone can get up there and sing like Elvis, you know."

"All right, all right. Sorry. I didn't mean to imply it doesn't take talent."

Yogi smiled. "I know you didn't."

So forgiving. He rarely held a grudge against an individual, though for the past thirty-six years he'd held a deep-seated resentment and dislike of the U.S. government no one had been able to alter. Only a few had tried. It had something to do with the sixties draft, the Vietnam war, and Orwell. At least he wasn't discriminating. He hated Republicans and Democrats alike. He also disliked drug companies, huge corporations and their CEOs, and "corrupt journalists." The list was much longer, but Harley tried not to dwell on it. On the plus side, Yogi loved his family, children, animals, and lost causes, not necessarily in that order.

All in all, she'd begun to discover that her family wasn't as bad as she'd always thought. Or maybe it was just that they weren't that much different from other families, in that they had their quirks that didn't always coincide with societal rules. They just didn't bother hiding them.

"So," she said, "who can I ask about the disqualification?"

Yogi thought for a moment. "I'm not sure. The organizers of the event would know, of course, but they'd never discuss it. Maybe you could ask Claude Williams."

"Claude Williams?" Aha. The man both Elvises were supposed to meet. "Who is he?"

"He's in charge of publicity."

That made sense. The victims wouldn't have questioned a postcard with his name on it. So, that either meant the killer was also an impersonator, or had intimate knowledge of the way the competitions were run. It was a toss-up. An Elvis or an employee.

"Any idea where I can find Williams?"

Yogi shook his head. "Nope. You might try looking for him at a concert. He's usually there with a camera."

The official competitions started soon. Competitors would be coming in from all over the world, and so would people coming to commemorate the day Elvis died. A serial killer on the loose would definitely be bad for the tourist business. Evidently, this serial killer picked on Elvises only, so he had to be a part of the competition, and Preston Hughes was beginning to look like a prime suspect.

"When's the next concert?" she asked her father, and Yogi smiled.

"Tonight. We've been having them every night, sort of a warm-up to the Super Bowl. Gives us all a chance to try out our acts, work on what needs to be changed."

"So you think this Claude Williams will be there tonight?"

"It's possible. He's been coming to a lot of them. Seems nice enough, I guess. Diva says he's greedy."

"Why did she say that?"

Yogi shrugged. "You know your mother. She's always saying things. Half the time I don't know what she means."

"I have complete empathy. So, maybe I should show up tonight and talk to him."

Yogi frowned. "Wait a minute—I'm not sure I like you doing all this kind of stuff. It always seems to involve danger. Do you have any idea how that scares us? How scared we are for you every time you get mixed up in this kind of stuff? For God's sake, Harley, you just got stabbed!"

"Tell me about it. This time, though, I'm staying away from anyone who even looks at me wrong."

Yogi stared at her shoulder, still bandaged although she'd abandoned the clumsy sling. "I don't think you're doing such a good job. Why don't you get Bruno to go with you?"

Harley sighed. "His name is Mike, and he's working on an undercover case."

"Then take your brother."

Looking at the couch where Eric slept with soft snores and green hair, she shook her head. "I don't think he'd be that helpful. Besides, he probably has a gig of his own."

"Not tonight. I don't want you roaming around town when some killer's out there. Take Eric with you."

"What could that beanpole do even if I did run into the killer? Offer him a toke?"

Yogi reached over and shook Eric. "He's wiry. Stronger than he looks. I'll feel better if he goes with you."

Appalled, Harley stared at her brother in dismay when he opened sleepy blue eyes and looked up at her. "Hey, dude," she said with a sigh of resignation.

He blinked. "Hey, cool chick."

Yogi said, "Get up and go with your sister to protect her."

Sitting halfway up, Eric yawned. "Where's she going?"

"To an Elvis concert."

Eric's eyes got wide with horror. He looked from Yogi to Harley. "*Chiiiick!*"

She smiled. Sometimes there were perks in the most unlikely of circumstances.

Nine

Harley rolled her eyes at her brother. "It's not like I'm not a little tired of going to Elvis concerts myself. The least you can do is shut up about it. Let me concentrate on my driving, all right?"

"But, chick—*Elvis?* You know that ain't my thing. Couldn't you have gotten someone else to go with you? Diva could have come along instead of me."

"She has to help Yogi with his costume. You know that."

"Why not Cami? Or that Bruno guy?"

"Cami's at work and *Mike* is, too."

"I've been hijacked by an Elvis terrorist," he muttered.

"If you don't shut up, I'll sign you up to sing *Hound Dog.*"

"Wouldn't do you any good," Eric grumbled, but he finally stopped complaining. He put on his earphones and turned up his CD player. Thank God. He'd whined all the way from the house, and she was about ready to put him out on the corner.

Any corner. But in this neighborhood, he'd get mugged. Especially wearing black baggy pants with a dozen zippers and shiny chains, a black *Slayer* tee shirt, and green hair standing straight up on his scalp that looked like a Bermuda lawn that needed mowing.

"I need to practice saying 'I love my family' several times a day," she said, but Eric didn't hear her with his music turned up. She could hear his music though, guitar riffs, drums, and bass all mangled together. It sounded like a train wreck.

When they pulled into the hotel parking lot, Eric stopped using her dashboard as a drum set and gave a pained look at all the cars crowded together. "Are there this many weirdoes?"

"Have you looked in a mirror lately, dude?"

Eric flipped her off and she returned the salute with a grin.

Some things never changed. After several round trips through the lot she found a parking slot at the very back again. Why did that seem to be the only place she could ever find? She debated not taking it, but the vapor lights had been replaced and it was fairly bright. Besides, it seemed to be the only one left. "We're looking for Claude Williams," she said when they were inside the concert, this one apparently a family night as a few dozen kids ran around screaming and the lights were up.

Eric looked around in dismay. "I'm not a kid person."

"Really. And you have so much in common. You start asking a few people if he's here tonight, and get them to point him out. Say you want him to promote your band or something."

Eric gave her a horrified look. "Chick! You gotta be kidding."

"So lie. I know you can do it. Remember the gig you're supposed to have the last night of the Elvis competition? I happen to know your lead singer's going to be out of town that night. I'll keep your secret, but you have to cooperate."

"Chick, you're not playing fair."

"Get over it. Take that side of the room. I'll start here." Harley found Williams after only two questions. A middle-aged man with a balding head and thick glasses, he was very cooperative. She showed him her copies of the postcards received by both men, and he shook his head.

"I never sent those, as I told the police just a little while ago. Must be some kind of error on the part of the concert organizers. Any interview would be conducted openly, not secretly. We aren't affiliated in any way with the actual competition. These concerts are just for the performers to refine their acts, give them a little more stage experience and entertain others who revere Elvis and his music."

"Would you know anyone who might have sent them by mistake?"

"No, we have a small staff for these concerts. Just me and my wife, actually. I can't imagine who else would send these."

Well, she'd expected as much. Someone was using his name as a lure to get the victims to take the vans he specified. And it had to be someone who knew about Claude Williams.

"How long have you been doing these concerts, Mr. Williams?"

"Oh my . . . let me see. About five years. Just a part-time occupation, of course, but once a year I throw myself into it."

He smiled genially.

"Do you ever perform? I notice you've got the Elvis sideburns."

Williams chuckled. "On occasion I've been known to get on stage, though most of the time I'm better at taking photographs and promoting."

"What's your favorite Elvis costume?"

"Um, I'd have to say my favorite is the black leather of his sixty-eight tour, but it's not the most flattering for me, so I usually wear the white jumpsuit. I even have the eagle one. A reproduction, of course."

Williams wasn't quite six feet, but close. He looked a little under a hundred seventy-five pounds, but in an Elvis outfit, that might easily be misjudged. Harley put him on her short list of possibles.

Just as she opened her mouth to thank him for his time, Eric grabbed her elbow. "Chick! You're not gonna believe this— Bruno's here in an Elvis outfit! Can you believe it?"

Harley tried to cut him off, but Eric paid no attention. He just kept talking.

"Man, that beats everything I've seen, an undercover cop playing Elvis. Did you know he did this kind of stuff?"

Gritting her teeth, Harley got out, "No, I'm sure you're mistaken. You probably just saw someone who looks like him."

"Oh no, I'd know that dude anywhere. It's him. His pants are too tight to stash a gun, though. You gotta come see this."

Williams looked shocked, and Harley wondered if that was a flicker of anger she saw in his eyes. Or fear? Damn. She'd known better than to let Yogi talk her into bringing her brother. "Thank you for your help, Mr. Williams," she said calmly.

She waited until she was several yards away before she grabbed Eric by the arm. "You idiot! Why'd you have to say that out loud?"

Eric looked surprised. "Say what?"

"That there's an undercover cop here, you moron!"

"I didn't say that, I said Bruno—oh. Guess I did. Sorry, chick. I was just so surprised to see him decked out in black leather and Elvis hair I didn't think that he might be . . . uh . . . working."

Harley sighed. "I understand. I had the same reaction. It's just that it was a bad time to say that when I was talking to a possible suspect."

"That bald guy? He doesn't look like he could kill a can of Coke."

"It's guys who look like that who're the worst. Let's go. I got the information I came for, so I don't have to torture you any longer."

Eric shrugged. "That's okay. I'll wait until Yogi does his bit onstage. It'd make him happy for me to stay."

"You know, sometimes you act human."

"Don't get used to it."

While Eric joined their mother, who was fussing over Yogi's costume and hair to get it just right, she went out into the hall and pulled out her cell phone. Three kids came screaming by as she dialed, and she cupped her hand over the phone. She got Morgan's answering service, as she'd expected.

"Hey. Sorry about this, but your cover's been blown. Claude Williams knows there's an undercover cop here tonight. Just wanted to let you know."

She hung up and stared at the ugly wallpaper for a moment. He'd be mad about it, and so would Bobby, but at least they'd been warned. And at least it hadn't been all her fault.

After the concert ended, Eric walked her to her car. The vapor light was burning brightly over it, and he said, "If you're okay, I'll ride home with Yogi and Diva."

"I'm fine. It saves me a trip."

Once out of the parking lot, she breathed a sigh of relief. Stupid to get so nervous, but the last week hadn't exactly been the most reassuring time of her life. Her shoulder still ached, and she wondered what it would have been like if the cut hadn't been so shallow, if it had been deeper than just a slice across her upper arm and shoulder.

When her cell phone rang, she knew who it was before answering. She let *Dixie* play a moment before giving in to the inevitable and pulling over into an empty parking lot to answer.

Morgan sounded calm. "Would you mind telling me who blew my cover?"

"Is it that important? I'd rather not be a tattletale."

"Probably not, but humor me."

"Eric came with me tonight. He recognized you."

There was a moment of silence, and then Morgan said, "I should have known. Diva and I agreed that we wouldn't tell Yogi, but we never thought about your brother."

"Diva knows? Wait. That was a stupid question. Of course she'd know. She always does. She's very observant, not to mention her special talents. So I take it Yogi doesn't know?"

"Apparently, he's not very observant."

Harley sighed. "True. I don't fall far from his genetic tree."

"I wouldn't say that."

"You don't have to say it. I recognize my limitations. I just can't do much about them."

"Work a little harder at it. So who did Eric tell?"

"Claude Williams, who promotes these concerts leading up to the big competition next week. Williams is on my shortlist of possible suspects, by the way, since he had opportunity and his name was on the postcards sent to the first two victims."

She paused. "But you probably know all this."

As usual, he didn't confirm or deny. "I take it you're still poking around in this despite your promise to Baroni."

"I didn't promise him I'd stop. I just promised I'd be careful, and anything I found out I'd share with the police. I'm doing that."

"Do you have a death wish? You've already been stabbed. Whoever is doing this isn't playing around, Harley."

"I know that. Why do you think I'm taking precautions? But I'm already involved in this whether I want to be or not. I'm an eyewitness, remember? Lydia and I are the only ones left who might be able to identify this guy, and he's already tried to get rid of me. I hope you're keeping a close watch on Lydia. I'm worried about her."

"Unlike you, she doesn't leave her house these days. Why don't *you* try that?"

"Maybe I should, but I don't like the thought of just sitting and waiting for some killer to show up at my front door. I'd rather be unpredictable."

After a moment of silence, Morgan laughed softly. "Well, I can't say you aren't that. I've never met anyone as unpredictable as you."

"I'd say thank you, but I'm not at all sure that was a

compliment."

"Neither am I. Look—be careful, Harley. If anything happened to you, I couldn't stand it. Okay? Just . . . be careful." Mike hung up before she could respond, and for a moment she just sat there. It almost sounded like he cared. Really cared. Damn him. Why'd he have to go and be confusing like this? She didn't want to think about him. She had to think about these murders, and not let herself get distracted.

And then she thought about him saying almost the same thing and got really irritated. She didn't want him being right. She preferred righteous indignation. Being wrong was the pits.

When she got home she pulled out a yellow legal pad and drew a line down the middle of the paper. She headed one column Williams and the other one Hughes. Then she listed beneath each one the opportunities and possible motives. It was a very short list.

Williams had opportunity, being involved in the concerts, but Hughes had motive. She'd have to dig into their backgrounds, find out what she could about each now that she'd narrowed it down to those two as possible suspects. And of course, find out the identity of the third victim and if he'd received a postcard as well. For these things, she'd need Tootsie's help.

Sam jumped up on the counter where she sat with her legal pad, and plopped down atop it to look up at her with slitted eyes and a soft purr. She tried to move the pad from beneath him but he wouldn't budge.

"Why is it you always want to sit on my newspaper or writing pad when I'm busy, and ignore me when I'm trying to get you to play?"

Sam's reply was a tap on her pencil. Then he bit the eraser, going into some kind of feline ecstasy at the taste of rubber, while his expensive cat toys remained untouched in the basket.

She leaned close to him.

"You're being a pest," she said, and he only purred louder.

"Apparently that's part of your charm. I seem to prefer difficult blue-eyed males with absolutely no hope of being civilized."

Dixie began to play, and she abandoned Sam to dig her cell phone out of her backpack. It was Lydia.

"Harley, I just remembered something about the Elvis on my bus," she said with a note of excitement in her voice. "It's possible that I'm wrong, but I don't think so, as it really did look like him. Do you think I should mention it to the police?"

"Of course. What did you remember?"

"It's the oddest thing, and it was so long ago it's taken me forever to think of it, but then I just did. It came out of the blue, just a thought, you know, and then I knew it had to be him since who else could it be?"

A little impatient, Harley said, "Well for heaven's sake, Lydia, who is it?"

"Well, I'm not positive, but—Harley, hold on a minute, will you? The utility guy is here. We're still having problems with our electricity."

Harley could have screamed with frustration, but instead chewed on her nails. This could be something that'd lead to the killer. Unless Lydia was off on one of her "TV turns into reality" moments. That had happened before. Once she'd related an entire story of someone being killed by a falling stone gargoyle, only to say later it was an episode of *Sherlock Holmes*.

Pacing, Harley went to the French doors looking out over her balcony and Overton Park. Lights marked the roads that were closed at night, and in the distance, a lion roared. She heard Lydia speak to the utility guy but didn't catch the words. It sounded like she picked up again, and Harley said, "Lydia? Lydia?" Then her cell phone went dead. Damn. Of all times! She probably needed to recharge it. It took her only a short time to plug it into the charger and bring up Lydia's number and redial. Lydia's phone rang. And rang. She might be trying to call her back, so Harley hung up and waited. Five minutes passed before she tried again. Still no answer. No answering machine. Just the ringing that went on until the phone company cut it off. She looked down at her cell phone and saw that it was fully charged. Maybe it hadn't cut her off after all.

That annoying prickling on the back of her neck urged her to call Morgan as she grabbed her car keys and headed out the door. "Lydia's not answering her phone," she said when he answered. "Someone needs to check on her."

"So maybe she's in the shower."

"No. I was talking to her and she said she'd remembered

something about the Elvis on the bus. Then she said the utility company was at the door and we got cut off."

"I'm on it."

The line went dead. Harley jumped the last three stairs to land in the foyer and ran out the door to her car. She didn't like what she was thinking and hoped she was wrong. Oh God, let her be wrong.

When she got to the spacious house on Audubon, police cruisers were in the driveway and on the street with flashing blue lights. Her stomach dropped. Maybe they were just checking things out. Lydia would be on the front porch shivering and saying silly stuff in her squeaky voice while the police looked for a prowler that didn't exist. Maybe everything was all right.

Then she saw the crime scene unit and knew. Nausea sat in the back of her throat, and she couldn't move. She sat there at the curb for what seemed an eternity and just watched. It didn't seem possible. Police coming and going, lights set up, uniformed officers investigating, looking in bushes, fingerprinting doors. It was a surreal nightmare.

A tap on her driver's door window startled her and she jumped. Then she saw Bobby. She let down the window and he bent to talk to her. "You okay?"

She nodded yes, but suddenly tears were streaming down her face and she felt stupid. He handed her a cloth to use as a hanky and she took it. Bobby looked sympathetic. "I didn't know you two were that close."

"Neither did I." She shook her head and said, "We weren't close, really. I was just worried. She was so upset and scared. Did . . . did she suffer?"

"It was quick."

She nodded and took a deep breath. "Morgan told me the police were watching her. How did it happen?"

"They were watching the sides and front of the house. The back is fenced, opens up onto a drainage ditch, lots of brush back there."

She remembered the open French doors the day she'd gone to visit Lydia. "I should have said something. I saw the back doors open . . . I should have told her to make sure they were locked up."

"Don't start blaming yourself. Harley—"

"I know. I know what you're going to say. You're right.

Morgan's right. But now she's dead."

"That doesn't mean you killed her, or could have done something to stop it."

She thought for a moment. "Two witnesses who might identify the killer—Lydia and me. The killer just got rid of one, and I'm next."

Bobby didn't say anything, and Harley knew he recognized the truth as well as she did. After a moment, he asked, "Did Lydia say anything important to you?"

Harley shook her head. "She was going to, but then the knock came at her door. She did say she'd remembered something about the Elvis on her bus, but it'd been a long time."

"That's all?"

"Except that it looked like him, so it had to be him. Something like that. I should have listened more closely."

Bobby nodded. "We'll need to get a formal statement from you. Tomorrow will be soon enough."

"Have you noticed it's only Elvis impersonators he's targeting? I think he's mad at the contestants. Or organizers. Maybe it's someone who's been disqualified. Like Preston Hughes."

"Maybe. We've got our theories." Bobby straightened. "There's nothing you can do here tonight. Go home, Harley. I'm sending a unit to make sure it's safe. Don't bother arguing with me." He paused. "The killer could be watching us now, watching the investigation, disguised as an average spectator."

It was on the tip of her tongue to say something tacky when he bent and leaned in the window again. He smelled like aftershave and coffee as he chucked her under the chin. "Hey, as much as you piss me off, I don't want anything to happen to you."

Her smile felt wobbly as she said, "Yeah, who would you have to complain about if I was gone?"

The unit he sent with her checked out her apartment, opening closet doors and cabinets, even checking behind the shower curtain and on the balcony. Then they told her to use the deadbolt before they left. She locked up behind them and leaned against the door. Poor frightened Lydia. Poor *foolish* Lydia. She hadn't taken the simplest precautions of keeping all the doors locked. If she had, Harley wouldn't have been able to scare her in the shower that day. That must be how the killer got into the main house. What had

Lydia remembered about him? Whatever it was, it'd gotten her killed.

Harley shivered. Sam, who'd stayed hidden while the police officers checked everything out, emerged from his hiding place with a soft *miaoow*. Or what passed for soft with him. Harley picked him up, and for once he didn't try to get away but let her hold him.

Cami had been right when she'd said having a cat could be nice. Sam must sense how upset she was and was trying to comfort her in his own way. He rubbed his head under her chin and purred so loudly his entire body vibrated. She stroked his back and went to her chair to sit down, holding him against her chest as she tried not to think about anything at all.

A knock at her door sent Sam bolt upright. He leaped from her lap, leaving claw marks on her arm, and disappeared behind the TV.

"So much for sympathy," she muttered as she went to her door. She peeked out the hole in the middle and then slid back the deadbolt. "Come on in. You can help me pour hydrogen peroxide over my wounds."

"How did you get wounded again?" Morgan shut the door behind him.

"Sam-sympathy gone bad. The knock on the door scared him."

"Oh. Sorry."

The scratches weren't bad. Taking care of them took just enough time for Harley to recover from her surprise at seeing Morgan at her door again. It felt awkward.

"So, what are you doing here?" she asked once they were back in the living room and he had refused her offer of a Coke. He perched on the arm of a chair and crossed his arms.

"Just thought you might need a friend."

She nodded, a little irritated by the tears that stung her eyes. "I'll be fine. Lydia wasn't a real friend, just an acquaintance, but it still hurts to think of the way she died. She was always so frightened and didn't even want to be a tour bus driver, but her uncle wanted her to learn the business from the ground up. I felt bad for her then and even worse now."

"What do you think she wanted to tell you when she called?"

Harley narrowed her eyes. "Wait a minute. Are you here on a

friendship basis or just trying to get more information out of me?"

"Friendship." Morgan met her gaze steadily. "Don't answer if you don't want to. It's just the cop in me trying to figure out what she knew that got her killed."

"Okay. I believe you." Harley plopped into her chair and ran a hand through her hair. It probably stuck up like railroad spikes, but she didn't care. "She said she'd recalled something about the Elvis on her bus, that it'd been a long time but she'd just remembered."

"And she didn't say what had been a long time?"

Harley shook her head. "She didn't have a chance to. All the other victims have been Elvis impersonators," she said after a moment. "Lydia is the first one who isn't. Could it be a random murder, a burglary gone bad or rape or some other horrible crime, or is it linked to the Elvis murders? That thought keeps going through my mind. And of course, Bobby pointed out that we were witnesses who might remember the killer, too. How could the maniac think no one else might have noticed him on that bus? The vans were full of tourists. Any one of them could remember him."

"The descriptions they gave are basically the same as the one you and Lydia gave. Maybe the perp thinks you have more reason to remember him. Could it be someone you work with?"

That thought hadn't occurred to her. She stared at him. "Why? If it ruins the company, we're all out of a job."

"That doesn't always matter. Maybe it's a former employee. Anyone leave on bad terms? Was there an argument with management?"

"Not that I know about. You'll have to ask Tootsie that question. He's been there a long time and he'd know. I've always thought Rhett Sandler has the personality of a biscuit, but he's not the kind to kill someone. Of course, not many of us like Mr. Penney, but it's not so bad that anyone would want to kill people over it."

"You'd be surprised."

"So you're checking out all the Tour Tyme employees?"

Morgan shrugged. "Just theories. Look, I don't want you to stay here alone. Think you could stay at your parents' awhile?"

"Oh please. I can't leave Sam alone, and King would be delighted to have a new toy. That wouldn't work at all. Sam might hurt him. Imagine Yogi's horror."

"Any other relatives? Your grandparents? Your aunt?"

"I'd rather take on the Killer Elvis. Look, I'll be fine here. Really."

"I'm sure you won't be surprised if I disagree."

Harley sighed. "I've got Mace and a cell phone. I have deadbolts. *And* I can't identify the killer."

"He may not know that. He's already tried to kill you once. He did kill Lydia."

She shuddered. That was very true. "Excellent point. All right. I'll go stay with family tomorrow."

"Out of town would be best."

"You're just trying to get rid of me."

Morgan smiled. "Only for a little while."

When he stood up, Harley tried not to focus on distracting things like the way he looked in a tight tee shirt and jeans. Or the way his eyes lingered on her a little bit longer than necessary, as if he was remembering their nights together. *Lord.* She'd been planning a hot bath, but maybe she should make it a cold shower instead. That crooked smile of his always did her in.

"Take care of yourself," he said, "and lock the door behind me."

"Right. You, too."

Well, she thought when he was gone, she'd really sounded lame. Her shoulder hurt and her head had started to throb right behind her eyes. Maybe she should take an aspirin. And chase it with a bottle of wine. This day had been too much.

Instead, she took a cold shower, chased an aspirin with Coke and went to bed. Tomorrow always seemed to come before she was ready.

Ten

"Hey, Harley Jean! I haven't seen you in a while. How you doing?" Mrs. Shipley called across the street from Harley's parents' house on Douglass, and Harley managed to wave back.

"Just fine, Mrs. Shipley. You sure do look nice today." That was code for "not as bizarre as usual" when it came to Sadie Shipley. A widow in her sixties, she preferred flamboyant hair to match her clothes, a style that often drew startled glances from the uninitiated. Neighbors were accustomed to it, however.

Today she was almost subtle. Bright yellow hair complemented her bright yellow long tee shirt and knee-length knit capris, and she wore plastic sandals with big yellow daisies atop each foot. She made Harley think of marshmallow Easter Peeps.

"You home to stay, Harley Jean?"

Not wanting to drag out the conversation, Harley shook her head and kept walking up the sidewalk to the front porch.

"Just staying a few days."

"You'll have to come over for some Karo pecan pie while you're here, Harley Jean."

Actually, that didn't sound bad. Mrs. Shipley made the best pie around. "I will," she called as she got the front door open without dropping Sam's cat carrier. He'd been very vocal during the fifteen minute drive, and had ruthlessly expressed his displeasure with her efforts to get him into the carrier. Cami had made it seem so easy. Of course, she'd had much more practice.

Once inside, Harley set the carrier on the coffee table next to half-finished necklaces and dream-catchers while Sam kept up a yowl loud enough to peel bark off trees. Diva came from the kitchen to greet her.

"While you're here we can cleanse your aura and make you feel better with Reiki," she said calmly, somehow able to be heard even over the cat's howling.

"Aura cleansing is fine, but no Reiki. That's too much like torture. I can't believe it does any good for anyone but orthopedic surgeons who charge big bucks to put people back together after they've had it done."

"You're thinking of Shiatsu." Diva smiled. She never took offense at Harley's skepticism. "I know something that will relieve your tension and help your headache. Here. Give me your hand."

After putting her backpack on the coffee table next to Sam, Harley held out her hand. Her mother's cool fingers found the pressure points on her hand and wrist. Using her thumb and fingers, she pressed gently, and oddly enough, after a few moments Harley's headache eased.

"I don't know how you do that," she said.

"It's not a secret. Anyone can do it. For instance, I apply pressure to move the body's energies along established pathways, or meridians. Facial pain or headaches can be relieved by applying pressure to the hand, because at that point a meridian connects the two areas. Each meridian links a number of areas of the body. By applying pressure, you direct the energies to heal the body."

Harley uncrossed her eyes. "Right. I'll try to remember that."

Diva released her hand after another gentle squeeze. "Yogi's in his workshop. He's nearly through with the bigger windmill he's been working on."

"I'll go out and see him after I take Sam up to my bedroom. Maybe he'll stop screeching once I get him out of this carrier."

"Animals are like people. They don't like being imprisoned."

After setting up his litter box and putting out his food and water, Harley opened the carrier door. Sam burst out like a cream and brown rocket. He streaked past the litter box, full food bowls and water, and out her open bedroom door. For a startled instant, she crouched beside the empty carrier with her mouth still open, the soothing words she'd started to say still unuttered. It hadn't gone at all like she'd planned. Cami had assured her he'd hide under her bed or a piece of furniture before he got brave enough to come out for his food. Apparently, Sam had not been informed of that.

There wasn't any sign of him in the hall or upstairs bathroom. Her brother's and parents' bedroom doors were closed. That meant he'd gone downstairs. A crash from below confirmed it.

Harley arrived in the kitchen just in time to see that Yogi had fixed King's pet door. King pushed through it at about the same time Sam bounced off the kitchen table and headed for the opening. They met nose to nose.

King was delighted.

Sam was not.

He performed a series of intricate cat karate moves with slashing claws and guttural snarls that startled King and sounded like something out of the *Exorcist.* Then he was gone, back into the dining room. A little late, King started to yelp. Chaos ensued as Yogi arrived to rescue his dog.

By the time Harley found Sam and got him back to her bedroom, she was sweaty, bloody, and panting. As soon as she released the cat, he disappeared under her bed. She knew where he was because of his high-pitched moans. Leaning back against her closed door, she began to think this hadn't been such a good idea. She should have nailed her doors shut and stayed home.

The unmistakable sounds of Sam hacking up a hairball under her bed confirmed that. When she had enough strength, she'd put him back in the carrier and return to her apartment. It'd be better than watching the door every moment to make sure cat and dog did not meet again.

"You're making this difficult, you know," she said to the cat. "You got along just fine with Cami's dogs. King's not so bad. Most of the time. Some of the time. You could overlook it. We won't be here that long. I hope."

There was no response from Sam, but that wasn't unusual.

After a moment, Harley got up and opened the door, intending to go to the bathroom to wash her face and scratches. King darted between her legs and into the bedroom, immediately finding Sam under the bed. Shouting for Yogi, Harley grabbed the dog by the tail to keep him from the cat. A scuffle ensued. "This isn't going to work," Harley said when Yogi finally got King back into the hallway and Sam was on top of a tall bookshelf spitting globs of saliva at the ceiling fan. "I knew better. I'm going back home."

Yogi looked worried. "Maybe you could just leave the cat in your apartment with lots of food and water, and I'll go check on him every day."

"No way. If this nut job is crazy enough to kill Elvis right in front of a van full of tourists, he's crazy enough to hurt my cat. And you. I'm not willing to risk it."

Diva settled it. She called Nana McMullen and asked if Harley and Sam could stay with her for a few days. Nana was delighted. Harley was less so.

"Doesn't she live in a nursing home?"

"Whispering Pines. It's assisted living. Very nice. Like condos in a mall setting. Nana has a two bedroom place with a screened porch. Meals are served in the main dining room, there's a beauty shop, doctors on staff, and buses to all the local stores."

"Don't forget three trips a month to the casinos," Yogi said, and Diva smiled.

"That's true. Nana does love the slot machines."

"There's always someone there," Yogi added, "and they lock the doors at night and no one goes in or out unless they're checked first. It's the perfect place to be safe."

Even though her parents sounded a lot more enthusiastic than she felt, Harley gave in. She hadn't seen Nana in a while, and she did enjoy her most of the time. But staying in a community of elderly people didn't sound like something she'd want to do for long.

"I'll give it a try," she said reluctantly. Maybe it wouldn't be so bad. After all, she'd get a lot of rest. Older people took plenty of naps.

"About damn time you came to see me," Nana said, dispensing with any civilities in her usual manner. At nearly eighty-six, Nana McMullen resembled a quintessential elderly Southern lady, small and white-haired, her pale skin thin and soft, and her eyes a bright blue. But there was nothing fragile or prim about her. She'd grown up during the Great Depression, borne her first child at fifteen, outlived three husbands, and lost none of her snap.

Harley grinned. "Glad to see you too, Nana. I've missed you and wanted to visit."

"Bullshit. You're only here because you're trying to hide. What, you think I don't read the newspapers or watch TV? Doesn't matter why you're here, I'm just glad to see you. Is that a cat?"

Harley set down the carrier. "His name is Sam. He and King have personality conflicts."

"That dog is demented. Cute, but crazy. Fits right in. See if Sam likes my screened porch. There are lots of birds flying around the feeder outside that he can watch."

"Sam is picky, but as long as there's not a dog trying to wear him as a furry hat, he should be okay."

Sam was better than okay. Immediately intrigued by the abundance of birds at the feeder, he crouched atop a wicker table to stare at them and make little noises low in his throat. Probably the feline version of *"Come into my parlor."*

After Harley set up the litter box and put out his food and water bowls, she went inside to find Nana in front of the TV, swearing at a baseball game.

"Who's your favorite?" she asked in a lull, and Nana looked up with something like surprise on her face.

"Atlanta, of course. Though I like our home team, too. Ever been to a Redbirds game?"

"Uh, no. I've been to AutoZone a lot, though. You know, with tourists."

"Yeah, why the hell did you take that job? You're smarter than that."

Harley shrugged. "I hated corporate banking. And they hated me. It wasn't something I was suited for. It was just the first job I got after leaving Ole Miss, and I was too dumb to move up in the company, anyway."

"Hah." Nana poked her with a finger. "You were always the smart one. You just got sick of it."

"Maybe that too. Thanks for the vote of confidence. Lately I've been feeling pretty damn stupid."

"Well you're not. You just need direction. Not like Darcy's two girls. Dumb as sock puppets, and with personalities to match. Ha!" She leaned forward in her rocker. "Brian McCann is pitching. He's a leftie. Got a pretty good strikeout record. Those Cardinals better watch out." Nana clicked off the TV. "Come on. Lunchtime. Let's go eat."

After sitting in the main dining room where they were served baked chicken, cornbread dressing, and green beans, Nana filched some fresh fruit and they went back to her apartment.

"Still got my own teeth," she said with a smile of smug satisfaction, and then bit into a pear. "So, how's it going with that hot cop you're sleeping with?"

Accustomed to Nana's bluntness, Harley shook her head. "Not going at all right now."

"Did you dump him?"

"No, we're just taking some time off for a while."

Nana looked at her shrewdly. "Right. It's all this murder crap, isn't it. Doesn't look too good for a cop's girlfriend to run around stumbling over corpses. Bet he dumped you, didn't he."

"Don't try to sugarcoat it for me," Harley said wryly. "You don't need me to tell you what you already know."

Nana waved a hand in the air. "It will sort itself out. You'll see."

"Now you sound like Diva."

"That girl has always been sharp. Isabel never could see it. Thought there was something wrong with her." Nana shook her head. "When Deirdre was just a little girl, I tried to tell Isabel that she had the sight, but Isabel would have none of it. Called it hocus pocus. I can't say I understand it myself, but my mother always seemed to know things before they happened, too. Spooky at times and downright scary at others, but not to be dismissed. But then, Isabel always wanted things to be just right. It's not a bad trait, just limited. I don't think Isabel's ever quite forgiven me for telling Deirdre to be who she is instead of what someone else wanted her to be."

Harley thought about Grandmother Eaton wanting her little girl to fit into a preconceived mold and Diva fighting against it, a nonconformist because she couldn't be anything else. No wonder Diva accepted whatever Harley wanted to do with such equanimity. She'd felt the sting of disapproval too often and didn't want to pass it along.

"What did Grandmother Eaton want Diva to be?" Harley asked, sitting in a thickly padded chair across from her grandmother.

"Isabel wanted both her girls to marry well. She'd married well, and Paul isn't a bad sort, even if he does stay gone too much. But Bel has always put too much stock in money and social position. Want a beer?"

"A beer? Is it cold?"

Nana laughed. "Yep. Don't have a washer and dryer here, so I have to keep it in this tiny little ice box. All those years of drinking it warm, now it tastes funny cold."

Harley got Nana a beer from one of those small apartment-sized refrigerators that saved space but had plenty of room for whatever Nana wanted to put in it. Like beer.

"Why did you drink your beer warm, anyway?" she asked Nana.

"My mother lived with me, and I didn't want her to know I liked a beer now and then. Of course, she had to know. She always knew things." Nana chuckled. "Still, it made me feel better, so I kept doing it even after she died."

"So what's the reason Grandmother Eaton doesn't like Yogi? He doesn't have money?"

"Part of it. Most of it was that Deirdre ran off to marry him even after she was told to have nothing to do with him. Felt like he'd stolen her daughter and brainwashed her in to living in a cult. It was sixteen years before Deidre came back, and Bel never has quite gotten over it."

Harley thought of her early years in California, moving from commune to commune, free in many ways, but constricted in ways that had meant little to Diva but a lot to her. She hadn't liked the looks they got in some towns, the derisive stares and comments when they went into stores. *Hippies. Trash. Thieves. Gypsies.* All those words had hurt. When Yogi had inherited his parents' house in Memphis, it was Harley's dream come true. Not that she wanted to be just like everyone else. She didn't. She liked her individuality, but nothing beat indoor plumbing.

"I don't think Diva has gotten over it either," she said after a moment. "She doesn't say it, but I think she misses Grandmother Eaton."

"Probably. It doesn't matter how much you disagree, there's no bond like that between a mother and daughter. Even when they don't want to admit it. Foolish stubbornness, I say. I never let Bel try that nonsense with me. Kenneth, neither, though sons are more likely to tell you just how they feel instead of sulk."

"How is Uncle Ken?"

"Doing really well. Lives up north with the Yankees in Virginia."

"Last time I heard, Virginia was below the Mason-Dixon line."

Nana snorted. "Right. You ever been up there? They sound like Yankees and eat like Yankees. Can't even cook grits properly. I don't know what they do to their barbecue, but it's not right, either. Tastes awful. I liked their biscuits, though. Best I ever had, and that's saying a lot. It's a pretty place, too, some of the most beautiful mountains I've ever seen. Rivals the Smokies."

Nana had been born in west Tennessee nine months after her father had returned from World War I. Her sturdy Irish ancestors had first settled in Memphis in the early 1800s, eventually moving out to the country right before the Civil War. Nana still called it the War of Northern Aggression, as her parents had done, and their parents before them. Stories passed down through generations told of the hard struggle during those war years, and Nana still had a big cardboard photograph of the large house the Jordans had once owned. It had four columns in front like Tara of *Gone With the Wind* fame, but wasn't as elegant. A dogtrot right down the center of the house provided cool air during the melting hot summers, with a door open at each end to allow in breezes, and big transoms over the top. Nana's great-grandparents and grandparents stood in front of the house with big smiles. Next to that framed photograph on her wall hung an after-the-war photo that showed the solemn family group in front of a white picket fence. A small two-room house sat behind the fence—once the overseer's cabin on their thirty thousand acre Tennessee estate, and after the war, home to three families. Hard times hit when taxes were raised so high only carpetbaggers could pay. As the story went, when the men who came home after the war saw what was left to them, they spent the rest of their days sitting on the front porch talking of how it'd have been if the South had won, while the women took in washing and worked gardens. But of course, that was from the women's point of view. The men no doubt had their own version.

"No," Harley said, "I've never been to Virginia, but I can tell you a lot about California."

"Those folks out there are a bit wild, aren't they? Just do what they want when they want. Must be the heat. Like here. Speaking of crazy, when do we start hunting down that idiot who's killing all the Elvises?"

"We? Hunt down? Nana, I'm not leaving here, and *we* certainly aren't going anywhere."

"We have to be back before seven-thirty," Nana said, getting up from her chair and going into her bedroom. Her voice drifted out. "They lock the doors then. I'm changing into my tennis shoes. Be ready in a minute."

"Nana, we're staying here. Remember? It's safe here. There's a killer loose, and I'm on his short list."

Appearing back in the doorway, Nana put both hands on her hips. "Don't be silly. There's nothing to be gained by being a sitting duck. Time to take the bull by the horns. No time like the present. And any other dumbass saying I can think of that'll make you see it's stupid to be the rabbit when you can be the fox."

Harley stared at her. Nana was a force to be reckoned with. But she'd met her match.

"This is insane," Harley muttered under her breath as they waited at a red light. Nana sat in the passenger seat looking like a sweet little old lady, when she was really the wolf dressed up as Little Red Riding Hood's grandmother. She wore a flowery dress that hit midway between her knees and ankles, a string of pearls around her neck, a white hat with pink and blue flowers atop her head, and two hundred dollar running shoes on her feet. She held a white wicker purse with wooden handles on her lap. White gloves covered her hands.

Dear Lord. It was the Terminator disguised as Opie's Aunt Bea.

"Not at all insane," Nana said calmly. "I can protect you."

Harley fought the urge to break into hysterical giggles. "Nana, you're barely five feet tall and weigh maybe eighty-five pounds, though I grant you that your hearing seems to be excellent. You can't protect butter. How do you expect to protect me?"

Opening her wicker purse, Nana pulled out a .38 Smith and Wesson with pearl handles. "Smitty here beats a fist fight every time."

The light turned green, but Harley couldn't summon up the energy to press the gas pedal. She felt faint. Horns honked behind her, and finally she dredged up the will to move forward, but the Toyota bucked and died when she didn't hit the clutch in time. More honking. She fumbled a moment, and then got everything moving right.

"Do the supervisors at the home know you've got that?" she asked when they were a little bit down the road, her knuckles white on the steering wheel. "And put it away, please."

"It's not a home. It's a retirement community. And to answer your question, no they don't and don't you dare tell them. I'll know when it's time to give it up, just like I knew when it was time to give up driving. Of course, I've had cataract surgery since then and I see better than ever now, so maybe I'll get me a car. Something snazzy." Nana slid the pistol back into her purse and snapped the latch. "I've been handling firearms since I was ten years old. Started out with a rifle, but that's too big to carry in my purse, of course."

"Of course. So where do you keep your Uzi?"

"Don't be a smartass. I used a .22 to hunt game back then. Buckshot makes it too hard to clean. Could pick a squirrel off a tree limb at twenty yards without thinking about it. Shot rabbits, possums, and raccoons, too, though I didn't much care for the meat off the last two. Deer meat now, that's something I miss. And sassafras tea. Grew wild around our house when I was young, and it smelled so sweet. They used to make root beer out of it, you know, though God only knows what they put in those drinks now. Chemicals, probably. Rot your innards out, not to think about what it does to your brain."

"Apparently, one of us in here has drunk too much root beer. Do you have any idea what can happen if we get stopped by the police and they find that gun in your purse?"

"I do. Not a damn thing." Nana looked smug when Harley glanced at her to see if she was having some kind of stroke.

"I've got a permit."

That took Harley aback for only a second. "To carry concealed?"

"Yep. You may not remember, but my second husband, Ed Sheridan—you never met him—was a deputy sheriff. Died of a heart attack when we were having our morning fun on the kitchen table. Try explaining to the medics why your dead husband's lying on the kitchen table with his bare ass up in the air and his ding-a-ling hard as a brick sometime. I've had better moments. Anyway, he got me the permit to carry concealed back when some yahoo was threatening to kill him and his family after Ed arrested him for armed robbery."

Harley's head swam. This was more than she wanted to know. Yet it explained so much about her family tree. "Isn't there an age limit on those permits?" she asked weakly.

"You'd think there'd be, wouldn't you? But not that I know about. I've still got Smitty and I've still got my permit. So don't worry. You're safe with me."

That was subjective. Harley slid a nervous glance toward the white wicker purse. "Is that thing loaded?"

"What the hell good would an unloaded pistol be to anyone?"

"Uh hunh. Can you make sure it's pointed in the other direction? Just in case it goes off by accident."

Nana snorted. "The only guns that go off by accident are those carried by children or fools, and I'm neither of those. But if it makes you feel any better, I'll put my purse on the floor."

"It does."

"So, where are we going first?" Nana asked when her purse was safely between her sneakers.

"I haven't thought that far yet." Truth was, she had, but that was before Lydia had been killed and she'd turned chicken.

Cluck cluck.

"I say we find out how all those Elvises got on buses that the killer was on. Couldn't be by coincidence."

Nana could be really sharp.

"The first two were sent postcards inviting them to a special TV interview. I imagine the last one was, too." Harley thought a moment. "I gave that information to Bobby, so I'm sure he's already checked up on it."

"Bobby? That skinny Italian kid I used to see hanging around your house all the time?" Nana pronounced Italian as "Eye-talian."

"That's the one. He's a detective now, and he isn't skinny anymore."

"Still cute?"

Harley thought a minute and nodded. "Most women think so."

"Who knew there were so many hot cops in Memphis? I bought one of their calendars a while back, you know. Those six-pack abs and bulging biceps made me want to lick their photos."

"You're a dirty old broad."

Nana smiled. "I know. It's always the quiet ones, isn't it?"

"You've never been quiet."

"But I do look like a sweet little old lady, and that fools people into thinking I am. Works every time."

Harley braked to avoid hitting a Mercedes that cut in front of her. "I didn't know you could be so devious, Nana."

"It's one of my best virtues. Don't let anyone tell you that life's fair and you should always play by the rules. You'll get your ass kicked if you do."

"So what do you suggest?"

"Make your own rules. Be fair, objective, kind, and as generous as you can afford to be. If someone tries to hurt you or yours in any way, take them down hard."

"Good God. My Nana is really Dirty Harry."

Nana only smiled.

Maybe Nana still went by pioneer justice, but there were pesky little things like rules of conduct in the modern world that frowned on that sort of thing. Not that it wasn't tempting.

There just had to be a compromise between the two.

"I'll make a deal with you," Harley said. "You keep Smitty tucked away, and we'll make a stop or two just to check some things out."

"Sounds good," Nana said with satisfaction. "Just let me know if you need Smitty."

"I will." Harley rolled her eyes. Like that would ever happen.

"The library?" Nana demanded in disgust when Harley parked in front of the big library on Poplar Avenue. "This isn't detective stuff."

"Sure it is. There're some things I have to look up on the Internet. You can go in a dark corner and read dirty books while I do my work."

Still disgruntled, Nana followed her inside, after their brief discussion about the wisdom of taking a loaded pistol into the library where children were had ended in the gun being locked safely in the Toyota's glove compartment. At least she'd won one battle with Nana. A red-letter day.

It didn't take too long to find out what she needed to know—if an hour and a half wasn't too long. Tootsie could probably have found the information in less than ten minutes, but she didn't know how to hack into web sites like he did. Just about the time Nana turned rebellious and threatened to go into the music room and do a hootchy-kootchy dance to *Ragtime Gal*, Harley slid off the seat and said, "All right. I'm done. On to the next adventure."

"If this is your idea of adventure," Nana muttered, "I'd be better off playing strip poker back in the dining room."

"You frighten me, Nana."

That seemed to please her and she smiled. To those who didn't know better, she could be an old darling, one of those elderly women that sang choir in church every Sunday morning, and baked cookies and knit sweaters for the homeless. Right down to her pretty lace collar beneath the string of pearls. No one would ever suspect Nana was Outlaw Annie in disguise.

"So who lives here?" Nana asked when they pulled up in front of a nice East Memphis home, a gray stone sixties modern with a red door and sharply angled roof. "The perp?"

"A suspect. I see you keep up with Law and Order."

"And CSI. I take turns watching one and taping one. So? Is this where the perp lives?"

"Suspect. Maybe a suspect. Let's just say, a person of interest."

"Ha!" Nana looked gleeful. "Give me your car keys a minute."

"You're not thinking of driving, are you?"

"Of course not. My license expired. Wouldn't want to break any laws."

Harley handed her the keys, then immediately regretted it when Nana unlocked the glove compartment and took out her pistol.

"*Oh God.* Put that thing away. We're not going to a shootout. We're just going to talk to this guy a little bit."

"You never know. Better safe than sorry. A penny earned is a penny saved—" She paused and frowned. "Wrong cliché. Well, you know what I mean."

"I'm afraid I do. Look, Dirty Harry, put up the pistol. You're going to get us in trouble."

Nana stuck the pistol into her wicker handbag and snapped it shut. "A bird in the hand is worth two in the bush."

"I'll keep that in mind when we go bird hunting. Put the gun back."

"That wasn't the right cliché at all. Damn. Maybe my meds are wearing off."

Harley felt faint. This was insane. She should never have let Nana talk her into leaving the home. Now she was in a car in front of Claude Williams's house, stuck with a fully armed senior citizen off her medication. She smacked her forehead with her palm. *What was I thinking?*

"Stop being so dramatic," Nana said calmly. "I'm all right. I just get a little confused at times. Nothing to worry about."

Before Harley could grab her, she had the door open and one foot on the curb. "Come on. Let's go grill him."

Ordinarily, now that she'd regained her senses, Harley would have insisted Nana get back in the car and would have taken her straight back to the home. But the red front door of Williams's house opened and out stepped Preston Hughes. Or a man who looked very much like the Preston Hughes in the Elvis competition photos she'd found on the Internet. Since he was dressed in jeans and a shirt instead of black leather, there was a chance she was wrong, but it certainly did look like him.

Might as well forge ahead, hit two birds with the same stone. Lord. Now she was thinking in clichés like Nana.

Williams looked surprised to see her again, and Hughes looked angry, but that could have been because of the conversation he'd been having with Williams. They'd seemed to be arguing.

"I hope I'm not intruding, Mr. Williams," she said as pleasantly as possible, "but I had a few more questions I wanted to ask you on behalf of the company. This is my great-grandmother, Mrs. McMullen."

That left the way open for Williams to introduce Hughes, which he did. Just as Harley had hoped, her suspicion was confirmed. Nana smiled sweetly and bobbed her head just like an old darling would do. The fraud.

"So very nice to meet you, Mr. Williams. My granddaughter has told me all about you."

Since she'd done nothing of the kind, Harley stepped in quickly. "I was very impressed with your photos I saw on the website—wait a moment. Preston Hughes? Aren't you always one of the winners in the big Elvis competition every year?"

Hughes nodded briefly. "Never the big winner. Not yet. I'd

hoped to correct that this year." The look he gave Williams was scorching.

Williams began to sweat, beads popping up on his forehead and bald crown. "As I've explained to Mr. Hughes, I have nothing to do with event rules and regulations. Those are left up to the contest organizers."

"Regardless of long *friendships*," Hughes said softly, and Williams looked distressed.

Interesting. Harley ruled out Williams as a definite suspect, but now her suspicion of Hughes was stronger than ever. He looked absolutely furious. The tension was so thick between the men that Harley poised to grab Nana and run before fists started flying. And before Nana showed them Smitty.

"Good friendships are like spring flowers," Nana piped up brightly, "needing lots of rain to bloom."

Both men looked at her. Harley wondered how many pills she'd missed.

Reaching out, Nana patted Hughes on the arm. "You'll see, young man. There's not much in this world that matters more than family and good friends. A quarrel shouldn't change that."

Hughes took a deep breath, and some of his tension visibly eased. "Maybe you're right. It's just that this is something I've wanted for so long that I've been willing to do almost anything to get it. I won't give up until I win."

He gave a short nod at Harley and Nana, a glance at Williams, and walked to his car in the driveway.

When they were back in her car, Harley looked at Nana. "You were great. A reminder of their friendship kept them from fighting. That was really sweet."

Nana snorted. "It was all crap. But whatever works, I always say."

"An excellent philosophy." Harley started the car and headed for Whispering Pines. She'd had just about all the fun she could handle today.

Williams lived on Shady Grove not far from the Racquet Club. The neighborhood had big, older homes, stately trees, and an air of comfortable if not lavish living. It wasn't too far from the Eaton home. Harley took Mendenhall south. The street turned into Mt. Moriah when it crossed Poplar, confusing new residents and even longtime Memphians not used to the area. The Half-Shell seafood restaurant was on the southeast corner, not far from a health food store and cat rescue. The Tobacco Shop on the southwest side sold newspapers from all over America and across the Atlantic, and a few from across the Pacific.

"Where are we going?" Nana asked when they got close to Park Avenue. "I feel like some pizza."

Damn. "I thought you'd be tired by now so I'm taking you back to the home."

"Retirement community. I'm retired, not crazy, dammit."

"Sorry. Retirement community. Don't they serve pizza at Whispering Pines? We can order takeout."

"Got my mouth all set for Memphis City Pizza. It's on the corner of Park across from the Eastgate Shopping Center. Isabel took me there once."

While Harley was trying to imagine Grandmother Eaton sitting in a pizza place with a pitcher of beer and a pepperoni slice, something bumped them from the rear. It knocked her little Toyota forward and she barely missed hitting the car in front of her.

"What the hell?" She looked over at her grandmother. "Nana, are you all right?"

"Of course I'm all right. That's what seat belts are for."

Harley started to pull the brake and turn off the ignition to get out and assess the damage and maybe swap licenses with whoever hit her, when another bump shoved them forward so that she hit the car in front. Dammit! She looked in the rearview mirror. The car behind was black and had tinted windows, so she couldn't see who was inside. Weren't tinted windows supposed to be illegal now?

Before she had time to dwell on that, another hard hit from behind threatened to make a sandwich out of her car, and wouldn't do too much for the passengers inside, either.

Nana, holding on to the dash with both hands, looked at her. "That guy's deliberately hitting us!"

Her heart thudded so hard against her ribs it hurt.

"Where are the cops when you need them?" Nana grumbled. "Probably at that doughnut shop we just passed."

Harley only half-listened. The black car revved its engine and she braced for another hit. They were hemmed in by traffic on both sides. The vehicle in front was a big Ford truck that had a trailer hitch sticking out on the back. If the cars in the turning lane moved, she could make a dash for the tire place on the corner. Fortunately, she already had plenty of experience dodging cars on Poplar.

Then a loud explosion blew out her back windshield. Instinct made her duck and grab for Nana to push her down in the seat. The Toyota engine whined.

"Dammit, you're messing up my aim," Nana said crossly, and Harley looked at her. She had her gun in both hands and was taking aim again.

"Jesus, Mary and Joseph, give me that!" Harley grabbed for the weapon just as it went off again. This time, the bullet took out their attacker's windshield. It was safety glass and cracked all the way across. It looked like crushed ice and when she looked, she couldn't make out the driver at all.

Other drivers honked, yelled, ran red lights and up on curbs, and the black car took off around a Taurus and headed down Park. Even if she'd wanted to follow him with Nana in the car holding a pistol that had probably belonged to Al Capone, her car bucked, groaned, and died. It was probably best. What would she do if she caught him?

Nana looked over at her. "If he didn't have that tinted glass, I'd have got him. I can shoot a squirrel at twenty yards."

"I've heard that."

Nana looked pleased.

Eleven

Something kept tickling her nose. She couldn't breathe. A steady weight pressed down on her chest, and Harley came straight up in the bed gasping for air and ready to fight her assailant.

Sam, dislodged and disgruntled, held on to the quilt with claws firmly attached. He yowled a complaint that registered in Harley's sleep-fogged brain and she peered at him blearily. "Don't you ever sleep late?"

Apparently not. Sam leaped to the floor and stalked toward the closed door, then looked at her over his shoulder and gave another loud yowl. Food and doody time. Yawning, Harley gave in and staggered into Nana's small kitchenette that consisted of a refrigerator, microwave, and one of those heavy-duty coffee pots that looked like it came from the fifties. After letting Sam out onto the screened porch and feeding him, she started toward the coffee pot, determined to figure out how to work it.

To her surprise—and relief—it was plugged in and the coffee brewed. Nice. That meant Nana was already up. So where was she? There was no sign of her in any of the rooms. It wasn't that big of a place, just two bedrooms, a large bath, the living room and kitchenette. Maybe she was already out visiting or having an early breakfast. Or doing a hit for the Mob. Yesterday hadn't been that much fun. Especially when Bobby showed up. Apparently he'd heard about it on his police radio and decided to add to the joy. At least they hadn't been charged with anything, though Nana was pretty upset that they'd taken her gun. There was an ordinance against firing weapons in the city limits it seemed, though that didn't seem to slow the gang-bangers much. Nana said it was age discrimination and she was going to sue.

Harley had gone to bed with a headache and the intention of sleeping until noon.

But it was nice outside this early, she had to admit when she took a cup of coffee out onto the porch to sit in one of the lounge chairs and watch Sam watch birds. The tip of his tail twitched in perfect harmony with the odd little noises he made.

A lovely, fresh breeze came in through the screens, smelling of recently mowed grass. Leaning back, she just enjoyed the fragrant coffee and tranquility for a moment, letting her mind drift. As it seemed to do lately, it eventually drifted toward death and murder. She'd become a ghoul. How interesting. She wondered exactly when this change in her personality had shifted from just being a little out of synch to being completely bizarre. It must have been sudden. Maybe finding Mrs. Trumble dead in her own dining room had put her over the edge. Whatever it was, she had no idea how to get rid of it. Might as well do the best she could until it went away.

So she began to try to piece together the fragments of information into some kind of pattern. It was like constructing the quilt on Nana's guestroom bed. Sooner or later, all those random scraps of details should come together into something recognizable.

For the moment, Williams was at the bottom of her suspect list. Hughes was at the top. He had motive, means, and opportunity. He was furious about being disqualified from being an Elvis competitor this year, he'd know the other contestants and be able to dress up and blend in with them, and he lived and worked in Memphis so would have opportunity. Also, he fit pretty closely with the descriptions from tourists and drivers, and even though she couldn't say with certainty it was him, he could be the extra Elvis on her van, too. And the guy who'd hit her car yesterday.

There was something else, a vague memory of something familiar . . . it had importance, she just knew, but what was it? Someone had said something familiar that passed her at the time, but triggered a warning bell. Damn. What *was* it?

"You look lost in thought," Nana said, opening the door onto the porch and stepping out. "Unfamiliar territory?"

"Well, aren't you just precious this morning." Harley tilted her head back to look at Nana. "What is that getup you're wearing?"

"My jogging outfit. Like it?"

Nana turned like a runway model, holding out the edge of her flowered skirt that was so transparent no one could miss the flesh-colored leotards beneath, nor what looked like knee-length drawers. A light gray sweatshirt, rolled down white tube socks, a sweatband around her forehead, and expensive running shoes completed the picture.

"It's adorable. Why not wear jogging pants, though?"

"A lady of my age just doesn't do that. It isn't seemly."

Harley looked at her. Apparently, wearing flesh-colored leotards and carrying a loaded .38 was considered seemly.

She shook her head. "I'd hate to see the men's dress code here."

"Don't be a smartass." Nana sat in the chair next to Harley. "Breakfast is at seven-thirty. Want to join us?"

"Isn't there a late breakfast?"

"Only for the slugs. You're young. Deal with it. We've got work to do."

Oh no. Harley narrowed her eyes. "What are you talking about?"

"Well, you've focused on Hughes as your prime suspect, haven't you? Don't deny it. I saw that look in your eyes yesterday when he said winning was something he'd wanted for so long, he'd be willing to do almost anything to get it. Rang a bell for you, didn't it?"

"Damn. How did you do that? I've been sitting here trying to think of what it was that's been bothering me, and you just spit it out. That's it, though. You're right. The Elvis in the taxi at the concert said almost the same exact thing to the taxi driver. I thought I recognized him, so it must have been Hughes. He was the one on my van. I'm certain of it. Almost certain. And he was probably the one who tried to shove us off the road yesterday."

Nana nodded in satisfaction. "So chickie, let's go!"

"This wasn't what I had in mind," Nana said resentfully when they stood in the West Precinct waiting on Bobby to get off the phone. "I thought we'd do a little snooping on our own."

"That leads to scary things. It's better this way. Trust me."

Nana snorted. "And here I thought you had pioneer spirit. You're taking the easy way out."

"I prefer to think of it as the safe way out. It's a little unnerving being held hostage at gunpoint."

"What's wrong with being unnerved a time or two? Good for

the blood. Gets it running."

Before Harley could give her opinion on running blood and all the reasons being unnerved couldn't possibly be good for a person, Bobby hung up the phone and beckoned for them.

Nana, looking like an old darling again in a print dress with lace collar, her hose rolled up and held by garters barely visible beneath the long skirt, and wearing plain, sensible shoes on her feet, took the first chair and settled into it with her white wicker purse in her lap. Minus Smitty.

"Did you find out anything about the car yesterday?" Harley asked Bobby when she sat down in the chair opposite his desk. "Did anyone get his plate number?"

"The car didn't have any plates. We're looking for it." He looked over at Nana. "And how are you today, Mrs. McMullen?" he asked in a loud voice.

"Pretty pissed off at the moment. And it was my late husband who was deaf, not me. Do I get my gun back today?"

"I'm afraid not. We're checking things out," Bobby said in a more normal tone.

"My lawyer says you can't keep it. I have a permit."

"Then I'm sure it'll be given back to you soon."

"So why haven't you caught this killer yet? Seems to me you should be glad of a little help instead of telling my granddaughter to stay out of it."

Bobby blinked. Harley smiled. Apparently he'd forgotten about Nana McMullen and how blunt she could be.

Bobby leaned forward and said, "This is a police matter, Mrs. McMullen. While we're always glad of citizens' cooperation and information, any kind of interference in an ongoing investigation is discouraged."

"Good Lord. Do you always talk like you've got a stick up your ass? I remember you, you know. You were a skinny little Italian kid with a swagger and more tricks than David Copperfield. And I remember that Fourth of July picnic when you used a toy bow and arrow to shoot a string of lit firecrackers up into the trees so that a flock of nesting blackbirds flew out and crapped all over our barbecue, too. Then there was a time you put a black snake in the Anderson's swimming pool, and the time—"

"Yes, you've got an excellent memory, it seems," Bobby

interrupted while scowling at the officer sitting behind the next desk who was laughing so hard he kept snorting through his nose. "But we have rules. And laws. They're designed to keep Memphis citizens safe. If everyone went around investigating carjackings, robberies, and murders, there'd be chaos. And mayhem. It needs to be left to the police."

Nana looked like she was ready to say something guaranteed to put Bobby in a bad mood, so Harley quickly said, "I have information about Preston Hughes that might interest you."

Bobby's expression immediately changed to his cop-face. Harley couldn't tell if the name was familiar to him or not.

"What information?" he asked.

She gave him the yellow sheet of legal paper with her pros and cons written on it. She'd updated it to include Hughes's comments to the taxi driver. He scanned it and nodded. "Thanks."

Harley stared at him. "Thanks? That's it?"

"What, you expected flowers?"

"Something more flowery, maybe. Like, *This will help*, or *Thanks for taking the time to make sure I got this information.*"

Bobby stood up. All she ever saw him in these days were suits, when once he'd been the tee shirt and scruffy Levi's type. Oddly enough, both styles looked good on him. Not only could she understand her friend Cami's attraction to him, occasionally she remembered their brief fling with a fond smile.

Not today, however. Today, she remembered with satisfaction the time she'd beat him to a pulp when she was fifteen because he'd pushed Eric down. No one shoved her little brother around except her. That was the cardinal rule. Of course, if she'd known Mr. Baroni would give Bobby another whipping when he got home, maybe she wouldn't have done it. That didn't seem quite fair.

Bobby said, "Okay, thanks for taking the time to make sure I got this information. If it leads to an arrest, I'll make sure you get the Crimestoppers cash. Is that better?"

Feeling slightly guilty when she recalled causing Bobby trouble a long time ago, she said, "Much better. Only give the cash to Nana. She's really the one who remembered what he said."

Nana beamed. "Hot damn!"

The greedy gleam in Nana's eyes promised a trip to the casinos in her future, and Harley just smiled. Sometimes things worked out fairly well.

"So, you really think Hughes is the one?" Nana asked on their way home, and Harley gave a shrug.

"He's the most likely one. All the murders except Lydia's are related to the competition."

Nana was quiet for a moment. Then she said, "So I wonder why he killed Lydia?"

"She must have known him. Seen him on the buses before, or maybe even at one of the big competitions."

"And that's why he tried to kill you and run us off the road?"

Harley shivered. "Must be."

"That doesn't make sense."

"What do you mean?"

Nana turned in the seat as much as the seat belt would allow and looked at her. "There are all those tourists on these buses, yet the only two witnesses the killer seems worried about is the two of you. Why is that?"

"I don't know. Probably because he thinks we paid more attention and can identify him. Poor Lydia."

"Wasn't there a third bus driver? What about her?"

"The police are keeping an eye on her, and she has a big strong husband hanging around the house. I imagine the killer's not as anxious to tackle all that."

Nana went quiet for a moment. Then she shook her head.

"Still, it doesn't quite add up. I'll think about it a while, then let you know what it is."

"So now you're not so sure it's Hughes?"

"He seemed right, but now I've been thinking about baking ingredients."

"Baking ingredients?" Harley wondered if Nana's meds had stopped working again.

"Yep, like in a cake. A little too much of this, not enough of that, and you've got a cake as flat as a fritter and hard as a brick. I'm wondering if Hughes is a fritter."

"You're just worried you won't get your Crimestoppers cash."

"Maybe. It sure would come in handy at the casino." Nana seemed sad about that, so Harley changed the subject to Aunt Darcy and her girls, since that always gave her something to talk about.

When they got back to Whispering Pines, Nana insisted upon introducing Harley to her friends and acquaintances. There were quite a few of them. Nana obviously had a full social schedule. Jogging around the indoor track in the mornings, playing cards or shuffleboard, a swim in the indoor pool, trips in the Whispering Pines vans to the local shopping malls, movies, doctor appointments, and down to the Tunica casinos, were just a few of the daily activities. Plus three meals a day served in the dining room or taken to their own apartments. Not a bad life. Old age obviously had its perks.

When Harley mentioned that, Nana agreed. "Definitely. Not as expensive as you might think, either. Though drawing pensions from three dead husbands helps out a lot."

Holding glasses of iced tea, they sat on the screened porch with Sam. Harley lay in the lounge chair, while Nana sat in her favorite wicker rocker with fat cushions. Sam was glued to window screens watching the birds. He'd hardly touched his food. Apparently, there were some things he liked better than flaked tuna bits in sauce.

"Of course," Nana added reflectively, "it took me a long time to get here. And it wasn't always fun. Not that I minded the bad times so much. Made the good ones that much better."

"Were there ever times you wondered if the bad outweighed the good?"

"Never. Not to say there weren't those times when I'd be thinking the good better hurry up and come along before I got too squirrelly, but it eventually did. Always does. You just have to recognize it when it gets there. A lot of folks I've known are so busy whining about how unfair life has been that they never even see all the good things they've got. I might feel sorry for them if it didn't make me so blamed impatient. Foolishness." Harley thought about that. She wondered if Nana was talking about Grandmother Eaton. Or maybe Darcy's daughters, Madelyn and Amanda.

"One of the things I learned," Nana said, "is if you're going to let past heartbreaks and disappointments ruin your present, you're not going to have a future that's worth spit."

"You're a wise woman, Nana."

"Yeah? Tell that to my stockbroker. But then, he wanted me to invest in Enron."

"So why aren't you wearing a dress?" Nana looked Tootsie up and down. "Harley tells me you're prettier than most women she's ever known."

Tootsie smiled. "I knew I couldn't outshine you, so I didn't even try."

"Bullshit," Nana said, but looked pleased.

Since Nana had a poker game waiting on her in the recreation hall, Harley and Tootsie went out onto the community's covered front porch to sit in the big wooden rockers.

"How's hard time at the home going?" Tootsie asked with a grin.

"Better than I expected. Although I've discovered that people in their eighties are far too frisky for me. Jogging, cards, shuffleboard, swimming—I can't keep up with them. I'm beginning to think they're really the Undead who never have to sleep. I'm exhausted."

"My grandmother was like that until the last few years of her life. No one can say she didn't know how to live. I still miss her."

Harley nodded sympathetically. Tootsie's grandmother had died several years before and left him a modest inheritance and a house in Midtown. Harley hadn't known him then, and he'd only mentioned her a few times, always with great affection.

"How's business?" Harley asked, even though she already knew.

"Down by forty percent." Tootsie looked glum. "Even with security guards on every van—and your friend Bubba gave us a great deal, thanks—we don't have nearly what we should this time of year."

"Look, I know you said you'd pay me even when I wasn't there, but don't. I don't need it. I still have money in savings since I decided that a decadent trip to the Caribbean isn't wise right now. See? And Diva thinks I never listen to her."

Tootsie laughed. "You don't. Not when you should, anyway. So, has she had any vibes on this thing? Who the killer might be? Why he's only doing this on our vans?"

"Go see her. If she can tell you anything, she will. Just keep in mind it's not like Ask Jeeves or Google. You might not get the answer you want, or even at all."

"Then it's *just* like Ask Jeeves or Google." Tootsie sat

thoughtfully for a moment. "You know, I think that's a very good idea. Will you call and ask her when would be a good time?"

"Yep. And even better, I'll go with you. Since we're both involved, she might get some really good vibes."

It ended up that Tootsie, Harley, and Nana all went to see Diva. A nice afternoon outing to visit your family psychic. Only recently had Diva started allowing people to come to her home for a reading, and only people recommended by someone she knew. Usually, her tarot card readings were done at the monthly flea market. She said too many readings drained her of energy and bruised her *chi*, or something like that. As many years as she'd been listening to it, Harley could never keep all those things straight. *Mantra, Tantric, chakra, chi*, all blended together in a litany of inexplicable terms that she never let register. That was Diva's thing, not hers—a disappointment to her mother and, she suspected, a relief to her father.

Diva's ecological statement was in full bloom, leggy weeds and trailing vincas straggling over the sidewalk and along the fence in front. It could have looked like someone had not taken the time to mow, but somehow, the pretty wildflowers looked more like a meadow, albeit one enclosed by concrete and unpainted pickets. Wind chimes hung on the porch stretching across the front of the house and tinkled in a light breeze, a welcoming sound. White concrete pillars stood sentinel on each side of the three steps up to the porch where Diva waited in a ladder-back chair painted with astrology signs, suns, moons, stars, and the planets. A similar chair stood on the other side of a small table draped with heavy tapestry cloth in muted jewel tones. Impressive. The paintings on the chairs were no doubt Eric's work. He was really talented when he wasn't being a total slug.

"No sign with a big red palm in the window?" Harley teased, and her mother smiled.

"Not yet. I've always thought those were tacky anyway. Hello, Nana. It's been a while since I've seen you."

As Diva got up to hug her grandmother, Harley noticed the glass globe in the center of the table. How nice. She'd bought that for her mother from Aunt Darcy's design shop, receiving the usual family discount of five percent. It hadn't done much for the hefty price tag, but the gift had pleased Diva enormously when Harley gave it to her.

Harley introduced Tootsie to Diva, and they shook hands. Her mother held his a little longer than necessary. She looked deeply into his eyes, one of those steady gazes that had always paralyzed Harley since childhood. It was like Diva saw all the soul's secrets, though she said that wasn't true at all.

"Hello, Thomas," Diva said, even though Harley had introduced him as Tootsie. "You're very welcome here."

Releasing his hand at last, she motioned for him to sit down across from her. Harley took Nana by the arm and suggested they go inside, but Tootsie looked up and said, "No, I want you to stay. You need to hear this, too, and like you said, both of us together may help."

Diva smiled. Picking up the tarot cards, she began shuffling them, then laying them out in what Harley recognized as some kind of Celtic Cross spread. Without looking at the cards, Diva spoke softly, her eyes closed so she couldn't even see Tootsie. That was always spooky to Harley. She'd wondered more than once if her mother had somehow marked the cards, but always felt disloyal when she did.

The first part of the reading sounded like a hundred others to Harley, with the chariot indicating a journey and swords indicating business problems, and the wheel of fortune promising it would soon be behind him. Then she abandoned the cards altogether.

In a husky voice that somehow sounded otherworldly, Diva said, "The past is following you, but it's not your past. You're caught in between. Elvis isn't dead, he's hiding. He finds you in the candlelight . . . but it's not really you . . . I can't quite see . . . "

She opened her eyes abruptly. "It's gone. Impressions and images can be so confusing. Sometimes I don't know what they mean. Do you?"

Tootsie shook his head. "Not all of them. The Elvis thing makes sense. The impersonator who's been killing the others has to be hiding. As for the past, I don't know what that would have to do with me if it's not my past."

"Perhaps it will come to me. Often it does, in my dreams or just out of the blue," Diva said with a shake of her head. "It's not always convenient."

"And sometimes it's just enough information to get you in

trouble," Harley said, and her mother nodded.

"That's true. There are times when things come to me so clearly, and then other times it's in a collage of images I can't interpret, because often they aren't what they seem to be."

"Damn spooky," Nana said, "if a psychic doesn't even know what she sees."

Diva laughed. "Nana, you're right, as usual." Nana smiled.

"*Wait a minute*," Harley said. "When you tell me that it's up to me to figure out what it is I'm supposed to do, that's only because *you* can't figure it out?" Diva's serene smile masked duplicity. Harley shook her head. "I've been suckered in, haven't I."

"All your life," Diva said, and laughed again.

"I'm crushed," said Harley, and flopped onto one of the porch chairs Yogi had purchased at a flea market and Eric had decorated with bright colors and designs. "But much wiser."

All in all, it wasn't a bad day. Nana and Diva laughed and talked over herbal tea, while Tootsie and Harley helped Yogi construct one of his windmill contraptions to sell at the next flea market. It was elephant shaped, and the trunk and tail spun with the wind. Yogi had also done another Eiffel Tower windmill—miniature, of course, only about four feet tall—and some flamingos and other birds. The one Harley liked best was the Elvis windmill. It was his last one, since the others had sold out, and when the wind blew hard enough, Elvis gyrated and his guitar spun. In his way, Yogi was an artist. That must be where Eric got his talent, though he didn't use it the way he should. Painting purple Picasso style body parts on their lime green van didn't really count. It did make Vanna distinctive, however. The vehicle was recognized all over Memphis.

When Eric wandered in, the house on Douglass was almost like a family reunion. Even Mrs. Shipley from across the street came over with one of her famous Karo pecan pies, and a Key Lime pie for Diva, her favorite.

"You out to catch you a man, Sadie?" Nana asked when the pie was almost gone.

Mrs. Shipley looked startled. "Lord, no. Why?"

"I've never seen so much daytime make-up on anyone not in vaudeville."

Harley gulped, but Mrs. Shipley just laughed.

"I'm just gilding the lily, Anna Mae, just gilding the lily."

"Looks to me like you tried to drown it. My sister Mary Jean used to put all that crap on her face, too. I never quite got the hang of it. She said I'd do better not to even try."

"She was probably right. Some people get along better with what the good Lord gave them, and some of us have to give it a little help."

Harley refrained from pointing out to Mrs. Shipley that she'd given a lot more than a little help, and thankfully, so did Nana. Actually, it was one of Mrs. Shipley's better days. She must have mislaid the trowel she usually used to apply her make-up. Even her colors were subdued, or what passed for subdued with her. The green capri pants and long top she wore were more pastel than vivid, and she'd left her hair alone and not dyed it to match, though she did wear a bright green ribbon through the red curls atop her crown.

Eric leaned close to Harley. "I can't decide if she looks like Christmas or something St. Patrick might have thrown up."

Tootsie obviously heard and started laughing, and since Harley didn't want to explain to the others why they were amused, she said it was time to start back to Whispering Pines.

"Before they lock me out," Nana said. "I turn into a pumpkin at seven-thirty."

After a brief discussion with Mrs. Shipley about the amenities at Whispering Pines, Nana got into the front seat of Tootsie's Acura and told him to see how fast the car would go on the way home. Fortunately, he didn't.

Mr. Fraser, the director of Whispering Pines, came out from his office when they entered the front door, smiling. "Looks like you've had a big day, Mrs. McMullen," he said cheerfully.

"Big enough. Now I'm ready for tonight's poker game. Ka-ching!"

While Harley stared at Nana and wondered if she could get on some of the meds she had to be on, the director continued, "It was very nice of your granddaughter to provide entertainment, but I thought you'd have wanted to be here, too."

Entertainment? Harley turned to look at him. "What entertainment?"

"Why, the Elvis impersonator you sent to give us a show. He

was unexpected—you really should discuss this with management first—but the guests loved him and he was a big hit. You should have seen the dining room. I thought Mr. Baker was going to snap his new hip out of joint."

"Uh, why do you think I sent an Elvis here?"

"Oh, because he said you had, and he left you something, too. Wait a moment and I'll get it for you."

When the director returned with a postcard, Harley and Tootsie exchanged glances. It was exactly like the cards sent to Derek Wade and Leroy Jenkins. The only difference was on the back, where the invitation read: *Soon. My time, my place, my choice.*

"Uh oh," Harley said, and Tootsie nodded. Uh oh, indeed.

Twelve

"No fingerprints at all?"

"Yes," Bobby said more patiently than usual, "the director's, yours, and Tootsie's."

Sitting across from his desk, Harley slumped in the uncomfortable chair. "Bummer."

Bobby cleared his throat. When she looked up, he had a worried expression. He said, "I knew this would happen. I should lock you in a cell for your own safety."

"Harsh. I'm being stalked by a killer again and all you can say is 'I told you so?' Thanks."

"That's not what I'm saying, Harley. Now he knows where you're staying. Maybe you should think about staying somewhere else."

"That's what I told Nana. She says I'm safer there than anywhere else, but I don't want her to get hurt."

"What? Thinking of someone besides yourself? I'm shocked."

Harley narrowed her eyes at him. "Don't be an ass. You know I'm not like that."

"I used to think so. Since you got this new hobby, I'm not so sure."

"It's not a hobby. It's a curse. If you'd tell me who you suspect, maybe I'd be a lot safer. Have you thought of that?"

"If you'd stay inside, you'd be a lot safer. Consider it. And I say that as a warning."

"You act like I'm the stalker, not the stalkee. I know there's a lot you're not telling me, and if you'd just stop treating me as the enemy, we could work together. Couldn't we?"

"No. You're an accident waiting to happen. Maybe you don't mean to be, but you blunder around making things worse and being a total disaster. Stop it. Before you get yourself killed."

"I'd love to stop 'being a total disaster,' but unfortunately, the killer isn't cooperating at all. It's not like I'm inviting all this, you know."

Bobby leaned closer over his desk, his tone intent. "That's exactly what I mean. You never send trouble engraved invitations. It just finds you."

"Other than recent events—which were totally unexpected and unwanted—name a time I invited trouble."

"You had to ask. There was the time you and Cami skipped school and auditioned for roles in *Hair* at the Playhouse Theater. Sister Mary Rita fainted and hit her head when she found you totally naked on the stage."

"That little rat Sherry Osborne had to go and tell her where we were, or she'd never have known. Besides, the actors in *Hair* were supposed to be naked. It was part of the play."

Bobby shook his head. "Then there was the time you skipped school and fell in a drainage ditch trying to jump across it, and Sister Elizabeth found you wearing nothing but a borrowed towel and washing your clothes at the Laundromat."

"My early childhood encouraged a lack of inhibition. I'm much more civilized now," she said with as much dignity as she could muster. "But I get your point. You're just being very uncooperative."

"I'm glad you noticed. Go away."

"All right. Since we're still meandering down Memory Lane, I remember the time you taught your five-year-old sister Angela a new cheer for the Little League Football team, and she got up in front of everyone with her pom-poms and shouted, 'Two, four, six, eight, everyone likes to masturba—'"

"What do you want, Harley?" Bobby cut in before she could finish, although she could hardly hear him over the detective at the next desk who was laughing so loud heads turned to look in their direction.

She smiled. "Just a heads-up on any new info you can share without breaking any police rules."

Bobby sighed. "Fine. Where can I reach you if I need you?"

"My cell phone. But if you mean where do I intend to stay until I find another place, I'll be at Whispering Pines."

"Maybe Nana McMullen is right. Maybe you're safer there than anywhere else. At least you're locked in after seven-thirty at night."

"I was thinking more along the line of others being locked out."

Bobby stood up. "Keep your cell phone charged. Do you have any pepper spray?"

"A brand new can of it. And an attack cat and a baseball bat. Nana believes in being well-prepared." She decided it'd be best not to remind him about Nana's .38. Bobby had a tendency to get a little jumpy about some things, and he might jump to the conclusion Nana had more guns tucked away.

"But you'll check out Preston Hughes?" she asked him from the doorway, and he nodded.

"We'll check him out. If it was him playing Elvis for the elderly yesterday, we'll know about it."

She hoped he was right. Hughes hadn't looked at all friendly when he'd left Williams's house, and now he knew about Nana.

Her imagination had conjured up all kinds of reasons for his visit to Whispering Pines, none of them pleasant.

Nana, however, seemed unfazed. "Come on," she said when Harley flopped down on the couch after returning from the police station. "Get dressed. It's almost time to go."

"Go where?" Harley opened one eye. Nana wore a striped dress with a belt and Peter Pan collar, white socks and tennis shoes, and instead of one of those flowery hats she favored, she had a Memphis Redbirds baseball cap atop her head. Sudden dread seized Harley. "A baseball game?"

Nana was almost dancing with excitement. "Yep! Memphis Redbirds at AutoZone park. It's Seniors' Day or some kind of crap like that. We got free tickets. The van will be out front in a few minutes. Hurry up and get dressed. Wear something cooler than jeans and a tee shirt. I'd loan you one of my skirts if you weren't so much taller. Don't you have any shorts?"

"I do, but the afternoon sun shining off my white legs would blind the outfielders. I'll just stay here."

"The hell you will. You need to relax. Safety in numbers. Now hurry up."

"I don't qualify as a senior. Give my ticket to someone else."

Harley might as well have been talking to a wall. Any argument with Nana usually ended in her great-grandmother's favor.

Before Harley knew quite how it had happened, she sat in the third row of a crowded bus with thirty-odd seniors all singing *Hinky, dinky, parley-voo* at the top of their lungs. They all wore wrist bands like hunting dogs' collars, a way to track them if they got separated from the chaperones. Except for Harley. Maybe she could sneak away and fall into a beer keg at the concession stand.

"Isn't this fun?" Nana yelled over the others, who'd begun singing *Do Ya Think I'm Sexy?* in quavering voices. Rod Stewart would be so proud.

"A blast."

The lie pleased Nana. She smiled and bobbed her head. Harley wasn't sure if she was more amazed by the fact the seniors knew all the words to a Rod Stewart song, or that she was the only one who wanted to take a nap. What happened to all that rest seniors were supposed to need?

The new AutoZone baseball stadium at Third and Union replaced the old one out at the Memphis Fairgrounds where the Memphis Chicks had once played. A gigantic metal figure in a baseball uniform greeted visitors at the entrance, with his bat drawn back in a swing. The tiled courtyard had ticket stands and pots of flowers. Tempting smells of popcorn, nachos, hot dogs and barbecue lured crowds to the concessions. Picnic tables covered by brightly colored metal canopies were bolted to concrete. A broad expanse of green grass for families with energetic kids looked over the outfield. Their comped seats were in a tier easily accessible by wheelchairs, the elderly, and vendors.

"It's the bee's knees, isn't it?" one of the men observed. A small man shrunken by time and arthritis, he squinted at players warming up on the field. "Is Mickey Mantle playing today?"

"Not today," an attendant replied with the tone of someone accustomed to questions from a different era. While all the elderly Whispering Pine residents wore electronic bracelets in case they got separated, accompanying attendants still hovered cautiously, like prison trustees watching over a senior chain gang.

Harley stopped worrying and started to enjoy the day. It was sunny but with a cool enough breeze that she didn't get too hot in her tee shirt and jeans. The usual smells and sounds that went with a baseball game even prompted her to join in when the seniors yelled *"Batter-batter-batter-batter!"* at the other team. It didn't matter who was playing or who won, it was just relaxing. As much as she hated admitting it, Nana was right. This was fun.

The mascot, a big giant redbird made of red and black felt and a few feathers, pranced along the edge of the field by the dugouts, waving at the fans up in the stands, and pretending to catch a foul ball. The Hot Shots cheerleaders dressed in red costumes danced energetically to *Take Me Out to the Ballgame,* then segued into *Walking in Memphis.* Some of the seniors started to dance. Sort of . . .

Harley decided it was a good time to find the bathrooms. Nana declined to join her, saying she was just fine. She probably wore Depends under that striped dress.

A lot of people roamed the wide corridors, going to the concessions stands, bathrooms, and buying souvenirs. The line to the ladies' bathroom wasn't too long, and when Harley came out of the stall, she was the only one in there. That was highly unusual. Normally, the bathrooms had lines as long as the stadium. Now it was so quiet that sound echoed. The organ music had stopped and the voice of the announcer sounded muffled through all the concrete. She washed her hands and dried them, muttering about the forced air dryers that never really got hands dry like paper towels did. It just made a lot of noise and blew out hot air, like some people she knew.

When she glanced around, the Redbirds mascot came around the tiled corner. Up close, it loomed even larger than it looked down on the field. Who knew there was a woman inside that big costume? It had to be lighter than it looked. Most of those costumes were pretty heavy, what with all the wire and heavy fabric. "What's up, chick?" she couldn't help asking. The mascot just looked at her. "Okay, guess you get a lot of jokes when you're wearing that. Sorry."

The stuffed yellow beak bobbed up and down. A really pale face could be glimpsed behind the mesh eye holes, eyeliner defining brown eyes. It had to be hot in that thing in the summertime. Harley felt uncomfortable. The mascot was probably waiting for her to leave before getting out of the costume to go into one of the stalls. Not even the handicapped stall looked big enough for that redbird. Harley rubbed her hands under the blowing air and ignored the unfriendly fowl.

The situation felt strangely out of kilter somehow. Like she was somewhere she wasn't meant to be. The dryer cut off and Harley gave her hands a final shake to get rid of any excess water.

As she turned toward the exit, something grabbed her from behind. Huge hands circled her throat and squeezed tightly.

Harley clawed at them frantically, but the more she tried to dislodge the grip, the tighter it got. Spots danced in front of her eyes, her ears rang, and the distinct smell of something almost sickly sweet stung her nose. She kicked at the sinks and tiled walls, managing to knock off one of the soap dispensers, then used leverage with her feet to throw her attacker off-balance. They both went down heavily to the tiled floor that smelled of disinfectant, and rolled so that the bird pinned her to the cold tiles. She jammed an elbow backward, aiming for the head, but hit something much softer. Bird legs flailed on each side of her and she heard a heavy grunt of pain. The grip slackened, but she was trapped under the weight of the costume. Felt and feathers blocked her nose and mouth, and a gagging sound came from somewhere. It might be her but it sounded like the bird was choking on its own feathers.

Then, as abruptly as it began, the attack ended. Weight lifted, and Harley caught a glimpse of tennis shoes where bird feet should be. Still sprawled on cold tiles, she heard a familiar voice shouting words no old darling should even know, much less say. The smell that accompanied those words burned the air. *Sulfur? No. Mace. Nana. Thank God.*

Coughing, she sat up, almost eye-level with Nana's striped belt.

"Are you all right?" Nana asked sharply, and Harley nodded. "Good. Get up. The bird's flown the coop, and we've got to catch that bastard!"

Harley's throat was too bruised to argue, and she stumbled to her feet to follow Nana out the bathroom door, staggering a little. Orange cones at the entrance and exit explained why no one else had come in on them. The redbird ran in a lumbering gait like a drunken hippo, the costume shedding feathers and huge feet slapping against concrete floors.

"Stop that chicken!" Nana shouted, but people just turned to stare, either thinking it was some kind of joke or not comprehending. Harley didn't blame them. The redbird disappeared around a corner with Nana in hot pursuit and Harley lagging behind.

When she caught up with her grandmother, Nana was standing in the middle of an empty corridor. She still had the can of Mace that had replaced Smitty in her hand. It'd been a good choice. There'd be no way to explain shooting the Memphis Redbird.

"We lost her," Harley managed to say in a croak. "Let's talk to the security guards."

"And tell them what? A giant chicken tried to choke my granddaughter?"

"Redbird."

"Whatever. This just ticks me off."

"I can tell."

Nana looked at her. "You sure you're okay? You're kinda red-faced."

"Lack of oxygen. I'm just fine."

"How'd you let that bird get near enough to choke you?"

"I didn't expect a woman to be inside the costume or to be a threat. Who knew?"

Nana snorted. "That was no woman."

"But . . . she was in the ladies' bathroom."

"And if I stand in a garage does that make me a car? I think lack of oxygen cost you a few brain cells, honey child. Come on. You need to sit down for a while."

"Probably." She thought for a moment. "I think I got him in the giblets with my elbow." That made her feel better, and not quite as stupid. "How'd you know where I was?" Harley asked on their way to the security office.

"I didn't. I saw the orange cones and figured there'd be no line in there, and then I saw you and that bird thrashing around. Damn good thing."

Oh yeah, Harley thought.

After they told the security guards what had happened and filled out a report, a chaperone from Whispering Pines arrived to escort them to the van. Those tracking devices apparently did the job. Just as they were leaving the stadium office, a police officer arrived.

"Hey, we just found the mascot tied up in a broom closet. He said someone knocked him out and stole the Redbird costume. We found the costume in the men's bathroom on level two."

Nana and Harley exchanged glances. That explained the assault. And also how vulnerable she was anywhere she went. Damn.

"Come on, Nana. We need to go."

Outside the stadium, kids shrieked, people laughed, and teenagers with big boom boxes on their shoulders strolled slowly by. A carnival atmosphere. Two blocks over lay Beale Street, with nightclubs that played everything from blues to the heavy metal at the New Daisy Theater. Peabody Place, the fairly new three story mall with upscale shops, a movie theater, and the requisite Starbucks was only a block away, behind The Peabody Hotel, billed as the South's Grand Hotel. Everyone from Hollywood movie stars to presidents stayed in the hotel that dated back to 1866, even though it had moved its location in the early twentieth century. The seniors waited near the corner of Union and Third.

The driver had gone to the garage to bring the van and would park in the handicapped spot right in front. Traffic must have delayed him. Some of the seniors sat down on benches, but Harley, Nana and a few other Whispering Pines residents stood on the sidewalk in front of the stadium. It could be just any late summer afternoon in downtown Memphis. Having been almost choked to death, Harley had a new appreciation of the mundane.

Cars inched forward on Union Avenue as the traffic light at Third Street changed. Harley watched a kid of about ten break into a routine in front of the stadium, dancing to the beat of a big boom box, doing gymnastic tricks that looked too impossible for the human body to perform. His friend held out a hat for donations, moving quickly before the cops could show to break it up. He managed to collect quite a few bills and some change before his radar picked up an approaching officer, and he, the dancer, the boom box, and the hat full of money melted into the crowd.

Smiling, Harley leaned forward to speak to Nana when something hard hit her between the shoulder blades. She lurched toward the street. Brakes screeched and a hot wind that stank of diesel fumes blew dust and grit in her face. Someone screamed. Harley grabbed at a thin shadow, barely managing to catch hold of a light pole before she ended up under a MATA bus. For a moment she just hung there, unable to move, blinking grit out of her eyes. If she flicked out her tongue like a frog, she could have licked a bug off the front of the bus.

It took a moment to recover, but she swung back to the sidewalk and pried her hands free of the light pole. The bus driver yelled at her to watch what she was doing. As the diesel engine kicked into gear and the bus moved down Union, Harley took a deep breath of fumes and turned around. Nana stood frozen to the spot, her eyes big and mouth open wide. Only one other person seemed to have noticed her near death experience.

Nana still stood with her mouth open, one hand lifted as if to drag her back from the curb. Right behind Nana, a man made strange motions with his hands. He had a white-painted face, heavily black-lined eyes with two painted teardrops under his left eye, and a dark red mouth.

Harley blinked.

A mime? He wore tight black pants and ballet slippers, a pair of black suspenders over a white shirt, white gloves, and a black bowler hat. The dark red mouth curved into a smile, and he put his palms out like he was trapped in an invisible box. A strong, sickly-sweet scent replaced the lingering bus fumes in her lungs. It held a hint of Mace. She glared at him.

"Did you just push . . . wait. It was *you!*"

The mime gave a quick bow, a tip of his hat, and then he skipped across Third Street in the direction of the river. Damn! Harley grabbed her grandmother's arm and pointed.

"It's the redbird, the guy in the costume! I recognize his heavy aftershave and Mace."

"Let's get him," Nana said immediately, and sprinted toward the corner.

"Wait!" Harley looked around for one of the chaperones, but they were busy gathering the seniors from the stadium entrance and herding them toward the van that had finally arrived. Damn it! Nana had already crossed Third in hot pursuit.

The light caught Harley and she had to stand on the curb and wait or be flattened like a pancake. She jogged impatiently from one foot to another. Just when she was ready to risk it anyway, the light changed and she bolted across the street, narrowly missing being hit by a car turning left on a red light. Idiot.

By the time she got across Third, Nana and her prey had jaywalked across Union, cutting between the horse-drawn carriages lined up at the curb and disappearing from sight.

Afraid for her grandmother, Harley did the same, again narrowly missing being hit. Obviously, she took after Nana's side of the family. Insanity had probably landed more than a few of her ancestors in straitjackets. Or early graves.

Out of breath by the time she got across Union without being run down, she took a chance and pushed into the door leading to the lobby of The Peabody. The gift shop lay to the left, the stairs leading to restaurants and another main door to the right. Unless the guy who'd tried to choke her had a room here, he'd probably just try for one of the exit doors.

Nana was just going out the door onto Second Street when Harley made it up the short flight of stairs. How the hell could that old woman move so fast? Harley was fifty-odd years younger but had a stitch in her side already.

"Nana! Wait a damn minute," she got out when she saw her great-grandmother pause at the corner on Union.

"He's circling around, Harley. Get the lead out and come on!"

"Why don't we just get a cop?"

"Do you see one?" Nana asked over her shoulder, scurrying down the sidewalk with her white wicker purse held to her chest and her tennis shoes a blur on concrete.

Harley finally caught up with her in front of the line of waiting horse carriages, and grabbed her arm, panting for breath. "Forget it. Let him . . . go. I can't . . . keep going."

Nana gave her a disgusted look. "The younger generation couldn't hoe a row of beans. Get up in this thing. We'll catch him."

Bent over with her hands on her knees and trying to catch her breath, Harley didn't look up quickly enough. She immediately realized her mistake when she heard a horse snort.

Alarmed, she was a little too late to stop disaster. There was nothing left to do but hop on when Nana clucked her tongue at the horse and started pulling the carriage out into traffic. Harley took a flying leap and landed on the running board. She clung desperately to the metal handles on each side to avoid the big wheels rapidly going faster.

"Have you lost your mind?" she yelled, clinging to the side of the carriage as Nana gave the reins an expert slap across the gleaming brown rump of the horse. "We'll be hung for horse-stealing!"

"They repealed that law. Shut up and get off the running
board and in here with me. Look for him. He's headed down
Union."

Harley managed to pull herself up into the driver's seat beside
Nana. She clutched at what would be a dashboard in a car and held
tight with both hands as the horse broke into a brisk trot. "Do you
know what you're doing?"

"Little girl, I was driving a team of horses when I was ten."

"While you were shooting squirrels out of trees, no doubt,"
Harley muttered, and closed her eyes when they nearly clipped a red
Honda at the corner.

"Don't be smart. Isn't that him walking down the street?"

Harley opened her eyes. Tight black pants and soft slippers,
suspenders, hat, white face, no feathers—yep, looked like the guy
who still wore the interesting blend of Old Spice and Mace. "Yes,"
she got out, holding tightly to the edge of the carriage. "Slow down!
What are you going to do, run over a mime?"

"If it'll help."

The horse and carriage increased speed. The mime glanced
over his shoulder and gave one of those fake, open-mouthed looks
of astonishment, but Harley didn't recognize him. He had on too
much white face paint, and eyes defined with black lines helped
disguise him. And he acted like it was all a damn game. He was
enjoying it just a little too much.

"Faster," she urged when he broke into a run, and Nana
obliged. Rubber horseshoes made a heavy muffled clack against
asphalt, and carriage wheels whined. Then the man cut through the
overhang of the Radisson and down the street by the Greyhound
bus station. Nana had no problem making the turn, and thankfully,
neither did the horse or carriage. Now the mime was running, his
feet slapping against concrete as they gained on him.

"Stop, you asshole!" Harley yelled, and grabbed the whip stuck
in some kind of holder on the front. Apparently, it was easier in
theory to work one of those than it was in reality. It popped in the
air, snaked back to wrap sharply around her arm, startled the horse,
and sent them racing headlong toward a parking lot fence straight
ahead. It was like watching a car crash, knowing it was going to
happen but unable to stop it. Harley flung an arm in front of Nana

and braced for the impact.

Just before they became one with the metal mesh, Nana managed to turn the horse. How she managed it, Harley had no idea. Those thin little arms had to be all steel. Tangled in the whip and holding onto the edge of the carriage for dear life, she was no help to her grandmother at all. Damn, did they really hit horses with these things? It *hurt*.

"There he goes," Nana hollered like a woman possessed, and Harley caught a glimpse of the mime turning the corner onto Fourth Street. Dear God. He was headed for Beale Street. He'd get lost in the crowd.

"If he gets past Gayoso we've lost him," Harley yelled back.

Nana sawed on the reins and the horse made the corner without clipping the curb. Much. A carriage wheel bumped over it and jolted Harley so that she nearly lost her grip on the metal rail along the front, and slammed her teeth down on the tip of her tongue.

"*Thit!*" she yelped, but couldn't let go of anything to see if she had any tongue left. It'd just have to wait.

By the time she got the whip untangled from her arm, they'd crossed Gayoso and Nana turned onto Beale Street. The killer mime was just ahead. Music throbbed, coming from open doors, a mix of rhythm and blues, rock, and heavy metal. The W.C. Handy House, a small structure moved there some years back by the tourist industry to honor the late blues legend, had a line out front. The street was blocked off to vehicles, and Nana barely missed one of the posts. A little farther down, the crowd got a lot heavier with tourists, street dancers, and drunks. Disaster loomed.

"Never mind, Nana. Let him go," Harley said, lisping, "Juth let him go. He'th gone anyway."

"Damn," Nana said, and slowed the horse to a walk, then a halt. "Probably a good thing. I think I've got blisters on my palms. Uh oh. Looks like we're nabbed."

Sirens blasted the air, and blue lights reflected off building windows. The *whoop-whoop* of police cruisers came from all directions. Nana's wrist bracelet beeped like a flock of roadrunners. Harley wondered if they'd let her wear a red or purple jumpsuit in jail instead of that awful orange color. It'd be so much more attractive at her trial and hanging.

Nana was right. Horse theft was no longer a hanging offense. However, that didn't mean they weren't in trouble.

Fortunately, Tootsie arranged bail and Nana's lawyer said he'd work it all out. Tootsie pulled up in front of the jail in his Acura as they came out.

Waving a hand like getting arrested and held at 201 Poplar was an everyday affair, Nana said to her lawyer, "Harley didn't have anything to do with it. Like I told those hardheaded cops, she was just trying to keep me from getting hurt. I forgot to take my medicine and thought I was back on the farm as a young girl again, driving my mama to church on Sunday morning."

Her attorney, a tall, thin man with shrewd eyes, looked at her and nodded. "An excellent defense, Mrs. McMullen. I'm sure the DA and I can come to some sort of agreement."

"Good. That's what I pay you for." Nana turned to Harley and Tootsie. "It's late and I'm missing my poker game. Let's go."

On the way to Whispering Pines, Harley turned to look at Nana, who was stretched out on the back seat with her eyes closed, and said, "You're a complete fraud. I'm amazed you haven't led a life of crime."

Unperturbed, Nana said, "What makes you think I haven't?"

Harley rolled her eyes and turned back around. Tootsie was making funny noises in the back of his throat that sounded suspiciously like laughter. Harley was not amused.

"It's been a horrible day. I've been attacked by a mime disguised as a giant bird—which the police were *not* interested in hearing, I might add—involved in a horse race against my will, had a whip wrap very painfully around my arm, then sat in a smelly cell with prostitutes and drunks. And no toilet. Believe me, after a day like that, a girl *needs* a toilet."

"Quit complaining," came the voice from the back. "You're out now, aren't you? Kids today have no stamina. In my day, we plowed twenty rows at sunup, then dug potatoes, picked beans, and cooked lunch for a dozen people, all before noon."

Harley refrained from pointing out the inaccuracy of Nana's claims. She just didn't have the energy.

"Mr. Fraser promised he'd unlock the doors for us," Tootsie said after a few moments in which he managed to stop making those irritating noises. "He said he's rather concerned about the recent activities."

"He's not alone." Harley drummed her fingers against the wood and leather of the dash. "I should find another place to go. Apparently, the killer knows where I am anyway. Bobby thought it'd be safe for me there since they lock the doors at night, but now I just don't know."

"You can come stay with me and Steve. We have a guest room. Since he's a cop, it ought to be safe enough for you."

"I'd have to bring Sam. Don't you have birds?"

"Yeah. Steve got them last year. They're Red Lorries, sometimes known as Scarlet Lorries. Beautiful, loud, obnoxious, and entertaining. Believe me, they can handle Sam."

"I'm not sure Sam could handle them. He's sensitive, you know."

Tootsie laughed out loud. "I've met your cat, Harley. He's as sensitive as a brick."

"He doesn't like loud noises. Seriously. He's been known to attack me for singing. It's not a good quality in an overnight guest."

"We'd live through it. Think about it. The offer is good as long as you want it to be."

That was the thing about good friends. No matter what the problem, they were there to help. "Thanks," she said, and he smiled.

Once back at Whispering Pines, Mr. Fraser had one of the on-site nurses check out Nana to be sure she hadn't damaged anything with her adventure, then suggested she go to bed and rest.

"Rest, hell. I'm missing my poker game. Besides, I rested on the way home."

With that, Nana was off to the recreation hall. Harley looked at a bemused Mr. Fraser. "I think Nana's reliving her teen years. Or the ones she never had. She's trying to make up for all she missed."

"Well," he said wryly, "she's doing an excellent job of catching up."

Harley promised Tootsie he'd get back his bail money as soon as she got to her checkbook and he waved her off, kissed her cheek, then left. Before his taillights were out of the gated driveway, Harley was in Nana's apartment and running bath water. The jailhouse stench had to go.

Still out on the screened porch, Sam looked pretty irritated that his dinner was late and it was too dark to see birds at the feeder.

"They're asleep anyway," she told him as she gave him more dry food with a scoop of wet tuna flakes in some kind of kitty sauce on top. "We're about to do the same."

After her bath, she remembered she hadn't turned her cell phone back on, and dug it out of her backpack. How nice that it was still working. Keeping it chained to her waist or safe in her backpack helped prevent the monthly expense of replacing them.

As expected, there were two messages from Bobby, one from Cami, and none from Morgan. The last message had Blocked Call on the Caller ID. She hesitated. A twinge in her belly told her to delete it without listening, but that wouldn't solve anything.

She took a deep breath and punched the buttons. It wasn't a big surprise to hear a strange voice that sounded disguised say, *"My time, my place, my choice. Expect it. You're dead."*

Despite being exhausted, she lay awake a long time that night, with Sam curled up beside her and sleeping soundly.

There were times it had to be good to be a cat.

Thirteen

"Why me?" Harley looked at Bobby. They sat in Nana's living room. "I mean, this guy is after me as if I did something to him, when all I've done is drive the damn tour bus."

"We've been through all that. I'll have the phone company do a trace. Here, take your phone. You'll probably need it." He looked up at her. "In spite of yesterday's stupidity, you're still safer here than anywhere else in Memphis unless we put you in a motel or hotel room, with a guard posted. Somewhere you can't involve an eighty-five year old woman in idiot schemes like stealing a horse."

Harley opened her mouth to defend herself, then shut it. He would never believe that Nana had been the one to steal the horse and carriage. No point in even trying.

"Right. I'll stay here, I guess. But he knows I'm here. He'll try again."

"Not if you keep your ass here and don't go out."

Harley frowned. "But how did he know I'd be at the ballgame yesterday? It couldn't be just coincidence. And the day before, he came here as Elvis. I know it. You know it. What I don't know for sure is if it's Hughes or not. But it can't be anyone else. Can it?"

"He's watching you. Maybe he has an accomplice, someone you wouldn't suspect?"

"Unless it's the old geezer on the second floor who tried to look down my shirt the other day, no."

Bobby grinned. "You might find another boyfriend here if you try hard enough."

"I'm not at a shopping mall for boyfriends, thank you. I thought this was an old folks' home but I think I've found the stars of *Cocoon*." Bobby looked blank so she explained, "You know, the movie where the old folks find aliens who share the secret of youth?"

He rolled his eyes. "Just be careful. My offer of police

protection still stands if you want it."

"Bobby, what if I go home to my own apartment?"

"I don't recommend it." He frowned. "You're not thinking of doing that, are you?"

"Well, let me run something by you. No one can really give a decent description of this evil Elvis. Yesterday didn't help. First he was a giant bird, then he was a mime—stop laughing, dammit—it's not enough to describe him or be sure it's Hughes. If I go home, and you have men stationed around my apartment, he's bound to show up sooner or later."

Bobby stopped laughing. "No. It's too risky. We had men posted outside Lydia's house, and look what happened to her."

"I know." Harley shivered. "Her funeral's tomorrow at Memorial Park. Maybe I should go, after all. If you have some cops pretend they're family members or friends, maybe he'll make his move then."

"You're offering to be bait?"

She nodded. "This guy's killed four people, and plans to make it five, if he can catch me. Nana had a good point when she said it's much better to be the fox instead of the rabbit."

After a moment, Bobby said, "Okay, attend the funeral. I'll set it up. But don't do anything on your own, you hear me? Just go to the funeral, do what you'd normally do, and let us take care of the rest. If you definitely recognize the guy who was in your van, signal."

"And the signal should be?"

"Switch your purse to your opposite shoulder."

"I don't usually carry a purse. My backpack is much more efficient."

"Then buy a purse. Or borrow one from your Nana. Someone will be watching."

It sounded simple enough.

Except for Tour Tyme employees who managed to attend, and Mr. Penney of course, there wasn't anyone in the chapel Harley recognized. Tootsie came, and Nana too. After the service, during which Harley learned that Lydia had graduated from college *magna cum laude*, they followed the hearse on the winding roads through the cemetery. Huge oaks shaded the quiet roads that wound through the grounds. Their cars passed a grotto built by a famous Italian sculptor a few decades ago. Inside the cave were carved depictions from the Bible, and glittering crystals studded the walls. Outside, a huge pond filled with fish spanned both sides of a small fieldstone footbridge. Flowers and balloons marked some of the graves they passed, and scattered mourners paid their respects. People often visited just to walk through the quiet grounds, though Harley had never understood that. Even with trellises, roses, stone benches made in Scotland, and the gigantic waterfall and fountains at the entrance, it wasn't like they could talk to the residents.

A green canopy had been erected over the gravesite to shade the family, and folding chairs covered in heavy twill lined one side of the casket which sat on the metal contraption that would lower it into the ground. Fake grass tactfully covered mounds of earth that would be pushed back over the grave once everyone left. A skirt of roses draped Lydia's coffin.

Harley hated funerals. They weren't so much for the dead as for the living, a reminder that the person was gone. Diva said death was just a door into the next world, that nothing was ever really gone, not even flowers and trees. If that was true, Harley figured the next world had to be pretty crowded by now.

When she bowed her head as the minister offered a prayer, Harley kept her eyes open and looked around at the mourners. It was a fairly large crowd. Lydia would be so pleased. Poor thing. It was really infuriating that someone had stolen her life. She'd never hurt anyone, just done her best with what she had. Mr. Penney probably felt guilty that he hadn't given in to her requests to work in the office, and he should. If he'd listened to her, she might be alive today.

The brief service ended and Harley stepped back from the crowd with Tootsie and Nana to look around casually, as if searching for someone. The killer should be here. Hughes would want to come and gloat, try to disguise himself so he could feel powerful. But there was no one here who looked like him. She couldn't even tell which ones were the undercover cops. Of course, the cops would recognize Hughes, too. After all, his picture was on the Elvis impersonator website, and they had a way of knowing that kind of thing even without her help. So why hadn't they already arrested him? They had to have collected enough evidence by now to make a case. Her identification would only be one more part of it. Bobby had always been careful about that kind of stuff, not wanting to falsely arrest a suspect until he had hard evidence. Even his arrest of Aunt Darcy had been more protective custody than an actual arraignment, and he'd turned out to be right about that. Maybe he just needed her to confirm what they already knew, and the more she thought about it, the more certain she became it'd been Hughes on her van for the first murder. All he had to do was show up today.

Family mourners remained under the canopy, saying their last good-byes. Lester Penney got up and went to the casket for a moment. When he turned back around, his cheeks had tear tracks. It surprised Harley, and then she felt bad about being surprised. Just because he was a hard-ass at work didn't mean he had no emotions. Being an ogre had little to do with being an uncle, after all. And maybe he felt bad about making Lydia do something that frightened her.

That was confirmed when Mr. Penney approached her and Tootsie. "Thank you for coming," he said, the ritual phrase at all funerals. "It means a lot to the family."

After their sympathetic murmurs, he took a deep breath and said, "I should never have kept making her drive. I just . . . I just wanted her to learn the business from the ground up, that's all." He made a helpless gesture with his hands out. "Lydia would have inherited my portion of it, you know. She was so smart. If she'd just believed in herself, had more confidence, I think she'd have done a wonderful job."

Harley said, "I always thought you'd bring your son into the business."

Mr. Penney's mouth tightened and his bushy caterpillar eyebrows lowered in a scowl. "No. I wouldn't. He has no desire to work with me anyway."

With that, Mr. Penney turned around and walked away, and Nana said, "Uh oh. I smell a family feud."

"Hush, Nana," Harley said.

Nana just smiled.

Tootsie said, "I'll explain later. Hey. Isn't that Hughes over there?"

Harley's heart skipped a beat and she turned in the direction of

Tootsie's gaze. Hughes had come. He hadn't been able to resist. Did the undercover guys see him? She fumbled at the strap of her borrowed purse and then paused. Something wasn't right. He looked different. Maybe the dark silk suit instead of white spandex studded with fake jewels made the difference.

Still, he had the long sideburns, same height, weight, and the profile looked very familiar . . .

She leaned down to say softly to Nana, "Is that the guy we chased the other day?"

"Where?"

"Standing by that tree."

"Damn, Harley, be specific. There are hundreds of trees around here."

Harley pointed. Nana lifted the delicate net that hung down from her black pillbox hat, with tiny flowers sewn around the crown and peered across the grass and gravestones. "Yep. Looks like him even without the tight pants. Get him to turn around and run. A good look at his ass, and I'd know for sure then."

"That's a possibility." Harley shifted her purse to her other shoulder and looked directly at Hughes.

Immediately, Hughes was surrounded by men in suits. He looked up in surprise, then with anger. Harley could hear his protests grow louder when she got close.

"Is this the guy?" one of the men asked, holding Hughes by the arm, and she nodded.

"Yes. It's got to be him."

"Is that a positive identification, Ms. Davidson?" the officer asked.

"Positive is a little strong. He looks different in an expensive suit than he does in spandex or tights, but it has to be—yes, I'm sure it's him."

"What the hell are you talking about?" Hughes demanded.

A cop obliged with, "Preston Hughes, you need to come downtown with us. We've got some questions for you about Lydia Free's murder."

Furious, Hughes resisted, so the officers got out their cuffs and prevailed after only a brief struggle. Then they read him his rights. Panting, Hughes glared at Harley. "I didn't murder anyone! I just came here because of Lydia. I met her at the competitions last year and she was a sweet girl."

Sweat popped out on Hughes's forehead. Dark blue eyes narrowed. "You did this, didn't you? Accused me of something I didn't do just so your father has a chance at winning? Well, it won't help him, I've seen his act and he doesn't have a chance in hell of ever winning. He's a big joke! I'll still beat him—I'll get you for this, you dumb little bitch!"

The cop turned him toward the road. "Time to go, Mr. Hughes."

Hughes wailed, "I didn't have anything to do with murder, I tell you!"

"Tell it walking," the officer said, and pushed him across the grass toward one of the cars lined up along the road.

Everyone was staring. Harley looked at Tootsie. "Well, that was tacky. How dare he say that about Yogi?"

Tootsie just rolled his eyes. "You have no sense of self-preservation at all."

"Well, at least he's going to jail. I don't have to worry anymore."

Nana looked up at her, squinting against the bright sunlight coming through oak leaves. "I guess that means you're not playing poker tonight?"

"I suck at cards."

"I know. But you're good for a laugh. I thought Gerald was going to pee himself when you thought a full house meant four of the same cards."

"So I get confused. I won that pot, didn't I? Besides, it explains why I never did that well at poker with Bobby. He didn't even have to cheat."

As they drove out of the cemetery, Harley saw a man standing with his back against a big oak. He must have been watching the funeral. For some reason, he looked strange. It gave her a creepy feeling and she didn't know why. She nudged Tootsie.

"Do you see that guy?"

"What guy?"

"The one standing under that oak across from Lydia's grave."

Tootsie looked that way, but the man had disappeared. Only empty space remained where he'd been standing.

"That's so weird." Harley stared at the tree. "He gave me a

funny feeling. Why wouldn't he come to the funeral instead of just watch?"

"A lot of ghouls turn out for funerals. I've never understood that. When my cousin died—she had muscular dystrophy— some guy no one knew kept sobbing and hugging people. It really was odd."

"It's amazing what some people do."

"That's why they have insane asylums," Nana said from the back seat. "It's where they keep the crazy people."

"I think they're called mental health institutions now, Nana."

"Doesn't matter what they call them, it's the same thing. It's where the crazy people stay."

No use arguing with Nana. She was always going to get the last word in.

Thankfully, Tootsie suggested they go out to eat somewhere, adding, "Not Taco Bell!" when Harley opened her mouth. They ended up at Corky's Barbecue not too far down Poplar Avenue.

Nana was in hog heaven—literally. She ordered and ate a rack of ribs that looked like half a pig, while Tootsie ate a barbecue sandwich big as a dinner plate. Harley ordered baked beans, slaw, and fried onion rings.

"There's something the matter with someone who doesn't eat meat," Nana said halfway through her ribs.

"I eat meat," Harley replied. "Just not that often. You have barbecue sauce on your nose. And your chin. And eyebrows."

Nana didn't even try to wipe it off. "That's for later. So what's wrong with you? Deirdre's idea?"

"Diva's a vegetarian. She encourages it, but doesn't try to push it on us. Except maybe for Yogi. She expects him to follow her diet. She says it's much healthier."

Nana snorted. "What's wrong with a little meat? When I was a girl—and don't roll your eyes like that, they'll get stuck—we ate everything off a pig. Snout, feet, brains, balls. We had to. If we were lucky enough to get meat in those days, we sure as hell made good use of it. Rendered fat is good for you. Look at me. I've eaten it all my life and I'm as healthy as a horse. Which, by the way, I've also eaten. Raccoon, possum, mule, squirrel, rabbit, deer—oh yeah, and fried rat."

"Nana!"

"Just kidding about the last one. Jeez, where's your sense of humor?"

"Speaking of," Tootsie said, and Harley saw from the glazed look in his eyes that he'd had enough of the conversational topic, "did they drop the charges for horse theft?"

"Mr. Griffin said he took care of it all." Nana nodded happily. "He always knows what to do. Smart as a whip, even if he does cost too much. Lawyers."

"My fingerprints are now on file," Harley said with a sigh. "And they've got my mug shot in the system. Not exactly a recommendation for future employment or my credit history."

"You're thinking of leaving Tour Tyme?" Tootsie sounded surprised.

"No. Not anytime soon, anyway. I'm just trying to figure out what I want to do with the rest of my life. I can't be a tour guide forever."

"Tell that to Carlton Chambers."

Carlton Chambers had to be pushing ninety, but his employment records claimed he was only eighty-three. Wizened but tough, he'd been driving for Tour Tyme since the company had been established. Before that, he'd been at one of the other companies until they went under.

Once, he'd driven for MATA, the city buses that were rarely full these days and had to be losing money annually. It was the only form of public transportation Memphis had, however, other than taxis or Nikes. And the downtown trolley that didn't go very far, but now streets were being torn up to extend the rails farther. Nana had said she remembered when they tore up the streets to remove the rails, spending too much taxpayer money when they were just going to lay them back down fifty years later.

"I can't see myself still hauling tourists around when I'm in my eighties," Harley said. "I'll have snapped by then. One too many Elvis weeks."

Tootsie grinned. "You'll make it. I have faith in you."

"If only I had that much faith in me. I guess you can put me back on the schedule."

"Now that the murderer's been arrested, it should be safe for you to work. Not that we've got that many clients left."

Tootsie looked discouraged.

"Things will pick up. After all, like you said, a Tour Tyme employee is responsible for the apprehension, and that'll play big in the papers. And on the news. Too bad a news crew wasn't there to catch it on video. That would have helped."

Nana leaned forward, over the now bare ribs on her plate.

"Alex and Marybeth should have been there."

"They're not reporters, Nana. They're anchors on that morning show, Live at Nine."

"Don't care. I like the way they talk. And that Alex is a cutie." She made a clicking noise with her teeth. "Why do you think Hughes was arrested for only one of the murders?"

"They're probably still gathering evidence," Tootsie said. "Just an eyewitness account isn't enough for an arrest. They need other things, like the murder weapon, fingerprints, opportunity and motive."

"So they must have all that stuff, huh, or they wouldn't have arrested him?" Nana asked.

Tootsie nodded. "They must."

"Good. Let's hope they keep him in jail and don't let him out. Wonder why he did it?"

Harley answered Nana's question. "He wanted to win the contest."

Nana shook her head. "Now he's lost everything. The idiot."

"Hey," Harley said to Tootsie, "what's the story with the ogre's son? Family feud? Drugs? Bad seed?"

"Some of the second, mostly the last. Larry's given Penney a pretty rough time. He's smart enough, just hates his dad."

"Normally, I'd say that's understandable, but I saw a side of the ogre today I didn't know existed. He never seemed to have a soft side, but he's really broken up about Lydia. So is Larry an only child?"

"No, just the only son. Penney tried to give him everything growing up. Best clothes, new cars, best schools—somewhere around twenty-three he decided his dad owed him all that and he shouldn't have to work for it. Penney disagreed. Junior got pissed, took off for Europe on his father's credit cards, and came back with an even worse attitude."

"Kids today." Harley thought about Larry Penney and wondered just how badly he hated his father. Enough to try to ruin him? She looked up at Tootsie and knew he was thinking the same thing.

Nana said bluntly, "I'd be looking at that kid, if I were you two. Kids brought up with that sense of entitlement rarely turn out well. Sounds like a sociopath to me."

Harley blinked. "What do you know about sociopaths?"

"What, you think I lived this long without learning anything? Take John Dillinger, for instance. Sociopath. Al Capone. Sociopath. I wouldn't rule out most of Congress, either."

Tootsie laughed. "You are such a darling."

"So are you, princess." Nana winked and clicked her teeth.

"Too bad you don't swing our way."

"If I did, you'd be first on my list."

"And I'd give you a run for your money, baby doll."

Harley looked at them with her hands on her hips. "Please, your mutual love-fest is leaving me nauseous."

After they left Corky's, Harley went back to Whispering Pines and packed her few clothes before tackling Sam. She'd need a rest before attempting to wedge him into his carrier.

"Sure you want to leave? You can stay another night or two," Nana said.

"I've paid my rent this month and hate to waste it, but thanks. Now that Hughes is in jail, it's safe for me to go home. And it's a lot closer to work. Maybe business will pick up again since the murderer's been caught. Tootsie's pretty worried about it. Job security isn't something to take lightly."

"Well, I hope it works out. That Tootsie is a nice girl."

"I'll pass along the compliment."

"Time for my shuffleboard tournament. Think this looks all right?" Nana turned for Harley to admire her outfit. She wore a soft blue sweatshirt under her pearl necklace, a long jersey skirt, and rolled down athletic socks with her running shoes. Atop her head perched an Atlanta Braves baseball cap.

"Perfect," Harley said.

"Good. I hate good-byes. Don't stay away so long next time."

"I won't."

Nana smiled and reached up to pat her cheek. "You're a good girl. I don't care what everyone else says about you."

"Thanks. Wait—who? What do they say?"

Laughing as she went out the door, Nana stuck her head back inside to say, "Psych!" then was gone.

"You're a terrible old woman," Harley said to the closed door, and smiled.

Harley went home, released an annoyed Sam into familiar territory, washed her scratches with hydrogen peroxide, and lay down across her bed. She fell asleep almost immediately.

It was dark when she woke. Only the nightlight in the hall provided any illumination. She felt drugged. It'd been a while since she'd been able to sleep soundly.

Yawning, she got up and went into the kitchen, where the nightlight over Sam's litter box put him in silhouette as he took advantage of the facilities.

"Nothing like the smell of fresh cat doody to wake a person up," she muttered, but Sam was still sulking over the indignity of being dumped rear end first into the cat carrier and didn't answer. He was like that sometimes. He'd get over it.

After getting a glass of iced tea, Harley went out onto her balcony to sit in the fresh air and wake up a little. It smelled like rain. Wind rustled the thick, leathery leaves of the huge magnolia and felt damp on her face. Wind chimes clanged nearby. Tammy Sprague next door must have hung them. It reminded Harley of Diva, and that made her think of what Diva had told Tootsie. It didn't make much sense, but that wasn't so unusual. There were times Diva was right on the money, but most of the time, she said obscure things that no one could figure out until later. Hindsight was twenty-twenty, as the saying went. Lord. Now she even thought in clichés. Nana was a bad influence.

Leaning her head against the back of the chair, she tried to connect the dots between what Diva had said and the killer. It wasn't easy. Some of it was obvious, like being caught between the past and present. Hughes was still mad at being disqualified, so transferred that anger to all things Elvis. Tour Tyme was caught between. And of course, the hidden Elvis only meant that he'd been in hiding since committing the murders. But the candlelight reference . . . What could that mean? The vigil or just that Hughes was in shadow?

A sudden shadow on the table next to her made Harley spill her iced tea and leap up from her chair. Heart pounding, a shriek caught in her throat, and then she recognized the reason.

"Sam, what are you doing out here? You know you're an inside cat. I signed an agreement promising not to let you outside. Cami would repossess you if I reneged. She said so. And I could tell she wasn't kidding. Now come on, go back inside and stop scaring the bejesus out of me."

Sam deigned to offer a reply, with a rather indignant *miaaow* loud enough to wake up the lions in the zoo across the road. Maybe it was his way of making up after a quarrel. She took him in with her and shut the balcony doors.

When the phone rang, Harley looked at the clock. A little after nine. She picked up the phone a bit warily.

Cami said, "I didn't wake you up or anything, did I?"

"If you mean by *anything* am I involved in something hot and sweaty, no. Unfortunately. I think I'm awake. My eyes are open, so it must be true."

"Not necessarily. I remember a sleep-over with your cousin Madelyn. She sleeps with her eyes open."

"Makes you wonder if she doesn't do that during the day too, doesn't it. So what's up?"

Cami hesitated, and then said, "I have a big favor to ask you."

"As long as it doesn't involve Elvis, I'm good with it."

"Are you sure?"

"Wait a minute. I recognize that tone of voice. It's your *This isn't going to hurt at all* voice."

"Well, it won't hurt. It'll just take up a little time. And space. It won't be for very long, I promise."

"Cami—"

"You'll be saving a life, Harley."

"Yours?"

"Possibly. Definitely Frank's."

"Frank?"

"Frank Burns."

A deep suspicion ignited. "Frank Burns, like in MASH on TV?"

"That's who he's named for, yes."

"Cami, tell me it's not another cat."

"It's not another cat."

"Thank God—wait. Or a dog?"

"Or a dog."

Harley closed her eyes and sighed. Cami really did take her animal rescue bit too far at times. Now she'd branched out into relatives. "Okay," she said. "But just for a few days."

"I knew you'd come through for me, Harley. We'll be there in forty-five minutes."

"If you collected dollar bills like you collect strays, you'd have more money than Donald Trump. Frank can stay a night or two, but he has to sleep on my couch. I don't give up my bed for anyone."

"That's okay. He's got his own bed."

Cami hung up before Harley could ask why a relative carried around his own bed. Uh oh. This did not bode well. She decided to be optimistic. Maybe it was a fish.

When she saw Cami lugging a big glass aquarium, Harley breathed a sigh of relief. It wasn't a crazy relative that Cami was trying to push off on her. It must be a fish. She didn't mind a fish sleeping over. Fish didn't make a lot of noise. Fish didn't require toys and cans of cat food. Fish didn't make stinky poop.

"Hey," Harley said, opening her door wider for Cami to get through with the ten gallon tank, "you should have asked for help. I'd have met you at the car."

"That's okay. I thought it'd be best if he was already inside when you met Frank."

Lifted brow time. "Does Frank have problems with strangers?"

"Not often. Strangers sometimes have problems with Frank."

Cami set the glass aquarium down on the coffee table. It was covered with a light blanket. Odd squeaky sounds came from it. The water filter? Rocks? Loud fish? Piranha?

Panting a little, Cami looked at Harley over her shoulder.

"Do you mind putting Sam up for a few minutes? It'll make Frank feel a lot better if he's not being stared at by a cat."

"I can understand that. Unless he's a piranha, he's probably not that fond of cats."

Harley shut an indignant Sam in her bedroom and went back into the living room. Cami had taken the blanket off the aquarium. Squeaking noises had turned to hisses.

"I never knew fish made sounds."

"They don't. Did you think this was a fish?"

Harley narrowed her eyes and tried to look around Cami into the aquarium. "It isn't? What did you bring over here? I'm not keeping another cat. Even kittens. Sam wouldn't like it. He's picky about who and what he likes."

"I know that. But he's only one cat, and I've got so many cats at my house that they really do make Frank nervous."

"He's a cat. Get him a mirror. He can get used to it."

"Uh, he's not a cat, Harley."

"A dog? Cami, I don't have time to walk a dog! I'm not home that much, and Elvis week is coming up. I'll be gone so long, and—"

"He's not a dog. Do you think I'd keep a dog in an aquarium? Jeez, Harley, get a grip."

Harley did a fake feint to the left, and then moved to the right before Cami could block her view. A long, skinny raccoon looked at her, blinking black beady eyes and twitching whiskers.

"I'm not keeping a raccoon!"

"Frank is not a raccoon, Harley. He's a ferret. M*A*S*H. Frank Burns. Ferret-face, get it?"

"I got it. He's not staying. Get it?"

Cami looked frazzled. Her blonde hair stuck up at odd angles, the tee shirt she wore had a rip and stains with mysterious origins, and her cutoffs looked more David Duke than Daisy Duke.

"Please, Harley. It's only for a little while. He's already been adopted, but she had to go out of town and can't take him until she gets back. No one else can take him. Everyone I know has too many cats or dogs, and Frank keeps getting loose."

"Oh, that's a point in his favor. Don't you have a cat cage?"

"Of course I do. Frank knows how to unlatch it."

Harley looked back at the aquarium. Frank twitched his whiskers and put tiny black paws up against the glass. Cedar shavings held some toys and two empty bowls, along with a few tiny dark pellets that she suspected weren't just decorations.

"What next, Cami? A llama?"

"No livestock allowed inside the city limits. They make good guard animals, though. I've always thought I'd like to have one."

Jeez. She actually looked serious when she said that. Harley shook her head.

"I know I'll regret this, but okay. Only for a few days!"

"Great. I brought some, but in case you run out, here's a list of foods he eats. You're the best, Harley. I owe you big-time."

Harley took the list Cami held out. "Damn straight about that. Wait a minute—what's this at the bottom of the page?"

She looked up. Cami had the door open.

"Gotta go. Feeding time at the zoo. Call me if you have any questions, okay?" Cami swept out the door and closed it behind her.

"Damn," Harley said when she reread the bottom of the page, "Cami!"

By the time she got downstairs and outside to the parking area, Cami's red taillights were at the end of the driveway. Who'd have ever thought Saturn coupes could move so quickly?

Apparently she banged the entrance hall door a little too hard when she went back inside. Sarah Simon opened her door a crack to peer out, one eye visible above the chain lock.

"Sorry," Harley said, and the door gently shut again. Strange girl. She hid like a groundhog all the time, tucked away in her apartment and only coming out to signal six more weeks of winter.

When she got back upstairs, the aquarium was empty. No sign of Frank. Sam kept up a yowl in the bedroom that sounded like fingernails on a chalkboard, and Harley went to the kitchen and opened the refrigerator. She took out a bottle of wine and didn't bother pouring any into a glass. After chugging a few swigs, she put the cork back in the top and the bottle back on the shelf and went ferret hunting.

She hoped the last line of Cami's list wasn't prophetic: *May poop in panty drawer.*

Fourteen

Morning came too early, as usual. Worse, rain pattered against her window panes, one of those summer rains that cooled Memphis only as long as it hung around. When it stopped, streets would be steaming like a nuclear reactor plant. Rain also brought out the worst in Memphis drivers, increased the workload on police, and made the streets as safe as the Indianapolis 500 home stretch. It was a day to sleep in, not a day to be out hauling tourists, but she got up anyway. When had she become so damned responsible?

She stumbled into the kitchen, fed Sam, checked his litter box, and made coffee. In that order. Any other order drew loud complaints from the feline quarter. Frank Burns was once more shut in the aquarium. He didn't look happy about it, but she'd finally found a use for that two-volume set of Shakespeare on her bookshelves. Wire mesh gave him plenty of air, she'd put a grape, a few ferret nuggets, and fresh water in his bowls before bedtime, and when she came home she'd check the pellet level in the cedar shavings. Maybe it wouldn't be so bad. Except that Sam seemed to view their guest as a threat. He growled low in his throat. He hissed at the glass. He hid under her bed. The last she didn't mind at all.

Since the weather promised a sauna effect guaranteed to melt make-up and gum up hair gel, she opted for the simple look. As usual. A brush of mascara over her lashes, a swipe of cherry flavored lip balm, and the "just laid" look for her hair. Tee shirt, khaki walking shorts, sports socks and white tennis shoes completed the professional yet comfortable attire of a tour guide.

"Y'all be good now," she said to the hiding cat and sulking ferret. "I'll be back."

Fortified with two cups of coffee and the cold end of a leftover bean burrito, she grabbed her leather backpack and headed out for the day. First stop—Claude Williams.

She found Williams at his office off Mendenhall, one of those three-story bland buildings a stone's throw from Poplar Avenue. Expensive new cars filled most of the slots. Her Toyota with the bashed in front and rear fenders looked a little out of place. Good thing she had insurance.

Williams's office was on the second floor overlooking the parking lot and Belmont Café. A young woman who looked almost old enough to vote greeted her at the front desk. She had light brown hair that swung loosely around her face, fingernails painted in three different colors, a short skirt, and canvas shoes that tied around her ankles. The desk was glass, with only a telephone, a pen set, a lamp, and a laptop on it. Very modern.

"May I help you?" the receptionist asked.

"I hope so, but I think I'm in the wrong office. Is Claude Williams here?"

"Your name please?"

"Miss Davidson." Always best not to give her first name. It saved time and the usual remarks she'd already heard a few thousand times.

Miss Jailbait punched a few buttons on the telephone console with her long curved nails, and in a few moments, Claude Williams came from the back to greet her. "Miss Davidson, what a surprise to see you here."

She smiled. "I hate to bother you at work, but I have a few questions. Just clearing up some confusion."

"Certainly. We can talk in my office."

The floors were light polished wood, the walls a creamy white, and furniture minimal. It looked efficient but not at all welcoming. Williams's office had a few plaques on the walls, a few framed pictures on a light oak bookcase, and a potted plant in the corner. His laptop hummed atop his desk.

"So what's this about Preston Hughes being back in the contest?" she asked when he'd shut the door. Williams didn't look at her but went to stand behind his desk and fiddle with a pen.

"His request for reconsideration before the board was approved," he said, not quite able to meet her eyes. "After all, Derek Wade isn't in the competition this year, so there shouldn't be any conflict."

Harley frowned. "Derek Wade isn't in the competition this year because Hughes murdered him," she said.

"That hasn't been proven."

"Not yet. The police have a different idea. Does Hughes know he's eligible to be in this year's competition?"

Williams nodded. "I told him the same night we had our discussion. After all, no one can say for sure who started the argument, and a man can't be disqualified just because he has . . . uh . . . an unpleasant personality."

That still didn't mean he hadn't murdered three Elvises. Or Lydia. Or had been stalking her. It just meant it'd paid off for him.

"So the squeaky wheel gets the grease, right?" she said. "Never mind. It seems he won't be in the competition this year anyway since he's in jail."

Williams's eyes narrowed a little. "He hasn't been charged and they can only keep him for forty-eight hours without charging him. In the meantime, perhaps it'd be best if your comments and questions didn't border on libel. You might find yourself on the wrong side of a lawsuit."

"Is that a threat?"

"Good heavens, no." Williams spread his hands out to his sides, and the genial smile was back. "Just expressing a friendly concern. Hughes hasn't been proven guilty."

"Uh hunh. I didn't know you two were so close." Williams's smile stiffened.

Maybe she'd been wrong to take Williams off her list, Harley thought when she left. The possibility of a team effort wasn't too much of a stretch. And Williams had been on her short list once. But what motive? What advantage could there possibly be to winning the competition that'd be enough to kill four people? Was the trophy filled with gold? The cash winnings weren't that much, not for two successful businessmen like Hughes and Williams. They might not be CEOs, but they made a lot more money than the cash prize offered. It just didn't make sense.

She mentioned that to Tootsie when she got to work. Plopping her backpack down on his desk, she crossed her arms over her chest and looked at him. "Well? What do you think?"

He leaned back in his chair. "Honey, I think it's time you stopped worrying about it. The police have Hughes in custody, and life can get back to normal. I've already booked four tourist groups this morning. My friend at the paper did a great write-up for us."

He shoved the morning paper toward her. "You're a hero again."

"Heroine. Don't you care that Williams may be getting away with complicity in murder?"

"In a word, no. If he was complicit in the murders, and I'm not saying he is, then Hughes is definitely the kill and tell type. He'll be quick to incriminate Williams and claim it was all his idea. The police are good at finding out that kind of thing. Besides, I don't care right now, as long as they got the right guy."

"Tootsie, I'm shocked. Where's your sense of justice? Fair play?"

"Renewed now that business is picking up." He pulled the end of his headset forward and punched a button on the console as three lines lit up at once. Harley sighed and opened the front page of the paper.

"Suspect Held in Elvis Murders" read the headline. It went on to say that police had an unnamed man in custody on suspicion of killing three Elvis impersonators and a Memphis Tour Tyme employee. *"Harley Jean Davidson, instrumental in the capture of jewelry thieves this past May and smugglers in June, identified the man on her tour bus as the killer of Derek Wade, 42, of Midtown,"* the piece read.

Then it went on to give a little background information, including the fact that Diva and Yogi had been frequent guests at 201 Poplar for things like picketing the meat-packing plant and protesting the wearing of furs. Good Lord. Was it a slow news day?

Not bothering to read the entire article, she debated calling Bobby and sharing her concern with him. That might turnaround and bite her in the butt. He had a lamentable lack of faith in her powers of deduction and a surplus of experience in her past failures. Maybe that could wait. She'd have to be certain before she went to him again, even though the success of being bait to catch Hughes had paid off quite nicely. Bobby too often saw the world in black and white. And he had a conveniently short memory.

"I'm keeping the security guards on the buses," Tootsie said when he had a moment in between calls. "Just for safety's sake. And to reassure tourists."

"Good plan. So do you need me today?"

"I'm calling drivers back in as we get booked. Charlsie quit. You can take her run from the Airport Inn to Graceland at three."

Harley wasn't surprised Charlsie had quit. She'd been really rattled. The possibility of being stalked by a murderer could be unsettling. She should know.

"Got it," she said, and took the printout of confirmed name she gave her. "Where does the security guard sit?"

"Wherever he wants."

"Sounds reasonable. Which van?"

"The ten." He hesitated. "It's parked next to Lydia's bus in the garage."

"That's okay. I'll have to get over it sometime."

It was harder than she thought. She kept seeing Lydia standing in the bus doorway, her face reflecting fear and horror as she babbled and then wound herself around Harley like she could protect her. She certainly hadn't done a very good job of it. It took a cold-blooded person to kill a harmless creature like Lydia. That only made her more determined to make sure Hughes got what he deserved.

The rain had stopped, and the streets were slick and littered with cars whose drivers obviously had never seen rain before, much less driven in it. The air was so muggy that she turned the van's AC on full blast.

The tourists were waiting at the hotel by the airport, a pretty happy group. Harley checked off names and matched ID photos to passengers, a tedious task she didn't mind doing at all. In spite of the wait, the group remained cheerful, a good sign. Surly tourists who complained about everything from the summer heat to long lines—like it was her fault—were a pain in the ass.

Their good mood raised her spirits, so that by the time they got to Graceland and she had them in line to get on the EPE bus to cross the street to the mansion, she was able to laugh at some of their jokes and banter. This was the kind of group she liked, there for fun and to appreciate Elvis, not to ridicule the man and his talents or his taste. After all, time had stopped for Elvis in 1977, and he'd have no doubt redecorated the Jungle Room sooner or later. Maybe he'd always have been a little over the top, but who knew?

Bubba's security guard, a man shaped like a square, with no neck but an impressive pistol on his belt, had gone to talk to someone he apparently knew. Another security guard, probably. He'd not said a single word the entire ride, but sat in the last row and pretended not to watch all the passengers. But Harley saw in her rearview mirror that he kept a close eye on everyone. Obviously, a jovial personality was not an employment requirement in the security business.

Harley went inside the coffee shop and ordered a Coke. She had some time on her hands before her group got through across the street, and she wasn't supposed to take them back to their hotel for three hours. Maybe Tootsie had another run for her, so she called him from a pay phone.

"God," he said when he heard her voice, "don't tell me—"

"No, everything's just fine. Hughes is in police custody, remember? I just wanted to see if you needed me for a short run. I've got three hours to kill. My cell phone lost its charge, so I can't even talk on the phone. If I sit here too long, I'll start thinking."

"That's never good. Let me see what I've got. Have a cold drink and I'll call you right back at this number."

Caller ID could be a wonderful thing. She drank a Coke, ate some fries, and was thinking about a piece of pie versus the slight tightening of her jeans during the days spent with Nana when the phone rang.

"Yo," she said into the receiver.

"I've got a quickie for you, and don't make any jokes about my choice of words," Tootsie said. "A group got stuck at the airport and all the other companies are booked, of course. Harley? Are you there?"

"Yep. You said no jokes so I'm just biting my tongue."

"Thank you. They need a ride and will be waiting at passenger pickup. Your contact name is Sam Elliott."

"The actor?"

"I should know? I ran his credit card and he checks out. Just pick them up and take them to the Ridgeway Inn on Poplar."

"It was a good idea to get in the taxi and limo service."

"Wasn't it? Don't speed, but hurry, okay? They're willing to pay fat corporate dollars for a ride now instead of having to wait for the next limo or hotel van."

"I'm on it."

She headed for the parking lot behind the tourist shops. It couldn't be *the* Sam Elliott, she was sure. This one was corporate and would be some potbellied bald guy making jokes that were stupid, but his employees would laugh anyway.

She got close to the van and unlocked it with the remote. It made a beeping sound. Then a loud blare from behind made her jump. The backpack fell from her hands, landed on the paved parking lot, and her cell phone popped out of its safe little pocket and skidded a few feet away. Before she could pick it up, the guy who'd startled her with his horn drove over it, coming so close to her that she had to flatten herself against the van to keep from being hit. What a jerk. He never even slowed down.

Harley stared at what was left of her cell phone. Apparently they weren't hardy enough to survive being run over. Sadly, she gathered up the remains. Another phone fatality.

While she was looking at the pieces of phone in her hand, a harrowing thought made her shudder. Had it been him? The Elvis killer? She flung herself into the van and locked the doors, sweating from more than the heat. An urgent need to get out of the parking lot made her hit the curb before she got to Elvis Presley Boulevard.

On her way to the airport, Harley realized that she hadn't even thought about finding the security guard. He probably hadn't missed her, either. It shouldn't matter. Hughes was behind bars and no Elvises had been murdered in over a week. Life could go back to normal. Whatever that was.

Obviously, the group had spent corporate dollars at the bar while waiting. A rowdy bunch, but in a harmless kind of way.

No mishaps slowed the trip to their hotel, conveniently located at the entrance to the interstate that'd take her swiftly back to Graceland. Ridgeway Inn was due to be torn down and replaced by something else soon, progress on the march. It was also across the street from Memorial Park Cemetery where Lydia had been buried.

Something—guilt, sorrow, or just curiosity—drew her gaze to the fieldstone walls that enclosed the cemetery lawns. Bright blobs of color looked incongruous, bobbing around in front of the walls, and she realized the colors were helium balloons held aloft by a white-gloved hand. Staring, her heart skipped a beat. Blood made a pounding noise in her ears so that she hardly heard the passengers disembark from the van and go into the hotel. Clutching the steering wheel with suddenly cold fingers, she looked at the painted white face and too-red mouth of the mime that had shoved her at the ballpark. It had to be the same one. He looked straight at her, red lips squared in a smug grin. Then he did a little dance, put up his hands to his face like he'd just seen something awful, and pranced down the sidewalk toward the cemetery entrance.

She stomped on the accelerator and peeled out of the parking lot onto Poplar. When she cut in front of a car to get to the cemetery entrance, the driver laid on the horn and flipped her the Southern salute. If she wasn't in a hurry she'd have returned the gesture, but the mime had skipped around the fieldstone wall and disappeared. Helium balloons rose slowly into the sky. She headed straight for them. He wasn't there, of course. He'd disappeared. Where in hell could he have gone so quickly? If it was Hughes, when had he made bail? Bobby should have warned her.

A road to the right led to the offices, chapel, and mausoleum. Straight ahead lay the grotto. The huge waterfall fountain separated the entrance and exit to the cemetery grounds. Cursing the lack of her cell phone, Hughes's release, and that tickling little warning at the back of her neck, she eased the van forward. A few visitors looked up when she drove slowly by, probably wondering if the cemetery was on the tour route now, but no mime popped up. He couldn't have gone far. How had Hughes known where she'd be, anyway? It couldn't be just coincidence he'd be there when she dropped off a group at the hotel across the street. He always seemed to know where she'd be. Damn.

There was something really strange about all this besides the fact she was trawling through a cemetery looking for a mime. As good as her imagination got at times, she'd never dream up something like this. *How* did he know where she'd always be? How had he known about Nana's retirement home, the ballpark, and now here? Something really screwy was going on.

A flash of white on the winding road ahead caught her attention and she turned the van. It started to rain again. A few drops hit the windshield, but not enough to turn on the wipers. She hit the power button for the window and let it halfway down. As crazy as it sounded even to her, if there was a liberal smell of too-sweet aftershave, she'd know it was Hughes. Apparently he didn't know he reeked of it.

All she smelled was rain, gas fumes, and wet asphalt. No sweet aftershave. Maybe she was imagining things. Or maybe he hadn't bathed in it this time. After all, he hadn't stunk of it when he went to see Claude Williams. She thought about that for a moment. Would it be something new he'd started, a sort of trademark or cover-up when committing murder? Maybe she'd ask Bobby if the smell had been in Lydia's apartment. Maybe there were two murderers. After all, she hadn't noticed the smell in her van with the first killing, but then, she'd been too unnerved afterward to notice much of anything.

She thought about that for a minute. Hughes could have an accomplice, but that wasn't very logical. Not many people considered murder an appropriate elimination of Elvis contestants. If there weren't two murderers . . . it had to be Hughes. Who else could it be? He was the only one with a solid motive. Besides, he was back in the competitions now so maybe he had a lot more to lose. In his twisted mind, if winning was all-important, he had to make it to the final competition. And Williams might be his partner. But what could be so damn important about winning an Elvis competition? It just didn't make a lot of sense.

Then again, this could be an unrelated event. It was entirely possible she'd annoyed any number of people. That seemed to be one of her talents. Maybe the mime had been a tourist on one of her tours that she'd had to put off the van. It happened on occasion. Anytime a surplus of alcohol and belligerence mixed, it usually ended in an eviction. She'd been hired as a driver, not a bouncer, but sometimes the two careers overlapped.

Whoever the mime was, he'd attacked her in the ladies' bathroom and tried to shove her in front of a bus outside AutoZone. That called for police intervention, no matter who he was. If she left to call the cops, he'd be gone when they got there. That was a given. No choice but to pursue and hopefully capture. Or at least identify. Then let the cops find out why he'd tried to kill her.

A gust of cool air blew into the window, smelling faintly like too-sweet perfume. Okay, it had to be the same guy. And he was close. She put down both front windows to get a cross-breeze going.

The van inched forward. Her backpack lay on the seat next to her and she pulled it close. If she saw him, she'd use her industrial strength pepper spray on him first, and then call Bobby. Except her cell phone had just been squashed. Damn. Okay. New plan. Juice him up with the pepper spray, and then use his suspenders to tie him up until she could call the police. Assuming he'd be properly and fully incapacitated, it should be a snap. If he wasn't, she'd empty the can on him and worry about the consequences later. Pepper spray wasn't lethal, was it?

No, just hideously uncomfortable, she decided. Now that she had a plan, she fumbled in her bag for the pepper spray with her right hand and steered with her left. Nerves made her stomach thump, and her heart raced like Jeff Gordon's souped-up Chevy.

The roads wound gently through the cemetery, sloping at times. Interstate 240 bounded the east side, Poplar Avenue the south, Yates on the west, and condos and houses on the north side. The neighborhood was upscale residential and high-end shops, with a sprinkling of doctor and dentist offices close to a Wendy's and Igor's Hair Salon. Igor cut her hair when she was flush with cash, as well as the hair of famous people like Jerry Lawler's wife. Ex-wife? It didn't matter. Lawler retained the title of King, as long as it pertained to wrestling and not Elvis. Too bad Lawler wasn't nearby. She'd appreciate a little help about now.

The road she'd been following came to a T. She paused, and then took the right hand turn toward the grotto. Dark clouds scudded overhead, oak branches swayed, and mixed in with the smell of rain and wet asphalt was that smell peculiar to cemeteries. Nana had said it was ivy, but Diva said it was the smell of sorrow lingering from those left behind. Nana's version sounded a lot more logical.

A white face suddenly popped up right in front of the van, startling her into slamming on the brakes. Van tires screeched, but fortunately she was going slow enough that the air bag didn't balloon out. She slammed the van into gear and bolted out the driver's door, pepper spray in hand, hot on the trail of the dancing mime. He managed to stay just ahead of her, and she was glad it had started raining hard enough that no one would see her running after some guy skipping along in tight black pants, ballet shoes, white shirt and suspenders, and wearing a black bowler on top of his head. They'd both be taken down to Memphis Psychiatric.

"Stop!" she yelled even though she knew he wouldn't. It just seemed like she should at least be yelling something at him.

He turned around and ran backward, doing that thing again with his hands pressed to his face and his mouth open like he was scared. That made her pretty mad. If she could just get close enough to this guy, she'd give him a shot of pepper spray that'd make those painted black tears on his face real enough, by God.

He must have read her mind. What looked like spiffy ballet pumps picked up a little speed. They had to be getting slick because of the rain, but he didn't miss a step over the arched footbridge that led to the grotto. A high rock wall rose behind the man-made cave. To the right of the grotto, some kind of storage area with a curved door and barred window had been carved.

Rain came down harder and thunder rumbled. It came down so hard and fast it looked like it was raining from the ground up. Puddles quickly formed and drenched her Nikes. Carefully-gelled spikes of hair clogged her vision like drowned worms. Weather never cooperated. Harley stumbled forward a few more steps, peering through the downpour, thinking that she must have been a Nazi in her former life. How else to explain all this bad luck? Or karma? Whatever it was, she should rethink letting Diva cleanse her aura.

She stopped. There was no sign of the killer mime. He could have climbed the rocks, but she didn't think so. Maybe he went behind the grotto. There was some kind of dirt path that went off to one side. Streams of runoff rain splashed down the rock wall in little waterfalls. Grass and plants flattened out under the force. So where had the guy gone?

Then he reappeared, white face looking like a disembodied moon in the pelting rain. It was bizarre. When he ducked into the crystal grotto, Harley smiled. Now she had him. There was no other way out of there. There should be an iron gate he could close to keep him in there until the police showed up. Everything had to be locked up at night because of vandals with the mental acuity of garden slugs who'd found it amusing to spray paint the crystals and the carved Biblical scenes. This time, their low IQs might work in her favor.

Gasping for air that wasn't full of water, she half-ran, half-slid across the footbridge and slammed shut the iron gate. It took a little work since it was hooked to the wall and heavier than she'd thought it'd be, but if he knew what she was doing, he didn't try to stop her. When she got the opening barred, she leaned back against it to catch her breath.

And damn if he wasn't right there in front of her. Outside of the cave instead of inside.

"How the hell . . . ?"

The dark red mouth squared into a silent grin. Every cell in her brain screamed at her to run, but her muscles didn't get the message in time. *Well, what a bitch.*

That was her last coherent thought before he pressed something against her arm and a numbing shot of voltage curled her hair and turned her into a flounder.

Fifteen

It was dark. The kind of dark that had to exist before the Big Bang. A musty smell filled the small space, and she had a hell of a headache. Harley tried to sit up, but her head hit a hard surface. Something soft cushioned her, but she didn't have room to roll over. No noise or sound provided any bearings for where she might be. Damn, it was quiet as a tomb.

No. That'd be too macabre. She shoved with all her strength at the lid over her but it didn't budge. *Okay, don't panic,* she told herself. No point in panicking. It couldn't be what it seemed to be, she just hadn't figured out yet where she was or how to get out. Panic would only make it a lot worse.

She sucked in a deep breath that smelled like dirt and tasted like death, and panic took over for a few minutes as she screamed until she was hoarse. When it subsided, she tried to stop shivering.

"All right," she said aloud so she didn't seem so alone, and her voice sounded muffled and heavy in the closeness, "I'll get out of this. Somehow. My karma hasn't been that bad. I'm nice to dogs and idiots. I love my parents. I visit the elderly."

Her voice broke a little on the last word. Tears stung her eyes. Her clothes were damp, her head still wet, and her toes felt squishy inside her shoes. She couldn't have been in here that long. Air must be coming in from somewhere. If . . . if she was buried, it wouldn't last long.

No nightmare had ever been like this. Maybe she should just go ahead and suck in all the air and get it over with instead of dying slowly. No, dammit. Something stronger than fear took over. She filled her lungs with air and let it out very slowly, a little at a time, then waited to take the next breath. Maybe she should breathe shallowly, but this seemed to work best.

Stale air felt warm and stuffy. After a while sleep tugged at her eyelids, but she kept them open even though she couldn't see anything. If she fell asleep, she'd never wake up. Not in this life.

That made her think of Diva's assurance that her spirit guides were always there. Maybe Diva's spirit guides were always on the job, but apparently her daughter's spirit guides were still gambling in Vegas. Unlucky in life and love, it seemed.

Morgan. She wondered if he'd miss her, or if he'd just be mad that she hadn't listened to him. That'd be Bobby's first reaction. Then he'd think of the past fourteen years and feel regret. As for Morgan, she had no idea what he'd feel. Or even if he'd feel anything. A month ago she'd have had a different opinion, but now?

Thinking of Morgan and Bobby and her own imminent demise made her breathe too heavily, so she focused on something else. She thought about Tootsie and wished she'd made out a will so he could have the last few silk dresses she owned. Cami would take Sam back, of course, and probably keep him the rest of his life since no one else could stand the cat. And the souvenir she'd brought home from that warehouse where she'd almost been killed would really make Nana happy. A wooden penis was just the kind of thing she'd find an appropriate bequest.

Okay. That wasn't focusing on something else. That was still thinking about dying.

She thought about her brother Eric and some of the stuff they'd done as kids, then how Diva and Yogi may not have been conventional parents, but they'd always been supportive. At least they weren't judgmental or prejudiced. Except for Yogi's distrust of anything to do with the government.

That made her think of some of their past protests at meat-packing plants and cosmetic manufacturers rumored to use animals as test subjects, and how she'd had to bail them out of jail. How many times? A lot. Then there were the protests they'd staged for animal rights. Human rights. And civil rights. Wasn't there something about gay rights?

It got harder to think and she concentrated on breathing in and letting it out slowly. Breathe in, hold, exhale. Breathe in, hold, exhale. It was so hard to keep her eyes open.

Earthquake. Damn, she was underground in an earthquake. What else could happen? And it was wet. She'd probably drown.

"Harley. Dammit, Harley, open your eyes! More oxygen, somebody give her more oxygen!"

Morgan? She opened her eyes, but everything was blurred. And wet. There was some kind of cover over her nose and mouth. Strangers crowded around looking down at her, and she got cranky and started shoving.

"Get . . . *off* me!"

Someone laughed. Morgan, she thought, but the crowd thinned some.

"Hey you," Morgan said, his face coming into focus.

"They're going to take you to the hospital to check you out, okay?"

"So . . . I have . . . a choice?"

"No. We'll talk later. Just keep breathing for now."

That sounded like a plan. She nodded and closed her eyes.

When she woke up again, she was on a gurney in the emergency room. Doctors said a lot of things, mostly how lucky she was they'd found her in time, and that she'd be fine with a little rest and a lot of air. They left, and Morgan stood at the side of her bed.

On the other side, Diva and Yogi huddled close by, looking worried. Harley realized it was the first time in years she'd seen that look on her mother's face.

"Fire my . . . spirit guides," she whispered, and like someone had turned on a light, a smile chased away the frown on Diva's face. Harley thought she'd never before quite appreciated how beautiful Diva was. Yogi kept a worried expression. They must have come to the hospital instead of going to the competitions. He still wore his Elvis costume, complete with cape, lacquered hair, gold chains, and long sideburns. How wonderful they both looked.

"If not for your spirit guides," Diva said in a husky voice, "I wouldn't have known where to look for you." Bells sewn into her sleeves tinkled as she dabbed at her eyes.

Yogi nudged closer, one arm around her mother's shoulders and his other hand reaching through the aluminum bars to touch Harley's arm. "When I find the guy who did this to you, he'll wish he hadn't, I promise!"

"So much for . . . being a pacifist," Harley got out with a weak laugh.

"Father first. Pacifist second. It's engraved on my tire iron."

"Take away his tire iron," Morgan said to Diva across the hospital bed. "I'll find the guy, and he'll wish that all he had to deal with was a tire iron."

"Yes," Diva said, "I know."

A little startled, Harley looked up at Mike. Blue eyes burned behind his half-lowered black lashes. Grooves deepened around his mouth. He put his fingers on her wrist and held it gently. His thumb made small, soft circles on the back of her hand. But she felt the tension in him, a slight vibration that said a lot more than his words. He had that look on his face again, the predatory one she'd first seen months ago when he was playing the part of Bruno Jett. Maybe he hadn't been playing a part after all. Maybe that was really him, and the more easygoing Mike was the disguise.

Harley's heart rate monitor beeped and she sucked in a lungful of oxygen. Probably her blood pressure spiked, too. She closed her eyes. *I need morphine before I say something stupid*, she thought hazily.

When the doctors released her, Morgan took her home.

She didn't ask anything, just rested her head against the back of the seat and relished being alive. Answers could come later. Right now she just wanted something to eat, drink, and lots of space around her.

Without asking, Mike stopped at Taco Bell. He ordered her two bean burritos, extra sour cream, and nachos and cheese. He handed her a large drink, and she sucked down half of it before taking a breath.

Wiping her mouth, she said, "God, that tastes good."

"Thought it might."

She looked over at him when they pulled out onto the street. He stared straight ahead. It'd stopped raining but the streets were still really slick. Memphis drivers who wanted to get anyplace without the benefit of a tow truck usually kept their eyes on the road in this kind of weather. Mike's jaw line sported what looked like a three day growth of beard, dark and bristly. A muscle in his jaw flexed a few times. He had a windbreaker on over his tee shirt, one of those navy colored ones with the police logo printed on it in white. It was impossible to tell what he was thinking.

It felt weird to be with him like this, their relationship—if it could be called one—having gone south. At the same time, there was a level of comfort in being with him. Like nothing could get to her as long as he was close. It wasn't a dependency thing as much as an acknowledgment that his survival skills were a lot better trained than hers were—case in point, being zapped by a mime and buried alive. Morgan would have never let that happen to him.

Neither said much until they went into her apartment.

"What's that?" Morgan asked, peering into the aquarium on her coffee table, and she remembered the ferret.

"Frank Burns. He's only temporary."

"I don't have to ask to know where you got him. He looks like a skinny raccoon."

"That's what I said. Don't take Shakespeare off the top. Frank's a flight risk."

"Sit down before you fall down," he said, and he didn't have to say it twice. She flopped back into her stuffed chair.

The tantalizing fragrance of Taco Bell increased with the opening of the white sacks. Intrigued, Sam waited impatiently for his portion as Morgan pulled out her burritos and his chalupas.

"So how did you find me?" she asked when her burritos were just greasy spots on sheets of Taco Bell paper, Frank had gobbled his way through a teaspoon of mushy refried beans, and Sam cleaned chicken chunks from his whiskers. "There are lots of graves out there."

"It wasn't easy. Diva found you."

She arched a brow. "You asked my mother?"

Morgan licked melted cheese off his thumb. "She told Tootsie that you were in grave—if you'll pardon the pun—danger. Seems like she had a vision of you in trouble, stuck in a close dark space where there were a lot of headstones. Figuring out where the headstones were was easy once I heard you'd gone to Ridgeway Inn right across from Memorial Park. Finding you once we got there wasn't quite so simple."

"I thought you didn't believe in Diva's visions."

"I think I said mumbo-jumbo, but this time it worked out. We found your van and tracked like Apache scouts to the place where he'd dragged you. Geronimo couldn't have done it better."

"Hunh. It's all a little hazy, so where did he bury me?"

"You weren't buried. You were in a broken coffin under a lot of brush ready to be hauled away. I figure he didn't have enough time to do any digging or find an empty grave. It felt more like a crime of convenience instead of premeditation."

"I'd have been just as dead." She wadded up her burrito papers and stuffed them in the empty sack. "How did he know where I'd be? That's the third time he's known where I am. I'd like to know just how he's doing that."

"So would I." Morgan frowned. The muscle in his jaw flexed again. "He has a pipeline to all your activities, it seems. Who else knows your work schedule?"

"No one. Usually not even my family. Tootsie does, of course."

Morgan lifted a brow, and Harley shook her head so hard her eyeballs rattled.

"No way. Tootsie would never be involved in anything like this."

"Anyone else at the office have access to employee schedules?"

"No. Besides, my schedule lately has been hit and miss, not regular. Like today, Tootsie gave me a pickup at the airport while I waited—omigod! What happened to the tourists left at Graceland?"

"They got some extra time with The King. When Tootsie called Diva, he said he'd had to send someone else after them, and asked if she knew where you were. That's when she told him about her vision."

"And he called you."

"Right." Morgan leaned back into the cushions of her overstuffed chair. It was a big chair, covered in white and off-white stripes. He dwarfed it. Sprawled with his long legs stuck out in front of him, he looked more like a coiled spring than relaxed. He had his jaw clenched so tightly the muscle kept twitching. "So, any problems with any of the other employees there? You have a disagreement with anybody?"

"Just Rhett Sandler, who does the payroll. But everyone's had a disagreement with him. I think it's his only form of entertainment, screwing up paychecks and hours. We get along okay most of the time."

"Think this Sandler would feel the same way?" He gave her a

look that showed nothing but mild curiosity. She knew better.

"Probably not, but if you're saying he'd try to kill me, why would he kill passengers on our vans? That doesn't make sense. Unless he thinks he'll make more collecting unemployment."

"Maybe Sandler has a grudge against management. Maybe he wants to ruin the business."

She thought about that. "It's a possibility, but I wouldn't know why. Ask Tootsie about the ogre's son. Rumor is they don't get along that well."

"I think I'll do that."

She didn't doubt it.

Sam stepped into her lap from the arm of the chair and curled up. Vibrating with a steady purr like a massager, he reminded her that she'd made it home alive. Horrified tears stung her eyelids and she blinked furiously. Crying was off-limits. It was something other people did, not her. Dammit.

"You okay?"

Morgan sounded really concerned, and that only made it worse. She nodded.

"I'm just fine," she said between her teeth.

"So I see." He got up and went into her kitchen. He came back in a few minutes with a glass of chilled white wine. "Drink this."

"Only because you insist." She tossed it back in three swallows. Morgan looked down at her with a slightly raised brow, then took her glass and refilled it. This one she slowly sipped. The French doors to the balcony were open, white sheers shifted in the warm wet breeze, and the scent of damp grass and magnolia blossoms teased the air.

"I don't like Hughes trying to kill me," she said when Morgan got a Coke and sat down in the chair across from her. "When did he get out of jail? And why didn't someone tell me?"

"Hughes? He's not out. He's been charged with fraud."

"Fraud? Not murder?"

"Not murder. Details to follow, so just be patient, okay?" She stared at him. "Then who just tried to kill me?"

"Beats me. I thought you might be able to shed a little light on that."

"You're the cop. I'm just an innocent citizen. Okay, not exactly innocent, but undeserving of being stalked by a homicidal maniac."

"I agree." The muscle in his jaw flexed again, but he looked calm enough. Maybe there was something to that old saying about still waters. Or was it muddy waters? Nana would know. Or not.

"So," she said, "either I'm being stalked by two killers, or Hughes is just a pissed-off guy with the right motive, no alibi, and bad luck."

"I'm beginning to think the first."

"Great. I feel so much better."

Morgan leaned forward in the chair and clasped his hands while he looked at her intently. "Think, Harley. Someone obviously knows you and wants you out of the way. Who'd want to see you dead?"

"Besides ex-boyfriends, a cheerleader when I was in junior high, my old boss—and quite possibly my current boss—and you, I can't think of a soul."

He sat back. "I don't want you dead. I just want you to quit finding the dead. It occurred to me that you made a few enemies this past spring, but if they'd wanted you dead, you'd already be dead. Besides, they wouldn't bother killing a few Elvises just to annoy you."

Harley had to agree with that.

"Anyone else?"

"Well . . . okay, this is probably nothing, but Tootsie and I were talking about the ogre and why he preferred Lydia to his own son joining the family business. Seems like Junior has a few behavior problems and grudges against his father."

Morgan gave a noncommittal nod. "I'd heard something like that."

"Then I'm telling you nothing new. As usual, you're way ahead."

Morgan's cell phone rang, and he answered it with the usual "Yeah," then got up and went out onto the balcony to talk in low tones she couldn't hear. Dammit. Undercover stuff could be very intriguing. Of course, curiosity had a lot to do with it, too. Who was he talking to out there? Did it have to do with her, or with the other case he was working?

"It's impolite to talk on the phone in front of guests," she said when he came back in.

"I'm the guest."

"That's even worse."

A faint smile tucked in one corner of his mouth. He looked tired.

"I don't want to leave you here by yourself," he said, and looked at her.

"I'll be fine," she lied. "I can lock my doors. I have an attack cat. And Mace."

"Yeah. That's great. Your brother will be here in a few minutes."

She scowled. "I'm *fine!*"

"Then play cards with him. I'm not leaving you here alone."

She said a few things that weren't very nice and stood up. While she'd planned on telling him exactly what he could do with himself, a sudden rush of blood from her head to her feet made her stagger and say something that sounded more like *"Urk!"* Morgan leaped forward and grabbed her arm to steady her.

"Sit down, okay?"

"Only because I want to," she said, reeling like a drunk.

He did the cop equivalent of an eye roll. "Fine. I don't care why you do it. Just sit down. Sit!"

She sat.

Eric arrived thirty minutes later. He wore baggy black pants, a *Slipknot* tee shirt, and did a handshake with Morgan that reminded Harley of hand games little girls played. Then he looked over at her.

"Chick, you really need to stop hanging around with the wrong people."

"Good advice. I wonder why I never thought of that."

Eric grinned. "I brought a Jackie Chan movie and my sleeping bag."

"Don't get too comfortable. You're not staying long," she said. "And what did you do to your hair?"

"Chick, this is the real color. Don't you remember?" He ran a hand through his dark brown hair. It was thick and coarse and looked normal. He'd trimmed it but left his sideburns a little long and had the beginning of a beard.

"You look like a Hell's Angel."

"Oh yeah, speaking of that, my car's on the blink again, so I borrowed your bike."

"You *what?*" She sat up straight and her voice rose an octave. "You're on *my* bike? Have you got a death wish?"

"Chick, I can ride a bike. I won't get hurt."

"Oh yes, you will. I'm going to strangle you."

When she stood up, Morgan stepped between them. "Hey, you don't need to get physical."

Harley lunged around him toward Eric, but her brother evaded her, slithering away with a look of surprise on his face.

"You idiot," she yelled at him, and he held up his sleeping bag to fend her off.

"Jeez, chick, settle down. I didn't hurt it. Go look for yourself if you want."

Panting a little, Harley glared at him. "It's paid for. If that bike has one scratch on it, I'll kick your ass from here to Canada."

Eric held out the key, keeping the sleeping bag up as a shield. "Check it out. It's fine. Damn, chick, you need some meds or something."

"Let's go down and look at it if it'll make you feel better," Morgan said. "You feel well enough to do that?"

"It's amazing what an urge to kill does for your health." She looked at her brother.

Morgan steered her toward the door. "I'll walk you down there and we'll check it out."

Mr. Lancaster had excellent security lights outside the door, two 400 watt lamps that came on at dusk and went off at dawn. The front door that faced the street had one of those gas lamps that didn't illuminate much, but that door usually stayed locked anyway. Everyone used the back door that led to the parking lot.

Harley's bike was next to Morgan's car. Chrome gleamed, the black and gold tank had that expensive glow, and the seat looked unharmed. Eric had left the helmet on the back bar, and she picked it up. This was her pride and joy, the Harley-Davidson Softail Deuce with over-under exhaust and a Twin 88 cam. It usually stayed in Yogi's garage with a canvas tarp over it, since no car could fit in there anyway with all the paint cans, PVC pipe, and assorted junk gathered through the years.

"See," Morgan said, "it's just fine. Feel better now?"

"Almost. Little jerk. He knows I don't like anyone else riding my bike."

"That might be my fault. He said your parents were gone and he didn't have a ride, and I told him to get here any way he could."

"So now I have to kick both your asses. Just as soon as I feel a little better."

Morgan grinned. "Yeah, that should be fun."

"Don't get too cocky. I've been known to inflict damage. Ask Bobby. I have ways."

"I'll keep that in mind." He took a couple of steps forward, pinned her back against his car and boxed her in with a hand against the car on each side of her head. He leaned into her, closing the height difference, his belly bumping hers. With the light behind him he was silhouetted, but there was no missing his intention.

Maybe she should have pulled away, but she didn't. Instead she got that tingly feeling in the pit of her stomach again, and it went all the way to her toes.

When he kissed her, the tingly feeling escalated into electricity strong enough to power all of Midtown. As if she wasn't already lightheaded enough. Damn him. He put his hand up her shirt and stroked her bare skin, fingers sliding upward. Everywhere he touched, her skin got hot enough to melt. She put her arms around his neck and held on. Oh yeah. She'd missed this. A lot.

They stopped kissing after a minute. Or maybe it was an hour. Whichever, when Mr. Diaz drove up and parked his car in the garage, it seemed best. He lived in the apartment just below the Spragues, worked at FedEx and kept odd hours. If he'd noticed them necking like teenagers in the parking lot, he didn't mention it, just nodded in their direction and said hello as he passed by. He was medium height with black hair and skin the color of aged oak, had a slim build, usually wore slacks and knit shirts, and kept pretty much to himself. He also had a really cool car, a new Mustang hardtop convertible. Speed and beauty.

"I'll watch until you're back in the building," Mike said, and Harley looked up at him.

"Okay."

He smiled and kissed her again, quickly and lightly this time, just a graze of his mouth against her lips. She hoped she wasn't drooling.

Like he'd said, he watched until she was back in the building and the door closed behind her before he fired up his car. Harley flipped the night latch on the door and went upstairs. Maybe being without oxygen had done some permanent damage. Why else would she let him just kiss her like that and then leave? It'd been his idea to take a break. It should be her idea when and if to stop the break. That's the way it went. There were rules about that sort of thing.

Before she got her apartment door open, she heard what sounded like a scuffle going on inside. Then Sam let out a shriek and she shoved open her door, barging inside ready to do battle.

Eric—or the back half of him—stuck out from under her coffee table. He seemed to be wrestling with something. And it sounded like he was losing. Sam was on top of the table looking like a Halloween cat with back arched and unearthly noises coming from his throat. Harley shut the door.

"Dude, what the hell are you doing?"

"I'm chasing a rat."

"A rat?"

"Yeah. It ate all your fish, but you forgot to put water in the tank anyway."

Harley looked back at the coffee table. The wire mesh top to the aquarium lay on the floor next to Shakespeare. Damn. She looked back at her brother.

"That's not a rat. It's a ferret. It belongs to Cami, and she'll be really ticked off if you've hurt him."

Eric sat up, banged his head on the underside of the coffee table, and then crawled out. "That explains the mask he's wearing. I thought I was seeing things."

"What have you been smoking?"

Rubbing his head, he looked up at her. "Just cigarettes. I've given up weed."

"Uh hunh."

"Seriously, chick. I'm thinking of getting into politics, and I hear they give drug tests."

Harley rolled her eyes. "Have you been talking to Prince Mongo again?"

Prince Mongo was a local Memphis eccentric, the only white man she knew who wore dreadlocks, sandals, loose baggy caftans in mismatched stripes and polka dots, and claimed he was from the planet Zambodia. He'd opened a bar downtown, and every year he

ran for mayor. He had a loyal following who voted for him, but
he'd never come close to being elected. Maybe the city wouldn't
have a financial deficit if he had been, but that was one of those
things that would never be known for sure.

"No," Eric said, "I haven't talked to him in a few months. You
don't think it's a good idea?"

"What I think is a good idea is that you help me find Frank and
get him back in his nice little home. I promised to keep him safe."

"Right. I'm on it." Eric stood up and brushed cat hair from his
black pants. Or maybe it was ferret hair. "Who's Frank?"

"The ferret."

Eric grinned. "Like in Frank Burns? That's funny."

"Hilarious. What direction did he go?"

"That way." Eric pointed toward her bedroom.

Harley got an uneasy suspicion. She went into her bedroom
with Eric and Sam following. A scrabbling noise came from her
dresser. When she opened her underwear drawer, a pair of red
bikinis leaped out and streaked across the floor. Inside them was
Frank Burns.

"Chick!" Eric leaped back.

"Catch him! He's headed for the living room!"

She didn't want Frank getting cedar shavings—or anything of
a pellet nature—on her best "do me" panties.

Sam stood in the small hallway outside the bathroom, fur
sticking straight up on his back like a bristle brush. He sounded like
a leaking tire. There was no sign of her panties or the ferret.

Eric peered around the door frame. "Where'd he go, chick?"

"My guess is he's in the bathroom. Sam keeps staring in there.
Just go in and close the door and you can catch him."

"Why me? I'm not going in there. Ferrets bite."

"You let him loose, you go in there after him. And I hope he
does bite. You idiot. Why'd you take the top off his cage anyway?"

"How was I to know? Who keeps a glass cage with a ferret in it
on their coffee table?"

"Well, obviously I do." Harley put her hands on her hips.

"You're not getting out of this. You let Frank out. You put
Frank up. Got it?"

Eric got that look on his face she remembered from their
childhood. Diva called it his "focused" expression. Harley called it

mulish when she was being kind, jackassed when she wasn't.

"Chick, chill out. It can't get far."

"I don't want teeth holes in my bikinis, or ferret poop either. Get the ferret!"

He started to say something and stopped. His blue eyes made a laser cut right into her brain. "Good thing for you that you just got out of the hospital, or I'd tell you where to put that ferret."

"Yeah? Don't let that stop you. *Chunko.*"

Chunko was her nickname for him when he was little. Until he reached five, he'd been built like a fireplug, stout and solid. Then he'd started growing up but not out, and decided he didn't like being called Chunko anymore. It was a guaranteed red flag.

"Bubble butt," he said back, another red flag.

"Snake snot."

They faced off, both pretty irritated by now. Then Eric suddenly started jumping up and down and shaking his left leg.

He made one of those high-pitched noises that always sounded so weird when a guy made them, almost like a shriek. Harley stepped back, a little startled.

"Dude, what is your problem?"

For a minute he just made those odd noises and slapped at his leg, then he unbuckled his belt and the baggy black pants fell to the floor. He wore Sponge Bob boxers that went almost to his knees. She started to laugh, and then she caught a glimpse of red silk at his feet. It was moving.

"My Victoria's Secret! Catch him!" She grabbed for the panties but Frank had them all wrapped around his head. His pink nose, masked face, and tiny feet were tangled in one of the lacy legs, but that didn't stop him from being too fast for her to catch. He darted toward the living room and disappeared under a chair.

Sam skittered sideways across the oak floors onto the rug, still making that guttural sound low in his throat, fur sticking up like it'd been gelled. Sam took his duties as Guard Cat quite seriously. Frank stuck his nose out from under the chair and looked at Sam. Black, beady eyes were rimmed by expensive red silk. Sam's eyes were blue slits. They made angry sounds at each other.

Harley climbed over the arm of the chair and crouched, waiting for Frank to come out so she could grab him. And snag her panties. The damn things had cost her over thirty dollars, and she sure didn't want a ferret wearing them before she could.

"Stand guard on this side," she said to her brother, but Eric was inspecting his legs for scratches and bites and didn't even answer. Just like a man.

Sam approached the chair in a crouch, stalking the ferret, and Frank ducked back under it. Harley watched the other three sides of the chair.

"This would be a lot easier if you'd help," she muttered in Eric's direction, and about that time the ferret made a run for it. She dove over the arm of the chair, grabbed panties and handfuls of furry ferret, and hung on. Sam tried to pounce and she fended him off with an elbow while trying to get to her feet. It was not the easiest thing she'd ever done, but finally, she got Frank back into his glass cage with the lid on top and without the red panties.

Ferret and cat both looked relieved. Eric looked worried. Harley looked at her panties.

"Damn. Ruined."

"Do ferrets get rabies?" Eric asked.

"Probably. You should get the shots just in case."

"Chick!" He sounded so alarmed that she sighed and shook her head.

"Cami would make sure he had all the shots he needs to have, so I'm sure you'll be just fine. There's some hydrogen peroxide under the sink. And pull your pants up when you're through looking for wounds, if you don't mind. Sponge Bob is winking at me."

Life, she decided a half hour later, when they had the Jackie Chan movie on TV and bowls of microwave popcorn with extra butter in their laps, was returning to normal. Tomorrow she'd worry about the killer. Tonight, she'd let Jackie Chan handle that kind of thing.

Sixteen

The finals for the Elvis competition were in just a few days. Yogi had made the last cut and was beside himself with joy. Not only that, the finalists were to be allowed a special place in the Candlelight Vigil this year, a ceremonial parade to the gravesite with their lit candles, a solemn procession to pay respects to the King of Rock and Roll.

"You'll be there, won't you, Harley?" he asked.

She looked at him, unable to refuse but wishing she could. It was always so crowded. "Yes. I'll be there, since I'm working that night anyway."

Yogi's smile stretched across his face. "Good. I want my family to be with me to share in the moment. It's always so emotional."

That's what she was afraid of. It always made her a little squeamish to see her father weep, and every time he went to Elvis's grave, he became very emotional.

"It's not just the loss of a great singer," he'd once explained to her, "it's the loss of the man himself. Elvis touched so many lives. Maybe most people saw him as a celebrity, but he was always that shy Mississippi boy with enormous talent being wasted in third rate movies and songs. I really think that's what killed him in the end, his disappointment."

Diva always said Elvis had just decided to go home.

Whichever it was, Harley dreaded being caught up in an emotional whirlpool. No matter how festive the crowd, once they reached the gravesite the mood immediately changed to sorrow. Very few were unaffected. Even her. Like Yogi said, it was such a waste of promise.

Tootsie, it seemed, had second thoughts about Harley attending the candlelight vigil.

"Are you sure you want to take that run?" Tootsie asked

doubtfully when she went in to work.

"Of course not. But the police are watching Hughes very closely."

"So I hear."

She tapped her foot thoughtfully. "I can't help wondering how he managed to show up at the cemetery with helium balloons and a bowler hat, though."

Tootsie pointed out the obvious. "No one can prove it was him. His fingerprints weren't on the balloons, the grotto's too damp, and concrete doesn't show fingerprints well. Besides which, they'd have to match them with the thousands of people who pass in and out of the cemetery, and that's nearly impossible."

"So you're saying they aren't even looking? And how do you know all this technical stuff, anyway?"

"I didn't say they aren't looking. They'll check for fibers or prints on the coffin you were in. Sorry about that," he said when she flinched. "Sore subject, I see."

"Only when I think about it. Do you know all this kind of stuff from listening to Steve, the invisible man?"

"He's not invisible, just rare. Okay, let's work this out another way. I'll list the pros and you list the cons."

"Easy enough. I'm sure Hughes is an escaped murderer."

Tootsie blew out a heavy sigh. "You want to try this or not?"

"Sure. Your turn."

"He was wearing white gloves." Tootsie paused. "And he was out on bail. He had time."

"But how would he know where I was going? He'd have had to be in his costume following me around. He might have been able to get to the cemetery across the street and then stand out front to catch my attention, but it would have to be close timing. What if I'd gone to The Peabody? Or the Hilton? Or just stayed there at Graceland?"

"Apparently, he's very flexible." Tootsie paused to take a call, and Harley rocked back and forth in the office chair next to his desk. The chair squeaked an annoying rhythm.

It just didn't make sense. It left too much up to chance, and Hughes seemed to be more organized than that. Now that the police were watching him very closely, as well as Williams, they had to be nervous. If they were working together, why try to destroy the very business that gave them the most access to their victims? It'd seem much more sensible, if killing an Elvis impersonator could be called sensible, to kill one of the contestants in the confusion and noise of a contest, not in a tourist van. Especially when the least thing could delay or prevent the victim from even getting on the van.

None of it made much sense to her.

"Tootsie," she said when he had a break between phone calls, "is there anyone who might hold a grudge against the ogre? A personal grudge?"

He thought a moment. "Well, there is the guy who went to prison for embezzling several years back. He got ten to twenty. Penney prosecuted him, even though he'd been his partner."

"I remember you mentioning that a time or two." She frowned. "Think he'd try to get back at Mr. Penney?"

"It's a moot point. He's still in prison."

"Maybe you should check and see if he's still there. Remember the last guy we thought was safely tucked away? States have a bad habit of paroling criminals before they finish serving their time."

"It is a problem," Tootsie agreed. "I'll check. Meanwhile, you see if Bobby's following up that angle already."

"Oh no. You call him. Lately, we don't seem to get along that well."

"Bobby's just worried about you."

"Of course. That's why he keeps threatening to put me under the jail. His concern isn't very comforting."

Tootsie's lips pursed. "Maybe he just has a funny way of showing it."

"You'd think I'd be used to that by now."

"Wouldn't you? Okay. I'll call Bobby. Meanwhile, why don't you forget the candlelight vigil and just stay home? I've already given your run to Jake anyway."

"Give it back."

"Darling, are you never happy? I seem to recall you begging me to give you any run but the candlelight vigil not so very long ago. Now I've given it to Jake and you're still unhappy. 'Perversity, thy name is woman.' It's no wonder I have alternate preferences."

Harley stood up. "You have alternate preferences because you're narcissistic. Don't look at me that way. You just think men are prettier. Which I understand, because I think they are, too."

Rolling his eyes, Tootsie said, "Please do us all a favor and don't go spouting that theory to anyone else. You're liable to set back any progress by at least a hundred years."

"Live in fear." She made a face at him. Another idea had occurred to her while watching Tootsie talk on the phone and schedule tours on his computer.

"Just how secure is the MTT computer these days?" she asked. "I've been watching you enter the driver's name, times, destination, number of passengers, estimated return time. Actual return time is entered later, after we punch in at the garage and the card registers time and driver. This new method is pretty thorough. Would anyone else be able to access this information?"

Tootsie stared at her. Then he nodded. "Yes. A good hacker could get in without too much trouble. Especially this older computer that Penney insisted on using instead of a new one with all the firewalls. God, why didn't I think of that? I've been so preoccupied with everything, I haven't even thought about checking for hackers. Damn, I'm so stupid! Of course, that'd be a perfect way to find out where the vans are going to be and who they're picking up, and where they're going. I log all that info in here. It helps with payroll. I probably need to check with Rhett, too, to make sure no hacker has accessed the financials."

"So, if changes are made, like my trip to the airport and the Ridgeway Inn, and you put it in the computer, a hacker would be able to find that out?"

"All he needs is a laptop and wireless Internet. He could do it from his own car."

"Or from under his rock, I presume. Well, that's a start. Another angle for the cops to check out."

Tootsie nodded slowly. "Maybe they've already done that. They asked a lot of questions after the first murder, you know, schedules, how we keep track of our vans, guides, and all that."

"And of course you told them about putting it all into the computer."

"But if the police suspect that's how the killer is accessing information, why haven't they done something? Oh, wait. Of course. I've been so rattled I didn't even think about it, but they must be gathering evidence, trying to track him before he kills again." Tootsie looked disgusted. "I should have already thought about that. And Steve should have mentioned it, the bad boy."

"Oh please. You know cops never tell secrets. Not even pillow talk works."

Tootsie arched a brow. "Then you just aren't doing it right."

"Let's not go there, since I'm not doing *it* at all right now. So there's a way to trace who's getting information from your computer without you knowing it?"

"Oh yeah. They leave fingerprints. No, not that kind. I just need a little time to find out."

Harley nodded. "Meanwhile, I think I'll go visit Nana. I'd like to ask a few more questions about the Elvis who showed up that day." When she reached the office door, she turned and said, "And don't forget to ask Bobby about Claude Williams. There's just something about that guy that really bothers me. Maybe he figures into this somehow."

Tootsie, already on the phone, gave her a wave to indicate he heard her, so Harley went to her car. Heat saturated asphalt and bounced off metal vehicles, reflecting sunlight like microwaves that made Harley feel like a baking potato. This was the time of year the Mid-South lived up to its reputation of Sunny South. Savagely sunny. Northern visitors found it difficult to breathe, while Southerners stayed inside. Most residents felt that if Mother Nature really wanted to sauté civilization, there wouldn't be such things as swimming pools and margaritas. Harley thought that an excellent philosophy. Both sounded good right now.

Nana wasn't in her room, but Harley hadn't really thought she'd be. Maybe the secret to living forever had something to do with not wasting time thinking about it. One thing about Nana—she wasted little time sitting around.

The assistant director of Whispering Pines sat at his desk, and he looked up with a pleasant smile when Harley stepped into the main office. "May I help you?"

"I hope so." She took the cushioned chair in front of his desk without waiting to be asked, giving him her brightest smile.

"My great-grandmother is a resident here, and the family is very pleased with all the extra activities planned for them. Would it be possible to get some information on just how these outings are arranged? I know some of them are planned by your office, such as inviting entertainment, but others, such as baseball games, must take a great deal of planning. Am I correct?"

"Indeed you are, Miss—?" He obviously didn't remember her, odd in one way, considering her participation in chaos at the ball game, but a relief in another.

"Davidson."

"Harvey Wiltshire." Harvey blinked rapidly behind his glasses, pale eyes shining. He had brown hair, with the kind of hairline men often got that looked like soil erosion on both sides, and a narrow strip of thinning hair stranded in the middle. Thin, with an occasional nervous tic in one eye, his nice smile made up for any other deficiencies.

It didn't take long for Harley to find out that the Elvis had just shown up out of the blue and presented the director with what had seemed to be a Paid in Full invoice for his services. The donor, of course, was supposed to be H. J. Davidson. Though it was unusual to allow an impromptu act to perform, since the Elvis had already gathered a crowd, they let him continue. As for the Seniors' Day at the Redbirds ball game, that was a regular outing, posted on bulletin boards and printed on the backs of monthly menus given to the residents. The names of all residents leaving on outings on their buses were entered into a computer and printed out for drivers and chaperones.

"Would you have entered my name as well?" she asked. "Since I was just a visitor?"

"Of course. We at Whispering Pines do like to be scrupulously careful with our residents, and return with *everyone* who goes on our outings."

"Thus the GPS bracelets, I guess. Handy."

"Davidson," Wiltshire mused slowly as if just remembering her temporary residence and the stir she'd caused, "it's *you*, isn't it?"

Time to go. She stood up

Harley thanked him nicely for his time and went to look for Nana. Wide halls were quiet, the framed paintings and copies of the masters on the walls deliberately chosen for their soothing, peaceful subjects. Lots of tall windows let in daylight at the ends of the halls, cozy chairs arranged for comfortable seating. She noticed little of it, mind busily mulling over possibilities.

So it would be easy for anyone who came to check out the

facilities or visit a resident to know about scheduled activities. It seemed like a lot of work to go to when it'd be easier to just show up at Memphis Tour Tyme or the garage and shoot her. It kept coming back to one thing. The killer wasn't that worried about risky situations or he wouldn't have killed three Elvises in vans full of tourists, not to mention poor Lydia living in a rented room in someone else's house.

Nor was he timid about trying to choke *her* to death while in a public restroom. Or wait in a cemetery across from her destination, knock her out, then bury her alive. She shuddered. That was a memory she wouldn't be able to escape for a long time.

This killer was bold, an opportunist as well as organized, and with a firm goal in mind. He went out of his way to publicly kill. For thrills? A challenge? Or was he deliberately trying to ruin MTT business. If he was, he was doing a pretty fair job at it. No telling what he'd do next.

Suddenly, Diva's warning popped into her mind: *You might want to skip the candlelight vigil.*

Most of the time she did her best to ignore her mother's frequent warnings and enigmatic comments. Nearly thirty years of experience had taught her that she'd go crazy waiting for it to happen, look for the worst behind every daily event, and then when it happened, she still wouldn't expect it. Clear predictions would be very nice. Diva just never had any. Her "visions" always seemed to come in odd fragments.

But since her mother was often uncannily right, maybe particular attention should be paid to the candlelight vigil. If the killer meant to strike again and Diva was right, it'd be then.

"Harley, what are you doing here?" Nana looked surprised and pleased. "Come to play poker again?"

"You mean lose at poker. No, just dropped by for a minute. Do me a favor, all right?"

"That depends. I might have a hot date later." Nana made a clicking sound with her teeth.

"Just keep your date here, will you? I don't want to worry about you, and it's too risky for you to be running around town."

"Wouldn't be so damn risky if I still had my gun. When is Bobby Baroni going to give that back to me? I'm about ready to call his mother."

"That's an excellent idea. I have her number. Meanwhile, just promise me you won't leave these grounds for a while, even with your new boyfriend."

Nana studied her face a moment, and then shrugged. "Sure. We'll just fool around in my room instead of go to the casinos."

Harley hugged her. "That's a girl!"

"Anything for you, kiddo. Ah, there's my new guy now. Want to meet him?"

Even if she'd wanted to, there was no time to say no. Harley turned to meet Nana's newest conquest. Not much taller than Nana, Rico Alvarez reminded Harley of Cesar Romero, the Latin star of the fifties—if Cesar had lived to be a hundred and twenty. Slightly shriveled, with dark skin and eyes and a broad smile, Rico's grip was strong when he took her hand and bent over it, a move that startled and concerned Harley in case he couldn't straighten back up. Yet he did pretty well, she thought, as he stood straight again and spoke with the slightest trace of an exotic accent.

"It's very nice to meet you at last, Miss Davidson. Your grandmother has told me so much about you."

Nana nudged him with her elbow. "I'm her *great*-grandmother."

Rico's eyes widened as if in surprise. "It cannot be! But, you are so fair and lovely, I never dreamed you to have been a child bride."

"Bride at fifteen, mother before sixteen. We worked quick back in those days, too." Nana winked at him, and it was obvious they shared a close secret. Maybe even an intimate secret.

Harley blinked. Was that kind of thing possible at their age? Since it wasn't a topic she wanted to think about, much less pursue, she said, "Mr. Alvarez, I trust you'll take good care of Nana for me. She's a family treasure, you know, and we want to keep her safe."

"But of course. It is my great pleasure to watch over so lovely a lady. Anna is a special person. Are you not, my dove?" He slid his arm around her waist and winked.

Nana got all giggly, transfixing Harley. It seemed she wasn't immune to masculine charm either, a family trait that could be very disturbing.

Leaning close, Nana said to Harley in a loud whisper, "I like the ones with a bit of the devil in them."

"Apparently we have a lot in common."

After Nana made that clicking noise with her teeth again, Harley left Whispering Pines. It was going to be a hot time in the old folks' home tonight, she bet.

Since her Toyota had been so cruelly treated, an old friend of hers was trying to put it back together in his shop. Sammy had always been good at fixing things as long as they had pistons and plugs. Other talents might elude him, but he could rebuild a carburetor and replace struts in half the time it took most mechanics. And best of all, he was honest. Didn't charge for what he didn't do, didn't overprice his parts and charge out the wazoo for picking them up from the auto supply just down the street like other garages did. The Toyota was in good hands, and she knew if it could be put back together, Sammy would do it.

Meanwhile, he'd given her one of the cars he loaned to customers, a Chevy Malibu that had seen better days, but with an engine that purred like a tiger. There was no loss of power, even though the car was the color of rust and primer. A definite incentive to quickly pay your mechanic bill and retrieve your own car, probably part of Sammy's strategy. He may have quit high school, but he was no dummy.

"I've got an idea," she said to Tootsie when she got back to the MTT offices.

"I can't believe I'm asking this, but what is it?"

"If the killer—I think it's Hughes, but it could be the ogre's bad son—is tracking my schedules through the computer, set me up for a run where he might try again."

"No way."

"Yes, way. Listen, the cops can be waiting for him with me. Or instead of me. At this point, I don't care which. It's getting nerve-wracking waiting for some guy with a knife and a grudge to jump out at me from behind the hedges."

Tootsie looked thoughtful. "Maybe I'll talk to Steve about it. It might work. What did you have in mind?"

"The candlelight vigil."

"You're crazy. That place is always chaos, and you want to add to it? No cop would agree to that."

"No, wait, see, it'd be perfect. There's a huge crowd there every year, and I'll be up at the front with Yogi, since he's been chosen to lead off the line. The head candle, so to speak. I'll be visible, the guy will make his move, the cops can hide behind the door that looks over the pool and grave area, or even in that little crescent-shaped thing where mourners sit. The killer jumps me, and the cops jump him, *bam!* It's over."

"And if the killer jumps you, the cops can't find him when he blends in with the crowd—*bam!* You're dead."

"You have no imagination, girlfriend. Yogi will be there with me, and believe me, for a pacifist, he can get very vicious." She paused. "Look, the guy won't be able to resist. He's the kind who obviously likes a challenge. Why else would he be so bold about the murders? They're always in public places, except for Lydia, and even her murder was committed in a house full of people who didn't hear a thing. And Lydia must have known this guy. She called me right before he killed her to tell me that she remembered him from somewhere. It could be Hughes, Williams, and yes, sad though it might be, even Larry Penney. Some sons are so ungrateful."

"Or just the opposite. My cousin Andy used to beat up people who insulted his dad."

"Well, I don't think we're dealing with a good son here. So, what do you think? Should I do it?"

Tootsie thought about it for a moment. "Only if I go with you."

"Do you really think that's wise? Remember Diva's warning?"

"Yes, and she also said it'd turn out all right."

"I don't remember that part."

"You were stuffing pie in your mouth. Besides, I can get vicious myself when needed."

She didn't need Tootsie's reminder about the karate. "Okay. Just don't wear a nightlight again. Wear something low-key."

"I will be the very *soul* of discretion."

Seventeen

It was a really good plan. Bobby didn't like it at all, but that wasn't unexpected. She'd been a willing lure before, so he got overruled. When Graceland's gates closed for the evening, they tested the wire and gave Harley detailed instructions on how to get out of harm's way when it went down. If it went down. They ran through every possibility with her.

"Remember, you don't know this guy," Captain Baker said, "so keep on your toes. Suspect everyone."

"Don't worry, I already do. I'm set to go. Shouldn't I have a weapon?"

Baker looked at her, an expression in his eyes like he wondered if she might be a little unbalanced. "No."

"It might come in handy, just in case."

"The wire is enough."

"Oh yeah, I can always use it to strangle him if things don't go well."

It was a joke, but Baker didn't understand the humor. Lights from the house reflected in the pool and off his glasses. Tall, a little bit chunky, with a square jaw, big nose, and thin lips, he looked like he didn't laugh much at anything.

Bobby, standing near the fence around the Perpetual Garden where Elvis and his parents rested, said, "I told you this isn't a good idea. She's a magnet for disaster."

Baker turned to look at him. Bobby wore an expression that didn't bode well for Harley. He'd just have to get over it. She was tired of looking over her shoulder. It made her nerve-ends buzz. She wanted this guy, whoever he was, behind bars. "Don't listen to him," she said to Captain Baker as she removed the wire from around her neck and gave it to him. "He's just mad because he's not running the show."

Bobby looked dangerously close to an explosion. Belatedly,

she remembered his Italian temper. Best to beat a swift retreat.

"I'll be running along now, Captain. I still don't know if it's a good idea not to tell my father about this, but I'm sure you know what you're doing. See you here at six tomorrow night."

She almost made it to her car before Bobby caught up to her.

"Halt or I'll shoot," he said, and since she wasn't at all sure he was kidding, she stopped.

"Oh. Hi, Bobby."

"What the hell do you think you're doing, Harley? Don't you have any sense? You've always been nutty, but this beats anything you've come up with yet."

Nutty? She stuck her face close to his. "Hang around. I'm sure I can beat this without a sweat."

He leaned back a little. "Why don't I doubt that? Damn, Harley, have you got a death wish?"

"We discussed that a while back, and you already know the answer. I can't keep waiting for this guy to find me at the right time and place. If I don't do something, he will."

"So you're saying you don't trust the MPD to catch the killer and that you think you can do it better, right? I mean, after all, you've had what, three months experience at finding bodies, and no training at all."

"Obviously, your captain thinks I'm useful or he wouldn't agree with me."

"Baker doesn't know you. I *do*."

"Not as well as I thought you did. Why do you think I'm doing this? He's going to kill again, Bobby, and maybe again and again. He's killed three people and I'm next on his list. Do you really think I'll just cower in my room and wait for him to come get me? That's not my style."

"You have no style, unless you count stupidity as stylish."

They were in each other's face now, glaring at each other in the glow of an overhead vapor light in the parking lot across the street from the Graceland mansion. Elvis fans already crowded the area in preparation for the candlelight vigil tomorrow night, and many sat or stood by the mansion's fieldstone walls covered with scrawled names and dates and poignant farewells to Elvis.

"You're an ass, Bobby," she said through her teeth, and he nodded.

"I know. But I'm an ass who cares if you get killed."

That took some of the wind out of her sails.

"I hate it when you do that," she said. "How can I stay mad?"

"I hate it when you treat police procedurals like a video game. Just stay alive, Harley."

Sighing, she said, "I will. Like it or not, I'll be fine."

"Is that one of Diva's predictions?"

"One of mine. I can't ever figure out Diva's predictions until it's too late."

"We have that in common. Come on. I'll walk you to your car." He slung an arm over her shoulder and walked her into the parking lot behind the shops. "You're asking for trouble when you park back here, you know."

"I know. But I had police protection. Like I do now."

"Where's your car?"

"Sammy has it."

"You've got one of his loaners?"

"I'm afraid so."

Bobby grinned. One good thing about their long friendship, they had their arguments and feuds, but once they blew up at each other, they often forgot why they'd argued.

"Let me guess. Is it the sixties VW Bug still painted with yellow and purple flowers?"

"That one was taken. I got the Malibu. It's over there." Rust and primer stood out even under vapor lights. "Runs like a bat out of hell, though."

"Sammy's a genius with engines."

Harley got into the car while Bobby looked in the backseat to satisfy himself no one was hiding. "Go straight home and lock your doors, will you?"

"Okay." She shut the car door and rolled down the window.

"Would it be against your professional judgment to tell me why the MPD thought it necessary to use undercover so quickly in this case? In two days, Morgan was swiveling his hips and onstage howling like a hound dog. I thought things like that took a lot of time to arrange."

Bobby's shrug was noncommittal. "Cases work differently."

"Don't tell me, then. I'll find out soon enough anyway."

Shaking his head, he stuck his hand in the window and rubbed his knuckles over her chin. "I have every faith that you will."

Somehow, that made her feel better. She wasn't sure why. Maybe because he expected her to succeed, even though he didn't recommend it. There were times Bobby reminded her why she still hung around him. Then there were the times here minded her why she got so irritated with him.

"Just like I have faith you'll end up in trouble and need rescuing again," he added.

Harley's feeling of good will instantly evaporated.

She rolled up her car window so fast he jerked back his hand before it got caught between glass and frame. Engine roaring to life, she slammed the Chevy into gear and screeched off.

By the time she reached the parking lot of her apartment to change clothes for the Elvis competition, Yogi had called twice on her cell phone. Maybe she'd been looking at the whole broken cell phone thing wrong, she decided. Not having one might be a real advantage at times.

"Yes, I'll be there, I promise," she said, trying to hold the phone between her ear and her shoulder, and failing. "Just running a little late. As usual."

Yogi sounded excited. "I'm one of the five finalists! Five of the best—such an honor. Oh, and your mother says to meet us on the far side of the bar. This year is going to be special, I just feel it. Can you believe that it's here again so quickly? Should I sing *Suspicious Minds*? I've always done that one well, but then, maybe I should do another one since so many others sing that song. Oh, and—"

"Take a toke and calm down, Yogi," Harley advised. "If you don't, you're going to get up there and sound like you're in fast forward. Damn!"

"Are you all right?"

"Yeah, just dropped my dinner and stepped on it. I'll probably eat it anyway. Look, I'll see you there, okay? Think positive."

Juggling her new cell phone—still on its long tether to her belt loop—backpack, car keys, dry cleaning, and takeout, she kicked shut the car door and hoped she hadn't forgotten anything. If she had, there wasn't much time to do anything about it.

It took some doing to open the heavy outside door that had one of those pneumatic door closers, but she got into the foyer without doing major damage to herself. Getting up the stairs was an accomplishment in itself, with plastic-wrapped clothes dragging—why did she bother paying to clean clothes she'd probably never wear again?—and her squashed takeout dripping marinara, as she clenched car keys between her teeth and fumbled one-handed in her backpack for her door keys. Obviously, she had not thought ahead.

After finding the ring of door keys at the very bottom of her backpack, she stuck one in the brass deadbolt, gave the door knob a twist, and nearly fell inside. Light through the French doors eased the gloom. She slung the dry cleaning over the back of a chair, leaned to toss the takeout to the counter, and dropped her backpack to the floor, all in a practiced motion.

"Sam, you handsome man," she crooned, "I brought your favorite, cheesy bread. Come on out, kitty kitty kitty."

Frank Burns made ferret noises, a scolding sound like *chi! chi! chi!*

"All right, you can have some, too. What the heck's the matter with this light now? I swear, Mr. Lancaster needs to do some serious repairs around here."

The wall switch that turned on the pretty Tiffany-style lamp with dragonflies in jewel colors of deep red, green, blue and amber did nothing. She flipped it a few times as if determination would make the electricity work. Deep shadows filled the apartment's corners, the only light coming through the open French doors. She paused. Open? Uh oh.

Silence pressed down, heavy and thick. There had to be someone out on her balcony. Heart thudding so hard in her chest it felt like a missing engine, she fumbled for the cell phone attached to her belt loop. 911 was the first number in her Quick Call. Little green numbers glowed as she lifted it high enough to see. They made these damned things so small now it was hard to find what she wanted, much less hit the right button . . . ah. There it was . . .

A hard chop to the back of her neck sent her to her knees but didn't knock her out. She let out a yell like Tootsie had that night, a "*Hi-ya!*" meant to intimidate. It came out more of a gurgle, but she didn't let that stop her. She rolled to one side, the sharp pain in her left arm and shoulder reminding her that she still hadn't completely recovered from being stabbed. Nothing hampered her feet, though.

When the dark figure leaned over, she kicked up with both feet and caught him right in the middle of his chest. He slammed back against the wall. Harley reached out, grabbed something heavy and threw it in his direction, then scrabbled to her feet and tried to get her breath even as she reached for another weapon. The second volume of Shakespeare followed the first one. It hit the wall instead of her attacker, the sound more of a splat than a thud.

A lamp fell over, shattering when it hit the floor, and she hoped it wasn't the Tiffany lamp even as she leaped toward the French doors. Since the killer stood between her and the hallway door, any port in a storm would do. Another loud crash as something hit the floor, and the killer started cussing. After a couple of hops, Harley nearly reached the open doors and balcony. Then she snagged on something that gave a sharp tug at her waist and pulled her off-balance. She went back onto the floor hard, hitting her head against something solid. Lights exploded in front of her eyes and everything went hazy and wheeling, a kaleidoscope of stars, bars of light, and shadows.

Helpless, dizzy, she dimly realized how vulnerable she was but couldn't dredge up the energy to move. The world was already spinning so fast around her, like having one too many drinks and holding on to the floor to keep from falling off.

Still in her fog, yet aware of sound and movement, a high-pitched yowl seemed vaguely familiar. More cussing followed the yowl, and as Harley tried to sit up, she caught the movement of something small and dark flying toward the French doors. Then it disappeared. From behind her, a hand landed on her right shoulder, grabbed a fistful of shirt, and hauled her to her feet.

"Stupid bitch," he said a little breathlessly, "you're more trouble . . . than all the others . . . put together."

Harley jammed her elbow backward into his stomach. His grip on her shirt loosened so she brought the heel of her Nike down hard on his instep. He let go of her shirt and grabbed her by the arm, jerking backward as he swung her around. She bit him. Hard. Teeth sank into the fleshy part of his forearm and she held on until he managed to shake her loose.

Cussing, he hit her so hard with the back of his other hand she saw stars again. Knee-jerk reaction set in when he pulled her forward, and she jabbed her knee up and into the estimated area where it might do the most damage. He screamed, a high-pitched yowl like a cat's, and doubled over, but still held tight to her arm. Just when she thought about biting him again he yelped, then thrashed around slapping at his leg and cussing. A dark shape crawled up his leg to his back and hung off his tee shirt, and its beady eyes reflected light through the open doors. Sam!

It seemed like the perfect time for a defense move. Harley grabbed his thumb and pulled back hard, he let go, and she headed for the door. It was still so dark she could barely see to find the door knob, but she finally got it open. A wedge of bright light fell into the room and she paused. *She had him.* She had the killer right here. She had to keep him here until help came. But how?

Her breath came hard and fast but she managed to grab the chain holding her cell phone. It had nothing on the end but a distorted metal link. Damn, damn, *damn!* Breathing hard, she turned around just in time to see the killer grab Sam off his back and fling him across the room. Her breath caught in her throat.

"Sam!" There was no answering yowl, no angry hiss. Propelled by fear and fury, she launched herself at the man staggering toward the French doors. "If you hurt my cat, *you're a dead man!*" she yelled as she collided with him. He didn't answer but kept going, and she leaped onto his back, wrapping her legs around his waist and her arms around his neck. Sickly sweet aftershave stung her nose, and his wiry hair tickled her chin.

"Oof!" he said when she landed on him. He staggered a little and then grasped the edge of one of the doors and held on.

Harley beat at his head, then grasped his fuzzy hair and yanked hard. Her momentum took her backward when his head came off. She screamed and let go, falling from his back onto the floor, and then he was gone.

About that time, she heard the sound of sirens, and boots stomping up the stairs. Someone had called the police, a little too late. She squinted at the head she still held. A rubber mask, complete with hair. It figured. *Elvis.*

"I can't find my cat," Harley said for about the twentieth time, and Bobby let out a long sigh.

"He probably got out the open door. He'll come back. Cats always come back."

"Sam's an inside cat. He's never stayed outside. Cami will be upset. Hell, *I'm* upset! I've looked everywhere, and called and called . . . " She put her face in her palms, muffling her voice. "Just like a damn male, always running off."

"I'm going to ignore that. Are you finished?" he asked one of the guys that had made her change clothes and put the ones she'd worn in one of their paper bags, then checked her teeth when she mentioned that she'd bitten her assailant.

"No usable hair with follicles," the CSR said, and Bobby turned back to her.

"Just answer a few more questions and you can go look for your cat, okay? Tell me one more time what the guy looked like."

She looked up. "You don't really listen, do you, Bobby. It was dark. He wore a mask. I never saw his face at all."

"But after you pulled off his mask, what did you see?"

"The back of his head."

"And he was how tall?"

"Damn, *I* don't know, I didn't take time to measure. I just thought that I should try to keep him here, and then he threw Frank across the room—"

"Frank?"

"Frank Burns. The ferret. I'm keeping him for Cami. I thought it was Sam, but it wasn't. By the way, when you do find the guy, he's going to have ferret fang marks all over his back and leg. Oh, and my teeth marks. Don't forget that I bit him on the arm. They already took impressions, so when we do get this guy, they can match my teeth with his bite mark. That stuff tastes nasty, by the way."

Bobby let out another long sigh. "Come home with me, Harley. I have a nice pullout couch, I'll even make you breakfast in the morning. Waffles. With pecans. Your favorite."

"Another time. I have to be at Yogi's competition tonight, and it's probably almost over by now. He'll be wondering where I am."

"Harley—"

"I *promised*, Bobby. I have to go. You know I do."

"All right. I'll put an extra guard on your apartment."

She started to argue, then thought about it and nodded. "That'd be nice."

After she'd called Cami to come help look for Sam and make

sure Frank hadn't been hurt despite his apparently quick recovery, she went into the bathroom to clean up. *Eek!* Not even the most expensive gel had ever made her hair stand up like that before. A big red mark still showed on her cheekbone where he'd hit her, and she had a scratch on her chin. Collateral damage.

By the time Cami got there to check over Frank, who seemed quite unconcerned about the evening's excitement as long as he had treats and toys, Harley had cleaned up as best she could and put on a clean pair of jeans and tee shirt. There wasn't much she could do with the hair.

Cami stood just inside the door and looked at the mess in the living room. Frank's tank tilted oddly, but that was because the coffee table did, too. "Your housekeeping skills really need some work, Harley."

"I know. But at least my Tiffany lamp is all right. We just have to find Sam. I'm going to make my appearance for Yogi, then come back as quickly as I can to help look, okay?"

"He's probably not far, maybe in the bushes or on another balcony. Don't worry about him, Harley. He'll be just fine. Sam knows how to hide."

"A skill I haven't quite mastered, it seems."

"But at least you fought off the killer."

"That's right, I did. Without needing to be rescued." She turned around, found Bobby standing by the balcony talking to a uniformed officer, and smiled. "Hey, Bobby, I didn't need rescuing!"

He looked over at her. "What the hell do you call *this?*"

"Late. By the time you guys got here, I had it all under control."

"The hell you did. We found you cowering on the floor."

"Did you find the killer? I thought not. Maybe he got away, but he didn't kill me." She turned back to look at Cami. "I feel better now. Thanks. Just find Sam for me and my night will be complete. Oh, and please keep Frank out of my panty drawer, will you? He's grown too fond of red lace bikinis. He and Tootsie would get along very well."

Harley got to the contest just in time to see Yogi perform.

Instead of the white jumpsuit, he wore fifties-style trousers and jacket. A guitar was slung across his body, and he grabbed a microphone on a stand, his posture reminiscent of one of Elvis's first concerts. He belted out the lyrics to *Heartbreak Hotel*. Smiling, she leaned against the bar and watched. Really, he did quite well at sounding like Elvis. No one would ever be able to duplicate Elvis's distinctive voice and style, but that wasn't the point anyway. This was more homage than imitation.

"He's pretty good," a low masculine voice said in her ear, and she didn't even have to turn around to recognize the voice.

"Yes, he is. Did you make the finals?" She took a deep breath and leaned back against the bar to look up at Morgan.

He had a mustache and beard, but it'd never disguise those electric blue eyes or that killer body. A blue pullover shirt molded to his broad chest and tucked into his black shorts. Long, bare legs were muscled and hard.

"Unfortunately, no," he said. "Someone blew my cover."

"That's terrible," she said with all the innocence she could muster.

"Yeah. What happened to your face?"

"A little accident."

"And your hair?"

"Even bigger accident. So why are you here if your cover's been blown?"

"It's the damnedest thing. I got assigned to keep an eye on you for the next two nights."

"I'll just bet. You should have been on the job a little earlier. You might have caught the killer."

"I'd heard that."

"Which explains your presence here, of course. And I thought it might be my charm."

Morgan's mouth tilted. "So who rescued you this time?"

"Well now, it's the damnedest thing. *No one.* The killer got the worst of the deal and took off for parts unknown."

"So now you think you can take care of yourself just fine, I see."

"I don't do too badly."

He blew out a disgusted sigh that was far too reminiscent of those she heard from Bobby. "*Riiight.* Never mind," he added when she put her hands on her hips, "just think of me as your temporary bodyguard, here to guard your body."

"Guard my body? I assume you don't mean in the more familiar manner."

"That part's up to you."

"Odd, I don't remember being given that option before."

Morgan just looked at her. A tingle went to her toes. She tried to think of something smart to say, but all that came out was, "What happened to my other bodyguard?"

"He's off-duty. I've been assigned to keep you safe."

"So who's going to keep me safe from you?"

"You're safe. For now."

That could be either ominous or promising, and as she was trying to decide which, music crashed in the room, people clapped appreciation, and up on the stage Yogi caught a pair of what looked like panties flung at him. Harley stuck her fingers in her mouth and whistled loudly a few times. Maybe he heard her, since he looked in the direction of the bar and grinned. Really, Yogi certainly knew how to have a good time. In fact, she couldn't recall when her parents worried a lot about life events, though they did protest those they disliked. Often vehemently.

She looked back at Mike.

His attention was no longer on her. Something across the room had caught his eye, and he looked suddenly intent, muscles taut. He said, "Don't go anywhere yet," and disappeared into the crowd that surged back and forth toward the stage like ocean surf.

Harley put her hands on her hips. So much for watching out for her. Any bodyguard who got distracted so easily needed to be guarding someone else. She headed toward the right side of the stage, where Diva should be. Her mother's shining pale hair stood out in the crowd, swinging from the crown of her head down her back in a French braid. Stray wisps framed her face when she turned to look at Harley.

"I knew you'd make it here in time."

"Then you were the only one. I probably broke ten traffic laws getting here."

Diva put an arm around her shoulders. "And now you're here."

"Is Yogi going to win?"

"Yes, but not the competition. Don't worry. It really will be all right."

"Okay. Uh, did you notice my face, by any chance?"

Diva smiled. "Don't you feel better knowing that you didn't need to be rescued?"

"Actually, yes. I do. Not only did I get to say an *In your face* to Bobby as well as Morgan, I feel like I finally managed to redeem myself."

"The ways of the universe are many and mysterious."

At times, Harley expected her mother to add *Grasshopper* at the end of her sentences. But she only replied, "They must be."

"Would you like to come to a yoga class next week? We're having it in the living room."

"No, thanks. Turning myself into a human pretzel has never been one of my favorite activities."

"A pity. You were very limber as a child. It would do a lot to relax you. And I'm serving willow bark tea."

Ugh. "That's just aspirin in its liquid form. You may need it after the class."

Diva smiled her serene smile, and then turned as Yogi reached them. Elation put a big grin on his face. "That was my best performance ever!"

"It certainly was," Diva agreed. "Soon, everyone will remember you."

Yogi looked pleased and Harley had an uneasy flash of memory. Diva had said that before, and it hadn't exactly sounded like a good thing. But maybe it'd be all right. Or maybe not.

"Don't go to the vigil," she said abruptly to her father.

Yogi blinked. "Why not? It's an honor, all five finalists leading thousands to the garden. I wouldn't miss it for anything. Why wouldn't you want me to go?"

Harley honestly couldn't say why she felt a sense of foreboding. That was more Diva's specialty. But Diva devoutly believed in good karma and the universe. Harley didn't.

"I don't know," she said when it seemed like Yogi really did expect an answer.

He came close and patted her on the shoulder.

"That's all right, sunshine. I don't have to win. This has been my best performance ever, and I'm happy."

Harley looked to her mother for confirmation, but Diva wasn't much help. Even in the dim lights of the club, with all the din and chaos around them, Diva looked serene and beautiful. It was easy to see her as she'd always seen her mother, beautiful, almost mystical, with a graceful way of moving confidently through the world, as if nothing or no one could rattle her. Maybe that's what Harley should strive for, that sense of peace with herself and her world. So far, it eluded her. But that didn't mean it always would.

"Yogi," Eric said, shouldering his way through the crowd, "you're the *king*, dude. You're the king." He and Yogi did that hand thing Harley never could quite figure out, not that she had the least desire to do so. Then Eric looked over at her. "Cool chick. Who's been chewing on your hair?"

"I can't believe you have the nerve to say anything to me about my hair. Especially when you look like you've been peed on by a rainbow."

Eric stroked a hand across his hair, bright blue and yellow streaks vivid against his natural dark brown. "You don't like it? It's only temporary."

"Keep dying your hair and it'll be only temporary, too." Harley looked over at her father. "I can't stay long, only until they announce the winner. Sam's gone and I have to find him."

If anyone would understand the urgency about looking for a lost pet, it was Yogi. After all, it'd been the abduction of the larcenous King that had first sent her entire family into the world of jewelry thieves and murderers.

"Sam is fine," Diva said. "He's with the groundhog."

"Groundhog? You mean, like the animal?"

"No, I don't think so." Diva frowned slightly. "It just popped into my head so I said it. I'm not sure why."

"Good thing I don't always say what just pops into my head," Harley muttered, then said, "I'll see what I can figure out. I'm glad he's okay."

A microphone crackled and popped, and the contest organizer announced it was time to count down to the winner of this year's competition. All attention turned toward the stage.

It occurred to her as the tension in the room grew palpable that this was rather like the flip version of Miss America competitions, only without the bathing suit contests. Morgan could have won on looks alone, although he'd probably have been eliminated when it came to the congeniality portion. Yogi would have won that.

Thinking of Morgan, she wondered just where he'd gone. he'd lost track of her body and she was almost ready to go. Not that she was nervous about leaving alone.

Okay, she *was* nervous about leaving alone. Recent events suggested it was a bit risky to run around by herself. Whatever this killer's identity, he had to be certifiably insane. The fact that he'd waited for her in the dark privacy of her apartment wasn't at all what he was supposed to do.

Either he was changing tactics or getting desperate. Neither of those options made her feel any better.

Thankfully, her attention was diverted from grim speculation by the excitement from Yogi as only he and Preston Hughes were left as contestants. Hughes had been pitch-perfect, but didn't have the heart Yogi did. Maybe that was just her opinion—like the opinion she had that the man was probably a bold, vicious killer. He should still be in jail. She hadn't a clue why he was here as if he had no problems at all, when he should be wearing an orange jumpsuit in a cell with a big guy named Bubba as his significant other.

Then the announcer named Yogi as the first runner-up, and he gleefully went up the stairs to the stage and took his bow as if he'd just been named Leader of the Free World. It never ceased to amaze Harley that Yogi let few disappointments bother him. The crowd roared its approval of his shimmy, shake, and curl of his upper lip, so that Hughes's acceptance of the trophy and title of King was almost overshadowed.

"You were wonderful," she told her father when she'd finally made her way through the crowd to his side, and gave him a kiss on the cheek. "If Hughes hadn't made bail, you'd have won this one."

Yogi's broad grin acknowledged her faith in him. He looked jubilant. "Next year, the title. Tomorrow night, the candlelight vigil. Don't forget."

"I won't." As if she could. She'd already set herself out as bait once, but caught the wrong fish. Maybe this time she'd get it right.

Eighteen

Morgan followed her home, driving an undercover car police used to escape notice. Until he showed up at her side as she got ready to leave, she hadn't seen him since he'd blown her off. He'd had some lame excuse that he'd been watching over her the entire night, but he must have hidden really well.

He parked the battered gray Pontiac right in front of her building. Not exactly what she'd consider unobtrusive, but maybe that was the point. Harley parked in back next to Cami's Saturn, and by the time she cut off her headlights and locked the car Morgan stood by the back door.

"Looking for anyone special, sailor?" she asked breezily, and he shook his head.

"Just doing my job, ma'am." He opened the door for her. "I'll be out here all night, in the heat with the mosquitoes."

"Is that a hint to be invited inside?"

He just smiled.

So much for that. Not that she wanted him to come inside. Really. Okay, so she did, but it had nothing to do with lust, just security. Mostly, anyway.

"Better move your car if you don't want to be seen," she advised. "Or is that the idea?"

"It might be a deterrent. Run along inside like a good girl so I can skulk back to the car to watch over you."

"I feel so safe." Prompted by an inner devil that usually got her into trouble, she stepped closer to him and playfully ran her fingers down the front of his shirt. "And I'm much more fun when I'm a bad girl," she added huskily, and saw heat flare in his eyes. A muscle leaped in his jaw and just when it seemed as if he was about to say something, she ran the tip of her tongue over her top lip and stepped back. "'Night, copper."

If he answered, she didn't wait to hear it but scooted inside and up the stairs. One more second standing on the stoop with him, and she'd have said something she'd probably regret.

The door to her apartment was locked and she used her key. Cami stood in the middle of the living room, surrounded by wreckage that looked as if she'd attempted to tidy up. Her short blonde hair had damp streaks in front of her ears and on the nape of her neck, and she looked completely frazzled. She turned to Harley.

"I've looked everywhere for him. It's dark now, but I went out looking while it was still light. I guess I could again. I have this flashlight, and should be able to see him in the dark. It's the eyes, you know, they shine like flat circles—if he's gone across the street to the zoo, he might end up as a snack for the lions. Oh, I can't stand this."

Harley said quickly, "Diva assures me that Sam is just fine. He's off somewhere with a groundhog."

Cami blinked. "A groundhog? Like the animal?"

"She doesn't think so. You know Diva. All her messages are so cryptic. I keep thinking I should know, but the only thing that comes to me right now is the mole that King's been after in Mrs. Shipley's yard. There's something else I'm supposed to be remembering, but it's not coming to me. God, what a mess. Sam could be hiding somewhere in here, for all we know."

Broken glass, shards of a lamp, and something she didn't want to look at too closely on one of the chair cushions, turned her usually-neat apartment into a rubbish dump. It was obvious Cami had done what she could, but it needed a complete overhaul.

"You know," Harley reflected aloud, "if I'm going to keep getting involved in situations where people feel compelled to try to kill me, I really need to get indestructible furniture. Or a maid."

"Or a security guard stationed at your door."

"Even better. How very practical of you."

"Where can we look next?" Cami ran a hand through her hair, and sweaty strands stuck out like Dagwood Bumstead's hair. "I've searched every cabinet, drawer, under your bed—by the way, that's not a good place to store Old Faithful."

"Old Faithful? Ah. Yes. Well, I haven't really needed it in a long time, and forgot about it being there. The batteries are probably run down by now. I should get some more in this time of need, I suppose."

"Better clean it first. It's pretty dusty. But much more discreet than that wooden penis you keep on your dresser."

"That's a souvenir, a reminder to duck when people are shooting at me."

"You need a reminder for that? Jeez, Harley. But back to the problem at hand. Do you still think Sam went over your balcony?"

"I'm fairly sure. He was really spooked. We'll look outside."

Cami glanced doubtfully at the French doors, now closed and locked. "I don't know . . . "

"It's safe. Morgan's hiding out there waiting to pounce on any evil Elvis that comes by. Pretend you don't notice him. I think he's sensitive about getting his cover blown."

After searching inside, they went outside and searched in the bushes again, each armed with a flashlight. Privet hedges stretched on one side of the yard, and bushes next to the building were kept neatly trimmed at waist-high level. The front yard gas lamp put out enough feeble light to barely see the green and white caladiums thriving in scalloped flowerbeds, but it was too dark to see the vivid hues of red and pink begonias. Dark shadows made a huge pool beneath the low, spreading branches of the magnolia tree. Sam could be anywhere.

After crawling under the bushes next to the building, calling *kitty, kitty, kitty* as softly as she could so no one would call the cops on her at midnight, Harley sat down on the bricked front stoop. She cut off her flashlight and blew out a frustrated breath.

Over at one side of the house, Cami still made her cat noises, strange sounds she interspersed with *"Here Kitty"* calls.

"What was *that?*" Harley asked Cami when she gave up and came to sit on the front stoop beside her.

"Cat in heat noises. Sam doesn't know he's been neutered."

"Sounded more like cat being strangled noises." She shuddered and made a sign from her forehead to her chest, then crossed herself.

"Catholic school training sticks, doesn't it," Cami said with a sigh. "But don't worry about that happening to Sam. He takes care of himself really well."

"I know. So does Frank Burns. I should take lessons from the animal kingdom."

"It'd help both of us. I'll set the trap I brought and bait it with some tuna flakes, and you check it first thing in the morning."

"It's not one of those things that traps his paw, is it?"

"Lord no, Harley, you know better than that. It's humane, a cage with a trap door. Once he gets in to eat the food, the door snaps shut and he's trapped."

"Try Chinese rather than tuna," Harley suggested. "He particularly likes shrimp fried rice."

Cami stood up. "No wonder Sam loves you. He'll just have to take what I brought with me this time. You can use egg rolls or sushi or whatever if he's not in it in the morning."

"The only sushi he likes is salmon. My favorite is the California roll."

"Somehow, I'm not surprised."

After Cami set the trap, sliding a can of reddish tuna flakes just for cats to the back of the wire mesh cage, they situated it next to the house behind the bushes, and at the foot of the white trellis that held some kind of climbing greenery. They crawled out of the beds and brushed dirt and mulch from their hands and legs. The gray Pontiac still sat under a streetlight at the curb.

"I wonder if that's how the killer got down so quickly," Harley mused, staring at the trellis she'd never really paid attention to before. "It looks pretty sturdy, not like the cheap, flimsy ones."

Cami turned to peer at the white trellis against the shadowed brick. "More than likely. The police were down here earlier pouring plaster into footprints."

"Ever efficient." Harley couldn't resist one last call of *kitty, kitty, kitty* before they went in, but there was no answering miaoow or indignant yowl. "Strangely," she said, "I don't want to go to bed without Sam there to irritate me. He likes to bite my feet when I wiggle my toes."

"Kinky. But I told you that you're a cat person."

"As much as it pains me to admit it, you must be right."

After Cami left, Harley worked on straightening up the apartment. Police had dusted for fingerprints that left a fine black powder over everything, a complete bust since the guy had worn gloves. They'd taken a few things with them, but she had no idea why. Maybe they thought they'd find fingerprints or DNA. If they wanted DNA, they should have taken Frank with them. He probably still had bits of the killer between his teeth.

"Don't you, Frank?" she leaned over the tank and asked. "Do you still have bits of the bad guy between your sharp little fangs? Or is that red lace I see?" She peered closer into the tank, but Frank obviously had other things on his mind. Cami must have given him more treats, because he barely paid any attention to the face hanging over the top of the tank. She wondered how she must look to him, magnified by the glass, and her face a collage of fleshy spots between wire mesh. Not that he seemed to care either way, as long as he had a piece of apple and a few raisins. Those *were* raisins, weren't they? *Eww.* Maybe looking close was a bad idea.

Straightening up, she decided the rest of the mess could wait. Tomorrow loomed long and fraught with apprehension, anyway. A good night's rest, if not sleep, would go a long way toward keeping her coherent. Besides, with Morgan outside her apartment watching over her, it was about as safe as it could get.

That led to thoughts about how safe she'd be if Morgan was inside her apartment instead of outside, and that line of thought was dangerous. Maybe not so much to her body as to her peace of mind. Well, maybe just a little to her body, since it still got these heated tingles in parts she'd rather not think about right now. Hmm. It could be time to dust off Old Faithful, but it still wouldn't compensate for the real thing.

She fanned her face with her hands. Time to think about something else. *Anything* else.

After a hot shower and thorough shampoo, she brushed her teeth, put Neosporin on all the cuts she'd sustained during the struggle, and put on a pair of men's boxers she'd bought at Target. Great to sleep in, she'd discovered. A moment's deliberation about the risks of being awakened unexpectedly led her to put on a wife-beater just in case. The sleeveless tee shirt covered her and wasn't uncomfortable to sleep in. Then she went to her balcony and called for Sam again, just on the off-chance he might pop up and say *Here I am!* in cat-speak.

He didn't.

She locked the French doors and shoved a chair in front of them, then triple-checked the locks on the hall door. A precaution. She wasn't really scared, just prepared. Yep. It was always smart to be prepared. "A good thing," as Martha Stewart would say. Only she usually meant Crepes Suzette or baskets of painted pine cones, not arming herself against a killer.

While the lock on her bedroom door wasn't as sturdy, it'd at least slow an intruder long enough to give her time to shake her canister of Mace. After a moment's thought, she took the wooden penis off her dresser and put it on the nightstand, too.

All she needed was Nana's gun and she'd qualify as a mobster.

But a girl could never have too many weapons these days. So now she had her cell phone within easy reach and Morgan's number at the top of the list, and the house phone positioned just right. She was ready for anything.

Then, clad in her Looney Tunes men's boxers and the kind of tee shirt men who beat their wives usually wore, she went to bed and tried to relax enough to sleep. Of course she lay awake a long time, tensing at any strange sound, half-expecting an Elvis to leap out from the shadows. Out in the living room, Frank chuckled to himself. She considered bringing him into the bedroom, not so much as an attack-ferret, but as company. It felt precariously solitary, an unfamiliar and uncomfortable feeling she didn't like at all.

Tomorrow, this would hopefully all be over, with the bad Elvis in custody. All she had to do was stay alert. Still, her stomach clenched and her heart thumped.

She squeezed her eyes shut and pretended she was back in California that long-ago day Yogi had held her on his shoulders so she could release a balloon above the Golden Gate Bridge. She'd been four or five, but she still remembered it as vividly as if it had been yesterday. It had been a red balloon, bright against the blue sky as it soared toward a light drift of clouds. They'd watched it until it was only a tiny speck in the distance, pushed by wind currents to the unknown. For her, it'd been a magical moment that she'd held close, though she wasn't sure why. Maybe it had something to do with being free, though she'd never really felt constraints in her childhood. Yogi and Diva believed in letting children discover the world at their own pace. While Eric thrived on that kind of thing, she'd yearned for more structure.

And for indoor toilets. Living in a commune with outdoor showers and toilets had been free, but also free of life's amenities. That's when she discovered that she must be a hedonist, because she liked her comfort too much. It'd been quite a relief to move to Memphis and a real house with indoor plumbing. Maybe she didn't lie under the open sky and stars anymore, but she didn't worry about snakes crawling into bed with her, either.

Life had its perks.

Sleep didn't come quickly. For a long time after the apartment was dark and quiet, she lay awake. Fragments of conversations flew at her like bats in the night. *A groundhog. Hughes on bail bond. Williams has an alibi. Penney's son might want to hurt his father.* Then: *"The past is following you, but it's not your past. You're caught in between. Elvis isn't dead, he's hiding. He finds you in the candlelight . . . but it's not really you . . . "*

What on earth did Diva mean by that? It seemed like she should know, and something hovered just beyond reach, teasing her. How maddening. This had to stop or she'd never sleep. She closed her eyes and focused on the balloon again, the polished blue of the sky and clouds scudding by, the feel of the wind in her face and her father holding onto her legs so she wouldn't fall from his shoulders to the ground. The balloon rose so high, higher and higher as she watched it drift away . . .

Suddenly, a hawk appeared in the sky right next to the balloon. It soared on wind currents, wings outspread as it glided toward the balloon. Talons pierced the thin rubber and the balloon popped with a loud noise she heard clearly. Shocked, she yelled at the hawk to go away, but it was too late. Shreds of bright red fell from the sky and the hawk made a keening sound like laughter.

Yogi swung her down from his shoulders to the ground. He bent, scooped up a rock and threw it at the hawk. The hawk dove toward them from the sky, screaming furiously and looking like a small feathered bomber. Instead of aiming for Yogi, the predator went straight for Harley.

Shouting angrily, Yogi threw himself in front of her and took the brunt of the attack. Talons sunk into his shoulder as he fought the creature. Harley rushed at the combatants, not sure what to do, but knowing she had to do something. Sharp talons raked her, and she screamed but didn't let go until the hawk lay on the ground with a broken wing. Yogi started shaking her.

"Harley! Harley! You're all right, wake up!"

She jerked upright in her bed, heart still pounding hard as a jackhammer. Light stung her eyes and she blinked, but instead of

Yogi, Morgan shook her. She sucked in a deep breath.

"What are you doing here? And how did you get in?"

He shrugged. "Easily enough, if you know how. Did you see anyone?"

"No. It was just a nightmare, I guess." She shuddered.

"Well, it scared the hell out of me. I thought maybe Kirkland had let the perp get by him."

"Who's Kirkland?"

Morgan sat down on the end of her bed. "The back door guard."

"Oh. So I rate two guards?"

He grinned. "Not so much you as the killer."

"Well, that's deflating. And here I thought I might be important."

"Only to some of us, babe."

Her eyebrow rose. "I note that you included yourself in that group."

Instead of replying, he bent forward and kissed her hard on the mouth, his hands moving to her shoulders, then up to cradle her face. Oh boy. There went that tingle again, all the way to her toes.

"Want me to send Kirkland home?" Mike asked right about the time her bones melted to jelly. His mouth was still close to hers, too close, and his hands had moved from her shoulders to the front of her wife-beater.

"I suppose I'd be safer with you inside than outside," she managed to murmur.

"Not really, sugar, not really."

"I take it our break is over?"

"As over as it can get."

"Send Kirkland packing."

He did.

"You look pretty mellow for someone who's going to be bait in a little while," Tootsie said when she showed up at the office the next morning. He squinted at her. "Ah. You got some."

"Got some what? Oh. Why do you think that?"

"You have that—"

"I know, that 'just laid' look. Honestly, you'd think I was

wearing a sign or something."

"I'm assuming you were with Mighty Mike Morgan. Are you two back together?"

She flopped into an office chair and it wheeled several feet before she stopped it. Using her heels, she dragged it back toward the desk. "Who knows? It wasn't mentioned. We, um, had other things to talk about."

Pursing his lips, Tootsie said, "I'm quite sure."

She ignored that. "I suppose you've heard all about last night's excitement."

Tootsie punched a buzzing button, sounding a bit harried as he tried to fit in more tourists to the already busy schedule. Another nice article in the *Commercial Appeal* had helped business and lessened fears about MTT being unsafe.

"Of course, I did," Tootsie said when he'd finished the call. "I think the entire police department heard about it. Steve said this is the weirdest case they've had in a while."

"Weirder than the city coroner having a bomb fastened to his chest with barbed wire? And then being charged with doing it himself? He got acquitted eventually. Can you imagine anyone would wrap themselves in barbed wire?"

"No, but that was a few years ago. We're talking recent." He ran his hands through his hair and retied it in a ponytail at the nape of his neck. Faint lines furrowed his brow. "I know you're set on this thing tonight, but I'd rather you reconsider. It's going to be so crowded, and I just don't see how the police can protect you that well."

"Of all people, I'd think you'd have more faith in the MPD."

"I have faith in the police, just not the sanity of a killer. This one's got to be crazy to do what he's done. He doesn't care if it's in plain sight, and the really scary part is that he's gotten away with it so far. Rather clever of him to disguise himself as Elvis in a crowd of Elvises, but I'm not much in the mood to admire his planning."

Harley would have answered, but Rhett Sandler chose that moment to appear at Tootsie's desk.

"You were right. Someone's hacked into the computers," he said in his nasal monotone. "I don't know how much information they managed to access."

Despite his impeccable gray suit, black-rimmed glasses, and

natty little white handkerchief sticking up out of his breast pocket, he looked distraught. It wasn't that easy to tell, since he rarely had any expression at all. Emotions were mostly expressed with his eyebrows, black fur that blended in with his glasses. Now they met in the middle over his nose.

"This one, too," Tootsie said. "I put up some firewalls, but a smart enough hacker can still get in if he's determined enough." He blew out a heavy breath. "Just what we need right now."

"Did you ever find out if the guy who embezzled MTT is still in prison?" Harley asked.

Tootsie nodded. "Locked up tight at the white-collar spa in Millington. He's probably in their library or working out with weights. Hardly payback for nearly sucking the well dry."

"Yes," Monotone Man said, "a good thing you came along to invest."

Harley looked from Sandler to Tootsie. "I *knew* it! No wonder you've been so panicky. You stand to lose money, too."

Tootsie's mouth pursed, and the look he gave Sandler should have scorched his professional strength gray socks. "How indiscreet of you."

Sandler's expression didn't change. "My apologies."

Harley smiled. "One mystery solved. Next thing I know, there'll be an actual Steve-sighting to prove he exists."

"How droll of you," Tootsie said, but she could tell he wasn't angry, only annoyed at being outed as more than a mere employee.

"I'm sure you'll share your reasoning for being so secretive." She waggled her brows.

"Don't hold your breath."

Harley smiled.

Sandler said, with what passed for impatience, "I've traced the identity of the hacker, but the police must become involved now."

"Yes, the police will definitely be involved." Tootsie paused, and then added, "I have a feeling that they already know more than we do anyway."

"Quite likely," Sandler said, then pivoted on his heel and walked back to his office down the hall.

"Have you ever noticed that he walks like a penguin?" Harley mused.

"I'd describe it as more like he's got a stick up his ass. But he's good at what he does, so I have no complaints."

"So the last guy who had his job stole a lot of money?"

"Quite a bit. If not for my investment, Penney would most likely have folded. Fortunately, we came to an agreement—that you are *not* to tell any of the other employees. I prefer being one of the rank and file, not one of the bosses."

"That's so modest of you." Harley crossed her legs and swung a foot back and forth. "Tell me about the last accountant. Did you know him?"

"I met him several times. I started out here as a driver, and when my grandmother died she left me a tidy sum that I decided to invest here and there. Unfortunately, Horton objected. It got tense around here for a while, but then he got caught embezzling so it didn't matter."

"How'd Horton get caught?"

Tootsie looked a little uncomfortable. "Well, I'm the one who discovered the discrepancy when the books were examined before I invested. It was supposed to be routine, but it turned out to be a nightmare. Horton didn't take it kindly."

"I imagine not." Harley swung her foot a little harder, thinking. "So Horton—every time I hear that name I think of the Dr. Seuss book, *Horton Helps A Who*—went to prison?"

"I thought it was *Horton Hears A Who*."

"Whichever. Anyway, I take it he went to prison."

"Ten to twenty. He's been there four years now."

"You checked and he's still there, but he has motive to want to ruin MTT. Maybe he's on work release?"

"Not from prison, no. I checked. What would he have to gain anyway?"

While Tootsie answered another incoming call, Harley mulled this new possibility. Really, he seemed like the most likely candidate, other than Hughes or Larry Penney.

"There's no shortage of suspects," she said when Tootsie finished the call and typed in the information on the computer.

"Horton could have had a partner in crime, maybe, and just didn't rat him out. Maybe it's his partner who's doing this."

"What would he gain?"

"Revenge."

"By killing innocent people? That's pretty sick."

"As you've said a few times, there's no shortage of sickos in the world."

"Lord knows I've met my share of them," Tootsie muttered. "Still, it's impossible for Horton to be behind this. Prisons usually monitor prisoners' mail pretty closely, and honestly I just don't think he's slick enough to carry it off. Vengeful enough, maybe, but not the kind who could sit in a van full of tourists and stick a knife in one of them."

"But if he has a partner?"

Tootsie shook his head. "No evidence of one. Besides, Horton's too greedy to share."

"Maybe he figured better some than none."

"Not Horton. He made less than $40,000 a year, but he had a huge house in Countrywood, a couple of really expensive cars, and his kid went to the best private schools. MTT didn't make enough to support that life-style and share it with anyone else."

"Okay, you've convinced me. It's not him. Bobby says it's not Hughes, so unless it's just a wacko out to rid the world of Elvis impersonators, it has to be the ogre's son. How old is he?"

"Twenty-eight. I've got a photo of him somewhere." He rummaged in the desk drawers then pulled out a folder of photos. "Company picnic. He's standing beside Penney."

Harley stared at the photo with interest. "I didn't know the ogre could smile. Good thing he doesn't do it too often. It looks strange."

Larry Penney stared unsmiling at the camera. He looked to be near six feet and pretty thin. Maybe it was the drugs. "It could be him," she said slowly, "he's about the right build."

"I don't think it's him. He's in and out of rehab too much to spend time plotting murders."

"Who's this guy?" She tapped her finger against the photo.

Tootsie peered at it. "That's Horton. His youngest son is right beside him."

"How old was he in this picture?"

"Somewhere around twelve, I think."

"Maybe he's the one."

"I doubt it. He moved to Hawaii with his mother."

"He could have come back, you know."

"From *Hawaii?*" Tootsie stared at her in disbelief. "Who'd

want to move from Hawaii?"

Exasperated, she put her hands on her hips. "Then we're all out of suspects."

"So it seems. Aren't you relieved? Now you can stay home tonight."

She rolled her eyes. "You're as bad as Bobby. Pretending we're out of suspects isn't a good enough reason not to go all-out to catch this guy."

"I see you won't be swayed. I'll pick you up at six."

"Remember, wear something discreet."

"Darling, I told you, I'll be the very *soul* of discretion."

Harley stared at Tootsie. "You call *this* discreet?"

Unruffled, he gave an elegant shrug of one shoulder. "Don't you like it?"

"Who are you supposed to be?"

"Priscilla Presley, of course."

"Ah. Now I see it. Who else would it be?"

Tootsie wore a wig, the light brown bobbed hair liberally streaked with maroon, looking very much like Elvis's ex-wife now wore her hair. From what Harley could tell, he also wore a black leather miniskirt, a gorgeous luminous bronze silk blouse and expensive Prada heels.

"A bit much with the heels, don't you think?" she asked, but he shook his head.

"Not at all. Priscilla has style."

Harley slid into the buttery-soft leather seat and closed the car door. "I feel underdressed. You should have told me you'd be in disguise tonight."

"Girlfriend, you're always underdressed. And someone has to be in disguise, since you've decided to paint a bulls-eye on your back."

"Surely you're not talking about my shirt."

Snorting, Tootsie put the Acura in gear and took off from the curb outside her building. As he sped off, Harley looked back, and to her surprise, saw Sarah Simon peering out her living room window. Wow. That was a rare sighting, rather like Punxsutawney Phil. If Sarah was seen, there was sure to be six more weeks of Elvis festivities.

"Yes," Tootsie said, turning onto Poplar, "I'm talking about your tee shirt. Could it *be* any more noticeable?"

"You're one to talk, Priscilla. Besides, green is a good color for me."

"Neon green? You look like a leprechaun puked on you."

"Since you're kind enough to worry if I get killed, I'll refrain from mentioning your black leather miniskirt, even if I do think you'd be right at home on the back of a hog with some guy named Mad Dog or Killer."

"As intriguing as that sounds, I'll blend right in tonight. I predict I'll even be asked to sign autographs."

"Modesty dies a quick death in your company, I see." Harley leaned her head back against the seat. "Besides, this tee shirt is loose and hides the wire I'm wearing. A police woman wired me up, but I got this shirt in New Orleans. A rather pithy motto, I think."

"*You shuck 'em, I'll suck 'em* refers to crawfish or oysters, I presume."

"Well, of course. Not that I will, though. I don't like either. I just like this tee shirt."

Sunlight glinted off the Acura's hood and into her eyes, and she lowered the visor. "Damn. I forgot my sunglasses."

"We don't really have time to go back. I think I have an extra pair in the glove box."

Harley found a pair of bright red cat-eye sunglasses crusted with rhinestones. She put them on and turned to look at him. "Look at me. I'm Elton John."

"*Sir* Elton John." He glanced at her. "Come to think of it, there is a strong resemblance."

She said something quite rude and sat back. "I can't believe I forgot my sunglasses. I lost track of time while I was hunting for Sam, I guess."

"Still no sign of him?"

She shook her head. "No. He's probably at the zoo teasing the lions and standing in line for his cut of their dinner."

"Sam's too selfish to share. He also likes his creature comforts. He'll be back."

"Unless he's gotten lost, or hurt, or . . . " She didn't want to think about the implications. "We're supposed to meet Yogi and the other finalists at the Heartbreak Hotel, and then take a van from there up to the Perpetual Garden."

"If it wasn't for the killer lying in wait to slaughter us all, I'd be excited about this. I've never been to Graceland."

"What? You've never been to Graceland? As many times as you've booked tours, given the spiel, even driven the vans, you've *never* been in the mansion?"

"Not once. I did go around back one time looking for a lost German and found him sitting in one of the cars—EPE was polite about it, but not at all understanding, I might add—but other than that, I've never crossed the threshold."

"Amazing."

"Isn't it? Tonight will be another adventure for me."

"Let's hope that's all it is."

Tootsie looked over at her, and she knew they were both thinking the same thing. Tonight it was going to be "do or die trying."

Yogi and Diva were waiting for them at the Heartbreak Hotel. The large pink structure sat just across the street from Graceland, convenient to tourists and much safer than walking the area at night. Sad to say, this neighborhood of nice homes and quiet living had gradually turned into a collage of car lots, Elvis-related tourist traps, and high-traffic that lured more than just people who came to honor their idol. When Elvis was still alive, it'd been an upscale neighborhood called Graceland, the white mansion being just one more nice house among several big houses set back on wooded lots from Highway 51. The mansion had been named for the neighborhood. Who knew that one day it'd be an icon recognized around the world? After his mother died and Vernon wed again, Elvis bought his father and his new wife a house on the next street and put a gate through the back fence for easy access. Vernon Presley died after Elvis, and the gate no longer existed.

Despite silent reassurances that everything would be fine, Harley's stomach knotted and her heart thumped an escalated beat against her ribs. When they walked into the hotel lobby, Yogi saw her and Tootsie immediately. He came toward them through the crowd, his eyes a little wide when he looked at Tootsie.

"You look just like Priscilla," he said.

Apparently, he was right, because people stared at them and whispered, and a few clutched autograph books a little tighter, as if poised to advance.

"Except for the Adam's apple," Harley pointed out. "And he's taller."

"Small details," Tootsie said with a smile. "You should have come as Lisa Marie."

"Then how would the killer recognize me?"

"Good point."

"Is, uh, everyone here?" Harley asked her father.

He said Eric couldn't come. "A music gig tonight. Train crash music."

Harley looked at her mother. Diva smiled. "The cards say you'll be fine."

"Great." She barely refrained from rolling her eyes. She'd never had much faith in the cards. It just seemed preposterous that painted card stock could tell the future. Harley had decided that Diva really used tarot as props for her own uncanny abilities. Years of experience should have convinced her that Diva possessed a sixth sense, but pragmatism always interfered. Maybe it was she who was different, not her mother.

But what if Diva was wrong? It could happen.

Still, Harley felt much better when she finally spied Morgan. He drifted through the crowd aimlessly, never looking their way. The dark beard and mustache wouldn't fool anyone who knew him well, but maybe the killer would be too focused on her to notice.

That thought made her stomach jump again.

"It's about to start," Yogi said excitedly, and Harley turned to see Claude Williams at the hotel doors, escorting Preston Hughes and the finalists toward a waiting van.

Williams gave a start when he saw Harley and Tootsie, his eyes going big as goose eggs at the Priscilla look-alike.

"You . . . you're not Priscilla," he said, after surveying Tootsie.

"Tonight I am." Tootsie smiled and batted his fake eyelashes. "Make-up magic."

A fan rushed forward and held out a notebook. "Ms. Presley, will you please sign this for me?" she asked. "It's such an honor to meet you!"

Tootsie gave Williams a wickedly impish glance and said "Of course. What's your name?"

"Emma Rutherford."

He took the pen and book she held out and signed with a flourish, then gave it back to her. "There you go, Emma. Thank you for coming to honor Elvis and his contributions to music."

"You'll get arrested for impersonating her," Williams said angrily when the happy fan went back to join her friends, and Tootsie shook his head.

"No, I won't. Not only is she a public figure, but I signed my own name. If Emma looks close enough, she'll be able to tell the difference, but I used lots of curls so it'll take a while."

Harley looked at him. "You're always surprising me. I never realized how entertaining you are."

"Baby, you ain't seen *nothing* yet."

"That I believe."

Once on the van, a little crowded with the impersonators and some of their families, it took longer than usual to cross Elvis Presley Boulevard because of the crowds. With dark closing in, everyone lit their candles as they waited at the iron gates with the musical notes on them. A few guards held back the fans as the gates opened and the van cruised slowly through, continuing up the gently curved driveway to stop in front of the mansion. An air of solemnity marked their descent from the van, as if they were at a funeral instead of a candlelight vigil for a man dead since 1977.

Several people were already there, the usual guards positioned for crowd control, ropes set up in front of the graves to guide people around so it didn't get too chaotic, and lights gleaming on the tombstones. Flowers, teddy bears, letters, cards, and even a sheet cake frosted with Elvis's likeness and dates of his birth and death, were placed around the markers. Three graves: Elvis in the center, his parents on each side of him. Behind the graves on one side was the pool, on the other the half-shell-shaped memorial where people often sat on the steps to meditate.

"Just act normal," Harley murmured to Tootsie, "and don't let on to Yogi that we expect anything to happen. You know how he is. He'd be sure to say or do something weird and blow it for us."

Tootsie patted the ends of his bobbed wig with one hand, his long fingernails painted blood red. "All we need is your Nana here to make things really interesting."

"Please. I'm nervous enough without the reminder of her hauling around a loaded pistol."

"Don't worry, you're wired for sound and there's bound to be enough cops here to pounce on the guy."

"I'm not really nervous. Honest."

"Bullshit."

"Yeah, you're right. Does it show?"

"Your secret is safe." He patted her arm. "There's your cue, girlfriend. Step on up. I'm right behind you."

There had to be several thousand people in the line that wound like a serpent down the driveway, out the gates onto the sidewalks, and down the street. Elvis Presley Boulevard had been blocked off, a precaution since a car had slammed into tourists a few years back. Only a single lane stayed open, and traffic guards directed the vehicles.

The gates swung slowly open and fans began the procession, walking solemnly up the hill. An eerie hush fell over the crowd.

Harley took a deep breath. "All right, Priscilla," she whispered. "Showtime!"

Butterflies square-danced in her stomach as she lit her candle, following her father and the other finalists. Preston Hughes headed the line, dressed in black leather. No one said anything as they walked slowly between the pool and the gravesites enclosed by black iron pickets.

It got so quiet Harley heard the thundering rush of blood in her ears as it raced to keep up with her rapid heartbeat. Every shadow beyond the lights looked sinister. Tall trees made black silhouettes against floodlights. If she tried to see past them, all she could make out were the bright spots in front of her eyes. Just as well.

Six Elvises stood ceremoniously in front of the graves, their lit candles wavering ellipses that illuminated their faces. Yogi stood right beside Preston Hughes, and as always, silent tears slid down his cheeks. He wasn't alone. Others had tears in their eyes. A magnificent tribute, she supposed, to a man who'd been a legend even in his own time.

Yogi stood a little straighter, and in his clear baritone began to sing, *"Amazing Grace,"* the hymn that had been one of Elvis's favorites rising heavenward past the tall oaks. Others began to sing, too, a swelling crescendo that would have been more moving if Harley wasn't so scared.

She tried to focus on her candle, but her peripheral vision kept waiting for a maniac to burst out of the trees or crowd to attack her. Rationality told her he'd wait until she was more accessible, but nerves stretched a little too tightly insisted that he'd succeeded in plain sight before and could do it again before anyone realized what was happening.

"Steady, girlfriend," Tootsie murmured when her candle began to shake a little too hard. "You're covered."

She kept her head down as if focused on the candle and graves. It'd be nice if she could spot at least one of the undercover cops, but maybe that was the point. If she could find them, so could the Killer Elvis.

Everyone started singing, and Tootsie nudged her with his elbow. "Participate. Sing."

"You've never heard me sing," she muttered to her candle. "I frighten crows."

"No one will notice. Just move your lips."

The Elvises began to move around the graves, up the steps to stand with their candles on the top step of the colonnaded half-shell. Harley saw Yogi wipe his eyes. She looked toward her mother. Diva remained on the fringes of the crowd, standing by a tall planter, but if she'd been trying to hide, she failed. Diva always stood out in a crowd. Not just because she wore long skirts with bells and tie-dyed tunic tops, but because she still looked as young and beautiful as she must have looked back in the seventies.

A slight breeze lifted long strands of Diva's blonde hair, and tiny bells tinkled as she lifted her arm to push it behind her ear. Harley couldn't hear the bells, but she saw them shimmy and knew from long experience the sound they made.

While her mother moved to stand below Yogi and the other impersonators, fans filed past in what seemed to be an unending line. Ellipses of light flickered in the cool breeze that made the night bearable, faces mostly sober and reflective as they passed by the graves.

Harley and Tootsie stood to one side, Harley with her back next to the planter and not far from the concrete shell occupied by impersonators and EPE employees. Somewhere in this crowd were undercover cops, and it was both comforting and unnerving that she had no idea who they might be. She'd tested her wire before leaving home and knew it was in good working order. The police already knew the range and were in position. All she had to do was bait the killer.

With that in mind, she eased away from Tootsie to amble along the edge of the concrete walkway. The grounds of Graceland were a river of light. The well-lit highway and shops across the street were mostly hidden by the trees and a high stone fence. To her right was the mansion, lit up as if Elvis was home. Behind that was the old office, the building dark now that no tourists were visiting. Next to it was the studio where Elvis had spent many nights singing with the Jordanaires. A three-rail fence separated the backyard from the pasture where a few horses still grazed. At night, subdivision lights glowed beyond the pasture and high fieldstone fence that surrounded the property. The horses were only black silhouettes against the streetlights.

A sudden chill raked down her spine and she didn't know why. Hair rose on the nape of her neck, and her muscles tensed.

Nothing looked amiss. Fans were still weeping and singing, candles still flickered, and the air was still heady with fragrance from flowery wreaths. Red and white roses, carnations, gladiolas, and even tulips flanked the graves. Teddy bears and handwritten notes were tucked among the flowers.

Harley edged toward the shadows, hoping the undercover guys noticed her. If the killer was here, he was being very cautious. Maybe temptation would draw him out. Guards focused on the fans to make certain they kept behind the ropes.

Sometimes an overeager mourner tried to slip beneath the ropes to place a tribute directly on the graves, but the guards discouraged that. If they didn't, the graves would disappear under a mound of stuffed animals, letters, and whatever other tributes the fans thought appropriate.

As *Amazing Grace* ended, Yogi segued into another Elvis song. Beside him, Preston Hughes looked furious. Harley smiled. Hughes probably felt like Yogi had stolen his thunder, but if he'd taken the lead Yogi wouldn't have been able to. Anyway, Yogi hadn't intended any insult by it. It wasn't in his nature to be malicious. He was probably just so swept away by the vigil festivities he couldn't help himself.

There was no sign of Williams, and she wondered if he was

present at all. There was something going on between those two, she just couldn't figure out what. Hughes still seemed the most likely to kill, and Lydia would have known him from previous contests. Of course, she'd have known Williams as well. That gave both of them a good reason to kill her, if there was such a thing as a good reason to kill anyone. Motives for killing Elvis impersonators, however, were known only to the murderer.

But why kill *me?* Harley mused. *I obviously can't identify him or he'd already be in jail.*

The only identification she could make would be if he popped up looking like a mime or stuffed into a giant Redbird costume.

Or if he still wore that strong, unpleasant aftershave. She wondered if he knew how distinctive it was, or if he even realized that he smelled like he'd bathed in a vat of it.

A lot of things went through her mind as she waited for terror to strike, most of it things she'd rather not think about at all. An hour passed, then two, and then a string of unbearably boring hours as she watched Elvis mourners file past. Of the finalists, only Yogi remained under the gentle curve of concrete.

He always stayed until the last, and had always come home bleary-eyed and exhausted but exhilarated. Yogi liked to wring every drop of emotion from his annual bout of grief and adulation. Diva had better sense. She'd gone home a long time ago.

So had Preston Hughes.

A hand touched her shoulder and she jumped, heart in her throat. When she whirled around she bumped into a uniformed guard. He caught her and said, "We think you should stand over there, ma'am, out of the way." He indicated the shadows beyond the ropes with a glance in that direction.

"In the dark? Can you still see me?"

"Yes. I'll check on you. Don't worry."

The trouble with undercover cops was that she could never pick them out of the crowds. A uniformed guard should have been easy to recognize, but she'd never thought the police would do that. She'd thought the undercover guys would be disguised as fans, but maybe this made better sense. Who'd suspect one of the guards? It was too obvious.

Harley waited a few moments, so as not to make it too obvious she'd been directed to go to a different spot. The crowd had thinned out, though more fans still moved in the slow, steady procession.

It was rather comforting to know the police were so thorough and close by. Even if she *was* wired, there were too many things that could happen if left on her own. A sidewalk led to the back of the mansion and to the recording studio where awards filled every available space on the high walls. To discourage tourists wandering away from the vigil, the lights were off and it was dark as she ambled casually toward the shadows behind the mansion.

A cool breeze eased the night's heat, and hungry mosquitoes had her slapping at her arms and face. Even with bug spray, the damn things found her irresistible. If only the rest of the world felt that way.

The guard had disappeared, but she thought she saw an undercover cop she recognized. It had to be the guy Morgan called Chainsaw. She didn't know what his real name was, and since it made her a little queasy to even think about how he might have gotten that nickname, she'd never asked.

Chainsaw, or his twin, looked in her direction. Like Morgan, he sported a beard, but he was easy to recognize because of his size. He was about the width of a side-by-side refrigerator, and a little taller. A little beyond him stood Tootsie, looking definitely out of place in his disguise as Priscilla. He kept tugging at the back of his skirt, and she had a momentary fear he'd brought along a weapon of some kind. Then she realized he was adjusting his thong underwear. He'd been complaining about it earlier, grumbling that the damn panties rode up and chafed him where he was the tenderest. She'd tried not to roll her eyes, but failed.

A sense of the ridiculous had always had the power to amuse her, and the sudden thought that no stranger would believe it if she told them she was waiting in the shadows for an Elvis impersonator to kill her, while a man dressed up as Priscilla Presley was one of her bodyguards and her father wore a white jumpsuit studded with fake gems and wept by the grave of a man dead over thirty years. It sounded pretty odd. *Preposterous*, a stranger unacquainted with her would say, and she'd have to admit that they were right.

Still, the reality of it struck her as quite funny, and she couldn't hold back a bubble of laughter, even though that seemed strange, too, standing alone in the shadows and cackling wildly to herself.

The police listening to her must be wondering if she'd cracked under the pressure.

Then two things happened at once. A woman began yelling that her purse had been stolen and someone grabbed Harley from behind and clapped a hand over her mouth. Just before the gloved hand covered her nose as well, she recognized the strong smell of aftershave.

Struggling didn't do her much good. His arm around her ribs and chest held her too tight. She clawed at the hand over her mouth, desperate to breathe. Blood pounded loud in her ears, and little lights exploded in front of her eyes, while candle flames and spotlights did a weird dance. It felt as if her lungs were bursting. Pinwheels of light whirled faster and faster until they turned into a single light that smothered the shadows. Then a buzz sounded and a shock went through her. All her muscles turned to jelly. Abruptly, darkness swallowed the light.

Then . . . nothing.

Nineteen

Harley woke with a start. It was dark and her head hurt. So did her throat. She tried to speak, to ask where the hell she was, but it came out as a smothered croak.

"Ah, you're awake," a voice crooned, and she blinked her eyes in an attempt to make sense of the shadows.

Tape covered her mouth, but thankfully not her nose. She could breathe, but it was obvious he didn't want conversation. Something bound her hands behind her, and her feet were tied so tightly her circulation was cut off. So she glared in the direction of the voice to show her contempt.

He chuckled. "Still defiant, are you? You've caused me a great deal of trouble, you know. Not like the others. They were quick, easy, foolish. You, though. You've been a challenge. I like games. I always win, but you've been quite a test of my abilities."

Leaning forward, he was a black silhouette against the faint glow of lights behind him. She blinked to clear her vision, heart pounding so hard in her chest he had to hear it.

Harley swallowed hard, hoping the guys listening to the wire heard his confession, as well as figured out where he'd taken her. It had better be soon, or she was going to be his next victim.

Surprisingly, he ran the back of his fingers over her cheek, chuckling again when she flinched. "Do you think I'm going to kill you? Not here. After the last time, I want to make sure nothing can go wrong. Besides, I'm enjoying myself."

She glared at him, but he found that amusing, too. "I like that you're not going to make it easy for me. I noticed you on the van, you know, how confident you were, like nothing in your life had ever gone wrong. Like you'd never been left stranded, alone, with the important things in your life jerked away so fast you hit the ground hard. It leaves you stunned, hopeless. Furious."

He leaned closer, so she could see his eyes behind the Elvis mask. They were dark and glittering, with an almost fanatical light so evil that she couldn't help a shudder.

Another chuckle came from behind the mask. "I'm enjoying this too much. Vengeance is sweet."

Then he stood up and went to stand beside what she could now see was a door with blinds that blocked out most of the light. Faint light revealed some kind of uniform. He eased aside two of the slats to peer out.

"They haven't noticed you're missing. I think it's time."

Harley realized they were in what had been Elvis's office. Now it was a tourist spot, and during regular hours had a running video of Elvis being interviewed on a TV behind the desk, talking about his stint in the Army. It was an old black and white film that flickered, but Elvis was so young and handsome and shy that it was one of the best interviews of him she'd ever seen.

If only she could get some of the duct tape off her mouth, she could mutter where they were so the cops listening to her wire would know she was in deep trouble. She wiggled next to the desk and scraped her face against the side. It didn't seem to help much. Keeping one eye on the killer looking out the window, she rubbed against the edge of the desk until her cheek burned. When the Elvis looked around, she stopped.

Another chuckle came from his direction. "The first thing I did was get rid of that wire. It's in the bushes where the cops can't see it, but it's still recording the vigil so they won't realize you're missing for a little while longer. I'm missing a chance to get rid of that pervert in the leather skirt, though. This would be a perfect opportunity to kill him as well, but he's still standing too close to the crowd. Everyone's looking at him in that ridiculous getup, and the risk's too great. But tonight you were easy enough."

Harley just stared at him. Her wire was gone. *Damn, damn, damn!* Real fear oozed through her veins. No one had missed her, which meant no one was looking for her. Once he got her away from Graceland she was doomed. Of course, if he got too panicky he might kill her right here and leave her body on the cold floor. It'd be easy enough. He still wore the guard's uniform.

He couldn't be the one who'd asked her to move back a little bit, because she hadn't smelled that awful aftershave. Were there two killers? Maybe this guy and Hughes?

They both had motives, insane as they were. One for vengeance, the other for triumph. It couldn't be for money. There'd been no demands made and nothing that she could see to gain, unless Rhett Sandler had come up with something about the payroll computer being hacked.

A burst of noise made the fake Elvis turn back to look out the window again. Harley worked at the restraints on her wrists while rubbing her face against the corner of the desk. She finally got a corner of the duct tape over her mouth free. She scrubbed harder at the corner of the tape until it only covered half her mouth.

Her head still throbbed and her stomach sat at the bottom of her throat. The Elvis had turned to look outside again, and she sensed his growing tension. One of her Catholic school prayers came to mind, the Our Father whirling round and round in her head. If she was going to die, it wouldn't hurt to remind God that she *tried* to be good. Most of the time. Some of the time.

Okay, infrequently, but most of her sins were venial ones. Surely He'd take that into account? Then, just to be on the safe side, she reminded the Earth Mother that she didn't litter or defile the earth. Diva would be so proud. She firmly believed that Native American respect for the earth and environment went hand in hand with a strong belief in a Higher Power.

Then the deadly Elvis turned back to stride toward her, and all thought went completely out of her head. Fear took over, a thudding apprehension making her numb. She strained at the stuff binding her wrists. It didn't loosen. Then instinct took over. When Elvis leaned over her, she did the only thing she could. She hit him squarely in the crotch with both feet. It worked.

He went down like a sack of potatoes, bent over and retching. Harley knew she'd only disabled him temporarily. When he recovered, he'd most likely be in a nasty mood.

She skidded across the floor like an inchworm until she reached the door. Miraculously, she somehow got to her feet. Behind her, Elvis groaned, but the retching had stopped. She had to do something quick. So she banged her head against the glass window of the door, buffered a little by the blinds. It didn't break. She hit it again, harder this time. Her eyes crossed but the window burst with a loud sound. An alarm immediately blared with a *whoop whoop* sound.

Sticking her head close to the gaping hole, she hollered as loud as she could, "Help! Help! Fire! Fire!" The last came from the safety course Mr. Penney had insisted the employees take. The reasoning was that people often ignored the cry for help, but usually responded pretty fast to the *Fire!* thing. Not that anyone would hear her over the shrieking alarm. Thankfully, someone did. Not the undercover cops she expected, but Yogi. He hit the door with his shoulder, but the deadlock held. Panicked now, Harley bent to try to turn the little knob with her chin. That didn't work. Elvis's gasping had stopped. She turned her head sideways and used her teeth. That worked. Yogi burst into the office.

"Are you all right?" he asked as he brushed past her.

Harley had seen murder in his eyes, and she said *Yes* as fast as she could with her teeth and mouth still smarting.

Yogi barely listened. He bore down on the Elvis, knocked him back to his knees and kicked him. Hard. Elvis grunted and tried to get up, but Yogi kept kicking him in the stomach, the face, his rib cage.

This is a pacifist? Yogi? Harley yelled at him to stop before he killed him, but Yogi ignored her. He kept making growling sounds deep in his throat, sounding like King when he cornered one of those big leathery rawhide toys he liked to chew into a soggy lump.

She hopped on her bound feet toward her father. Maybe she could distract him from killing the guy, though it did seem rather justified. From long experience, however, she knew the cops wouldn't agree. They usually looked askance at that sort of thing.

"Yogi!" she hollered again, as close to his ear as she could get since he kept kicking the Elvis sprawled on the floor. "Stop or you'll kill him!"

Panting, Yogi said, "Sounds good to me."

"Agh!" she said back.

About that time, the cavalry arrived. The first thing they did was pull Yogi away from the bloody thing on the floor.

Someone turned on the lights, and she tried to see who the Elvis was since his mask had come off. He looked vaguely familiar, though it was hard to tell because of the swelling, blood, and shoe imprints on his face.

Cops got busy, hauling the Elvis to his feet, slapping handcuffs on his wrists and reading him his rights. If not for

Morgan, they may well have taken Yogi in, too. Assault and attempted murder charges wouldn't help her father's life-style. After convincing his fellow officers that Yogi had only acted in defense of his daughter, Morgan turned to look at her.

"Hi there," she said through swollen lips. "Fancy seeing you here."

"Why do you always go for the crotch?" He didn't sound really mad about it. He must have been thinking of their first encounter, when she'd kicked him in the crotch, too.

"It just seems the right thing to do," she said.

He smiled. "Rules according to Harley."

"Yep. Always seems to work."

"You know, I may just leave you tied up. It's kind of sexy."

She lifted an eye brow. "I'm not really into the bondage thing."

"The longer I know you, the more it seems appropriate. Insurance against your uncanny ability to get in trouble."

Rather indignant, she said, "Trouble always finds me, I don't go looking for it, you know."

"It's the same thing. By the way, you've just been rescued again."

"Well, if I had to depend on my guards, I wouldn't have gotten rescued at all! Breaking the window is what helped. That I did all by myself."

"So you did. Guess I'll untie you, though it's against my better judgment."

She tried to blow a raspberry but her lips didn't cooperate. She settled for a glare instead.

Just as Morgan got her wrists and ankles loose, a loud noise came from outside the door. "I'm one of her bodyguards and I'm going in! Move out of my way or I'll have to get ugly."

One of the cops stuck his head into the office. "There's a woman—or guy—out here who says she's—*he's?*—a bodyguard. Looks like Priscilla Presley."

"Let Priscilla in." Morgan sounded amused.

Tootsie burst into the room. His wig was askew, and he clattered across the floor on high heels. "Are you all right?" He looked anxious.

Harley coughed. "I'm fine. Honest. Just a little bruised."

He still looked worried, but he calmed down a bit. Then he

looked at the unmasked Elvis and his eyes got really big. "Jimmy Horton? *You're* the killer?"

Jimmy Horton. His face was so battered it was hard to tell if he was even human, but apparently Tootsie knew how. Horton glared at Tootsie. "If it wasn't for you, my father never would have gone to prison, you queer!"

"Sticks and stones. And it wasn't me who got him into prison. He did it all by himself."

"He'd have made things right. You wouldn't listen, you or that bastard Penney!"

"Just how would he have made things right? He didn't have any of the money left that he stole. He'd spent it all, down to a couple of thousand. Hardly enough to cover the couple hundred thousand he took."

"You didn't give him a chance. You had to drag the cops into it. I had to watch while he went through a trial and got sent to that hell of prison. Every time I visit him, he's got new bruises, new cuts. He doesn't deserve that."

"You'll forgive me if I don't agree," Tootsie said. "He committed a crime and a jury decided he'd done it. It wasn't exactly a shock since he'd left so many clues."

"No one would have noticed if not for you!"

Tootsie looked at him for a minute, and then asked, "So you think killing innocent people is a good payback?"

"*I* didn't do anything. Whoever did ruined your business, though. Obviously it was too damned easy to hack into your computers and find out what they needed to know. Seems like you aren't the great computer whiz you pretend to be."

Tootsie ignored that. "But what did Lydia ever do to you?"

Horton shrugged. "Nothing. I didn't do anything to her, and you can't prove I did."

Harley felt like smacking the smug bastard. She took a step forward, but Morgan grabbed her arm. "Don't worry. He'll get what's coming to him."

Sneering, Horton said, "You won't find any evidence that can convict me."

Morgan smiled. "I think the DNA we got from one of the crime scenes will be enough to send you to prison for a long, long time."

Horton stared at him, obviously stunned. "No, that's not—"

"Lydia caught you. She got skin under her fingernails when she tried to fight you off. You should have been more careful."

One of the officers took Horton roughly by the arm and shoved him toward the door. As they passed by him, Tootsie swung his heavy purse and hit Horton a good clip on the chin. Horton staggered sideways and Tootsie hit him again.

Then an officer caught his arm. "That's enough, Priscilla."

The last thing Harley heard Horton say was that he'd have all their badges, that he hadn't done anything wrong. She turned around to look at Morgan and Tootsie.

"He's nuts. Can he get off on an insanity plea?"

"Doubtful," Morgan said. "He was sane enough to plan a complicated series of murders. Besides, no prosecutor would allow it."

"Good. He deserves to fry. Is Tennessee a death penalty state?"

"Vicious little thing, aren't you."

Harley nodded. "Only when necessary."

Morgan grinned. "You're something, you know that?"

"Yes. It's one of my better virtues."

Tootsie took her home. Her apartment was still a mess, but Frank seemed happy enough. He made chuckling noises in his glass tank, and nibbled on some ferret food.

"Home sweet home." Harley collapsed into one of her overstuffed chairs. It tilted to the right. A brief examination revealed a broken leg. *One of the hazards of getting mixed up with a serial killer*, she thought.

"Sit up," Tootsie said as he hovered over her, and she looked up at him.

"What's that?"

"Neosporin, a warm washrag, and bandages. I'm going to clean you up and take care of your face. Then I'll put some ice on your mouth. You look like a duck."

She sat up in the tilting chair and muttered, "Flattery will get you anywhere."

After Tootsie did his doctor routine he offered to stay a while, but she waved him off. "I'm fine. Go home, Priscilla."

Grinning, Tootsie hefted his Jimmy Choo purse and left,

telling her to lock the door behind him. She did, then went out onto her balcony and called for Sam. He didn't answer. Where was he? Was he lost and gone forever? The thought depressed her and left tears in her eyes. She sniffled.

"I'm getting to be too much like Cami," she sighed, and went back inside. The sight of his litter box didn't help. As late as it was, she decided to go down and look in the trap under the bushes to see if he'd been fooled into going for the can of tuna.

He hadn't. The trap had, however, snared a raccoon that didn't look at all happy. It curled tiny fingers in the wire and stuck its nose through one of the small squares. Beady eyes looked at her hopefully. She tried not to notice.

"Are you the little beast who gets into the garbage dump all the time? You make quite a mess, you know. I shouldn't let you go."

She let it go, of course. It sprang out from the trap and attached itself to her leg. She screeched. That scared the raccoon so badly it fell off her leg. Then it took off for wherever it was urban raccoons went.

A little shaken, Harley didn't bother to reset the trap. Apparently Sam wasn't coming back anytime soon. If at all.

When she went back into the apartment building and stepped into the entrance hall, a door opened. Sarah Simon peered out through the narrow space between the chain-locked door and the door frame.

"Did you lose a cat?"

Harley's stomach jumped. She nodded. "Yes. A loud Siamese. Have you seen him?"

Sarah nodded. "He's in my bathroom. Come and get him. He won't use the newspapers."

Sam is used to more pleasant living arrangements, Harley thought as Sarah closed the door and undid the chain.

Sarah's apartment was piled high with magazines and newspapers. It was clean but cluttered, with stuff sitting everywhere. A big-screen TV sat against one wall, and a huge chair had been placed in front of it. Tables held more figurines and magazines.

"How did you find him?" Harley asked as she followed Sarah through the maze toward the bathroom.

"I didn't. He found me. I heard him scratching on my window screen, and when I saw it was a cat and not a murderer I let him in. My cat died a few months ago, and I thought maybe the fairies sent me a new one."

"Uh huh," Harley said. Sarah might be nuts, but at least she didn't seem homicidal. It did explain a lot of her behavior.

Sarah opened her bathroom door and Sam shot out like a rocket. His fur stood straight out and up, and he looked *pissed.*

Halfway across the room and somewhere in the maze, he must have noticed Harley. He came back a little at a time. When he peered around a stack of *Victoria* magazines, he saw Harley and his eyes narrowed into blue slits. She couldn't tell if he was happy to see her or just mad because she'd taken so long to come get him.

"Are you sure that's your cat?" Sarah asked doubtfully, and Harley nodded.

"Oh yeah. I can tell by the bad attitude."

Sam minced over to her and hissed, then leaped up so that she had to grab him or risk his claws raking down her front. He started to purr and rub his whiskers against her face, and then dug his claws into her arm.

"I think he's ready to go home now," Harley said as she carefully dislodged him from her forearm. "You don't know how grateful I am that you took him in. If there's ever anything you need, just let me know and I'll do my best to help out."

"There is one thing," Sarah said. "You could stop having murderous maniacs up to your apartment. The neighbors are talking."

"Will do."

Harley left, crooning to Sam as she went upstairs. As soon as she unlocked her door and stepped into the living room, he made a leap from her arms and a mad dash under her bed. She didn't much blame him. It must have been an exhausting few days for him.

Before she went to bed, Harley called Cami and told her Sam was back. "In good shape and as ornery as ever."

"Oh, I'm so relieved. Where was he?"

"In a neighbor's apartment. Sarah Simon. She thought the fairies brought him."

"What?"

"True story. Oh, and the killer's in jail. I'll tell you all about it when I come out of the coma I'm planning, okay?"

"Come out of it soon. I can't wait to hear."

When Harley hung up, she staggered toward her bedroom and collapsed on the bed. She debated a bath and changing into a pair of panties, but fell asleep before she could bring herself to do more than lie there under the ceiling fan.

A heavy weight on the side of her bed woke her with a start and she reached out for some kind of a weapon, her heartbeat escalating into a *Flight of the Bumblebee* pace.

"Hey, I'm part of the cavalry," a familiar voice said, and she flopped back onto her pillow.

"How the hell do you always get in through a locked door?"

"Simple. I still have the key you gave me."

"Oh. I could have shot you, you know."

He bent and kissed her until her head started to spin and tingles popped up in vital places. "You don't have a gun," he said after a moment.

"You don't know that."

Morgan curled his fingers into hers and pushed her arms up over her head and deep into her pillow. "Yes I do. If you did, you'd have shot Horton instead of kicking him in the crotch."

"I liked kicking him in the crotch. He was obviously a slow learner. I did it a few times."

"Are your lips still swollen?"

"Tootsie put ice on them. I'm good to go."

"How handy," he murmured deep in his throat. "Want to take a shower with me?"

"Are you saying I stink?"

"Yeah. But that's okay. So do I."

Before she could think up an appropriate insult, he lifted her into his arms and walked toward the bathroom. It took him no time to strip off her clothes and his, and they were in the shower with hot water beating down on them and slick soap making things nice and slippery.

"I thought you wanted your space," she murmured through the pelting water.

"I just said that so you wouldn't snoop around in my case too much."

"And what was your case?" She shuddered when he slipped

his hands down over her well-lathered body.

"Hughes and Williams. They were running a scam on the charity and the tourists."

"I knew it! I *knew* there was something wrong about those guys!"

"Sometimes you scare me."

"You love it."

He laughed softly. "I guess I do."

It was the best shower she'd had in a long time, Harley reflected a few hours later as her bedroom started to get light enough for her to see the wet towels on her floor.

Mike was asleep. That was okay. He'd worked pretty hard these last few hours. She smiled and turned over to throw a leg over him. Not a bad ending to the night.

Not bad at all.

Diva called at noon. "Yogi's on the front page of the paper. He's credited with capturing the serial killer. I think you should come over and congratulate him. Most of the neighborhood has shown up this morning."

"So he's famous, huh."

"As I told you he'd be."

"You're scary."

Diva ignored that and said, "It'd be nice if you'd stop by to pick up Nana on your way. She wanted to be here, too."

Harley closed her eyes. Serenity was so short-lived.

"I'll pick up Nana," she heard herself sigh, and Morgan turned over and started doing things with his fingers that made her speechless.

"I'll expect you in a few hours," Diva said, and Harley hung up. Her mother knew too many things she'd rather she didn't.

She didn't show up at Whispering Pines until 3:00. Nana met her in the lobby.

"It's about damn time you got here. I was just thinking about a quickie with Julio."

Harley winced at the images that summoned. "I thought his name was Rico."

"Oh yeah. So it is. No matter. Let's get out of here, chickie."

Chickie and Nana got to the house on Douglass Street by

three-thirty. Eric met them at the curb. "When are you going to get your car back?" he asked. "This one looks pretty ragged."

"It's a theft deterrent. And I get my car back day after tomorrow. Once I raid my savings account."

"Stop chattering and come inside," Nana said as she opened the gate in the picket fence, marching up the sidewalk. Long-stemmed sunflowers banged against her head and she shoved them to the side. Bumblebees swarmed around her baseball cap. She took a few swats at them and they buzzed off. Not much intimidated Nana.

Yogi met them at the door. His chest was all puffed out and his knuckles had a few cuts. He must have taken some swings at Horton.

"I hear you're famous now," Nana said.

Yogi nodded. "So everyone says."

"You captured that killer, didn't you? Good thing. He was starting to get on my nerves. Is that Sadie in there? I hope she brought some pie."

Without waiting for an answer, Nana went into the kitchen. Harley looked at her brother and Yogi. "Now do you understand why I couldn't stop her from stealing that horse and carriage?"

"Cool chick, no one can stop Nana when she's set her mind on something," Eric said.

Yogi grinned. "She told Diva she wants her gun back. I hope they don't give it to her."

"Don't worry. Bobby isn't too anxious to arm her again. Things happen."

"That's a relief. Did you see the morning paper?"

"Not yet." Yogi held it out and she scanned the headline. "Hey, you're really famous."

Shrugging, her father said, "Not quite the way I thought I'd be, but I guess this is pretty good."

"You saved my life! I think it's much better than pretty good."

Yogi's grin got so wide she thought his face might never be normal again.

"Come on into the kitchen," Eric said. "There's pie and cake. Aunt Darcy sent over some of those good cookies Janet makes. They have lots of icing on the top."

"I'm sold."

They wandered into the kitchen where Sadie Shipley sat on a stool by the breakfast bar and told anyone who'd listen that she'd always known Yogi had it in him to tackle a killer. Yogi rolled his eyes but didn't say anything. Diva just smiled her serene smile.

Harley stuffed her mouth with Janet's cookies. No one made them better. Aunt Darcy was the bomb; Janet was worth every penny she paid her to cook and clean. Darcy had changed a lot in the past months and become much nicer. Madeline and Amanda still had a ways to go.

A pleasant buzz filled the kitchen, reminding Harley of her childhood. Diva had never closed her door to anyone. Over the years, a long line of hippies, drifters, and the adventurous had been invited inside. Some of them, Harley recalled, were former residents of the communes they'd lived in from time to time. It was a mystery to her how they'd found her house, but maybe Diva gave off some kind of vibe that drew them in.

"This isn't sweet tea," Nana said, looking into the glass she'd been given. "What is this crap?"

Diva said calmly, "Chamomile. It's soothing."

"It's crap. Use real tea. This stuff tastes like watered-down flies."

While Harley was trying to figure out if chamomile really did taste like watered-down flies, Morgan showed up.

Nana immediately got all flirty. "Hey handsome, where'd you come from?"

Morgan took it in stride. "Midtown, Mrs. McMullen." He looked over at Harley. "Baroni said to tell you he still expects you to show up and give your statement."

"Bobby Baroni?" Nana snorted. "He still hasn't given me my gun back yet. I'm thinking of suing the entire police department."

"I hope you have a good lawyer."

"I do. He's a real pip."

"By the way, Nana, I brought you something." Harley held out a flowery gift bag.

Nana looked at it suspiciously. "It's not something unpleasant, is it?"

"Why on earth would you think that? It's just something I think you might like."

Nana took the bag and peered into it as if afraid the contents might bite. Then her face lit up. "Hot damn!"

She pulled out the gift and waved the wooden penis in the air. Mrs. Shipley looked puzzled, then shocked.

"Anna Mae? Is that what I think it is?"

"Yep, and a good, big one. Not that I can do anything with it, but it does give me nice memories. Oughta give Rico something to work towards. Why'd you give this to me, Harley?"

"When I was in that casket and vault, I wished I'd made a will. Then I thought—why wait? I'd just give it to you now."

"Did you leave me your bike?" Eric looked hopeful until she shook her head.

"I'm keeping that for a while longer."

Silence had fallen, with Mrs. Shipley still looking shocked, Nana gloating, and Morgan looking bemused. Diva must have thought it was time to say something innocuous.

"Would you care for something to drink?" Diva asked Morgan, and before he could answer Nana said, "Don't drink the tea. It tastes like crap."

Yogi handed Mike an organic root beer. "Try this."

"Thanks. There a lot of talk about you down at the precinct."

Yogi's eyes got wide. "Are they going to charge me with something?"

"Nothing like that. You were pretty amazing. Especially since you didn't know if Horton was armed. He could have had a gun, or used the knife we took off him."

Yogi went pale. "He had a *knife?*"

"A good-sized one. Could have done a lot of damage."

Swallowing hard, Yogi said in a weak voice, "Well, I had to save my little girl."

"You did a bang-up job. Horton's going to be in the hospital a day or two."

"Come along, officer," Harley said, and took him by the arm. "Let's go sit on the porch."

One of the swinging settees was covered with flowery cushions, and they sat on that. It was a nice afternoon as long as they stayed in the shade and under a ceiling fan. Cicadas sang and crickets made chirping noises. The hum of bumblebees mixed in with the other sounds. They sat for a while in silence, until Harley got drowsy.

"This root beer isn't too bad." Morgan took another drink from the bottle.

She roused. "It tastes like crap."

They both laughed at her imitation of Nana. Then Morgan leaned close.

"We could sneak out of here if we're quiet."

"I can't. I brought Nana and I have to take her home."

"Eric can do it. By the way, there's something I've been wanting to ask you."

Her stomach got tight. Surely he wasn't going to ask her to move in with him, or elope, or anything that crazy. That was something she wasn't at all sure she was ready to do.

He didn't. Instead he asked, "Why does your brother have a normal name and you don't?"

"I do too have a normal name. It's just that Harley and Davidson sound funny said together. Besides, Eric doesn't exactly have a normal name."

"What's wrong with Eric as a name?"

"Nothing. But his middle name is Toke."

"Strangely enough, that's not very surprising. So go get Toke to take Nana home. I've got something I want to do with you."

"Does it involve Mr. Happy? I've already seen a lot of him today."

"Not Mr. Happy. Though you could appreciate my efforts a little better."

"There's always another chance for personal growth, grasshopper."

"I love it when you talk Ninja to me. Come on." He stood up and took her hand. "Go tell Toke he's the designated driver tonight."

Morgan drove his red Corvette. He stuck a CD into the player and turned it up. Then he took her to the Tom Lee Park that overlooked the Mississippi River. They parked in the lot next to the bluffs. Dusk had begun to fall. The river rushed past, as it had for centuries, and barges glided through the currents leaving cone-shaped wakes behind. Jewel played on the CD, and her husky voice sang about lost love.

"How did you know I liked Jewel?" Harley asked.

"You have her CDs all over your apartment."

She rested her head against the back of the seat. Slowly, her earlier tension faded away and was replaced with a sense of peace. The fiery ball of sun sinking beyond the horizon made streaked patterns in the sky. In the distance, cars streamed across the M-shaped bridge that would light up the night when it got darker. It felt like the tension from everything she'd been through oozed out from her feet and through the car mats onto the pavement below.

Morgan reached over and took her hand, rubbing his thumb over her wrist. He didn't say anything and she was glad. Speaking would ruin the moment. They sat there until the sun left only a faint gleam, staining the sky red and turning the clouds blue. Lights popped on the bridge, so the M was much more visible. A few other cars had shown up. Some of the passengers got out to meander along the concrete walks edging the bluffs.

She was content to just sit there, the top down on the Corvette and a soft breeze blowing. After the last weeks, it was as close to perfect as she could get. Then Morgan handed her a glass of wine he'd taken from his small cooler in what could have been a back seat but wasn't.

Okay, *now* it was perfect.

A sip of chilled zinfandel made her sigh with pleasure. "I'm officially in love," she said.

"You mean you weren't before?"

"Maybe."

"Tease."

"If it works, why change?" Harley slid him a glance. He looked back at her with such a sizzling gaze that her mouth got dry despite the wine. That tingle headed south again, and the air held heat that had nothing to do with the weather.

Morgan smiled. "Sure you don't want to see Mr. Happy tonight?"

"Come to think of it, I would enjoy the pleasure of his company."

"Shall we go?"

"As fast as we can."

It was one of the best nights yet. Maybe she *could* fall in love. While she waited for it, she could certainly enjoy all the perks.

Until next time . . .

Afterword

I have, of course, taken liberties with certain dates and facts, as writers of fiction are prone to do. *Images of the King* is indeed the "Super Bowl" of Elvis competitions in August every year, with some very talented performers and dedicated organizers, none of whom are depicted nor resemble in any way the characters in this book. Most of the Memphis tourist attractions are accurately described, with a certain fictional license to fit my plot. If you've ever been to Memphis, you'll recognize many places, and if you haven't, I extend an invitation in the time-honored tradition of the South—"Y'all come!"

Don't miss Harley's next adventure!

CPSIA information can be obtained at www.ICGtesting.com
Printed in the USA
LVOW12s0223200214

374475LV00003B/120/P

9 781611 940992